ALSO BY LAILA LALAMI

Conditional Citizens

The Other Americans

The Moor's Account

Secret Son

Hope and Other Dangerous Pursuits

THE DREAM HOTEL

THE DREAM HOTEL

A NOVEL

Laila Lalami

Pantheon Books, New York

All rights reserved. Published in the United States by Pantheon Books,
a division of Penguin Random House LLC, New York, and distributed
in Canada by Penguin Random House Canada Limited, Toronto.

Pantheon Books and colophon are registered trademarks of
Penguin Random House LLC.

Library of Congress Cataloging-in-Publication Data
Names: Lalami, Laila, [date] - author.
Title: The dream hotel : a novel / Laila Lalami.
Description: First edition. | New York : Pantheon Books, 2025.
Identifiers: LCCN 2024050170 | ISBN 9780593317600 (hardcover) |
ISBN 9780593317617 (ebook) | ISBN 9780593702420 (open-market)
Subjects: LCGFT: Dystopian fiction. | Novels.
Classification: LCC PS3612.A543 D74 2025 |
DDC 813/.6—dc23/eng/20241025
LC record available at https://lccn.loc.gov/2024050170

www.pantheonbooks.com

Jacket design and illustration by Jack Smyth
Book design by Betty Lew

Printed in Canada
First Edition

2 4 6 8 9 7 5 3 1

For A. and S.,
who waited ten years

You're a good person; if you were in a position to stop disaster, you probably would. Whenever a woman's murder captures headlines, your first instinct is to ask why no one did anything about the cuts and bruises for which she sought treatment, the boyfriend's repeated violations of the court's restraining order, the alarming texts he sent, which laid out in detail what he planned to do. If a child's dead body is found in the park, you wonder aloud whether anyone had ever noticed the alcoholic father with a temper, the gym teacher lurking in the showers, the creep watching the playground from a bench. Picture the women. Picture the children. What if you could save them from these monsters? You don't even have to do anything; you've already agreed to the terms of service.

I

T HE DREAM CEDES TO REALITY, OR PERHAPS IT'S THE OTHER way around, and she pulls herself from the tangle of sheets and stumbles out into the hallway. There she waits, barefoot on the cold floor, until the bell stops ringing. She stands still, limbs straight, eyes fixed on a point in the middle distance; if Madison has taught her anything, it is that compliance begins in the body. The trick is to hide any flicker of personality or hint of difference. From white domes on the ceiling, the cameras watch.

The others line up alongside her, rubbing sleep from their eyes, squinting under the chrome-plated lights. The fixtures date back to 1939, when Madison was a public elementary school, enrolling as many as four hundred children every fall. Back then, the town of Ellis had a farming-tool factory, a movie theater, a thriving pool hall, two modest hotels, and natural hot springs that attracted tourists from ninety miles away in Los Angeles. A century later, the factory had shuttered, and the springs were dry. The school sat empty, its walls spotting with mold, until the city council sold it to Safe-X. Because of legal constraints on renovation, Madison's new owners had to keep the original lighting and metalwork, but they threw away the blackboards, stripped the state maps and alphabet posters from the walls, auctioned off the furniture, and converted the second floor into a ward.

When they brought her to her cot in 208, the smell of industrial floor cleaner made her ill. She wrestled with the window, her knuckles turning white before she noticed that it had been welded shut. But these days the smell of synthetic pine doesn't bother her as much. Living with strangers in bare rooms, showering next to them in open stalls, standing behind them in line for the comm pods—all these have taught her to be alert to more intimate scents. From four feet away, she can smell the cream her roommate rubs on her skin to treat the rash she developed in the jail.

The attendants bristle when one of the women calls Madison a jail. This is a retention center, they say, it's not a prison or a jail. You haven't been convicted, you're not serving time. You're being retained only until your forensic observation is complete. How much longer, someone will always ask. Depends, the attendants say. Some retainees stay just twenty-one days; others have to stay a bit longer. The attendants never call the women prisoners. They say *retainees, residents, enrollees,* and sometimes *program participants.*

Hinton comes through the gate seven minutes after six. There must've been some traffic on the highway, or a delay during the security briefing. This morning his hair looks freshly cut, bringing out his high cheekbones and bright, hungry eyes. But his fine features are muddled by the burn scar that runs along the base of his neck, just above the stiff collar of his uniform. The scar is a frequent subject of gossip at Madison. Some people say Hinton was injured in the Tujunga complex fire, which burned his house to the ground and killed his dog, supposedly a German shepherd. Others point out that the scar looks old, so it must be the mark of a youthful accident, a mishap with a firecracker, say, or a brawl around a campfire. Who knows? But the scar gives him substance, rescues his looks from bland perfection.

Unhurriedly, he makes his way down the hall. At 202 he berates two retainees for a towel lying in a heap on the floor. That it must have slipped from its hook on the wall doesn't matter; they're responsible for keeping their quarters tidy. There's another issue in 205, something about an overflowing wastebasket. But it's only at 207 that his vigilance pays off. He finds, under a blanket, a battery-powered night-light, smaller than a fingernail. Staying awake past ten is against the rules, everyone knows that. "You people amaze me," he says, whistling in mock admiration. From his breast pocket, he pulls out his Tekmerion and touches the screen to file a report. "It's like you're not even trying to lower your scores."

Two more steps and he'll be at 208. She can already smell the instant ramen on him, made with hot water from the tap and slurped at his desk before the start of his shift. Does he know he's the object of so much speculation? Does he care? Perhaps he gossips about the women, too, when he eats lunch with the other attendants or when they're bantering in the locker room after a long shift. One thing is certain: Hinton takes pride in his work, always handling device check in the morning rather than delegating it to a junior attendant. He never rushes through it, even when all the women are standing in the hallway, shivering from the cold.

No matter how long he takes to get to her, she doesn't lower her head to make it easier for him to reach behind her ear. It's a small thing, but it's what she can do to signal her resistance. He points the scanner at the back of her skull, and the scanner gives a beep, indicating that the neuroprosthetic on Retainee M-7493002 [username: Sara T. Hussein] hasn't been tampered with overnight.

She's about to turn around when he asks, "What's the matter?" His eyes are direct, unblinking. "You look a little off today."

How can he tell? But keeping her mouth shut is another thing Madison has taught Sara. A response, no matter how anodyne, might be used against her. She waits, hoping her face is blank enough, until he moves on to her roommate.

Now the day can begin.

It is a frigid morning in October, the morning of her thirty-eighth birthday.

FACING THE SMALL MIRROR ABOVE THE SINK, SARA PINS HER HAIR IN a tight bun. Emily has her shoes on already; she's assigned to kitchen duty and has to be there early, before the breakfast bell. The women who've been at Madison awhile have learned the value of a routine, but newer retainees usually go right back to bed after device check. They're still in denial about their situation, still going over every detail of what happened to them, hoping to pick out the moment that tipped the algorithm's calculations against them. They face the wall or stare at the ceiling, undisturbed by the sound of footsteps down the hallway or the roar of the leaf blower outside. In the evening, they come out of their rooms long enough to eat a meal, then resume their silent meditation. It takes a while to adjust to Madison—not just the facility, but the idea behind it, too.

The first adjustment is to time itself. Each day resembles the one that came before it, the monotony adding to the women's apprehension and leading them to make decisions that damage their cases. Some of them might refuse to submit to mental-status evaluations or provide urine samples on demand; others might get into heated arguments with the attendants. Yet the rare days that break with tedium are difficult in their own way: a phone call from a loved one or a visit from a lawyer can bring consolation just as often as heartbreak. So the monotony and the excitement weigh in different fashion on retainees. Sara marks time not by days or hours, but by milestones.

Like first steps.

Playing Peekaboo.

The word "Mama."

And now, her birthday.

She washes up, then takes a look around the room, making sure everything is put away according to regulation. On her shelf, encased in a plastic frame purchased at the commissary, is a photograph of her children in their high chairs. Mona smiles for the camera while Mohsin looks at the banana slices on his plate, his fingers poised over a piece. The picture is already outdated, but she likes the twins' expressions too much to exchange it for a newer photo. Next to the frame are a pile of letters, a book of stories by Jorge Luis Borges she borrowed from the library, and her notebook.

Sara resisted the lure of the notebook for as long as she could. Writing about her life at Madison seemed to her a form of capitulation—tacit acceptance that her retention was not a misunderstanding, which would be swiftly corrected when the appropriate evidence was produced, but the result of reasonable suspicions that the RAA might have about her. Naturally, she also worried that whatever she wrote could be held against her by agents who cared only about the data, not about the truth. Day after day she lay on her cot, ruminating about how she had ended up at Madison and how she could prove herself innocent of the violence they thought she was planning.

But there came a moment when she grew tired of staring at empty walls and her old habits prevailed. By training, she is a historian of post-colonial Africa, specializing in independence movements and border formation, but except for a few years when she taught at Cal State she hasn't worked as a historian. She's spent most of her career in digital archiving, work that doesn't require her to prepare lectures, allows her to write on subjects she finds interesting, and provides health insurance. Or did, anyway.

While she waits for the breakfast bell, she writes her dreams in as much detail as she can remember. In last night's dream, she's scrolling through her Printastic feed one day at breakfast when she comes across a 1954 photograph of Moroccan independence fighters misidentified as conscripts in the French army. It's an embarrassing mistake, which even a first-year student of African history wouldn't make, and soon she discovers, with abject horror, that it was posted from her account. Already there are dozens of comments, mocking or shaming her for the blunder. But no matter how many times she taps the Delete button, the picture stays on her feed and her device pings with new notifications—the high-pitched sound of her disgrace. The only way to delete the image is to remove it from the mainframe that sits in a bunker underneath her building. Stairs appear in front of her and she takes them two by two, her hand barely grazing the banister as she hurries to the basement. Then the stairs melt into quicksand and her feet sink.

Another dream about humiliation. Writing it down makes her realize that what stings most isn't the moment of public shame, but the silence of the people she thought would come to her defense. The feeling that she has been tainted and must be cast out is painful, reminding her of her first days at Madison, when she expected to hear that her friend Myra, with whom she used to hike in Will Rogers State Park most weekends, had come to her defense. All the way up to Inspiration Point, Myra would talk about how disgusted she was with the men she was dating and her plans to move to France as soon as she qualified for one of their reproductive-age visas. At the viewpoint, though, the sun-glazed Pacific would lull her into a dreamy silence. Then all the way down, she'd talk about why she could never leave the people she loved behind, people like Sara. It was a comfort to Sara each time, hearing that Myra treasured their friendship. As it happened, only her family has been in touch with her since she's been at Madison; everyone else is afraid that associating with her might damage their risk scores.

Now she goes to the window. If she cranes her neck a certain way, and puts her hands around her eyes to block the ceiling light, she can see a stretch of road bordered by creosote and, beyond it, a mountain. It's not much of a mountain, it's probably more of a hill, but it's covered with creosote and brittlebush that shiver at the slightest breeze. This morning the sky is cloudy. A flock of blackbirds gathers in formation, then breaks off again before disappearing from sight. Like Hinton, the old woman is a little late today. She lumbers to the bus stop weighed down by straw baskets, hats, and mats, her long, beaded earrings swinging with each step. An artist is how Sara thinks of the old woman, emerging out of her workshop three days a week to sell her original pieces at the farmer's markets in nearby towns.

Then the bus arrives, its brakes screeching as it comes to a halt. The old woman gets on, scans her face, and places her things on the luggage rack. The driver waits, watching in his rearview mirror as she takes a seat in the priority area, facing Madison. Can she see Sara from that distance? It's impossible to tell. But Sara likes to think of the old woman as a friend, a kind friend who checks in on her a few times a week.

She watches until the bus is out of sight and the scene resumes its tranquility. A solitary moment is rare at Madison and she tries to make this one last as long as she can, but she gives it up when the breakfast bell rings.

COMING DOWN THE STAIRS, SHE TURNS A CORNER LIT BY THE CYCLOPIC eye of a porthole window. The architects who designed Madison wanted it to be an avatar of the modern world: they gave it a flat roof, steel-pipe balustrades, and curved forms that evoked ocean liners cleaving the Atlantic at record-breaking speed. The walls would be sleek and white, the window frames an ocean blue. The Great Depression, the Dust Bowl, the Hoovervilles scattered across a sterile landscape—all these were in the past. The future belonged to science and progress.

On her way to the cafeteria, she passes the WPA mural at the entrance to the auditorium. The painting is the only piece of art in the entire facility, and for that reason it's not unusual to find a retainee or two standing at a distance to admire it. It was painted by Victor Arnautoff, and depicts a farm scene from the 1930s: hatted laborers kneel between furrows, picking lettuce, while in the background an overseer in blue dungarees leans against a rusty white truck. The colors are remarkably well preserved; the paint isn't exposed to direct light. Standing under the mural for even a moment feels to Sara like stepping back a hundred years in time. It's always a little startling to move from the artwork to the next hallway, one wall of which is lined end to end with bright computer screens that display the work assignments.

The cafeteria is busiest on Tuesdays and Thursdays, when eggs and potatoes are served for breakfast. Today is a Monday; the line is short. Sara waits for the facial recognition system to identify her, then picks up a tray. The oatmeal, or what passes for oatmeal, bubbles in a huge pot embossed with the logo of MealSecure. Emily ladles the grayish liquid onto Sara's tray, finishing off the serving with a decisive clank against the rim. She adds a slice of bread from a basket of barely defrosted toast and a fruit cup from the mound that sits at the other end of the counter. "Early bird special," she tells Sara, rubbing the rash on her face with the inside of her arm. No matter what cream Emily tries from the commissary, the rash clears then returns after a few days.

"Lucky me." Sara takes her food to an empty table under the windows. The oatmeal is gray and gritty; to get through it she has to cast about for a memory, and feed on it instead. A plate of fluffy beghrir, lavender honey in a dipping bowl, a pot of mint tea—a breakfast her mother used to make for her on mornings when she needed a little cheering.

The clock on the far wall says it's 6:33. The day ahead seems impossibly long, even with a second shift. The only thing keeping her going is the prospect of getting a card from Elias and the twins. They're not allowed to send her anything that isn't purchased from one of two commercial sites approved by Safe-X, but children's drawings are an exception, and she's hoping that's what they will send. Even if the twins' lines and scribbles have yet to take on easily recognizable shapes, the drawings seem to her to reflect their personalities, something that photos alone can't quite capture.

Where's Toya, Sara wonders, raising herself on her elbows and surveying the cafeteria again in case she missed her friend. About fifty women are eating breakfast at the moment, most of them old-timers who are inured to the taste of the food or don't have enough money in their accounts to buy snacks at the commissary. There's no sign of Toya, but soon enough Lucy and Marcela arrive with their trays, their lukewarm smiles, their idle talk.

Dipping into her oatmeal, Marcela says there's a new girl. "Came in around midnight."

Lucy's eyes widen. "You were awake?"

"I was just using the bathroom," Marcela replies, raising a hand in self-defense.

It's rare for someone to arrive at night, Sara thinks. Usually, the attendants bring in new women during the day, when the regular intake staff is on duty at Madison. They perform a medical exam; take fingerprints, DNA swabs, and other biometric information from those whose files don't already have them; and explain the rules that govern life at the facility. No cell phones or smart devices. No smoking. No loud noises. No loitering in the hallways. No excess property, defined as any item that makes a retainee's room look untidy. (Retention officers have full discretion in assessing tidiness.) No art materials unless approved beforehand. No identification documents, credit cards, or cash. No jewelry, save for plain wedding bands. Shirts are to be tucked in at all times. Dirty uniforms are to be turned in promptly for exchange. Et cetera.

It takes two hours to watch the video that covers the regulations, after which retainees are given a handbook of policies and procedures they must follow. Ignorance of a rule does not justify being exempt from consequences, which is why retainees are advised during orientation to read the handbook cover to cover. Breaking a rule results in being written up, being written up raises a retainee's risk score, and a higher risk score extends the retention period.

"So where's this new girl?" Sara asks, looking around.

"Don't know."

"You sure it wasn't a dream?"

Marcela runs her hand over her fade, still damp from the shower. From her elbow to her wrist a tattoo spells out SHARP JELLO, the name of her band, in melting orange letters. "I guess we'll find out."

Lucy finishes the diced fruit, scraping the bottom of the plastic container with her spoon to get the last drop. "You'd think they'd give us more today, seeing as it's a holiday."

"What holiday?" Marcela asks.

"Columbus Day."

"Is that today? I don't think they care."

"It's still a holiday."

"No one calls it Columbus Day anymore. It's Indigenous Peoples' Day now."

"I still call it Columbus Day. God, I'm so hungry."

With only a flicker of hesitation, Marcela gives her fruit cup to Lucy. These two make an odd pair: they have almost nothing in common. Marcela is in her twenties; Lucy is in her late fifties. One is a guitarist for an indie band from Bell Gardens; the other an accounting clerk for a real estate company in Sherman Oaks. Yet from the moment they started sharing a room, they became allies. That doesn't always happen at Madison. There have been disagreements between retainees and even a few fights, which resulted in longer observation periods for the retainees involved.

"Thanks, kiddo," Lucy says, peeling the plastic cover carefully so as not to spill any of the juice. Her face has broadened, and without regular visits to the salon her hair has gone gray. The changes make her look like an aging matriarch, with two ex-husbands and five squabbling children.

Finally the new girl walks in. She's tall and fit, and strides with great purpose toward the service window. She's late for breakfast, though, so she doesn't get a fruit cup, just the oatmeal and a single piece of toast. After getting her tray she surveys the cafeteria for a place to sit. When her gaze falls on the table by the window, Lucy slides over to make room. A new arrival is a nice break from the routine. "I'm Lucy Everett," she says after a minute. "This here is Marcela DeLeón. And that quiet gal over there is Sara Hussein. What's your name?"

"Eisley Richardson," the new girl replies. She has the voice of a talk-show host; every syllable is clearly enunciated. She hasn't yet learned to speak in a monotone whisper, blending her voice with the voices of others around her in order to make sound capture more difficult. Her first taste of oatmeal elicits a look of sheer disgust, but after a moment she eats her meal resignedly, as if completing an assignment.

"Food's terrible, but what doesn't kill you and all that." Lucy used to spend a lot of time on the phone with clients, and she thinks that makes her a good conversationalist. "So, where you from?"

"Los Angeles."

"No need to holler. How'd you end up here?"

Eisley shakes her head. "I didn't do anything."

"Jesus. Lower your voice."

"I didn't do anything." In a whisper this time.

Lucy nods. "Right. But what'd they say you were *going* to do?"

"Vehicular manslaughter."

"How long you here for, then?"

"Twenty-one days."

Even though Marcela and Lucy exchange knowing glances, neither one of them tells the new girl that few people are released at the end of their forensic hold. They're the lucky ones, Sara thinks, because almost right away they return to being CLEARS. But most retainees are QUESTIONABLES; they can't get their risk scores to decrease enough in twenty-one days, and they're slapped with extensions.

Sara looks up to find Hinton watching them—as if the neuro-prosthetics, the temperature sensors, and the cameras equipped with Guardian emotion-tracking software aren't enough. The system is never satisfied with the data it already has. It always seeks more, in new formats or from new sources, including human collectors. If Hinton catches something the cameras don't, he reports it on his Tekmerion. The more reporting credits he has, the more vacation time he earns.

"Where'd they put you?" Lucy asks the new girl.

"Room 258."

"No, I mean, what job?"

"I'm only here three weeks."

Sara picks up her fruit cup, dusting the lid with the palm of her hand. When she was admitted to Madison, she, too, had declined to work at one of the trailers that line the exercise yard. It took her a while to understand that refusing a job assignment allowed the algorithm to mark her as UNEMPLOYED. At Madison, unemployment is a negative multiplier of risk scores; it makes every violation of the rules significantly worse. "You should work," Sara whispers. With a glance at the clock above the service station, she adds, "If you go sign up right after breakfast, you can still make today's shift in one of the trailers."

But the new girl frowns at the unsolicited advice. She continues eating while Lucy interrogates her.

"Why'd they bring you in after hours, anyway?"

"What do you do for a living?"

"What's that tat on your arm mean?"

Each question is met with a shrug or an indecipherable grunt. What Lucy doesn't understand is that the last thing anyone wants to do when they walk into Madison is talk, least of all to other retainees. If Eisley is anything like me, Sara thinks, she's still in disbelief about her retention, convinced that it's nothing more than a mistake that can be rectified soon. She needs time to get used to this place, that's all.

They finish their meal in silence. The light streaming in from the windows is bright, hitting the tables in the cafeteria at sharp angles. Outside, the gardeners are trimming the bushes and clearing leaves, disturbing the crows that are digging for grubs. The retention center takes up an entire city block in Ellis, but to any cars driving past the main gate, Madison looks much as it did before its renovation. Safe-X even kept the paloverdes in the front; they shield part of the main building from view and, especially when they're blooming, add to its charm. There are no watchtowers, no steel doors, no concertina wire. But if Sara were to stray past the chain-link fence that surrounds the exercise yard, her neuroprosthetic would reveal her precise location to the attendants.

Before Madison, she never thought much about location tracking; she was too busy living her life. At this hour, she would be having breakfast with the twins, making up silly songs about bananas and blueberries, getting ready to drop them off at daycare on her way to work. Elias would be on the Metro to County/USC, listening to music on his earphones while going over his caseload for the day. After that weird virus swept through the country last year, there was a spike of children in need of speech therapy, so his schedule had become tighter. Still, he would check in on her before his appointments, ask her how she was doing or if he should pick up anything at the store before dinner. It was an ordinary life. To get back to it, she has to show improvement in her comportment, demonstrate that she can comply, that she's not a criminal.

Sara carries her tray to the racks by the service window. The new girl follows, putting her utensils in the appropriate bins and signing out at the exit station. Already she is learning the rules. The retainees have to eat what they're given, do what they're told, sleep when the lights are out, but they're considered FUO.

Free, under observation.

THE TROUBLE STARTED IN TERMINAL B, ON THE LAST FRIDAY before Christmas. Because of a power outage earlier that morning, the Customs and Immigration hall was packed with travelers—retirees in matching baseball hats, sullen teenagers in checkered pajama pants, toddlers trailing behind disheveled parents. Stepping off the moving walkway, Sara noticed a sign that advertised concierge exit for a hefty fee, but having already spent more than she should have on her trip she resigned herself to wait. The line for passport control snaked around the hall all the way to the back wall. *This might take a while,* she texted her husband.

"No phones allowed," an officer barked, pointing at an orange-colored notice that banned the use of devices. "Turn off your phone."

"I'm sorry, Officer," she said, putting her phone in the back pocket of her jeans. "It's just my husband. He can't find parking."

The officer seemed unconvinced. Sara felt his gaze on her for a long time, even as more stations opened and the line began to move at a steady pace. On the loudspeaker a male voice warned, first in English and then in Spanish, to maintain visual contact with your property at all times. Somewhere, a child wailed inconsolably. When Sara's turn came, she picked up her bag and shuffled toward Scout, which directed her to put her hand on his fingerprint reader, speak her name into his microphone, and look into his tiny green eyes. The cameras made her feel self-conscious; she wasn't wearing any makeup and her hair was a tangled mass of curls. "Report to Line B," Scout said.

Well, that was strange.

She took a step back and presented herself to the AI a second time, but Scout refused to process her. "Report to Line B," he repeated in his metallic voice.

As she joined the new line, Sara looked around her at the other travelers who had been selected for human inspection: a scruffy couple in backpacking gear, a woman carrying a sleeping infant, a handful of elderly people. On rare occasions, the AI still returned more than one face, which meant that an officer had to verify the correct match. Perhaps Sara's unruly hair this morning had caused a snag. Mercifully, the new line was short. In her pocket her phone buzzed again, but she resisted the impulse to answer it. With holiday traffic, it would take Elias and the twins a while to circle the terminal again and return to the pickup area. By then, she would be done. She handed her passport to the CBP officer, a middle-aged woman with a lineless face and thin eyebrows filled unevenly with pencil.

"Sara Tilila Hussein," the officer said, drawing out every syllable. "Did I pronounce that right?"

"Uh. Yes."

"Where are you coming from today, Ms. Hussein?"

"London."

"What were you doing there?"

"Attending a conference."

"And what is it that you do?"

"I'm an archivist. I work for the Getty Museum."

"Up on the hill? That's nice. I like the gardens there." The officer scanned the picture page of the passport, then looked at her screen, toggling from tab to tab. At the next station, an elderly couple presented their documents, got their stamps, and walked off to Baggage Claim. A few feet away, an airport employee pushed a woman in a wheelchair through the security gate.

"Is there a problem, Officer?" Sara asked, trying to keep impatience out of her tone.

"No," the officer said, though she kept the passport, holding it open with one hand while she used her mouse with the other. She seemed riveted by the information on her computer screen, which Sara found strange. For the past six or seven years, she had traveled to London for the same conference, flying the same airline, and landing in and out of the same airport, yet she'd never had to go through an additional passport check. It didn't seem that facial recognition was the issue. Was it because she had broken the rules when she used her cell phone? She put her bag down and rubbed the soreness from her hand. Standing under the white lights of the customs hall had made her warm, and she removed her jacket and scarf and stuffed them inside her bag. After a moment, the officer stood, raising herself on her toes as she looked beyond her glass-walled cubicle to the other stations. "Hernandez," she called.

Damn it. Sara shifted on her feet. This new delay meant that Elias would have to circle the terminal a third or a fourth time, with their thirteen-month-old twins strapped in their car seats. They would have woken up from their morning naps by now and would be screaming for the bottles that were tucked in the mini-cooler in the back, out of his reach. The phone in Sara's pocket buzzed once again, but she didn't answer it. She could imagine his frustration mounting as she ignored his calls and texts. He had spent the past five days taking care of the kids; she knew he was desperate for her to come home.

Officer Hernandez came inside the cubicle and stood behind his co-worker, whose name tag, Sara noticed now, said Hastings. "So check this out," Hastings said. Together, they stared at the computer screen. "It looks like a 55-60, right?" she asked, looking up at him for confirmation.

"Let me see." Hernandez took the mouse and started clicking and scrolling, moving at the same glacial pace as Hastings. Meanwhile, the people waiting in line stared and whispered amongst themselves. Sara felt as though she were being watched by a disapproving audience and, her performance having failed to impress, the heckling from the peanut gallery would start in short order. "Yes, 55-60," Hernandez said after a while. "That's correct."

With this verdict, both officers turned to look at Sara. At once she became anxious, even though she had done nothing wrong. Hastings said, "Ms. Hussein, you have to go to Inspection and Prevention. The elevator is down the hall to your right."

"What's going on?"

"It's procedure."

"What procedure?"

"Your risk score is too high."

"What? Why?" The last time Sara had seen her risk report was when she and Elias had bought their apartment, three years earlier. The bank had required a copy of the document before approving them for a fifty-year mortgage in their family-friendly neighborhood. She was marked CLEAR then. They both were. There had to be a mistake somewhere. But why did it have to happen at the airport, when she was already so pressed for time?

"The RAA officer will explain it you. Do you have any luggage to pick up?"

"No, I only have this carry-on."

"Great. Officer Hernandez will escort you."

"What about my passport?"

"Officer Hernandez will take it for you. Follow him."

Not a secondary inspection, Sara thought, after all these years.

WHILE THE OTHER TRAVELERS STOOD STARING, OFFICER HERNANDEZ stepped out of the cubicle with Sara's passport and asked her to follow him. He took her on the elevator to the second floor, then through a maze of gray corridors to an office marked RISK ASSESSMENT ADMINISTRATION. Two armed guards sat on either side of the door, scrolling on their phones, eyes glazed. Inside the office, a glass wall separated a waiting area from an interview room, where a young officer was talking to a redhead in a velour tracksuit. Hernandez placed Sara's passport in a sliding tray at the counter. "Have a seat," he told her.

"How long will this take?"

"Not long. It's just procedure."

"You still haven't told me what procedure it is," she groused. But by then she was resigned to the bureaucratic delay and sat down on one of the vinyl chairs to call her husband. There was no cell signal, though, even after she turned off and restarted her phone. She assumed Elias had given up on curbside pickup and tried the parking structure again. With any luck he would have found a spot and would be wrestling the kids out of their car seats and into the side-by-side stroller, hard as it was to maneuver in the airport. Wistfully, Sara thought about the lunch they were planning to have at Mimi's, a new restaurant that was supposed to have the best lomo saltado in town. She had made the reservation online the night before, a small gesture she hoped would make up for the inconvenience of picking her up at LAX on a holiday weekend. Now she wondered if they would be able to make it. Her phone said it was 11:45. Not impossible, she thought with deliberate optimism. If this interview took twenty or thirty minutes and Sepulveda wasn't backed up, they could be there by 1:30. The twins would be tired, but she could distract them with games on their tablets.

Sara put her phone in her purse and waited. She wasn't exactly a stranger to invasive searches at airports, from hand swabs for explosives at TSA checkpoints to detailed security interviews with hostile agents. When she was a child, her father made the family go to the airport three hours early every time they went on vacation, in order to allow enough time for the extra searches. He liked to plan for every eventuality, a habit that owed less to his training as a physicist than to the immigrant's chronic fear of anyone in a government uniform. Sara's mother resented this cautiousness—"why did we move here, then?" she'd complain—and regularly found ways to sabotage it. Sometimes, she would pack an innocuous item in three layers of tissue wrapping, forcing the agents to peel each one before discovering they were holding an old hairbrush or an eyeglass case. Other times, she would make a scene at the TSA checkpoint, loudly repeating each of the agent's requests in her thick accent and offering unsolicited help. "You missed the zipper pocket inside, Officer," she would say. "Let me show you where it is." "What about my laundry bag? Don't you want to search that?" Everyone would stare.

Mama was a character, Sara thought. A wonderful character.

Whatever Sara's father did to anticipate and alleviate the hassle, however, it never worked. He was routinely issued boarding passes with the dreaded SSSS code or called to the gate to undergo humiliating screenings in full view of the other passengers. One time, when he dared to complain that a second search at the gate was unnecessary, the security agent took it out on Sara and her brother, Saïd. They were eight and four at the time, dressed from head to toe in new hiking gear, excited to visit the Grand Canyon, where they were promised they could ride a mule. A big mule, with a saddle and everything. "Take off your shoes," the agent ordered them. Her brother's Tevas were green, she remembered, and hers were blue. Barefoot, they watched as the agent bent each shoe in half until it cracked. The Washi tape Sara used to put her shoes back together stuck to the arches of her feet, giving her painful blisters that lasted for days. The blisters were the only memory she had of the Grand Canyon.

Another time, when they were returning from their yearly trip to Morocco, they were held just long enough at Dulles International to miss their cross-country flight home, then released without explanation. The delay meant that her father couldn't attend a ceremony at which he and three of his Caltech colleagues were to be honored for their work on a new generation of Mars rovers. What made these experiences difficult wasn't that they never turned up anything and were a waste of time for all parties involved, but the gnawing feeling that her family's ability to go about their business was entirely at the discretion of uniformed officers. Though she was only a child, Sara felt a visceral fear every time she was in an airport.

But once the government deployed Scout at security checkpoints, the hassle disappeared. Sara was a sophomore in high school by then, and she noticed the difference during her soccer team's training trip to Mexico. All she had to do was present herself to Scout, and the AI instantly accessed her passenger identification, biometric information, and criminal records. The light turned green, and she was cleared through the checkpoint. No more long lines, no more questions. A new era of digital policing had begun, and young Sara Hussein, for one, welcomed it. It made transiting through airports fast and straightforward.

Until today, it seemed.

With nothing else to do, she watched the interview that was taking place on the other side of the soundproof glass. The young redhead spoke with so much raw emotion that her face turned pink. She pulled out a piece of paper from her purse and waved it rudely in the officer's face. Yet he kept his cool. He examined the paper for a moment, asked her some more questions, then gave it back to her and stamped her passport. She came out of the interview room, dragging a set of matching leather suitcases and cursing him under her breath.

Then it was Sara's turn. The officer retrieved her passport from the sliding tray and came to the door. This time, she took note of his name tag. Segura. Later it would occur to her that it was suited to his line of work. "Ms. Hussein?"

"That's me," she said, getting up.

"Please come in and have a seat."

There was a large desk with two computer monitors, but no personal items of any kind—no framed photos or potted plants or funny gadgets. On one wall was a screen that played a silent ad for luxury vacations in Hawaii, a detail Sara found puzzling. On the other wall was a brass plaque with an official seal and a mission statement too small to decipher from where she sat.

Now that she was across from Officer Segura, she noticed that his uniform was of a different color than the CBP officers downstairs—dark blue, rather than black—and that he carried no weapon. The patch on his arm said RAA. Next to his computer was a small, motion-tracking camera that was aimed at her face.

"So you're returning from London, correct?" Segura asked.

"That's right."

"And L.A. is home."

"Yes."

He asked for her address, occupation, and other personal information. Each answer she gave, he checked against the log on his computer. His thick, glossy hair was gelled into place and he had a tiny diamond earring in his right earlobe. Sara could easily imagine him out of uniform, in a hip jacket and jeans, sitting at a bar in Silver Lake. It made her feel more conscious of her present shabbiness. She was dressed for the cooler London weather, in jeans and an old flannel shirt with a button missing on the sleeve. Sweat stains were growing under her armpits. Fretting about the smell, she folded her arms.

"What happened on the London flight? It says here that the police were called."

So this must be why she'd been pulled into secondary. "That was a medical emergency," she explained. "Just before we pushed back from the gate at Heathrow, the old gentleman in the seat next to me started clutching his chest, like he was having trouble breathing. He was making this weird, throaty sound. I thought he was having a heart attack or something. So I buzzed the flight attendant, who got him help from a doctor a few rows down. The doctor said he should be taken off the flight before departure, but he refused. He really wanted to go to L.A., he said he was meeting his grandchildren for the first time. Anyway, there was an argument with the crew and in the end they called the police to remove him. The flight was delayed thirty minutes because of him."

"That's annoying," Segura said.

It had been alarming, too. The old man's face had turned brick-red, so much did he strain to breathe while also arguing with the flight crew. When the cabin chief told him he had to deboard, Sara could scarcely hide her relief. His situation might worsen when they were halfway across the Atlantic, and then what? But his rage at the order was immediate, and extraordinary. He turned on Sara for reporting his medical distress and by the time the Metro police took him away he was screaming at her about meddling in his private business. Had he accused her of something? Perhaps that was why the police encounter showed up on her risk report, even though it had nothing to do with her. All of a sudden she felt great bitterness toward the old man; she'd been trying to help him, and for her trouble he'd caused her to be pulled into an inspection.

"And who paid for your trip to London?"

"My employer. I was at a conference for work."

"All right," Segura said, dutifully typing her answer. Although he seemed to be in his late twenties, he had the posture of an aging office clerk, with a tight jaw and hunched shoulders. Ten more years of this, Sara thought, and he'll end up with chronic back pain. He clicked to a new screen and, frowning now, he asked, "Can you verify your social media usernames for me?"

"My social media?" She paused, trying to figure out what connection there might be between the police encounter at Heathrow and her social feeds. There wasn't any, as far as she knew. "Well, I have a Nabe account," she said, "but I rarely use it anymore. It's SaraTHussein, no hyphen or space."

He nodded. "Anything else?"

"Printastic. It sounds like you already know. Can you tell me what this is about, exactly?"

"The algorithm flagged you as an imminent risk," Segura said with great courtesy. His face betrayed no emotion; she couldn't tell if he trusted the algorithm or was just following protocol.

"Me, an imminent risk?" Sara said with a nervous chuckle. But the fear and frustration that she once associated with airports wrapped around her, as familiar as an old, ill-fitting coat. On Nabe, she followed the pages of different museums, posted the occasional comment about that BBC costume drama everyone was talking about, and kept in touch with friends from high school and college. Earlier that year she had gotten into a heated argument with a computer programmer who had been one of her neighbors when she was at Berkeley. Darren often volunteered to DJ at the parties that were held in the courtyard of their dorm. At the time, he had seemed apolitical, never offering opinions about the TA unionization efforts Sara was involved in, or the calls on university leadership to divest from water stocks. In many ways, he was indistinguishable from other students in the building.

After returning home to Los Angeles, Sara had stayed in touch with everyone she knew at Berkeley through Nabe, which was how she'd discovered his conspiracy-laced posts and his fanatical devotion to firearms. When Sara commented on one of his tirades about the Chinese with a correction, he replied within seconds, starting an argument that lasted all night and covered everything from the Boxer Rebellion to Tiananmen Square. Sara found the exchange so tiresome that she vowed not to engage with him again, but it didn't matter because Darren turned vengeful, reporting two of her archival photographs for nudity and causing her to be suspended from the site for three days. Once she regained control of her account, he reported her again, this time for spam because she had posted several links to a photography exhibit she'd helped curate in San Diego. She had to block him to stop the harassment.

But everyone had stories like this, didn't they? It was impossible to be on social media these days without encountering trolls, bots, cyborgs, scammers, sock puppets, reply guys, or conspiracy theorists—people who were best avoided, ignored, or blocked. She wasn't foolish enough to have posted threats or incitement against Darren, or anything remotely relevant to a law enforcement officer like Segura. Besides, Sara's account was locked.

On Printastic her feed was public, but it was purely professional, devoted to archival images about her areas of scholarly interest. She was excited that the Getty had acquired an important collection of photographs from the Rif War, which she expected to digitize and catalogue. She posted a lot of open-source pictures of rebel fighters from the era, hoping to attract followers who would later be interested in the exhibit she would curate for the museum. Occasionally, she posted brief items about significant moments in early twentieth-century Arab and Amazigh history. These, too, would be of little appeal to anyone outside her field.

Segura looked at her levelly. "Yes, Ms. Hussein. An imminent risk of a crime."

"Based on what?" she asked, her pulse quickening. She felt even warmer than she had downstairs and wished she could take off her flannel shirt. "Like I said, the thing at Heathrow was a medical emergency."

"The software conducts a holistic review. It uses a *lot* of different sources." A note of pride entered his voice, as if he'd had a hand in collecting the data himself.

Sara frowned. There had been no major change in her life since the last time she'd seen her risk report. She didn't lose her job, didn't get evicted, didn't default on a loan, didn't receive public assistance, didn't owe child support, didn't abuse drugs, didn't suffer a mental health crisis, any of which might have ticked up her score. And she didn't have a criminal record—wasn't that the biggest factor in calculating the likelihood of a future crime? "But I've never been arrested," she said.

"Right. I can see that," he replied, his eyes darting back to his screen. He hummed as he weighed the information before him, then turned to her again. "Let me see your phone."

Sara had read somewhere that CBP officers could legally search anyone's phone at the border, but the idea of handing over something so personal still made her uncomfortable. Besides, Segura worked for a different agency altogether, which made her doubt whether the directive he gave her was legal. "Why do you need my phone?"

"I'm just trying to figure out why you were flagged, Miss."

His tone made it clear that any hesitation on her part would only cause further delays. With a sigh, she unlocked her phone and handed it over. It was an older model, with a cracked screen she hadn't had the chance to repair yet. Segura didn't bother looking at her social media accounts, in spite of his earlier questions, but he took careful note of the apps she had—three newspaper subscriptions, a grocery delivery service, a baby monitor, a thermostat sensor, a word game, a sleep-aid tracker, and a dozen more she forgot she even had. Then he opened her photo library, and started scrolling. If he did this long enough, he would see the twins age backward from thirteen months, morphing slowly into the infants they used to be, so tiny and fragile that they had trouble latching when she nursed them. Scroll further down, and he would see her pregnant, her belly as big as a house, stretch marks spreading across it like vine tendrils. Scroll some more, and he'd find pictures of her in a bikini, on the last vacation she and Elias took as a couple. Scroll again—why was he still going through her photos?

She didn't know what he was looking for and she was fairly sure he didn't either, so the whole procedure left her feeling deeply violated, as if a stranger were standing at the window of her bedroom, looking in. It occurred to her that what Segura was checking wasn't so much her phone, but her compliance with his directive to hand it over. Would he have counted it against her if she had said no?

"I'm a museum archivist," she said after a moment. She wasn't sure why she mentioned her job; it was an instinct, born of the belief that a museum archivist couldn't possibly be considered a member of the lawbreaking classes. There had to be a mistake somewhere. After all, what use could she be to a criminal enterprise? Advise the higher-ups on best practices for organizing their records? The whole idea was absurd. "I've gone on this trip several times without problem," she said. "What's going on this time?"

"I'm not sure," he said, handing back her phone and returning to his screen. It seemed he was genuinely puzzled by her presence in his office. He opened her passport and leafed through it. "Who sent you here?"

"Officer Hernandez brought me, I think you saw him? But the officer who referred me here was Hastings."

"Oh, her." He shook his head slowly, the way an old monk might at a zealous novice. Why was he being so candid about his disappointment? Sara felt as though she'd stumbled unaware into a tangle of office politics. The last thing she needed was to get ensnared. Segura leafed through the passport again. She had the feeling he was about to stamp it, because he reached for the desk drawer with his other hand. This was how it had been in the old days, too, when her parents were pulled aside for inspections: a few questions, a whole lot of hassle, and in the end they were let go. At the prospect of her release, her stomach let out a loud growl.

Segura laughed. "You hungry, huh?"

"Sorry. I haven't had anything to eat since last night."

Just then, another officer came in without knocking. "Yo, Segura. Wheeler wants you."

"Now? I thought he wouldn't decide until tomorrow."

"Yeah, now. I'll cover for you."

"Can I go, then?" Sara asked.

But Segura was halfway out the door. "Just give me a sec," he said. "I'll be right back."

RISK ASSESSMENT ADMINISTRATION

The mission of the RAA is to keep American communities safe. We are committed to identifying public-safety risks and investigating suspicious individuals in order to prevent future crimes. Using advanced data analytics tools, we keep law-abiding Americans safe from harm, while also protecting their privacy. Our core principles are care, respect, and responsibility.

ORNING LIGHT SILVERS THE GLASS-BRICK WINDOWS OF the library. A sign taped to the wall above the return shelf says QUIET. Sara's footsteps are muffled by the carpeting, but its mustiness combines with the smell of old paper to tickle her nose, and she sneezes. "Bless you," someone behind her says in a stentorian voice. Alarmed, she turns around. The new girl has followed her here, the way a lost child trails after the first kind stranger it sees.

"Sorry," Eisley says, dropping to a whisper. "Bless you. I wanted to ask, can I send an email from one of these computers?"

"No." The five stations set up in the far corner allow retainees to access the news, Sara explains, and only from the few sources that Safe-X deems acceptable. "If you want to send an email, you have to pay for an account with PostPal."

"Oh." Eisley has sparse eyebrows, a blunt nose, a small mouth. A blank canvas of a face, a face about whom people would say that you couldn't pick her out of a lineup. She seems about as threatening as a fish on a bed of crushed ice. "I just... I want to email my husband."

"Sure. But you'll need an account with PostPal."

"Is it expensive?"

"It's $400 every two months."

"But I'm only here three weeks."

"That's how their billing system works. And then you have to rent a tablet from them to read your email. They'll explain everything to you when you open the account."

Eisley takes in the wood-paneled circulation desk, the three reading tables, the stacks where old books—some held together with tape, others missing a cover or a few pages—line the shelves. "Do I have to pay to read books, too?"

"No." The books come from a Minnesota-based nonprofit organization that wants to encourage reading across the country's crime-prevention facilities; it buys stock that shuttered schools and colleges intend to pulp and redistributes it to retention centers at no cost. The collection at Madison is small—fifteen hundred titles— but being the only public resource at the retention center it is also the most precious. "Those are free."

Someone has taken another seat at the computers.

"PostPal is right down the hall to your right."

Eisley leaves, finally.

Sara gets the last open spot at the computers. She likes to take her time with the national papers, which she reads with more care than she did before her retention, when she was so busy with the twins that she only glanced at the headlines on her way to work. This morning, a financial scandal implicating a ten-term congressman from Arizona dominates the front page of the *Los Angeles Times,* along with coverage of wildfires in Oregon, floods in Texas, and a blizzard in Ohio. Nothing terribly new. But below the fold she finds a report on OmniCloud's plans to buy an education technology firm whose software is used in K–12 schools across the country. OmniCloud wants to mine the data to help its corporate clients hire workers whose histories best match the positions they have open—or get rid of those who may not be ideal for the positions they already have.

OmniCloud continues to grow at an astonishing pace, Sara thinks, its only serious competition the Chinese conglomerate that a handful of senators want to outlaw. OmniCloud is always hungry; it can function only by feeding itself continually. Not for the first time, she's reminded of the dusty colonial censuses she consulted when she was writing her dissertation at Berkeley, each edition thicker than the one preceding it on the shelf. The earliest censuses were counts of populations in different territories of the British Empire, but as time passed the volumes expanded into a massive trove of information on colonial subjects, listing everything from their age and occupation to their marital status, and even their so-called infirmities. If she needed to find out how many able-bodied male workers there were in Gambia in 1930, all she had to do was find the right table.

Now it is her turn to enter the census, one digital step at a time, leaving traces she never intended to leave. Someday, when her children are old enough, they, too, will become lines in OmniCloud's giant database, every facet of their behavior catalogued and quantified and sold for purposes she can scarcely imagine yet. A fierce protective instinct uncoils inside her. She has to get out of this place; she has to shield them from the single eye and countless tentacles of OmniCloud—but how?

From his seat by the door, the attendant on duty is watching. Sara pretends not to notice, continues reading the news. The widow of a rapper she's never heard of is said to be preparing an auction of his art collection at Sotheby's. A review of the new play by Lynn Nottage declares it a return to form for the elderly playwright. Two VR creators are suing each other over copyright of their latest venture, after it was adapted into a dinner party game. Sara makes an effort to read arts and culture news, though there are days when she can't imagine ever going back to sitting in an office at the museum, cataloguing photographs or typing messages that begin with *per my last email*.

At least not for a while. In the fantasies of freedom she entertains late at night in her room, the place she keeps returning to is Mirror Lake, up in Yosemite. She used to visit thirty years ago, when she was a little girl, yet she remembers with startling clarity how it felt to sit under a view of Half Dome, with only the drone of bees and the whirring of grasshoppers in her ears. Back then she was too young to have a phone; she could still move without being tracked, speak without being recorded, play without being monitored. Gazing at the granite walls of Half Dome, she felt as small and anonymous as a speck of dust. Will it ever be possible to be that free again? That is what she wants to find out. She wants to lie on that lakeside again and see only nature from horizon to horizon.

She's about to start *The New York Times,* which has a front-page report on a looming Senate fight over the Crime Prevention Act, when Alice walks into the library.

Immediately, Williams stands up. His uniform is crisp, the bronze stripe on his sleeve still fresh. "Hussein," he calls, "time's up. Give your seat to Carter."

"I don't need the computer," Alice tells him. She wears a pale green headwrap, which she won an appeal to have returned to her, weeks after Hinton confiscated it. Over her uniform she has on a gray, pilling cardigan and a black cord from which dangle her reading glasses. She goes to the fiction section, running her finger against the spines as she looks for what to read next.

Sara returns to the standoff in the Senate over the renewal of a key provision of the CPA.

"The limit's twenty minutes," Williams says.

This isn't true. The signs that are posted at the entrance of the library say nothing about time limits on the computers; they list only the hours of operation and the kind of materials the computers will allow the retainees to access—newspapers, law journals, educational texts.

From the circulation desk, Ana watches, a hand resting on the mound of her belly. She knows there is no rule about time limits, but she can't contradict an attendant, not even a rookie, and risk the cushy library assignment she was given because of her pregnancy.

"Hussein." Williams is young; he can't be more than twenty-one or twenty-two. He used to work as an orderly in a mental health facility before getting hired here, but he's adapted quickly to Madison, enforcing rules he makes up on the spot.

Sara decides to let the matter drop. "All yours," she says. She takes the Borges stories to the return shelf and wanders into the stacks, looking for something new.

At 7:25, the work bell rings. She scans the book she selected and rushes out.

THE CEILING LIGHTS IN TRAILER D ARE DIM. SARA WALKS DOWN THE third row, where workers sit one after the other in front of screens, their faces bathed in blue. She stops at her assigned station, waits for the system to recognize her face, then clicks START. A movie clip begins to play. The question she has to answer is always the same: IS THIS REAL? She must choose one of three answers: YES, NO, or I CAN'T TELL. The work is part of a contract between Safe-X and NovusFilm, a studio that wants to improve the generative capabilities of its software.

The clip starts with an establishing shot of a home, then the camera closes in on the kitchen window, where a young woman is washing dishes at the sink. The scene is restaged in different landscapes and lighting conditions—a tiny house at sunset, a bungalow on a bright summer day, a log cabin cloaked in darkness. Again and again, the woman is shown washing dishes, her brows furrowed in concentration. Sara clicks at a steady pace. While the studio's AI performs well with geometric shapes, and can generate architectural styles from around the world, it has trouble creating realistic weather patterns. The snow on this thatched roof looks too symmetrical, she notices. The grass around that mobile home is too uniform.

IS THIS REAL?

NO.

At the bottom of her screen, a counter measures the time it takes her to respond to each clip. Longer response times suggest that the human interpreter is growing uncertain or unreliable, which is why each clip has to be viewed by a second retainee. Safe-X is responsible for maintaining the high work standards it committed to when it agreed to review 800,000 reels for NovusFilm.

The next set of clips shows a man driving along a winding road in different vehicles. A blue motorcycle. A vintage Volkswagen. A zippy sports car. NovusFilm customers will be able to choose from an array of options when they watch the action-adventure movie that the studio releases each season. Sara clicks at a steady pace.

IS THIS REAL?

YES.

Time passes. Her neck and shoulders start to hurt. Sometimes she finds it hard to tell whether she's looking at a real person, especially when the subject faces the camera and the lighting is good. Along with her response time, the counter at the bottom of her screen measures her accuracy. If she clicks on the same response too many times in a row, she could be deemed a bad employee—or worse, a saboteur. She has to consider each clip carefully, give a truthful answer. That means looking for details that stick out. Like this guy in a helmet, sweating as he ascends a hill on his bike: the braids on either side of his head are too parallel, too perfect.

IS THIS REAL?

NO.

The next clip is of a baby. A brown-haired boy, sitting in a barber's chair, wrapped in a nylon cape. He looks terrified; the yellow rattle that someone out of the frame is shaking seems to be an attempt at distracting him. IS THIS REAL? But now Sara is back in Madison's visiting room, on that warm January afternoon when Elias brought the twins to visit her for the first time. Back then he didn't know the best times to schedule his visits, so he'd gotten caught in monstrous traffic out of Los Angeles. "I'm sorry we're late," he'd said, standing up when she walked in behind Hinton.

Even with dark circles under his eyes, Elias seemed full of life, sated with freedom. All of a sudden she became aware of what set her apart from him, from everyone outside Madison, and was overcome with the reckless hope that he would break her out of this place. What they're saying about me isn't true, she wanted to say, take me home with you, *please* take me home. And when he put his arms around her it seemed to her for a moment as if he had, until the scent of hand sanitizer brought her back to the gray walls of the visiting room. "It's gonna be okay," he was saying. "It's gonna be okay."

"You don't believe them, do you?" she whispered.

He lifted her chin with a finger and looked into her face. Holding her breath, she watched him watch her. Did he wonder if, beneath the placid features he had known for years, she harbored violent urges? "No," he said. "Of course not."

On the quilted blanket he had spread out over the cement floor, Mona was playing with a set of plastic rings while Mohsin was trying to pull off one of his socks. "Hi, babies," she called as she kneeled beside them. She picked up Mona first, holding her close and kissing her over and over on the cheek. "Did you miss Mama?" she asked, wiping the little girl's drool with a bib.

Then she hoisted Mohsin onto her lap as well. How she had missed the weight of their wriggling bodies! "They smell so good," she said, resting her cheek against Mohsin's head. That's when she noticed his newly shorn hair. "You got it cut?" she asked Elias.

Before her trip to London, she'd been planning to take Mohsin to a kids' salon. She'd wanted to save a lock of hair, take pictures, add a page to his keepsake book. The extent of what was being stolen from her was beginning to reveal itself, threatening to bring tears, but she tamped down the impulse; she wanted to enjoy this visit with her family.

"It was getting into his eyes," Elias explained, his voice brimming with apology. "And he's so close to walking now, I didn't want to chance a fall."

"Right. Of course." She kissed her son's hair again, breathing in his delicious smell. "I wish I could've been there is all."

"I know." Elias put his hand on her knee. He asked how she was holding up, if she got over the cold she'd caught when she was admitted, if she needed more money in her commissary account. "They said if we didn't have cash, I could link your account to my credit card."

She shook her head; she didn't really need anything. At the other end of the room, Emily and her girlfriend sat at a table, heads bent over a document they were discussing, whispering in order to maintain a shred of privacy. Alice was standing by the vending machines, having what looked like an argument with her teenage son. Back then Sara still thought of the other retainees as strangers—strangers who might commit crimes—and she was afraid of them. So she kept to herself, hoping that isolation would lead to self-preservation.

"It's not gonna be long," Elias said, trying to sound encouraging. "Just keep your head down and follow the rules. Don't get into any more trouble. You'll be home soon."

"It's just that this place…" Sara's voice trailed off. This place is a nightmare, she wanted to say, except it was a nightmare that everyone else seemed to be dreaming as well. The table, the chairs, the blank walls of the visiting room were real, but reality itself had become slippery. Nothing seemed to penetrate it, flip it back into the world as she knew it.

The twins started to fidget. How did she look to them, she wondered, in an all-white uniform and with her hair tied into the severe bun mandated by the Safe-X handbook? Even her hands looked different, now that her rings, watch, and bracelet had been taken away.

Could they perceive, in their own limited ways, that something strange had happened to her?

Guilt began to prick her. Guilt at putting herself in this situation. Guilt at being away from the twins just as they were about to start walking. Guilt at having time to eat, and read, and sleep while Elias had to go to work and return home to teething, crawling twins. Even with help from his parents, it was too much for him to handle, surely.

Then Mohsin tried to climb down from Sara's lap. "Stay, baby," she begged, even as her son pushed her away. Aware of the cameras on the wall, she didn't dare insist. All she could do was put out her hand and wait for him to come back. Skin hunger, the experts call it. But hunger is ordinary, it's what people experience every day. Hunger can be satisfied immediately, and repeatedly. What she felt was different; it was starvation.

"He's a little cranky," Elias said as he took the boy from her and put him back on the blanket. Rummaging through the clear plastic bag that Safe-X made him buy, he took out a stuffed parrot. "It was such a long drive."

"What about you?" Sara asked her daughter. "You're not tired, are you?" Mona cooed, allowing herself to be hugged and kissed without complaint. After a while she tried to stand on teetering little feet. She seemed on the verge of taking a step, but changed her mind and thrust her arms up. Right away Sara scooped her up. "She's getting close to walking, too."

"It was nice of that attendant to help," Elias said.

"Who?"

"Tall guy who brought you. Hinton?"

"Hinton? What'd he do?"

"He helped me with the stroller and set up the blanket for me."

Sara shook her head. "That can't be him. It must've been somebody else."

"No, it was him."

That doesn't make sense, she wanted to say. Hinton is incapable of showing kindness, you must be mistaken.

But Elias's attention had already shifted to Mohsin. "Go back to Mama. Go say hi."

It took Mohsin a little while to relinquish the safety of the blanket. Sara had just sat him down on her lap again when a metallic voice came on the loudspeaker. "Hussein. Visit's over."

Sara pretended not to hear, held on to her baby boy until the warning repeated thirty seconds later. She stood as Elias picked up each child and walked out. She stood there a minute, looking at the door, her hands balled into fists.

IS THIS REAL?

I CAN'T TELL.

DESPITE SUCCESS, CHALLENGES TO CRIME LAW PERSIST

DISAGREEMENT OVER SMALL, BUT IMPORTANT PART OF THE CPA
PRESENTS A CAMPAIGN OPPORTUNITY AHEAD OF THE ELECTIONS.

By Alejandro Arteta and Lily Khan, with assistance from PressBot

WASHINGTON—A legislative fight is brewing in the Senate over the renewal of key provisions of the Crime Prevention Act, twenty years after the landmark legislation was passed. The battle is likely to become heated, with three prominent members eyeing it as a campaign issue ahead of the presidential elections.

The CPA was passed after the mass shooting at the Super Bowl halftime show in Miami, in which 86 people were shot dead on live television before the broadcast was pulled by CBS, and another 32 were killed off camera before the gunman was successfully apprehended.

The traumatic event, witnessed live by 113 million Americans, led to historic protests across the country. Democratic lawmakers called the Super Bowl massacre a "watershed moment" and demanded strict gun control, while Republicans seized on the findings of the FBI investigation to argue that the fault lay solely with the gunman, Luca Schmidt.

Mr. Schmidt, of Coconut Grove, Florida, left a long trail of evidence leading up to his crime: two domestic violence complaints filed by his mother; bump stocks and ammunition purchased on his personal credit card; a grievance against a team doctor for whom he worked as a lab assistant; angry texts about getting no respect from the football players; and online searches on ways to bypass stadium security.

Mining relevant information became the focal point of the CPA, which gives authorities broad access to private records and allows them to use commercial data analytics tools as part of their investigations. President Casey Graham charged the Risk Assessment Administration with identifying and detaining individuals who are likely to commit violent crimes.

In the twenty years since the law was passed, hundreds of potential murderers have been identified, and detained in public safety centers for investigation and prosecution. The dismantling of the notorious 53rd Street gang in Chicago, whose members had been waging a protracted war against rival groups, has been one of the RAA's biggest success stories.

The RAA has also been effective at preventing suicides by firearms, and is credited with saving tens of thousands of American lives per year, thanks to its rapid alert system.

But there have been occasional failures as well, including the case of Lana Delgado, the beloved stage actress who was mistakenly referred to a commitment clinic while she was receiving treatment for multiple sclerosis at NYU Langone, or Milo Coleman, the five-year-old child whose parents received a notification that they were to bring him to a public safety center. Cases like these, critics say, are evidence that the scope of the CPA should be more limited.

Polls show that the public remains supportive of the pre-crime legislation, with a majority (62%) viewing it as a necessary tool for law-enforcement agencies and slightly more than a third (34%) concerned about its reach.

The current clash in the Senate is about the ability of private detention contractors to issue extensions to the suspects in their custody, without the need for government approval, and the types of data that the RAA can legally use in its algorithms.

The battle does not fall neatly along party lines. Senator Adriana Jimenez (D-California) has partnered with Senator Jamie Hutchinson (R-Oklahoma) to denounce the reach of the CPA, which they say jeopardizes fundamental rights and increases government spending. They plan to introduce an amendment that would limit the authority of private contractors and prohibit the RAA from using certain kinds of private data.

Others, including Senator Cora Jenkins (D-Texas) and Senator Vicente Torres (R-Texas), argue that the CPA strikes an appropriate balance between safety and liberty at a time when criminals can unleash massive violence with extraordinary speed. "No one who watched those innocent people be gunned down on that fateful February day can sit by and wait for another massacre," Senator Jenkins told reporters.

Reached for comment, Risk Assessment Administrator James Wesley pointed to the 42.6% decrease in gun deaths in the last twenty years. Deaths by suicide plunged a dramatic 48%. "I think the numbers speak for themselves," he said.

S ARA'S PASSPORT LAY ON THE DESK, ASKEW. IF ONLY SEGURA HAD stamped it before he was called away, she would've been done with the security screening and on her way to passenger arrivals. But he'd left so quickly she hadn't had a chance to protest that her family was waiting for her downstairs, that she had reservations for lunch at a trendy place in the South Bay. The officer who'd barged in on the interview asked her if she wanted a cup of coffee; there was a fresh pot in the RAA lounge.

"No, thanks," she said, barely able to disguise her exasperation. She resented this interloper, whose appearance had caused her yet another delay. The longer this procedure took, the further away she was from lunch with Elias. "I don't drink coffee."

"No coffee?" He sank into the chair opposite her and sipped from a steaming mug, closing his eyes at the pleasure of it. "Man, I don't know how you do it."

She shrugged. Ever since she'd gotten a sleep-aid device, she rarely needed coffee, though she used to drink as many as six cups a day. Restful sleep had obliterated her cravings for caffeine. "The taste doesn't appeal to me anymore."

"The taste is the best part," he said, sipping noisily from his cup. He had thinning brown hair and a face drawn out of soft lines: round eyes, chubby cheeks, a bulbous nose. His name tag said Moss. Unlike Segura, he carried a huge weapon in his holster, which made him look a bit out of place, especially with that tanned couple frolicking on the big screen above him. A GLIMPSE OF PARADISE, the slogan read.

The ad taunted Sara. Although she had grown up in California, where the islands exerted a magnetic pull every winter break and summer holiday, she had never visited Hawaii. Every year, while her friends traveled to Oʻahu or Maui, her parents packed the family to Morocco, in the process trading Sara's teenage fantasies of tattooed surfers for the stark reality of gaping relatives. From the spectator she aspired to be, she found herself overnight an object of spectacle. Surrounded by aunts and uncles she didn't know, and cousins with whom she could barely communicate, Sara spent a few weeks each year like a defendant in a courtroom, answering questions about her hobbies, her grades, her friends, or else listening quietly while the adults compared, in minute detail, life in one country to life in the other.

For their honeymoon, Sara had suggested to Elias that they go to Kauai, whose evergreen trails she has long wanted to see, but he wanted to visit Prague. He had even found a way to pay for the trip with fellowship money he'd received for his graduate work in speech pathology. "All we have to do," he said, "is settle on the dates." Then he pulled out his phone to look at his calendar. Sara was taken aback; she'd expected they would have a discussion before deciding on a destination, but Prague was a fine idea, too, especially if it didn't cost them as much. "Okay," she said. Those were the good days, when a disagreement between them was nothing more than a chance to discover a new city together. They spent a week in Prague, rising from their hotel bed late in the morning to explore the Castle or take a stroll down thousand-year-old streets.

As time passed, Sara found it harder to overlook Elias's habit of making decisions without consulting her. Some of it was no doubt her fault. Once, when she kept dragging her feet about picking a new dishwasher to replace the one that kept flooding the kitchen, he ordered one online and installed it while she was at work. But another time, he traded in their old Toyota for a new Volvo without warning, only calling her from the dealership to sign the paperwork for the title. She was watching a film documentary on PBS, and she had to mute the sound to make sure she'd heard him correctly. "You did *what*?" she asked. "How can you buy a car without talking to me about it?"

"We did talk about it. Remember you said the Toyota was on its last legs? It needed to be done, so I did it."

"You didn't tell me you went car shopping!"

"It's not a big deal."

"Not a big deal? Are you fucking serious right now?"

"Sara."

"What?"

There was a shuffle of footsteps; Elias was stepping outside to continue the call. "We just replaced the batteries on the Toyota six months ago. And now it needs a new transmission. We can't keep spending money on repairs, it doesn't make sense. You said that yourself the other day."

"That's fine, but we should discuss it first. You can't just waltz into the Volvo dealership and pick one. We can't afford it, Elias. We can't." With the word *can't*, Sara's mind flashed to the red-lined box at the bottom of her student loan statement. When they got approved for a mortgage on their apartment, the broker had joked that the deal was held together by bubble gum and shoestrings. Didn't Elias realize how careful they had to be with money?

"Sure, we can. I got a fantastic deal from Lauren."

"Who the hell's Lauren?"

"The saleswoman at Volvo. We went to high school together. Remember that picture of the senior recital? She's the brunette standing behind me. Anyway, she posted about this incredible deal on Nabe, I messaged her about it, and she gave it to me. I need you to come down, so we can get the title sorted out. And can you bring me my blue jacket? They have the AC on full blast here, it's getting chilly."

This impulsiveness was a source of recurring tension between them, even though it was what had drawn Sara to Elias in the first place. She liked that he made decisions quickly, that he didn't spend hours outlining every possible scenario and its likely consequences, that he didn't care if he failed or made a fool of himself. The habit of caution was deeply ingrained in her, no doubt because she was raised by a scientist, but compounded, surely, by the simple fact that she was a woman. If she was catcalled or harassed while she was on a run, she took a different route the next day. If a colleague mistook a comment for a come-on, she analyzed what she'd said, trying to fig-ure out what word or turn of phrase might have given him the wrong impression. And after her experience with Nabe, she reread every post, no matter how trivial, before publishing it. To be a woman was to watch yourself not just through your own eyes, but through the eyes of others. Elias, on the other hand, was untethered from any judgment except his own, which she found exotic and irresistible all at once. She tried to quiet the voice inside her that told her Elias didn't need her—or didn't need her opinion, at any rate.

So whenever he talked about having a baby, she was reluctant. She could scarcely imagine him compromising on all the big decisions that came with starting a family, from picking a name and finding a pediatrician to choosing a daycare. They had their finances to consider, too; she wasn't sure they were ready to take on the responsibility of a child. Besides, they were young; they should be enjoying late nights and morning sex and impromptu trips out of the country, not saddling themselves with more responsibility.

But Elias didn't want to wait. Female fertility starts declining by age thirty, he would say, we have to start trying because it could take us a while. The back-and-forth lasted for six years, during which the subject became increasingly touchy, as likely to end in a fight as in extended periods of wounded silence. When Sara forgot to pack her birth control for a weekend in New Mexico, she wondered if it was not an unconscious form of abdication; she was tired of the protracted disagreements.

The twin pregnancy took them both by surprise. Sara developed morning sickness so acute she couldn't get out of bed, and on the rare days when she did manage it, spent her time fighting back her nausea. Elias, on the other hand, met the challenge with cheery aplomb; he repainted the guest room, set up the nursery, researched strollers and car seats online. You have enough on your hands, he would tell Sara at night, rubbing her back and helping her readjust the support belt that the obstetrician recommended. How did other women develop pregnancy glow? Sara couldn't even bear to look at herself in the mirror. Her skin was sallow, her ankles were swollen. Every morning, waddling out of the bedroom into the kitchen, she looked at the Nimble screen above the counter, which listed the days remaining to full term, and smarted at how many she had left. The constant reminders Nimble sent her about her low intake of iron and folic acid only added to her stress. The last month of her pregnancy was pure agony. She couldn't sleep, couldn't walk, couldn't rest until she went into labor. When she saw Mohsin, his head slick with afterbirth and his face tied in a disapproving grimace at the world he was entering, she understood, in a way she never had before, why the procedure was called a *delivery*. Mona came three minutes later, screaming at the top of her lungs as soon as the doctor eased her out of the womb.

If one baby was a miracle, two were a revelation. Nothing could have prepared Sara for how much her life would change after the birth of the twins. The sheer impossibility of soothing one baby while the other was screaming. The crushing guilt of it, too, for how could she ignore a crying baby? As if aware of how long he had waited for them, and how much he had wanted them, the twins soothed easily when Elias was in charge, falling asleep in his arms within minutes. But not with her. These tiny creatures depended on her, and yet she couldn't feed, burp, change, and put them back to sleep without making at least five mistakes along the way.

Time was no longer something she had in abundance, to spend as she saw fit, but a precious commodity that needed to be parceled out carefully. Something as ordinary as a meal or a shower required planning, deployment, and execution with military precision. Like a recruit at bugle call, she met each day with a mix of terror and resignation.

She pulled out her phone again. Though the cracked screen distorted the numbers, she saw that fifty minutes had passed; they wouldn't make it to Mimi's now. She was famished, and wished she hadn't slept through the breakfast service on the plane.

Across the desk, meanwhile, Officer Moss was sipping his coffee peacefully.

"Did you just start your shift?" she asked, more out of boredom than interest.

"Uh-huh. It's my last day on rotation this week."

"That must be nice."

"Got any plans this weekend?"

The casualness of this question irritated Sara. Of course she had plans—eating a leisurely lunch with Elias, taking a long shower when she got home, playing with Mohsin and Mona, reading to them before bed—plans that this officer and his colleague at the RAA were disrupting. Her irritation quickly boiled to anger. "Is there a supervisor I could speak with?"

"A supervisor? What for?"

"I've been here over an hour," she said. "The other officer was about to stamp my passport when he was called away. I really don't understand the reason for this delay."

"It's not gonna take much longer. It's just procedure."

"Procedure because my name is Hussein?"

"Ma'am. We're all professionals here."

"Then why don't you stamp my passport?"

"I don't review risk reports."

"I thought you said you were a professional."

Moss didn't speak to her after that. Once he finished his coffee, he started texting on his phone, occasionally smiling at his screen. When a teenager with an oversized scarf around his neck was brought into the waiting room, Moss repositioned his chair so that he could keep both the teenager and Sara in his line of sight. What did he think she was going to do? Make a run for it? It was all so ridiculous. She tried texting her husband yet again, but there was no use.

Elias was probably trying to keep the twins entertained while he waited for her at Arrivals. She felt bad about the lengthy delay. She had spent four days in London on her employer's dime, had gone to the Tate Modern and the V&A, had enjoyed dinners and conversations with other adults. She couldn't blame him if he was feeling tired or even resentful.

The door flew open, and Segura reappeared.

Moss stood up. "How'd it go?"

Segura shook his head, as if to say they'd talk about it later, when they were alone.

"Sorry, man. Anyway, lady's all yours." Moss headed for the door. "Oh, and Ms. Hussein here thinks you're profiling her."

Segura gave her a wounded look, as though she had greatly offended him by complaining about being detained for an hour without reason. "We're all professionals here."

"So I keep hearing," Sara replied. She should stop there, a voice inside her advised, but it was drowned out by her mounting exasperation at the repeated delays. "But I'll tell you, I have my doubts."

His eyes widened at her insolence.

"Can I have my passport now?"

"Not yet," he said, his tone sharper. He logged back in to his computer and made a production out of clicking from tab to tab on his screen. On the other side of the glass, a woman in a blue shalwar kameez was escorted in, followed minutes later by an elderly man with dreadlocks and a knitted skullcap. Sara felt conscious of this growing audience, watching her interview with as much curiosity as self-interest. "The thing is," Segura was now saying, "your risk score is above the acceptable threshold. People get flagged anytime their score is above 500. Yours is at 518. There has to be a reason for that."

But that's such a small difference, Sara thought. Only an hour earlier, he hadn't seemed too concerned and was on the verge of stamping her passport. Now that same score was a problem that required a satisfactory explanation from her. It was absurd. Yet his new tone intimidated her. Calm down, she told herself, and turn this around before it gets out of hand. The Crime Prevention Act allowed algorithms to predict criminal activity, but it still gave RAA officers like Segura a certain amount of discretionary power.

If only she could have a glass of water and something to eat, she would feel revived, she would be able to handle this better. She still didn't know why her risk score was above 500. Had she run a red light without realizing it? Had she neglected to pay for a parking violation? Had she left the grocery store without scanning all her items? Had her phone pinged near a political protest or some kind of public disturbance? She racked her brain, but couldn't think why her score might have risen above the legal limit. "I have no record," she said, her tone turning conciliatory now. "You saw that for yourself."

Segura ignored her. It seemed he was determined to prove just how thorough at his job he could be. After a moment he asked, "What's your connection to Zach Miller?"

"He's my cousin."

"Well, *he* has an arrest record."

This was news to her, and it took her a moment to process it. "I haven't seen him in at least twenty years," she said. "I don't know what he did to get arrested, but it has nothing to do with me. How do you know we're related?"

"DNA database. Like I said, the algorithm is holistic."

Sara didn't bother asking how the RAA had access to her genetic material. Her parents had made her take one of those DNA tests that her school sent home with every fifth grader—the idea being that children could be identified in case of an earthquake, a mass shooting, or even a kidnapping. But the data had been harvested and now it was being used to tie her to her knucklehead cousin. Zach was, what, forty-one or forty-two? They had been playmates when they were in grade school in Pasadena. She remembered him as an older, aggressive kid who loved playing the "zombie game," which consisted mostly of tackling her and her brother, Saïd, to the ground and trying to bite them. One day, he pushed her so hard that she fell face-first on the driveway, cut her lip, and chipped her front tooth. Sara's howls of pain drew her mother and aunt out of the house in their slippers. "What happened?" her mother cried.

Holding her bloodied mouth with one hand, Sara pointed at the culprit with the other.

"She fell," Zach said, palms raised in self-defense. "We were just playing."

"So it was an accident," his mother said.

With a feeling of grave injustice washing over her, Sara watched as Aunt Hiba downplayed Zach's attack. It was only horseplay, she said, girls should learn to toughen up. A little fall wasn't the end of the world. Sara's mother rushed her to the dentist for emergency tooth repair, but the bonding material wasn't properly color-matched and the fracture remained visible. For weeks after the incident, Sara refused to smile, sealing her rage with a stoic face.

A couple of years later, Zach's father sold some stock he'd been holding on to for a decade and moved his family to Florida. Why Florida, everyone asked. Taxes, he replied. He bought three apartment buildings and retired on the income, but within months he had an affair and everything went downhill from there. Zach was in middle school at the time and already getting into trouble: skipping classes, talking back to his mom, fighting with his sisters. The police were called a couple of times. When Sara's uncle died a few years ago, Zach inherited a sizable amount of money, but little savvy. He started businesses at an astonishing rate, usually closing them down a few months later, when he lost interest. The last Sara had heard, he'd bought a vintage car dealership in Orlando.

"But wait a minute," Sara said. "What does my cousin being arrested have to do with me? You can't expect me to be responsible for something I haven't done."

"It increases your chances of a future arrest. It's relevant data."

"No, it isn't. Being related to someone isn't a crime." She became certain then that she was being held without reason. Moss and Segura knew it, too. Her mistake—her foolish mistake, no doubt caused by hunger and jet lag—had been to protest against what was happening to her; she was expected to be quiet and docile in her encounter with officers, no matter what they said or did. This realization renewed the pressure she felt to defuse the situation, a pressure that only worsened her anxiety.

"Ms. Hussein, it doesn't help your case when you make a false statement to law enforcement."

"What false statement?"

"Your employer didn't pay for your airfare."

"Oh," she said, realizing as soon as the word left her lips that the camera must have recorded her shock. "Well, I can explain that. The Getty doesn't give us expense cards for conferences. I have to charge the plane ticket to my personal Amex and then file for reimbursement. But I can't get reimbursed until next week because the office is closed during Christmas. I can assure you that the museum is paying for this trip. They've paid for all my previous conferences."

A long moment passed, during which the only sound was the clicking of the mouse. Sara felt beads of sweat traveling down her back; the smell was impossible to disguise now. She wondered who was watching at the other end, parsing her facial expressions for signs of deceit. "Are you seriously considering that a false statement?"

"The algorithm considers everything. I told you that already."

"I did *not* make a false statement. It was just a manner of speaking. The museum is paying for this trip as soon as I give them my receipts."

He shushed her, then leaned closer to the screen. This behavior baffled Sara. Had she miscalculated when she gave candid answers to all his questions? She should've been more careful, she realized with mounting horror. Now it was too late; he was using her words against her. A moment later, Segura turned to her again, his face full of concern.

SAFE-X, INC.

Short-Term Forensic Observation Facilities Division
Facility: Madison
Location: Ellis, California
Timestamp: 10-08-09-34

Minutes compiled by: MeetingPro

The Safe-X staff meeting was called to order at 09:34 a.m.

Present: Chief Retention Officer ███. Senior Attendant Hinton. Attendants Jackson, Yee, and Ortega. Junior Attendant Williams. Case Manager Gardner. Administrative Assistant Doyle.
Absent: Nurse Flores.
Guests: None.

APPROVAL OF SEPTEMBER MEETING MINUTES

On a motion by CRO ███, with a second by Senior Attendant Hinton, the meeting minutes of September 8 were unanimously approved.

CRO REPORT

A shipment of medications bound for Safe-X facilities in California was lost to a pileup of automated trucks on the 5 freeway. CRO ███ has been working with Nurse Flores to acquire replacements for essential needs, but shortages are to be expected.

CRO ███ received four bids for the east wing renovation and expansion, all of them from local companies in Ellis. Given this competitive situation, he believes he can get the project completed at a reasonable cost, especially with added revenue from this month's resident survey. The renovation work will begin in the next two to three weeks.

The contract with PostPal for communication services has been renewed for another two years. CRO ███ is pleased to report that he managed to get a .2% rate increase on Safe-X's share of call revenue.

The cybersecurity awareness training was due October 5, but so far only Attendants Hinton and Yee have completed it. CRO ███ reminded attendants that this training is mandatory for all Safe-X employees.

ATTENDANT REPORTS

Senior Attendant Hinton reported that the earthquake, flood, and wildfire safety check was completed on October 1. The designated safety marshals noted that some emergency supplies are running low, including nitrile gloves, face masks, and plastic sheeting. Attendant Hinton said he had a complete list and requested funding to purchase the items.

CRO ███ said he would take each item under consideration, as the budget is tight.

Attendant Jackson reported that the work contracts are on schedule.

CRO ███ asked how many shifts are vacant at the moment.

Attendant Jackson responded that there were seven.

CRO ███ commended Attendant Jackson on improving her numbers over last month, but reminded everyone that the goal is zero. Attendants should be more proactive in encouraging residents to work overtime shifts.

Attendant Yee reported that the north-facing camera in the cafeteria is feeding shaky video to the main observation deck, and requests a replacement.

CRO ███ asked what happened to it.

Attendant Yee responded that Residents Toya Jones and Sara Hussein were attempting to catch a flying cockroach. Resident Jones threw her shoe at it, hitting the camera.

CRO ▓▓▓▓ asked did she catch it at least.

[Laughter]

Attendant Yee said yes.

CRO ▓▓▓▓ said he would order the replacement and charge the cost to Resident Jones.

NEW BUSINESS

CRO ▓▓▓▓ reported that he came across a video that Junior Attendant Williams posted on Printastic, where he appeared to be making jokes about this facility. Attendants Ortega, Jackson, Yee, and Hinton could also be seen in the video. CRO ▓▓▓▓ demanded an explanation.

Junior Attendant Williams responded that the video was made on his own time at Ray's Bar and Grill in Ellis and therefore doesn't constitute a violation of company policy.

CRO ▓▓▓▓ asked Junior Attendant Williams whether he is an expert on company policy.

Junior Attendant Williams replied that the video doesn't include explicit references to Madison.

CRO ▓▓▓▓ asked the attendants what terms they did use and why.

Attendant Ortega said he's only ever called Madison what it is, a Short-Term Forensic Observation Facility.

Attendant Jackson said she calls it "the house of detention" because she is from Brooklyn and also because Madison used to be a public school.

Junior Attendant Williams said he calls it "the asylum" out of habit, because he used to work at a mental health facility before coming to Madison.

Attendant Yee said he doesn't call it anything, and that he was only at the dinner because dress rehearsal for his play was cancelled.

Senior Attendant Hinton said he calls it "the hotel."

CRO ███ asked Senior Attendant Hinton why.

Senior Attendant Hinton replied that he likes to make every woman's stay memorable.

[Laughter]

CRO ███ said that he didn't mind if the attendants let off some steam on Fridays, but he could not allow the taping or posting of videos that reflect negatively on this facility, even if it's through nicknames, as it could be prejudicial to the company's reputation.

CRO ███ added that attendants might get sued *in personam* [click to add word to dictionary] for violating company privacy agreements.

Attendant Williams said he would take down the video.

CRO ███ reminded everyone that he is hosting a barbecue in honor of his son's return from overseas service this Saturday afternoon. All are invited.

ADJOURNMENT

There being no further business, CRO ███ moved that the meeting be adjourned. The motion was seconded by Attendant Hinton and carried unanimously. The meeting was adjourned at 10:06 a.m.

THE LAUNDRY ROOM IS PARTICULARLY DANK THIS AFTERNOON. It takes Sara a minute to adjust to the smell, but Toya is already at work, sorting through the mesh sacks in the wheeled cart. She acknowledges Sara with a nod. Though she isn't much of a talker, Toya is full of interesting information on a wide range of subjects when she does speak. She knows how much a ten-year-old lightly driven Tesla is worth, or what it costs to replace a broken picture window, or how often a particular neighborhood floods, details she picked up in the course of a twenty-year career as an insurance claims adjuster. After the complex wildfire in Tujunga three years ago, she was put in charge of supervising claims verifications at Sanctuary Insurance, a huge responsibility that should have led to professional advancement, but she was agitating for a union and the promotion went to someone else—an oversight about which she's still bitter.

Sara comes to stand next to Toya at the washers, helping her unpack the bags of white uniforms. Whoever decided on white wasn't exactly concerned about practicality, Sara thinks; she has to pour two heaping scoops of company-approved whitening chemical over every load. On the other hand, white reinforces the idea that Madison isn't a prison or a jail. In red or orange, the retainees might be perceived as dangerous inmates, the type that should be housed with convicted murderers or drug dealers. In brown or stripes, they might seem like petty thieves, shoplifters, or fraudsters.

But white affords other interpretations.

White is bland, sterile, therapeutic. White means their crimes can still be averted.

She brings more bags to the machines. Before her retention, she used to hate running the wash, but now the two afternoons a week when she's assigned to the laundry room are her favorite; working with her hands allows her mind to roam free. Toya fiddles with the thermostat on the wall, trying to keep the laundry room cool. Even though the numbers on the screen decrease to 65 degrees, there's no detectable change in the temperature. By the time the dryers are running, both women are sweating through their uniforms. Still, the steady thrum of the machines means they can have private conversations, which is almost impossible anywhere else at Madison. "I didn't see you at breakfast," Sara says.

"I was at the infirmary," Toya replies. "Trying to refill my blood pressure medication again." The last time she tried, Nurse Flores told her they had run out of the particular drug she needs. "I looked up a bunch of substitutes at the library."

"That's smart."

"Desperate, more like. But I'll take smart, too," Toya says with a grin. The gap between her front teeth makes her look much younger. She spends her meager earnings on hair dye from the commissary; the curls that frame her face look charcoal black. Sara has never asked how old Toya is, because she's come to suspect it's a touchy subject.

"When's your hearing?" Sara asks.

"Tuesday at 3:30."

Twenty-two retainees have been released in the time Sara has been at Madison. Nearly all of them had hearings early in the morning, at 8 or 8:30. From this small dataset, everyone has drawn different conclusions. Some people think that RAA agents tend to be more lenient when they've just started their day. Others believe the retainees with early appointments were well rested first thing in the morning, which allowed them to perform better on their mental-status evaluations. Yet others think that the freed retainees made good impressions because they wore immaculate uniforms, compared with those who had to go straight from their work assignments in the kitchen or the yard to the interview room. Retention makes everyone superstitious. "I can cover for you," Sara offers.

"They already told me I have to keep to my work schedule until it's time for the hearing. But thanks, I appreciate it."

Sara rubs her eyes. When she worked at the Getty she wore special glasses that protected against the blue lights of her computer screen, making it easier to sit at her desk for hours on end, looking at grainy photographs from the 1920s. By now, Jim Klass must have taken her name out of the office directory and assigned someone else to her project. These days it is Sara's replacement who rides the tram up the hill, enjoying the views of the Santa Monica Mountains on a brisk fall morning, then steps out onto the still-empty Getty plaza, where the plash of a water fountain welcomes her into a day filled with art and beauty. What a life it was! Sara can't believe she ever complained about the tram ride adding to her commute or about the cost of the caprese salad at the cafeteria or even about the tourists who periodically wandered into the research institute, looking for a bathroom. Then again, perhaps she has it wrong. Perhaps her retention presented the museum with an opportunity to cut down on the department's budget by leaving her position unfilled.

Either way, the world moves on without her.

Now she opens the hardcover she borrowed from the library, a nonfiction book called *When We Came Together: The Legacy of the WPA*. Toya is reading a hard-boiled novel by Chester Himes. She flips through the pages and pulls out something that she slides across the table. "Happy birthday," she says.

It's a handmade bookmark, cut in the shape of photographic film. "I can't believe you remembered!" Sara says, delight raising her voice to a higher pitch. "Thank you." She holds up the bookmark to the light to admire it. "It looks so real. The perforations must've taken forever. Where'd you find the card stock?"

"Container for the laundry soap."

"I love it," Sara says. "Thanks so much." She places the bookmark in her book.

A companionable silence falls between the two women as they read. The rest of the shift unfolds uneventfully, with only a minor interruption from Hinton, who makes a point of checking the laundry room while doing his rounds. Sara isn't sure what he's looking for; there's no chance of illicit activity in a cramped room like this, which is equipped with cameras and has no back doors or hidden corners. But Hinton likes to be thorough.

·   ·   ·

AFTER HER LAUNDRY SHIFT SARA FORCES HERSELF TO GO TO THE EXER-
cise yard. Around the perimeter there are still traces of the school's
playground—markers where the monkey bars stood, a line on the
wall that was used for handball practice, a pole from which a tether-
ball once hung. The breezeway still has handprint tiles, remnants of
a kindergarten art project called THERE IS ONLY ONE ME. As late as
thirty years ago, when keeping the school open wasn't considered
a fiscal liability for the district, the playground was filled with the
joyful noise of children. Now it's mostly quiet, even when dozens of
retainees are out on break; they are under strict orders not to disrupt
the work in the trailers that take up the northern side of the lawn.

She walks a couple of laps around the track, telling herself that
this counts as exercise, then sits on a bench under the sun. Marcela is
using the other end for a knee stretch. She's a friendly girl, Marcela.
It's hard to believe there's a restraining order against her.

The way Marcela tells it, her problems started when she reported
her neighbors for running an unlicensed daycare. She objected to
the business as a matter of principle, it was nothing personal. But
after the city shut down the couple's business and slapped them
with a fine, Marcela started getting noise disturbance calls from the
police whenever she rehearsed with her guitar or drums. On weekends, her neighbors blocked her garage door with their car, which
was a problem because Marcela came home late from shows and
was forced to circle the block each time, looking for street parking.
So when they cut down her Japanese maple, she snapped and took
a baseball bat to their fence. The footage of her on their doorbell
camera allowed them to obtain a restraining order—and shot up
her risk score. A few weeks later, while she was driving Sharp Jello's
band van, she was stopped for running a red light and was referred
to the RAA. The violent dreams she was having about her neighbors
landed her in retention.

With all the time she's had at Madison, Sara has been thinking
about her past, too, replaying one or another event that the algorithm could've used against her by giving it more significance than

it deserved: a joke she made on social media in a heated moment, a fight she had over a parking space in a grocery-store lot, a ticket scan she skipped because she was in a rush to catch the Metro. At the time, she thought these incidents were trivial, if she thought about them at all, but they were recorded on smartphones, documented in screenshots, or watched from hidden security cameras, then stored in online databases. She can't erase or escape her past: the incidents remain on OmniCloud, to be read, scored, and interpreted however the algorithm's designers intended. We blame the algorithm for our predicament, she thinks, but the algorithm was written by people. That's who put us at Madison. People, not machines.

Marcela sits on the bench. "Can I ask you something?"

Sara's eyes dart to the sentry post under the breezeway, where Jackson sits, arms folded, the silver stripes on her shirt barely visible in the shade. She stays out of the sun as much as possible, on account of the vitiligo patches on her elbows, and that means she's too far away to hear their conversation. The nearest Guardian camera is on top of the light pole, twenty feet away, but the hum of traffic from the highway must interfere with sound quality.

"You're a professor, right?" Marcela asks.

"Not anymore," Sara says, getting up and stretching her right leg. She doesn't really need it, but it makes her look busy rather than friendly. Even without sound, she has learned, camera footage can convey unintended meaning.

"But you know how to write official letters," Marcela insists. She leans forward. "Here's the thing. I asked to have my guitar sent here, but they told me I had to write an official request and explain why I need it. Which is like, I don't know, like asking me why I need air to breathe."

Sara switches to the left leg. Sooner or later every retainee comes face-to-face with Safe-X bureaucracy. It's a risky encounter, liable to lead you to break one rule while trying to follow another.

"So anyway. I wrote the damn petition, but they said I didn't provide sufficient justification." Marcela makes air quotes around *sufficient justification*. "And since you got your petition for the worship space approved, I was thinking, maybe you could help me write mine? It has to be a convincing petition. I really need my guitar. I need it."

"They don't care about that."

After another cycle of stretches, Sara sits on the bench beside Marcela. The truth is that she wouldn't mind helping with the letter, but she doesn't know whether it's against the rules to assist a fellow retainee with a petition. She has to check the handbook first. "Tell you what," she whispers. "Let me think on it."

SARA RETURNS TO THE SECOND FLOOR, FEELING WORN OUT EVEN though she hasn't exerted herself all that much. It must be the monotony; her body finds it as exhausting as her mind does. This afternoon is particularly slow. Walking into 208, she finds her room-mate working on her comic book. Emily spends all her money on pencils and paper, but she can't afford colors, which is a source of continual frustration for her. She's always telling Sara what shades of red or yellow she would have used if she had them, how much they would have added to the tone or depth of the work. The comic features a tightly clad mutant who fights supervillains using the fire-power in her hands, which ignite at will and shoot flames from as far as a hundred feet away. Emily is a firefighter; she takes pride in the fact that her renderings of flames, and all the damage that a fire can cause, are realistic. Why a firefighter is writing a comic about a pyro-maniac mutant, Sara hasn't asked. Every woman needs private pas-sions. Besides, Sara finds the sound of pencil on paper to be soothing.

Sara splashes cold water on her face, then sits on her cot, resting her back against the wall. Emily looks up from her drawing pad. "There's a new girl," she announces.

"Yeah, I met her this morning."

"What's she like?"

"I don't really know. She didn't say much."

From where Sara is sitting, she can see Eisley in the hallway, standing at the door of 207, with her hand resting on the jamb. Does she have a question about the rules? No, it sounds like she's asking where the television room is. "I think she's doing okay."

Sara goes back to her history of the WPA. The section she's reading is about how the Federal Writers' Project began to collect oral histories from thousands of former slaves. The narratives were recorded and edited in the 1930s by outsiders, a majority of them middle-class whites, yielding an archive that is both valuable and hopelessly limited in its ability to document how enslaved people survived under brutal predations. The chapter is engaging, but Sara has a harder time concentrating on the text as the afternoon device check approaches.

Finally the bell rings. Sara and her roommate step out into the hallway, joined a moment later by the women returning from the work trailers. This afternoon the attendant on duty is Yee, a younger guy with thick eyebrows who walks down the hallway in long, easy strides. As he makes the rounds with the scanner, he murmurs a polite thank-you each time a retainee's neuroprosthetic beeps. Sara is amazed by his ability to maintain his good humor; compartmentalizing has never been her strong suit.

Once the neuroprosthetic scan is completed, Yee rattles off from a list on his tablet the names of those who have PostPal mail today, then turns around to leave.

"Yee," Sara says, catching up to him. "You got anything for me?"

"Not today."

She shifts on her feet, fighting the urge to snatch the PostPal tablet from him and check it herself. "You don't have any mail for me, or a package maybe?"

"Nothing today. Were you expecting an email?"

"Yeah." Never mind her birthday. It's been nearly a month since she last heard from Elias, her calls and emails to him going unanswered. At first she thought he'd lost his phone, or that he was felled by a nasty cold, or that he was busy with a special project at work, but as the days turned into weeks, she's had a harder time interpreting his silence, deciding whether it's the benign reserve of a busy father or an early sign of estrangement. She's starved for news of him, news of home.

His messages are the only chronicle she has of everything she's missing while she's at Madison. Last time he wrote, he told her that their homeowners' association is giving him grief about taking in a paying roommate, saying he should've consulted with them and allowed them to vet the applicants. He's finished child-proofing the kitchen cabinets, and secured the windows, too. The twins are walking, the twins can use spoons, the twins play with toy cars. He thinks they're ready to start potty training because they wake up from their naps with clean diapers. Both of them are talking as well, saying words like *cup* and *milk* and *papa*.

As for Sara's own papa, every letter he writes is a variation on the same themes: he urges her to eat well, exercise, and rest; to work hard and keep out of trouble; and to stay away from the other retainees in order to avoid any entanglements that might have legal ramifications for her case. The advice makes Sara cringe; her father has never encountered a problem he didn't immediately try to solve through the application of personal effort. Responsibility—and its corollary, blame—were the principles on which he built his life and, after the passing of Sara's mother a few years ago, he has grown even more committed to them. But although his messages never fail to trigger bouts of guilt, Sara still likes receiving them, likes knowing that she is being remembered. Especially on a day like this. "It's, uh...I should be getting something today."

Yee scrolls through the list on his tablet again, then shakes his head. "Nope, I don't have you on here."

"Thanks for checking." A wave of disappointment washes over her as she walks back down the hallway, passing Emily on her way to the reading room.

Good evening, residents. This is your chief retention officer speaking. In honor of Indigenous Peoples' Day, we will be showing a new documentary about Mesa Verde National Park in the entertainment room. Showtimes are 8 p.m. and 9 p.m. Snacks are available for purchase at the commissary.

The water in Rooms 225 and 227 has been shut off due to a pipe leak. Residents assigned to those rooms will have to use the toilets in the locker room.

Starting tomorrow, residents assigned to Trailers A and B will be working on a new contract from Vox-R for the next four weeks, with evening shifts available for anyone else who wishes to work overtime. Trailers C and D will continue their work with NovusFilm.

Thank you for your cooperation.

THE INTERVIEW ROOM SEEMED SUDDENLY SMALLER TO SARA, the walls close enough to touch. Shock pulled her out of her body, and for a moment she felt as if she were floating above, watching the back-and-forth with Segura. How did it take such a terrible turn? I have to stop this, she thought as she returned to herself. Sweat ran down her back in a continuous stream, pooling at the waist of her jeans.

"It's your sleep data," Segura said, peering at her with fresh suspicion. "And I can't ignore that, not with the other flags I see in your file and your responses during this interview. I'm afraid I have to issue an order of retention." He pulled an evidence bag from the bottom drawer and began writing her name in block letters on the label.

"Wait a minute," Sara said, raising a hand. "Just wait. What are you talking about?" Her neuroprosthetic logged the time she went to sleep and the time she woke up, but that data could hardly mean anything. What did it matter to law enforcement if she went to sleep at eleven? Or that she woke up at four to feed the twins? Or even that she took occasional thirty-minute naps on the couch in her office? That was nobody's business. "What does my sleep data have to do with crime?"

"Some entries showed a high risk of violence."

"Entries? You mean dreams?" Sara's mind reeled, thinking about the consent forms she signed the day she got the implant. They said nothing about the sale of dreams to a third party, much less a government entity. If they did, then the detail had been concealed in incomprehensible legalese.

"Yes, Ms. Hussein," Segura replied, his voice dripping with condescension. "Dreams."

All her life Sara had been a good sleeper, quickly falling into slumber and waking up eight or nine or sometimes ten hours later with no interruption in between. Even on long flights, when she was squeezed into a middle seat with no adjustable headrest, she always managed to get some shut-eye. Her pregnancy changed all that. She couldn't get more than a few scattered hours of sleep each night because her back ached, or her legs cramped, or her feet swelled. Wrestling with her pillows to find a comfortable position made her heart race.

When she and Elias brought the twins home from the hospital, they agreed to take turns feeding them at night. But Elias had a Dreamsaver, so the minute he went to bed he fell asleep, and woke up from his four-hour nap as refreshed as if he had slept eight hours. Lucky bastard. He fed the babies all the milk she'd pumped, and cooed to them, and changed their diapers without ever losing his patience or good humor. Meanwhile, Sara lay awake, her nipples raw and painful, waiting for the next feeding or worrying about all the things she might've done wrong.

It was only then that she began to understand—no, to experience— sleep deprivation. She couldn't keep her eyes open during the day, no matter how much coffee she consumed, and started to forget every little thing. The water on the stove. The clothes in the dryer. Where she put Mona's pacifier, or Mohsin's diaper-rash cream. Whether she ate the fenugreek seeds the lactation specialist had recommended. She gave up breastfeeding, which allowed her to regain a bit of her strength, though it did nothing to fix her sleeplessness.

What is happening to me, she wondered. She moved through the day as if in a trance. She quarreled with Elias over the smallest, most insignificant things. Once, she ordered takeout from an Indian place a couple of miles from their apartment and forgot to pick it up because she was arguing with Elias about who told Nimble to send ten cases of sparkling water to the door. Another time, she put Mohsin on her bed while she went to fetch a box of diapers, got distracted by Mona crying in the other room, and forgot all about Mohsin.

She couldn't go on like this, she just couldn't. She'd been reluctant to get a Dreamsaver because she was squeamish about the proce- dure, but when she scheduled the appointment, a brochure appeared in her inbox that put her fears to rest. The original device had been designed in the 2000s to treat sleep apnea, and was implanted in a delicate surgery that required several days of recovery. Back then the only patients who were willing to take the risk were acute sufferers, whose lives were in danger from interrupted breathing. But over the years, the procedure became safer, the recovery time shorter. Longitudinal studies of the earliest implantees showed that their sleep not only improved, but deepened, giving them longer REM cycles. They performed better on memory tests, healed faster from wounds and bone fractures, and felt more rested and energetic during the day.

These benefits attracted the attention of Eric Hollins, a Silicon Valley medical entrepreneur. His team developed a new version of the neuroprosthetic that turned the side effect of longer REM cycles into a raison d'être, producing a device that was small, inexpensive, and easy to implant. It could give you deeper sleep, and in fewer hours. On the brochure, Hollins posed in white pajamas, with a halo around his head, his palm turned up in offering. In it was a minuscule implant, which he called the Dreamsaver. Imagine what you could do with more time, he asked.

Insomniacs who turned to Dreamsavers wrote five-star reviews where they sounded like the apostles of a new religion, eager to tell everyone the good news. From ER nurses to security guards, night-shift workers were huge fans of the device, whose effects included improved productivity and a drop in workplace accidents. Elias had gotten one a couple of years earlier because he was taking evening courses to improve his certifications, and needed the extra hours for school. The Dreamsaver came in handy when the twins were born. It was time for Sara to get one, too.

Within two days of implantation, she started to sleep restfully and regularly. She was able to function again. She didn't lose her patience when Mona refused to be put down in her crib, or when Mohsin soiled his diaper two minutes after she changed it. Each developmental stage became a cause for celebration, rather than relief. When she arrived at work in the morning, she was refreshed and ready for whatever the day held. In the evening, she was excited about playing with her children or catching up with her husband.

The Dreamsaver really did have a dramatic effect on her life—all of it positive.

"They're just dreams," she told Segura. It occurred to her that she might be hallucinating. Her mouth was so dry that she had trouble swallowing, and the hunger she felt was making her light-headed. "They're not real."

"Whether they're real or not is above my pay grade, Ms. Hussein. That's a philosophical question you can take up in your spare time. All I know is that they're among the two hundred data sources used by the crime-prediction algorithm and they've raised your risk score above the acceptable threshold." He slipped Sara's passport into the labeled evidence bag. "You've left me no choice."

Sara's hands were so sweaty by now that her phone slipped from them and fell on the floor. The screen cracked anew, in a different place. "You can't be serious," she said, picking up the phone and stuffing it in her purse. The conversation was taking a turn she was desperate to correct. "Dreams are random."

"Nothing is random," he said with frightening conviction. Didn't she know that dreams were windows into the subconscious? They showed connections between our thoughts and actions while remaining free of lies or justifications. They revealed our fears, desires, and petty jealousies with greater honesty than we would ever allow in our waking moments. They were valuable precisely because they exposed the most private parts of ourselves, from repressed memories to future plans.

"Okay, sure, but they're not crimes."

"They might *turn* into crimes. That's the whole point." The company that made the Dreamsaver had harvested data from millions of users, and trained an AI to look for patterns and make predictions. He cleared his throat. "Now, having reviewed the evidence, I've determined that you're an immediate risk, which is why I'm referring you to Safe-X for an observation period of twenty-one days."

"I'm a risk?" She wanted to scream. "To whom?"

"Elias Rosales," he replied, with another glance at his screen. "Your husband."

"My *husband*? That's ridiculous. I love my husband. Why would I be a risk to him? As a matter of fact, he's waiting for me downst—"

"—So you understand the urgency."

"What urgency? I would never hurt him."

"Well, we need to make sure of that. That's why you're being retained, Ms. Hussein."

"Retained?"

"Confined, isolated, quarantined. Whatever you want to call it."

Officer Moss walked in again, as if Segura had summoned him from an unseen button. "Ms. Hussein," he said, "come with me."

Sara looked from one officer to the other. For a brief moment, she wondered if this was an elaborate prank, staged for the amusement of their colleagues in the RAA lounge, who were watching from the other side of the camera. But the look on Moss's face crushed any hope of this possibility, however humiliating it would be in its own way. "You can't do this," she managed to say. To make it clear that she had no intention of going anywhere with Moss, she sat back in her chair and folded her arms. "I want to speak to a supervisor."

"I *am* a supervisor," Moss said with a little smile, his hand resting on his holster.

Sara realized then that she had misjudged him, that the softness in his features did not indicate compassion in his duties or reluctance around firearms. "Can you explain what's happening, then? Why is he saying I have to be retained when my score is only 518?"

"See, you've answered your own question. Your score is above the legal limit. Now stand up and come with me. We have a lot of people to process today and we're already running behind schedule."

"*Now* you're in a rush?" Sara asked, working and yet failing to keep her voice from rising. "I've waited more than an hour already. I'm not moving from here until I make a phone call. I need to speak to my husband. He's waiting for me at Baggage Claim and has no idea where I am. Or better yet, call him yourself. He can tell you I'm not a risk to him, or to anyone else. Just call him. You can get this cleared up right now."

"There's a phone downstairs," Moss replied. "We'll send him an official notice as well. Now bring your bag and come with me."

"Why can't you call him from here?"

Moss heaved a sigh. "This isn't a good start to your retention, Ms. Hussein. Like I said, you can make a phone call from downstairs.

But behaving like this isn't going to help your case. Right now, it's doing the opposite. Think of your score."

On the other side of the glass, the other travelers seemed riveted by the conversation. The woman in the blue shalwar kameez had her hand on her cheek and the teenager was leaning forward, resting his elbows on his knees, staring at her. Sara wondered whether they could tell what was happening. She wasn't sure herself.

"Come on. Let's go," Moss said.

Carrying her bag, Sara followed him through the waiting area, noticing along the way the concerned looks of the other travelers, united in their fear of ending up like her. Moss took her downstairs on the elevator, leading her to a small, white room where two hostile Safe-X employees immediately took away her phone, wallet, and keys, placing them in labeled envelopes. "I need to make a call," she said to one of them.

"This the correct name?" he replied, showing her the label on one of the envelopes.

"Yes, but I need to make a call."

"In a minute."

Only after her luggage was searched, and each item catalogued and stored in a Safe-X bin, did Moss walk her to a phone. The device was in a booth in the hallway, where RAA employees and Safe-X agents who were passing by could hear her. She dialed her husband, but after a few rings the call went to voicemail. She dialed a second time, but again he didn't pick up. "He's not answering," she told Moss. "Maybe he doesn't have cell reception."

"Is there anyone else you can call?" he said. For the first time, he sounded like he was trying to help. "We have a couple more minutes."

Sara wanted to try her father, but he had upgraded his phone and, although she had saved the new number on her mobile, she didn't know it by heart. She could summon the area code and the prefix, but try as she might she couldn't remember the last four digits. Now she pleaded with Moss. "Isn't there something you can do?" she asked. "My score is barely above the limit. I mean, your friend upstairs was going to stamp my passport before he was called away. Can't you just give me a warning or something?"

"I'm sorry," Moss said. "I don't review risk reports."

"Right, you already said." Don't cry, she told herself. Whatever you do, don't cry. "But you're the supervisor, aren't you?"

"It's just twenty-one days," he said, touching her elbow as if to console her. "And it's a retention center for dreamers, it's almost like summer camp. You go in, they watch you to make sure you don't do anything, and then you come out three weeks later. It's really not that bad. Some people might even think of it as a vacation. I mean, if it were me, I wouldn't mind getting a break from the old ball and chain, you know what I'm saying?"

"I just . . ." Sara said, swallowing hard. Then she turned to the dial once more. "I'll try my husband again."

"Too late," Moss said, looking beyond her at the double doors. "Transport is here."

THE BUS THAT PULLED UP TO THE CURB SEEMED TO HAVE BEEN BOUGHT at a salvage sale, hastily painted black, and imprinted with the logo of Safe-X. Through the barred windows, the other retainees watched as Sara was brought on board. As soon as she took her seat, a message played on the stereo, announcing that Safe-X was acting *in loco magistratus;* it was allowed to conduct a forensic observation of retainees and, if necessary, to discipline them on behalf of the government. There will be multiple stops, the disembodied voice continued. Your name will be called when we arrive at your designated facility. There will be no talking on the bus. If you have questions about your file, you can ask your case manager after you've been processed.

Sara was the last drop-off, in Ellis. By the time she walked into Madison, her legs could hardly carry her. Sitting in what she later learned was the gym, she had trouble following the orders that were lobbied at her by the nurse, the intake clerk, and the attendants who were in charge of orientation. They wanted her to submit blood, urine, and hair samples, wash with a medicated shampoo, and squat and cough while they watched, whereas she wanted to find out why she was here and when she could make a call. They recorded her weight, her blood pressure, and the date of her last menstrual period, while she kept asking why she had to stay three whole weeks.

It was as if the agents were speaking a foreign tongue, in which the only mood was the imperative, the subject never stated. She couldn't speak this language; she could only obey it.

Oh, but everything was so clear to her now. She should've been patient with Segura and Moss; instead, she'd been in a rush. Should've been quiet; she'd talked back. Should've followed directions; she'd resisted. She'd passed up so many chances to demonstrate her docility that she had only herself to blame for what happened. But still, it made no sense that her score was above the legal limit. Didn't Segura say that the algorithm used data from two hundred sources? She'd already corrected the information about the police encounter at Heathrow. Surely there was a mistake somewhere else. There was no other explanation.

It came to her then that she should never have taken Moss at his word and allowed herself to be escorted out of the interview room. Now she was in the custody of private contractors, who were totally uninterested in her legal case; all they cared about were the rules of retention, which had to be followed to the letter. Then, after the orientation was completed, they said it was too late to make a phone call and she had to wait until morning.

They escorted her to 208 instead, and told her to go to dinner.

But she'd lost her appetite, and the smell of the floor cleaner made her feel ill. She wrestled with the window for a while, then gave up and lay on her cot, covered with the thin blanket they gave her. How was it possible that so much could change in a single day? It felt like months since she'd woken up in London.

Try to stay calm, she told herself, even as fear whispered into her ear one horrific scenario after another. Try not to panic. Her experience as an archivist had taught her that human error was an inescapable part of any record-keeping program and that it could lead to misunderstandings, some trivial and others tragic. That had to be what had happened here. Time was not on her side, though. Unless the information was corrected quickly, it could become legitimate by virtue of its presence in the records.

By now Elias must have found out what happened to her. Would he believe their ridiculous claims about her? No, he loved her; he knew she would never hurt him. He would treat the RAA's retention order as the misunderstanding that it was and hire a lawyer to get her out as soon as possible. With the help of a good attorney, her case would be dismissed. She had done nothing wrong—a fact that would be easy enough to establish.

A short, stocky woman walked into the room just then, and sat on the opposite cot. Her neck was raw from scratching and on her right bicep was a tattoo of a firefighter in a helmet. "What's your name?" she asked in a whisper. "I'm Emily. Emily Robbins."

Sara turned to the wall. She couldn't bring herself to make small talk. All she could think about was how to secure her release from this terrible place, filled with people who might be dangerous. She tried to still her frenetic thoughts; the sooner she fell asleep, the sooner morning would come. Then she could speak to a lawyer, find out what happened, and petition for her immediate release.

But she was afraid to surrender to sleep. How could she be sure that her dreams wouldn't incriminate her further? The uniform shirt she had been issued was a size too small, making her so uncomfortable that she had to take it off and layer it over herself for added warmth. She should never have gone to that conference in London; if she'd stayed home with her children, none of this would've happened. She lay on her cot for hours, eyes wide open, until the lights went out. Later she couldn't remember what she dreamed; she had yet to keep a notebook. All she remembered was waking up in terror at the sound of the six o'clock bell.

Emily was already up, washing her face at the sink, splashing water all over the floor. "You'll get used it," she said when the bell stopped ringing.

Well, Sara had no intention of getting used to it; she didn't belong in this place. Sleep had revived her, and now she was even more determined to untangle the mess she'd landed herself in and get out of here. She put on her shirt and followed her roommate into the hallway.

Emily stood at attention. "Whatever you do, don't piss off Hinton."

Sara turned her gaze on the handsome guy coming down the hall. He was a little older than the two attendants who had conducted orientation, and carried himself with a gravitas that the three gold stripes on his sleeve appeared to corroborate. He seemed to be getting over a cold, because he coughed into his elbow a couple of times as he moved from one room to the next, telling the woman at 203 that she had a visit this afternoon, and the one at 205 that her petition to start a zine was denied. When he finally got to 208, he scanned the back of Emily's skull with a device that looked like an ear thermometer. As soon as it flashed green, she went back inside the room.

Then Hinton nodded at Sara. "Dr. Hussein, I presume." He looked beyond her at the cell, where Emily was already making her cot. "208 is very nice, you get a window."

"There's been a mistake," she began.

"Oh, there's no mistake."

"But I would never—"

"—The algorithm knows what you're thinking of doing, before even you know it. That's a scientific fact. A forensic hold is for your own good, it prevents you from acting on your impulses." Hinton pointed his scanner at the back of her skull, as he continued his little speech. She had to stay here until her behavioral observation was complete. Her lawyer, if she had one, would be able to meet with her in the cafeteria during regular business hours, but otherwise she was not allowed any visitors until after seven days.

"This can't be legal."

"Sure it is." The scanner gave a beep, and he stepped back. "Look it up, Doc."

"But you can't keep me in prison. I didn't do anything."

"Calm down. This is a retention facility, not the Château d'If."

Sara must've looked surprised at the reference, because Hinton let out a bitter laugh.

"What, you think I don't read?" he said, fixing her with his hungry eyes.

"No, no." He doesn't like me, she thought. Later, remembering this moment, she would realize he'd interpreted her surprise as disdain, and developed an immediate hostility to her. "I just…" she said, quickly changing directions, "I haven't been able to make my call yet."

"Downstairs," he said. "You get three minutes."

.   .   .

AN HOUR LATER SHE WAS IN A GLASS-WALLED COMM POD, PRE-WIRED with a security camera and audio system. In order to activate the phone panel, she had to slip her index finger through a vitals monitor, which tracked her heart rate. As she dialed Elias's number, she felt keenly aware that she was being watched, that whatever she said could be used against her, and that she had to make the most of the time allotted to her. These limitations were both stressful and contradictory, so that she fumbled with the numbers a couple of times before she could steady her hand and touch the right keys.

As soon as he heard her voice, Elias launched into worried questions. "Where are you?" he asked. "What happened? We waited for you for hours at the airport. We've been calling hospitals all night. Are you all right?"

In the background, Sara heard a chair being pushed aside and the buzzing of the Ambulator Exo-Legs her father had been using since his stroke four years earlier. "Is that her?" he asked. "Where is she?"

"You didn't get a notice from the RAA?" Sara asked.

"No. We didn't hear anything. We've been worried sick."

"I got detained at the airport," she said, her voice breaking. Being listened to with a kindly ear was such a release that the humiliation of the last twenty-four hours began to overwhelm her. She leaned against the glass wall, only to be startled by a male voice on the audio system warning her to keep off the glass. The order was repeated in Spanish, and she had to wait several precious seconds before she could hope to be heard on the other end of the line. "I got detained," she said, more steadily this time, "and they're keeping me under observation."

"What? Where?"

"A town called Ellis, in San Bernardino County."

"Ellis? I've never heard of it."

Sara's father let out a strange, throaty sound. To hear him muffling a cry made her aware that she had disappointed him, as she had so many times before. All his life he had tried to instill in her the immigrant's habit of caution, reminding her to follow the rules, avoid unnecessary attention, and give careful consideration to decisions she made. But once more she had misstepped, and was deserving of blame.

"But why are they holding you there?" Elias was asking, now for the second time.

"They're saying my risk score is too high. That I'm liable to commit a crime. They're keeping me under observation for twenty-one days."

"Three whole weeks? That's insane."

"The officers…" Sara wanted to call them assholes and bastards and motherfuckers, but she knew her call was being monitored and she was in enough trouble as it was. "The officers said I was an imminent risk to you. To you! Can you believe it? I tried to get them to call you so you could talk to them directly, but they said no. Anyway, can you get me a lawyer? I don't want to spend three weeks here."

"A risk to me?" He sounded puzzled. There was a rustling noise, as if he were moving his phone from one ear to the other.

"I was thinking, maybe you could ask that professor whose daughter you treated a while back. You said he taught in the law school, right? He might be willing to help, or at least know someone who can. It's not a complicated case. I mean, I haven't done anything. I want them to file a motion for immediate release."

The line was quiet.

"Hello?" Sara asked.

"I'm here, I'm just trying to process everything. This is just crazy."

"I know, I'm sorry. Just get me a lawyer, I want to get out of here. How are the twins?"

"They're okay, I think. They were exhausted when we came home last night. Mona's still sleeping. Mohsin's right here, in his high chair. He's eating bananas."

"But why three weeks?" Sara's father was asking in the background.

"I don't know," Elias told him. "That's what I'm trying to figure out."

The phone screen flashed with a message, warning her that she had only thirty seconds left on the call. "Listen," Sara said, her voice rising despite her best efforts. "Listen, can you just make sure to call a lawyer and see if we can straighten this out? I was thinking—"

Then the call dropped.

. . .

NO LAWYER CAME THAT DAY, OR THE NEXT. RACKED WITH DOUBT, SARA went to inquire about legal assistance at the Case Management office. It was housed in what used to be the specialists' room—where various therapists and special-ed teachers once met privately with students. That day, the office was festooned with colorful Christmas garlands that ran from one end of the counter to the other. Classic rock played at low volume from a radio on the shelf. Next to it, an aromatic candle burned in its glass case. The scent made Sara sneeze as soon as she approached the counter. The case manager pushed away from the desk on his rolling chair, making a show of trying to avoid any germs she might bring.

"I'm sorry," Sara said. "I'm allergic to scented candles."

"What is it?" he asked. He had heavy-lidded eyes that made him look sleepy, but the effect was counterbalanced by his protruding chin. The jacket he wore covered the name tag on his uniform; Sara couldn't tell if this was intentional. After she explained the reason for her visit, the case manager typed her name on his keyboard and a moment later shook his head. "I don't see a lawyer on the schedule for you."

"Are you sure?" Sara asked. "Can you check the spelling, please?" While he typed she thought of all the ways her last name could be transliterated—Hussein, Hosain, Hossein, and Hüseyn being the most common variants she had encountered over the years. There were easily a dozen possibilities, even without the addition of a definite article or name particles. Throw in diacritics and hyphens— and misspellings were bound to happen.

However it was spelled, the name had a musicality that eluded most speakers of English. When he'd moved to Caltech to take up a fellowship in astrophysics, Sara's father had tried explaining to his American colleagues how to pronounce his idiosyncratically Moroccan name, Omar Ait-Elhoussine. But the fricative consonants and clipped vowels brought a look of panic to the faces of even his most liberal peers, followed by valiant, but nearly always failed attempts at pronunciation. When he became a citizen, he changed his name to Omar Hussein. Sara was in preschool at the time and had barely learned how to spell Ait-Elhoussine when she had to be taught how to write Hussein instead. The change seemed pointless now, for here she was, asking a Safe-X employee to check the more basic spelling. "My name is Sara Hussein. H-u-s-s-e-i-n."

From the end of the hallway came the sound of rubber shoes squeaking. It was Hinton, doing his rounds. A moment later, he was standing beside her. "What's going on?" he asked.

"I'm just checking on my lawyer," she told him.

"Ah," he said, and walked away. But he quickly changed his mind and returned to stand next to her, as if he, too, were curious whether her family had hired a lawyer. Strands of Sara's hair had spilled over the counter, and he wiped them away delicately.

"I don't have you on the schedule," the case manager said, shaking his head. "Step back from the counter."

"What spelling do you have on my file?" she insisted, her heart filling with wild hope that this had to be the source of the mix-up that landed her here. They had flagged another Hussein. It had to be *her* dreams they found dangerous, not Sara's.

"Step back from the counter," the case manager said. He pushed away from his computer station and went to his file cabinet.

She leaned over the counter, so she could get a look at his screen. "I'm just trying—"

The electric shock from Hinton's gun knocked the breath out of Sara. She fell on the floor, her limbs writhing. She'd been so intent on the argument about her case that she'd forgotten she was a body, flesh and bone that could be brought to compliance at the touch of a button. Every nerve inside her throbbed, and a helpless moan escaped her throat as she tried to regain control of herself. Meanwhile the two attendants watched and waited.

The next day, when the lawyer Elias hired arrived, he informed Sara that her forensic observation at Madison had been extended by an additional forty-five days because Hinton had written Sara up three times—once for having a noncompliant hairstyle; a second time for resisting the orders of the case manager; and a third for loitering in the hallway.

Sitting across from Sara in the cafeteria, the lawyer spoke in the soothing voice of an older man, though he seemed about the same age as her. His scholarship was in property law, he explained, but her case was simple enough because she had no prior arrests, had a stable home, had a full-time job and two children. And while it was extremely rare for someone with a score under 550 to end up in forensic observation, the RAA had full authority to keep her in custody because the courts defined retention as precaution, not punishment. "Just follow the rules," he advised. "Get your score down and we'll get you out in a couple of months."

Sara is still waiting, 291 days later.

DREAMSAVER, INC. TERMS OF SERVICE

(EXCERPT)

§ 5.2

By using this product, you grant DI a worldwide, nonexclusive, royalty-free license to host, access, use, interpret, reproduce, process, adapt, modify, and transmit your sleep data for the purpose of operating and improving our services; measuring and analyzing the effectiveness of our products; and developing new technologies consistent with these terms. We do not share your private data with third parties, except as required by a legal enforcement authority or its designated representative. Your content remains yours, and you retain intellectual property rights over it.

2

THEY REACH THE SUMMIT IN THE AFTERNOON. WHILE ELIAS takes pictures, Sara drops her backpack at the foot of the rusty sign marked HULM PEAK and advances, knees weak, toward the railing. Beyond the steep drop-off, the valley is a sea of green, with majestic ponderosa pines stretching for miles in every direction. The sight of three-hundred-year-old trees never fails to bring her clarity; however great they may seem, her fears and joys and regrets and desires are ephemeral in the end. She stretches her arms, rubs the soreness from her back. From the mesh pockets of her backpack, she pulls out a bottle of water and a bag of trail mix. "Want some?"

"Thanks," Elias says, taking a handful of nuts. Then he turns his gaze on the horizon, where the sunlight has begun to dissolve behind white clouds. "It's getting late."

A mosquito hums in Sara's ear, and she swats at it before sitting down on a boulder nearby. "I told you it was a bad idea to take that detour. It added a couple of hours at least."

"It was pretty, though, wasn't it?" He unlaces and relaces one of his hiking boots, tying it off with a double knot. "Anyway, we should head back."

"But we just got here." She leans against the rock, runs her hand on a patch of moss, wondering what this type is called. Just the other day she heard a segment on the radio about how there were thousands of species of moss. Perched on a nearby tree, a bluebird is watching her with great curiosity, its head tilted in her direction.

Meanwhile Elias walks the perimeter of the viewpoint, taking a few pictures with his phone camera. Every time they go hiking, he takes dozens of photos; it's as if he's afraid of not remembering what the landscape looks like. He tells her again they should head back.

"The trail closes at sunset, and we don't want to get locked in the parking lot." When she doesn't respond, he presses. "Sara, we really have to go. Come on, I'll carry your backpack."

With a sigh, she gets up and follows. If only he'd listened to her, they could've had a leisurely hike, instead of whatever this was. A race to the top? The whole point of a hike is taking the time to enjoy nature. At least they're going downhill now, though she should be careful not to walk too fast, it will strain her knees.

It is a warm weekday afternoon, and the trail is empty. The drone of mosquitoes, the chirping and clicking of critters in the bushes, the crunching of dirt under their shoes—these keep them company as they get to the river. The water is fast, full of runoff from a recent snowstorm in the Sierras. Elias steps onto the bridge, an old structure made of uneven slats that dates back to the last century, with rope handrails that seem to have been added almost as an afterthought. Pulling out his phone from his pocket, he starts to take pictures again.

"I need a break," Sara complains from the bank. Her arms are dotted with red bites; she has to reapply bug repellent. She scratches herself, her nails drawing blood.

"Come on," Elias calls, motioning for her to hurry up. "We gotta go."

Why is he like this? Can't he see how miserable she is? It's too late for bug repellent, she needs the soothing gel that's in one of the backpacks.

She steps onto the bridge, and now he turns his phone camera on her. "Smile!"

The last thing she wants is a picture; her skin is on fire. "Get that thing off my face," she says, swatting his hand. The gesture knocks the phone to the ground, and Elias falters to the side. On instinct he reaches for the rope railing, but the two packs on his back unsettle him and in the blink of an eye he falls into the water, thirty feet below.

"Elias!" Sara shouts as she rushes to the railing. "Elias!" The river is loud, muffling her cries, and so fast that it froths like milk around the boulders. There's no sign of Elias anywhere; it's as if the water has swallowed him. Fear kicks her in the stomach. Who will believe me now, she thinks, pacing back and forth in a panic. She must dive into the river, even though she has a terrible fear of water, she has to save him. But just as she puts her foot on the rope railing, she is startled by a hand on her shoulder.

"Get up," Emily tells her. "Hinton's almost here."

Sara stirs. The lights are on everywhere; she's slept right through the bell. She drags herself up just in time for device check, then lies in bed again. The heavy footfalls of women heading out to the showers or to early work shifts tell her she should get up, too, follow her routine, stop her thoughts before they spiral out of control, but instead she pulls the blanket over her head and curls up on her side, wishing she could sleep forever—or at least until her ordeal is over. She wants to go back to the time before, be with her husband and children, do work that is meaningful to her, walk out in the sun whenever she pleases. With her eyes closed, she can still see every detail of that life, from the broken train set on the living room rug to the potted succulents on the windowsill of the bathroom. Lulled by these images, she dozes off again.

The sound of the leaf blower outside rouses her for good. She forces herself out of bed, washes up, then sits down with her notebook, unsure how to write about this dream. The truth is, she would never complain about a detour, or lag behind Elias, or need to have her backpack carried for her—she's a far more experienced hiker than her husband, having scaled every major mountain in California.

This dream, she writes after a few moments of deliberation, must reflect her anguish that Elias has been saddled with massive burdens since her retention started ten months ago—emotional, financial, familial burdens that are too much for him to bear alone. He has to manage everything by himself, and the slightest occurrence disrupts his fragile balance. But she still wants to help him, doesn't she, because she tries to dive in after him, even at the risk to her own life. Whatever crime the algorithm foretold she would commit against him, she knows she's innocent of it.

But despite a request from Adam Abdo, the attorney Elias hired after the first one left the case, the RAA has refused to turn over its predictive equation, arguing that it comes from proprietary sources. Abdo has to make his case with the data Sara makes available to him and with the risk-score report from the RAA. The algorithm in between—that is, the engine that converted raw data into predictions of criminal activity—remains a black box. Abdo can get information corrected if he can prove it is inaccurate, but he cannot challenge how one or another data point is weighed against others in Sara's file.

Keeping a dream journal has been a comfort these last few months. It has taught her to be in conversation with herself, to pay closer attention to the inner workings of her mind, to notice where imagination draws from emotion or intellect. What it hasn't shown her is how to discern the future. After months of scrupulously writing down her dreams she is no closer to figuring out what will happen to her or when she will be let out.

Perhaps she lacks that kind of insight because she is a historian, her eye cast on the past in order to explain the present. She must turn her gaze to the future instead, start thinking like a scientist, or better yet like a software engineer. Historians observe the world, and scientists try to explain it, but engineers transform it. Step by step, they've replaced village matchmakers with dating apps, town criers with social media, local doctors with diagnostic tools. The time has come for sages, mystics, and prophets to cede to an AI.

In this way, history marches on.

"LOOK WHO'S FINALLY UP," EMILY SAYS AS SHE REFILLS A PAN OF SCRAM-bled eggs at the service station. The hairnet pulls at her face, giving her a frozen look even as her cheeks are flushed from the heat in the kitchen.

"I didn't hear the bell," Sara replies. "Thanks for waking me." The clank of the serving spoon is enough to give her a headache, and the smell of frying oil isn't helping. Everything about today feels a little off. She faces the camera, waits for the indicator light to turn green, and picks up a tray. This morning a few apples are available as premium items for eight dollars per unit, but after a flash of temptation she decides she can't afford one.

She moves to the beverage station, where she gets water and herbal tea. (There are no caffeinated beverages at Madison, a deprivation she didn't notice when she was admitted, but now seems like another needless cruelty.) The light from the windows is gray, adding to the general cheerlessness of the stainless steel tables, the bare walls, the attendant station. Carrying her food through the noisy cafeteria, she looks for her friends, feeling a surge of relief when she sees them at a table by the far wall.

They're talking about books, a nice break from the gossip that usually animates the table. Alice is raving about an Octavia Butler novel she just finished, declaring it the best book she's read in ages. Since August, she's been keeping up with her children's schoolwork by reading the books their teachers assign to them. She found out about this particular one from her younger son, who is studying it in AP English. "It's called *Kindred*. You guys should check it out. It's sci-fi, but it's about real people, you know? People like you and me, not kings or princes or cyborgs or chosen ones."

"I used to live next door to Octavia," Lucy puts in. This brush with fame draws all eyes to her. She takes a huge bite of toast and smiles like a Cheshire cat.

"For real?" Alice says. "You're just messing with me."

"Why would I lie about something like that?"

What a strange thing to say, Sara thinks. There's a difference between saying someone's messing with you and calling them a liar. But retention tends to make people paranoid; they hear accusations even when none are intended. "I take it you're from Pasadena?" Sara asks, picking up her spork. "I grew up there."

"Yeah, but this was well before your time, I'm sure. My parents moved out when prices started shooting up, and I've lived in Crenshaw for the last thirty-five years."

"But Crenshaw's expensive, too," Toya says, shaking her head. "You can't find anything there anymore. My cousins got priced out, like, twenty years ago. I'm hanging by a thread."

"What part of Crenshaw?" Lucy asks.

"The black part," Toya quips. "What part do you think?"

Alice tries to bring the conversation back on track. "So what was Octavia Butler like?"

"Oh, she was very nice," Lucy says with a nod. "I was in middle school at the time, and she'd always wave when she'd see me riding my bike to school or skipping rope with my sister in the front yard. This was in 1997 or '98. She was already a big deal, you know. *Kindred* had been out for a while and the first *Parable* book, too. But then her mother died and she left town. Another family moved in next door."

The rehydrated eggs are even blander than usual. Sara takes a sip of water, careful to pace herself to make it last. The chatter around the table moves on to adaptations, with Lucy saying she wishes a virtual reality studio would do a new version of *Kindred*, because in her opinion the old one was too violent.

Toya snorts. "Too violent?"

Marcela tries to include the new girl in the conversation. "Have you read *Kindred*?"

"Nope," Eisley replies. "I don't like sci-fi."

This gets Lucy's attention. "So what did you say you did for a living?"

Eisley doesn't answer. She takes a bite of her potatoes, barely suppressing her disgust.

Lucy rests one elbow on the table, watching and waiting. She's not pestering Eisley this time, allowing the silence to stretch instead.

"I'm a fitness trainer," Eisley says after a minute.

Sara gazes at the new girl with anthropological curiosity. Her face is tanned, her biceps impressive. She could pass for a volleyball player from Hermosa Beach, one of those people who knows how to make a delicious vitamin smoothie or where to get the best deal on a bike, but has no idea who the mayor is. This initial impression is misleading, though, because her eyes communicate a weary worldliness. "I'm only here for three weeks," she continues, waving her hand, "and then I'm back at work."

"Right. Of course."

"So do you have any famous clients?" Alice asks.

"No, just normal people," Eisley says with a little smile. After a moment, she adds, almost reluctantly, "I work for FitClient."

Sara tilts her head in surprise. "And normal people have money for a FitClient trainer?"

"It's not about money," Eisley replies, with obvious irritation. She sounds like she's had to face the same misconception a hundred times and has grown testy about it. "I have clients in different income brackets. It's about priorities, really. My clients care about their fitness, and if you care enough about something, you're going to devote time and resources to it. It's a question of responsibility."

Toya perks up. "Responsibility? Responsibility's got nothing to do with it. People can't get decent insurance without good HF scores from one of the big companies, so there's a lot more demand for licensed trainers these days."

"I paid three grand a month for a basic plan," Alice says, suddenly full of passion. Her voice drops an octave, and she pauses to collect herself and readjust to the proper pitch. "The broker said I couldn't qualify for a better plan that covers my medications because I didn't log enough steps per day."

"See?" Toya says. "Health plans keep you guys afloat."

"I mean, yeah, okay. We get people who have to improve their Health and Fitness scores for whatever reason, but there's no downside to exercising. It's good for you." Eisley turns to Alice, who's slumping in her seat. "Take you, for example. You could exercise *after* work, if you really wanted. Then your HF score would go up, and your premium would go down."

"I lead convoys of autonomous trucks," Alice replies, draining the last of her tea. "You want me to do jumping jacks by the side of the freeway at four o'clock in the morning?"

Everyone laughs.

"On the weekend, then."

"I don't get weekends, necessarily. And anyway, on my days off I try to get some rest and spend time with my kids."

"But see, exercise would boost your stamina. And it's also good for your mental health, so why wouldn't you do it?"

"Because where's the fun in that?" Lucy says, her voice rising above its usual whisper out of sheer irritation. "If you have to do something, it's an obligation, it stops being fun. No one wants to be a hamster on a wheel."

"Well, actually, hamsters *enjoy* running on wheels."

What a chatterbox, Sara thinks. And with such strong opinions about fitness, of all things. Even after Alice complains that her boyfriend had to delay hernia surgery until next year, when he hopes to qualify for better insurance, Eisley counters that correct posture and guided exercise with a professional trainer could have prevented or mitigated his condition. She won't let it go. Who cares about fitness when they're all stuck here for the foreseeable future? But petty arguments like these are a form of entertainment at Madison; everyone indulges in them.

While Eisley is talking, Sara's gaze is drawn across the dining room. Victoria Aguilar, a skinny kid with tattoos all over her arms, is acting out a scene for the others at her table. It's some kind of mime routine in which she's running to catch a train. She's taking stairs two at a time, running down the platform, waving to the conductor when she collides with a pole and falls face-first on the pavement. Carefully she sits up and, eyes crossed, begins to walk in the opposite direction. Her tablemates erupt in laughter. She takes a bow, then returns to her seat.

Sara can't decide if she's amazed or horrified. In spite of all that happened, Victoria finds joy in a public performance of her private life, using it as entertainment for her friends. The Guardian cameras on the wall haven't deterred her from behaving exactly as she would outside these walls, making comedy by exaggerating details of her story. She seems unconcerned about drawing attention to herself or providing the attendants with data that might be used against her. Sara expects Hinton to be watching Victoria's little performance, but finds him staring at Eisley, who has brought with her some kind of pill, in its individual wrapping, and is preparing to finish off her meal with it.

Hinton has a gift for noticing even the smallest moments; it's a bit unsettling. This morning, his honey-brown hair is combed to the side, a nod to recent fashion. He takes good care of his appearance, and must find his gray uniform boring, an impediment to sartorial expression. All of a sudden he turns his keen eyes on her, and she drops her gaze, her face hot.

From the busing window comes the metallic clack of trays being stacked. The cafeteria is emptying slowly, with everyone heading to their work assignments. Sara is mopping up the last of the eggs with her toast when Marcela nudges her. "So have you thought about it? Can you help me with that letter?"

"What letter?" Eisley asks.

Sara stuffs the toast in her mouth, giving herself a minute to think. The Safe-X handbook, which she checked late last night, states that a retainee can file any petition she likes, as long as it pertains to her case only. There is some ambiguity in the phrasing, she feels. The rule doesn't say that helping a fellow retainee is forbidden, only that filing a petition on someone else's behalf is not allowed. But gray areas like this have caused her trouble in the past, got her written up even when she didn't know she was breaking a rule. She can't take that risk.

"You need help writing to your boyfriend?" Lucy asks.

"At least I have a boyfriend," Marcela snaps.

That's a little cruel, Sara thinks. After all, Lucy is a widow. Her husband died in a horrific car accident, which also left her badly injured. Eisley Richardson doesn't know this, though, and on hearing Marcela's retort she throws her head back and laughs.

"Hey, I was just teasing." Lucy raises her palms in self-defense. "I didn't mean anything by it, kiddo."

"And stop calling me that. I'm not a kid."

"All right, all right. I'm sorry."

Sara is taken aback. Lucy and Marcela have never had an argument like this before. What could have caused the sudden animosity? The chatter around the table stops. In a huff, Marcela takes her tray to the busing window and heads out. The bell rings a moment later and the rest of the women clear the table, under the watchful eyes of the cameras.

THE AC UNIT IS ON; THE AIR IS CHILLY. WITHOUT A WORD ORTEGA points Sara toward her station. She hurries, passing Eisley, who's squinting at her screen, her lips moving silently while she reads instructions on how to use the software. (So the new girl is smart, she signed up for a job right away!) Sara takes the last seat in the third row, beneath the wall bubbles that appeared after a freak rainstorm last July. She waits for the system to recognize her face, then launches the NovusFilm program.

The silence is monastic. The only movement comes from Ortega, who circumambulates the trailer every hour, though he is careful not to make much noise. If he needs to speak to a retainee for any reason, he taps her on the shoulder, and whispers into her ear. Nothing is to distract the workers from their tasks.

This morning Sara can't help but think about the last email she received from Elias, more than a month ago. She's read it so many times already that she knows it almost by heart. As always, the email begins with an update on the children. The twins are making more progress with plosives, he says, distinguishing *b*s from *p*s and *d*s from *t*s in everyday speech; Mohsin has become a pickier eater than Mona, but he's still reaching his milestones on the growth chart; both kids are starting to show an interest in insects. Then he shares a few miscellaneous notes. The papers for the second mortgage he took out on the apartment have come through, and he's been able to pay the lawyer's bill, including late fees.

Yet something feels odd about the email; it lacks a touch of the quotidian. Elias's parents take care of the twins four days a week, but they don't rate a mention, and neither does Sara's father, even though he must visit from time to time. There are no complaints about the noisy upstairs neighbor, say, or about his co-worker, who's in the habit of leaving dirty plates in the communal kitchen. It's as if Elias and the children live apart from everyone else. It could be that he's trying to limit giving out personal information, since incoming emails are read by Safe-X algorithms before they're released to retainees, but the details about the twins are almost clinical in their precision, as though Elias were describing strangers rather than his children.

These gaps and silences rankle her; they're starting to coalesce into a noisy and disturbing realization: Elias is growing apart from her. The last time they spoke there was none of the flow that there should be between partners, only the rancor of two people who find themselves jointly embroiled in a case that has dragged on unnecessarily for months.

Plus, it's been a while since he's booked time in the Virtual Conjugal Room. He used to pick fun meet-up places, like a checkered blanket under the shade of an oak tree, or a darkened corner in a busy Parisian café. The cost of these visits is outrageous, but somehow he's managed to make it work before, so why doesn't he make the effort any longer?

The old Elias wasn't so aloof. The old Elias maintained a running conversation with her, texting at random moments of the day to tell her he loved her, or sending her a picture of Mona sleeping on his chest, or calling to remind her to pick up bread on her way home. The old Elias was warm and funny and available, qualities that stood out from the moment they met, the summer after college. She'd moved back in with her parents and started working part-time at the Huntington Gardens gift shop, a job for which she didn't have much aptitude but that paid just enough to keep her afloat while she figured out what she would do next. Sara's mother, Faiza, was happy to have some help around the house. She would ask Sara to pick up the dry cleaning or fix the ceiling fan in the bedroom or take Mshisha, the family's aging cat, to her vet appointment. "Why don't you ask Baba to do it?" Sara would reply, her voice brimming with irritation.

Faiza's booming laugh would come from the porch, where she sat smoking Marlboro Lights and reading the newspaper in the afternoons. More often than not, the laughter would turn into a cough—an early symptom of the cancer that would eventually take her life. "Your father is too busy," she would say.

Sara's father, Omar, spent the better part of his waking hours thinking about space rockets. Even when he came home from work, his mind was still in his office at Caltech. There was no room for anything—or anyone—else. For years Faiza had shouldered the responsibilities of parenting almost by herself: not just school drop-offs, PTA meetings, or doctor's appointments, but also volunteering as an assistant soccer coach every summer. So she considered it natural that Sara should help at home now, especially as she was loafing around most afternoons. Beaten down by guilt, Sara would go pick up the dry cleaning or fix the ceiling fan or shuttle Mshisha to her appointment.

One day her mother found a baby picture of Saïd in the pages of an old book. She told Sara to go to the store for a frame, refusing to order one online, even after Sara pointed out how much cheaper and more convenient it would be. The store no longer carried much of a selection, and the few frames it had were on a low shelf in the back. Sara was on her knees, trying to reach one, when she was hit by a moving cart.

"Oh! I'm sorry. Are you all right?"

Sara stood up and rubbed her ankle where the cart hit it, wiping off a small trickle of blood. "I'm fine."

"I'm so sorry." The voice belonged to a tall, lanky man with bushy eyebrows and an easy smile. "I didn't see you."

"It happens a lot." She was five foot one, and was used to being overlooked.

"At least let me help you." He picked up her items, introducing himself as Elias Rosales. When he found out she was running an errand for her mom, he laughed and pointed at his cart, which was stacked high with storage bins his grandfather had sent him to pick up. They kept the conversation going through the checkout line, then in the parking lot, and later on the phone.

The new Elias is different, though. The new Elias has been forced to become sole breadwinner, single parent, and legal advocate. He's taken on these roles as best as he could over the last ten months: when it became clear that Sara's retention would last longer than they expected, he cancelled daycare, coaxed his parents into baby-sitting the twins, and found a paying roommate. But maybe this has left him with little time for Sara. She misses the companionship she gets from his notes, the illusion that she can hear his voice as she reads them. And along with the loss, there's also the worry, which she can no longer dismiss now that Elias hasn't been in touch in a month, that he's cut his losses and moved on from her.

The screen flashes; her response times and click patterns indicate that she hasn't been paying attention during this set of reels. Does she wish to restart?

Funny how everything at Madison is presented as a choice, even though the correct answer [YES] is already highlighted in green. All she has to do is click.

HER ROOMMATE ASKS HER IF SHE WOULDN'T MIND POSING; SHE NEEDS to draw her mutant superhero in a crouching position, waiting to leap on an opponent. A good distraction, Sara thinks, while they wait for the mail to be delivered. There isn't much room for movement in the space between their cots, but Emily insists on directing Sara, leading her by the arm to a spot under the window, where the light is more natural. "Right here," she says, positioning Sara's arms and knees as though she were handling a marionette. Then she returns to her pad and starts drawing, the pencil scratches filling the silence.

"Why did you name your character Rina?" Sara asks after a minute.

"Rina Campoy. It's an anagram for pyromaniac."

"But she's a superhero, right?"

"Fuck superheroes."

The sudden passion in Emily's voice intrigues Sara. She rests one hand on the floor, getting some weight off her knees.

"Don't move."

"Sorry," Sara says, resuming her position. "Why don't you see Rina as a superhero?"

"Because she knows she can't save everyone or be liked by every-one. What she really wants is to find other people like her, who can help her figure out how to have a normal life. Her superpower is a curse, see. She can't touch anything without setting fire to it, which means she can't be with her girlfriend, she can't hug her mom, she can't hang out with anyone without running the risk of turning them into barbecue."

The scent of the medicated cream Emily rubs on her skin reaches Sara. A pleasant, lemony smell. It's lucky that it's not a stronger fra-grance that triggers Sara's allergies, or else she would have to ask for a room reassignment, which would go on her record and could be taken as a sign of bad behavior. "How did you get started in comics?" she asks.

"I've always read them, ever since I was a kid. I took a drawing class in high school, but the teacher made us draw still lifes and I was too scared to say I wanted to draw something else. It wasn't until after I started working as a firefighter that I really gave it a try. Clara says I could do this. She says there's decent money in comics and I wouldn't have to risk my life all the time."

The college campuses and art museums where Sara has spent

most of her working life haven't taught her anything about the kind of work that Emily does for a living. She has no idea what her roommate's training involved, for example, or what licensing it required, but she does know that Emily began her training as a seventeen-year-old inmate in Lassen County, while serving a three-year sentence for assault and battery. Once she came out of jail, she finished high school, got an associate's degree, and went to work in the private sector, for a Los Angeles–based company called NaarPro. Everything was going well until an OmniCloud facial recognition system spotted her rushing out of a baseball stadium where a riot had broken out, and her risk score went up to 620. The RAA came after her for a recurring dream she had about assaulting her mom.

"You enjoyed being a firefighter, though, right?"

"Sure, at first. It's a great feeling when you evacuate people safely or save someone's home. There's no feeling like it in the world, really. But they keep pushing us on pay, even though we don't make anywhere as much as the state guys. I mean, why do it at that point? Why risk my life if I'm not even getting paid enough to put food on the table? Clara helped me understand that drawing was more than just a hobby, that I should make it a career."

"And you can make a living from comics?" Sara asks, careful to keep disbelief out of her voice. The hardship of her early years in academia has made her skeptical of relying on her passions. She loves history—studying it, interpreting it, teaching it—but after college and graduate school, the best position she was able to find was a part-time job at Cal State. She couldn't afford rent.

"Not at first. But Clara said she'd support me."

Clara this, Clara that. Does Emily have to drop her girlfriend's name into every conversation? Not everyone has a partner cheering them on, or visiting them every other week, or writing them all the time. From the framed portrait on the shelf, Clara peers at them, half smiling.

Sara keeps the pose for another minute before standing up. "You got enough to work with, right?"

"For now," Emily says. "Thanks."

Sara rests one arm on the wall and waits for the circulation to return to her legs. Outside, the sky is the color of a fresh bruise; it will be dark soon. Beyond the road, the bushes that dot the hill look dry and brittle. It won't be long before the next fire.

The bell rings. Sara and her roommate step out to join the other retainees for afternoon device check. All along the hallway, Guardian cameras whirr as they adjust to the women's positions. Wherever they go they are watched from lenses on the ceiling, their behavior scrutinized for the slightest infraction, their conversations monitored for clues of intent. A nod, a whisper, a joke: under the right circumstances, anything can be made into something sinister, to bulk up their files. At night their dreams are collected from their Dreamsavers, offering more evidence of all that is murky and suspicious in their natures.

That they have committed no crime is beside the point. In any case crime is relative, its boundaries shifting in service of the people in power. Once upon a time, adultery and miscegenation used to be crimes; now they aren't. Burning flags and collecting rainwater were once legal; now they aren't. A crime isn't the same as a moral transgression. The law delineates the former, never the latter. I have done nothing wrong, Sara thinks. It's only that the line of legality has moved, and now I'm on the wrong side of it.

Before her retention, she rarely thought about how much crime evolves, though the evidence was all around her. Elias's great-grandmother Róisín arrived in Ellis Island, a frightened teenage girl in the fourth-class cabin of a crowded ship from Ireland. The law declared her an immigrant, allowed her to settle in New York, to chase the American dream (that most seductive of fantasies). Twenty years later, Elias's grandfather Hernán crossed the border in the back of a truck. He was the same age Róisín had been, was fleeing the same circumstances, but in the intervening decades the law had changed. Now he was called a removable alien, a drain on public resources, a carrier of disease, a potential criminal who should be detained and deported without delay.

The law separates the permitted from the forbidden, but it doesn't require that a crime be committed before the agents acting in its name deploy the full force of their power. Police officers used to patrol neighborhoods they called "rough," stopping and searching people they thought were suspicious. Now they sift through dreams.

Yee is coming down the hallway, scanning the retainees one after the other. His face is flushed, as though he were embarrassed about something. One of the older women in 217 teases him about it, asks if it's because he saw her changing; another one says, don't flatter yourself. Yee shakes his head at their banter, represses a smile. Once the device check is completed he pulls out his PostPal tablet and reads the names of those who have mail.

Aguilar, he begins.

Brown.

Guerrero.

Kamau.

Sara retreats into her room, holding back tears.

From: SaraTHussein@PostPal.com
To: customercare@PostPal.com
Timestamp: 12-26-10-02
Ticket number: 3962

Describe the issue: My outgoing calls dropped after 30 seconds, but I was charged for 3 minutes. This happened four times in a row, and I used up $12 of the funds my husband sent me, without actually speaking to him for much longer than a minute. I would like a refund for the unused minutes. Thank you in advance for your help.

. . .

From: customercare@PostPal.com
To: SaraTHussein@PostPal.com
Timestamp: 01-03-11-38
Ticket number: 3962

Issue resolution: We apologize for the service disruption, which we are working to resolve. Unfortunately, we cannot issue a refund to your account because the minimum charge for any call placed from a PostPal comm pod is 3 minutes. If this doesn't serve your needs, we recommend using PostPal email, which does not have length limits. Please note that a usage fee of $10 per 30 minutes applies to the tablets in the reading room. Thank you for using PostPal.

. . .

From: SaraTHussein@PostPal.com
To: customercare@PostPal.com
Timestamp: 02-12-16-03
Ticket number: 4218

Describe the issue: An in-person visit with my husband was cancelled because PostPal incorrectly lists me as laid up in the infirmary. I waited for two hours before I was told of the cancellation and even longer before one of the attendants told me about the mix-up. Can you please correct my status in the system? I'm not sick and I want to see my husband.

. . .

From: customercare@PostPal.com
To: SaraTHussein@PostPal.com
Timestamp: 02-13-11-12
Ticket number: 4218

Issue resolution: We apologize for any inconvenience. We have investigated this issue and have corrected your status in the system. Thank you for using PostPal.

. . .

From: SaraTHussein@PostPal.com
To: customercare@PostPal.com
Timestamp: 02-26-16-33
Ticket number: 7462

Describe the issue: Your system is again listing me as unavailable for in-person visits. I'm not sick!!! This is the second time my husband and kids had to drive all the way out here only to be told that I couldn't see them. CORRECT MY STATUS. I checked with the nurse and she said the mistake is not on her end. So please just correct my status.

. . .

From: customercare@PostPal.com
To: SaraTHussein@PostPal.com
Timestamp: 02-27-11-06
Ticket number: 7462

Issue resolution: We apologize for the error. Your status is adjusted. Thank you for using PostPal.

. . .

From: SaraTHussein@PostPal.com
To: customercare@PostPal.com
Timestamp: 03-05-10-01
Ticket number: 8606

Describe the issue: The scheduling system is down for the second time this week. Doesn't your company want to make money?! Why is your service so shitty? I haven't been able to get a visit from my lawyer, which I'm pretty sure constitutes an infringement under the law. Fix your scheduling system!

. . .

From: customercare@PostPal.com
To: SaraTHussein@PostPal.com
Timestamp: 03-09-15-12
Ticket number: 8606

Issue resolution: We are showing a visit with an attorney on March 18. This ticket is marked as resolved. Thank you for using PostPal.

. . .

From: SaraTHussein@PostPal.com
To: customercare@PostPal.com
Timestamp: 04-20-12-11
Ticket number: 12106

Describe the issue: Outgoing calls dropped after 30 seconds.

. . .

From: SaraTHussein@PostPal.com
To: customercare@PostPal.com
Timestamp: 06-21-12-30
Ticket number: 13813

Describe the issue: Outgoing call dropped after 30 seconds.

. . .

From: customercare@PostPal.com
To: SaraTHussein@PostPal.com
Timestamp: 06-23-08-02
Ticket number: 12106

Issue resolution: We are working to resolve service disruptions. Thank you for using PostPal.

. . .

From: SaraTHussein@PostPal.com
To: customercare@PostPal.com
Timestamp: 06-27-18-15

Ticket number: 12145

Describe the issue: My balance shows $0 all of a sudden. I had $27 in there as of yesterday.

· · ·

From: customercare@PostPal.com
To: SaraTHussein@PostPal.com
Timestamp: 06-28-08-05
Ticket number: 12106

Issue resolution: Your balance has been corrected. Thank you for bringing this to our attention.

· · ·

From: SaraTHussein@PostPal.com
To: customercare@PostPal.com
Timestamp: 10-09-18-01
Ticket number: 17887

Describe the issue: Can you check that my account is still active? Except for a letter from my lawyer, I haven't received mail in a month. There must be a problem with my account.

· · ·

From: customercare@PostPal.com
To: SaraTHussein@PostPal.com
Timestamp: 10-10-19-05
Ticket number: 12106

Issue resolution: We are showing that your account is active. Thank you for using PostPal.

D URING THE NIGHT, THE SANTA ANAS BLEW IN FROM THE EAST, tearing branches from trees and lashing them against the windows. The air is dry, and tainted with dust. Weather like this makes some people uneasy, causes them to have migraines or lose their keys or get into arguments with loved ones, yet Sara wakes feeling unusually rested. Her head still cradled by her pillow, she takes a deep breath, slowly emerging from her dream. She is miles and years away from Madison, sitting at a cozy booth in a French bistro, waiting for her husband to arrive. It's extremely dark inside; it must be the young maître d's idea of mood lighting. She can't see much beyond her table, and she's even having trouble reading the menu, but the smell of meat braised in wine sauce is a harbinger of a great meal. God, she's starving. She was so busy at work that she didn't have time to get lunch. It doesn't matter what's on the menu, she'll eat anything. "Sorry I'm late," her husband says as he slides in next to her.

"It's okay," she replies. "I just got here myself." She leans in to kiss him. It is a deep kiss, a kiss that shows how happy she is to see him after an exhausting day at the museum, where the exhibit she helped research is about to open.

"I missed you," he says in her ear, and kisses her again, his mouth warm against hers. A moment later, he reaches between the folds of her skirt. It's unusual for him to do this in public, but the tablecloth hides his hand, and in any case it's so dark in this restaurant she doesn't think anyone will notice them. He runs his fingers slowly up her thighs, and when he comes up against her underwear she sits back, allowing him to slide it to the side. Gently, he opens her up. She's already wet, and he begins to touch her, his motions slow and circular. She is so turned on that she will climax quickly, she can already tell. But as her eyes adjust to the darkness in the restaurant, she realizes that the man who's pleasuring her isn't her husband.

It's Hinton.

She struggles to pull down her skirt and regain her composure. "How dare you?" she wants to scream, but what comes out of her mouth instead is a loud, helpless moan as ecstasy radiates all through her body. At a nearby table an elderly woman in a black coat has noticed what's happening; she whispers something in her friend's ear while pointing at Sara. Meanwhile, Hinton is kissing Sara's neck, telling her how much he wants her, how much he still wants to do to her, and she finds herself reaching for his belt.

Sara sits up in her cot, fully conscious now. What happened to her? She has been feeling lonely these last few days, lonely and miserable—but is she *that* lonely? Being held at Madison for this long has put her out of sync with herself. At the thought that this embarrassing dream, too, has been recorded, she drops her face into her hands. Everything that ought to remain separate is getting mixed up; she's losing her grip on reality. Then the bell rings, startling her.

Sara hates morning device check, hates the idea that she must be reminded of her detention the minute she's awake, that any respite from captivity must be crushed immediately. She doesn't feel ready to face Hinton. As he brings the scanner to her implant, she has to work on not drawing back from him. For some reason he smells like the outdoors today, like leaves or perhaps tree bark, conjuring images of a picnic at the park on a sunny afternoon. He's a handsome guy, no question about it, and the scar on his neck adds a touch of mystery, or perhaps danger. Again, the memory of the pleasure he gave her returns. Afraid that her face might betray her, she drops her gaze to the floor.

This was only a dream, she tells herself, a few billion neurons firing in her brain, speaking in a pictographic language that no one could claim to master, not even the makers of the Dreamsaver. Perhaps the Santa Ana winds are affecting her, the spike of positive ions messing with her moods. The truth is that, except for his looks, she finds everything about Hinton repulsive, and especially the satisfaction he seems to derive from his job. What kind of a man enjoys working in a place like this?

But what kind of a woman, a voice inside her asks, dreams about a man like him?

IF RETENTION HAS TAKEN EVERYTHING FROM SARA, IT HAS ALSO GIVEN her something she didn't realize she had lost: the time to read. Before breakfast, between shifts, during yard time, after dinner—minutes and sometimes hours she spends with her nose in a book, if only to ward off thoughts about Madison. Always she feels two contradictory impulses: to avoid thinking about her captivity, and thinking about it all the time. This morning she is on the third chapter of *When We Came Together,* which is about the Historical Records Survey, a little-known program that collected state, county, and local records, and archived the information on microfilm—at the time a state-of-the-art technology. The HRS was inexpensive, yet the valuable work it did stopped abruptly when the WPA was dissolved in 1943. There are still gaps in the national archives because the HRS was abandoned.

This is the kind of detail that makes the historian in Sara smile. If a record collection of the magnitude of the HRS, funded by the federal government and employing thousands of record keepers, can't provide a completely accurate portrait of the past, why should she believe that the database maintained by the RAA is reliable? It's an automated archive, but like ancient archives it, too, must have gaps. For starters, the RAA is missing information from all kinds of people: undocumented immigrants, people without fixed addresses, the few among the elderly or the disabled who don't use smart devices, along with cranks, hermits, bohemians, and objectors.

Come to think of it, the girlfriend of Sara's housemate at Berkeley was an objector. Back when Sara knew her, she was working on a Ph.D. in face recognition and seemed no different than any other graduate student in the Bay Area. Things changed when she won a large cash grant from the Scott Foundation. Everyone thought she would invest the money in setting up her own lab, or even use it as a down payment for an apartment, but instead she sank it into ten acres at the foothill of the Sierras, with a two-room cabin that barely had running water and electricity. She started spending all her time there, refurbishing the place modestly, buying non-smart appliances from thrift stores, and slowly getting herself off the grid. She even gave up her phone. Whenever she wanted to make a call or send an email, she had to ride her bike to the nearest town. Sara's house-mate, Leo, was sure this arrangement was temporary. "She's writing her dissertation," he would say, "she just needs peace and quiet to focus." He kept saying that right until his girlfriend dropped out of the Ph.D. program. Only then did he realize she was committed to analog life—and broke up with her.

This was twelve years ago. At the time Sara thought Leo's girl-friend was paranoid, but now the simplicity of her solution to the problem of surveillance is evident. The RAA can't claim she con-stitutes a criminal risk to anyone; she would never end up in a place like Madison because they wouldn't have much behavioral informa-tion on her, if any at all.

Now Sara wonders what an internet search might turn up for her name—if only she could remember it. It started with a *D*. The lines in Sara's book blur as her mind drifts to those long-gone years. Once, Leo's girlfriend helped Sara fix a bug on her computer and when she found out Sara's folks were from Morocco, she started talking about her grandfather, who emigrated from Fes to Montreal, and eventu-ally settled in Los Angeles, where he married an Algerian, like him an immigrant determined to make it in the Golden State.

Curiosity drives Sara to the library, where she waits for a com-puter station to open up. Though she can't remember the objector's name, she does remember her housemate's name, so she starts with that. She types "Leo Keane" and "Berkeley" and finds that he's now working for an asset-management firm in New York. He's sporting a shaved head these days, fashionable glasses, and dental veneers—a stark contrast to the bearded pothead Sara once knew. She adds dif-ferent years to the search terms until she lands on travel photos Leo posted fifteen years ago when he went to Colorado for spring break. And there is the objector, standing next to Leo, squinting in the sun-light. The caption says her name is Dani. That's it! Dani Senoussi. Armed with this information, Sara runs a new search, using differ-ent terms she can think of—"Berkeley," "face recognition," "com-puter science"—but aside from the papers Dani published when she was still in graduate school, there is nothing. It's as if Dani has disappeared.

Sara drops the spring break photo into ImageBank, narrows the focus to Dani's face, and hits SEND. There are hundreds of millions of pictures sitting in all kinds of databases, so it takes a full thirty seconds for the search engine to find a match. It comes from an accident report in Sacramento ten years ago. A motorist hit a cyclist and two pedestrians, one of whom was left gravely injured. In the picture, a couple of medics are wheeling out a gurney for the pedestrian, while the cyclist is standing next to her bike, holding one arm in the other. It is Dani, with shorter hair and looser clothes, except that the caption says her name is Mary Brown.

So she gave them an alias. A common name that will muddy search results. To preserve shreds of her privacy she'd had to put on the gray uniform of a generic identity. She uses fake credentials everywhere. Buys burner phones and dumps them periodically. Wears sunglasses or face masks wherever cameras are present, which is everywhere. The only reason Sara was able to find a picture of Dani is that the car accident caught her off guard—the bandana around her face slipped off while she examined the injury to her arm. A mistake, perhaps, made in the first few years of her new life.

The cost of this freedom is steep. Dani has given up the convenience of traveling by car, plane, or subway. She's stopped shopping in grocery stores that accept only electronic payments, which is nearly all of them. She doesn't receive state alerts about flash floods, wildfires, and earthquakes. She can't borrow large sums of money from a bank, or make significant transactions of any kind. She's even renounced the pleasures of sitting on a park bench with the sun on her face or swimming in a public pool on a hot day. It's a difficult life. Not to mention solitary.

But after all these years Dani might've found a solution to that, too.

Perhaps she's joined one of those offline communities that have sprouted up in smaller towns. Twenty-Thirders, they're called, because they log online only if needed, always from a secure connection, and for never longer than an hour per day. To minimize their digital footprint, they trade services and share resources, socialize almost exclusively with people who share their beliefs, and when-ever they go out they wear clothing that distorts their features. The media treats Twenty-Thirders mostly as objects of fascination or, more often, ridicule. The police, of course, are openly suspicious of them, because who would go to all that trouble just to avoid ordinary technology?

But to Sara the very existence of the Twenty-Thirders is a source of hope.

TOYA IS STANDING IN FRONT OF THE THERMOSTAT AGAIN. THE TEM-perature is set to 60 and a downward arrow blinks on the display, but the room feels a good thirty degrees hotter. "This fucking place," she mutters as she walks away. She opens a laundry bag and dumps its contents into the first washer, not bothering to spray any stains or check for forbidden items. She pours soap without measuring it, then slams the lid shut.

"I wonder if we should try it the other way," Sara suggests. "Set this thing to 75, see what happens."

"Go for it."

But it doesn't seem to make a difference; once all the machines are running, they're both sweating through their uniforms. They sit at the table. Toya has her detective novel open in front of her, but Sara can tell she's not reading because she hasn't turned a single page. "So how'd your hearing go?"

Toya shakes her head. Not a minute later, she's holding back tears. "When I came in," she says, "they were chatting about baseball, jok-ing around with each other like it was an ordinary day. I guess it was, for them. But when we got started, they laid out my whole life in front of me, bringing up shit I'd forgotten about, like the emails I sent to my cousin twenty-two years ago, telling him to wire me $3,500. I told them that he *owed me* that money because I'd paid for a trip he took to New York so he could do a training program there, and I really needed the cash for Christmas. But this guy at the table, he sucked his teeth like he didn't believe a word out of my mouth. Then he started talking about my gambling debts."

"What?"

"I know," Toya says. "But I told them, is having debt illegal or did I miss the memo? I mean, I got carried away on the slot machines in Vegas last year, but I didn't break any laws. It's none of their damn business how much I owe to anybody. Well, they didn't like that. One of them brought up this dream I kept having about burning down my house for the insurance money. He said my expertise was a liability."

"Did they show you the dream?"

"Nu-uh, they just described it. But I remember it anyway, because I had it a few times that summer. I'm sitting on my porch with a group of friends, enjoying beers and hamburgers. Then later in the evening, after everyone leaves, I tip over the barbecue grill right there on the porch and let the fire do the rest. But why the fuck would I do that in real life? I love my house. My folks busted their backs to buy it, and I can't afford to live anywhere else." She closes the detective novel, smoothing its dog-eared cover with her palm. "I tried to explain to them that I was under a lot of stress from the claims I had to settle last year. I mean, I had to listen to so many people talking about everything they lost in the Tujunga fire that I was depressed and anxious all the time. But they didn't care. They said the risk was real, and the fight I had in the exercise yard last month raised my score. So I got denied again."

Sara reaches across the table and squeezes Toya's arm. It's a terrible thing, being denied release, a terrible thing. She composes her face carefully before she speaks, because she has no idea if what she's about to say is true. "You're gonna get out of here." It's the only consolation she can offer. And in truth she needs to hear it, too. But what she really wants to say is that she understands.

To put the awkwardness behind them, Sara returns to the thermostat. "You feel a difference?"

"Nope."

"It feels like a hundred in here."

"At least."

"Why put it here, then? If they're going to set the temperature from the other end, why bother having this display here and letting us think we can set our own temperature?"

"It doesn't make sense. But then again—"

"They're just fucking with us." Sara bangs on the thermostat, presses the arrow button all the way down, bangs it again. None of it makes a detectable difference. There are moments when she feels like a guinea pig in a lab experiment, forced to submit to whatever tests the scientists have designed. How else to explain Safe-X's decision to heat a utility room? Or why the water in the showers is adequately hot only in the afternoons? Or that week in February when, without warning or explanation, the same dinner was served for eight nights in a row? Only after a fight erupted in the cafeteria did MealSecure return to a regular menu. "Fuck it," Sara snaps. She takes off her shirt, releasing a grassy funk, and sits in her bra.

Toya decides to take off her shirt, too, using it to wipe off the sheen of sweat on her shoulders and chest. "I wish we had some water."

Sara goes back to *When We Came Together.* A few lines into a section on visual artists, she comes across a mention of Victor Arnautoff, the artist who painted the mural at the entrance of the auditorium. She's surprised to learn that a lithograph he made in 1955, while he was teaching at Stanford, attracted national controversy. It showed Richard Nixon carrying a paintbrush and a bucket labeled "smear," and was intended for display at the San Francisco Art Festival, but was taken down after the curators received a phone call from the FBI. At one point, Arnautoff was even interviewed by the House Un-American Activities Committee for suspected communist sympathies, a charge that owed at least in part to his birth in Russia and his apprenticeship with Diego Rivera. Sixty-five years later, Arnautoff's work ignited another controversy, this time after a high school mural depicting George Washington as a conqueror of Natives and enslaver of Africans was denounced as demeaning to his victims. A petition circulated to remove the painting from the high school.

Too critical of a president, then not critical enough. How an artist's reputation changes in the course of a half century! Sara is used to historical reassessments, from the mild to the radical. When she wrote her dissertation she fashioned new arguments out of old facts, using as bonding material whatever evidence or context other scholars hadn't considered before. Reevaluating kings, presidents, or rebel leaders chipped away at their reputations as noble statesmen and helped advance scholarship. But over the years, she has seen that process expand, with more passion and less rigor, to other public figures, from actors and musicians to athletes and journalists. And now that every moment of our lives is monitored and documented, she thinks, it happens to all of us. Everyone can have an Arnautoff moment. Worse: everyone lives in expectation of an Arnautoff moment. She's having hers now.

The steady hum of the machines, combined with the heat, has made Toya listless. She gives up on the book and leans on the table with her head between her arms. Sara decides to let her rest while she puts in new loads of uniforms and folds the dry ones. Another hour passes.

It is almost the end of the shift when Hinton passes the laundry room on his rounds. "Jesus," he says from the doorway, "it's hotter than hell in here." His voice has the effect of an alarm. They both sit up, and quickly put on their shirts.

"Thermostat doesn't work," Toya explains.

"That's not an excuse to take off your shirts."

"It's not against the rules," Toya replies. If anyone knows what the Madison handbook has to say about shirts, it's Toya Jones. Her work in insurance long ago trained her to pay close attention to the fine print.

"Listen to you," Hinton says with an amused laugh. "You know the handbook by heart?"

"We're supposed to have our shirts on in common areas. This is a restricted area, no one can come here without authorization."

"No one's been here at all," Sara adds. Instantly, she knows she has made things worse. There is something about her—is it her personality? her manners? her elocution?—that seems to rub Hinton the wrong way.

He steps inside the laundry room, and casts an appraising look around him. The floor is swept clean, the soap boxes are on the shelf, the mesh bags hang from their hooks on the wall. A pile of clean uniforms sits on the folding table. Then his gaze settles on Sara, sitting with her book open in front of her. "So you're saying I'm no one?"

"I— No. I just meant, we didn't break any rules."

"Here's a rule: No one needs to see your flat rack. It's disgusting."

Sara drops her gaze to the floor.

But then Hinton picks up a fresh shirt from the pile. It's still warm from the dryer. "Put this on, too," he tells Sara.

She glances at Toya. What's this all about, she wants to ask.

"What are you looking at her for? She can't help you."

Sara draws a breath, she's about to ask why she's being told to put on a second shirt. But there is no why, she realizes, and the last thing she needs is to get in Hinton's crosshairs. So she takes the second shirt from him and pulls it on, though she has trouble fitting it over her own, it feels suffocating.

"Keep going," he says, handing her another shirt.

This time the shirt gets stuck around her midriff. Her face turns hot, her hair comes undone, her arms look like flippers.

"Atta girl." Hinton leaves, keys rattling on his belt.

After his footsteps recede down the hallway, Toya helps Sara get out of the makeshift straitjacket. "At least he didn't write you up," she says consolingly.

By the time they're done pulling off the extra shirts, Sara has bruises on her arms. Her face is slick with sweat, more from rage now than heat. No matter how many times she's had interactions like this, she can't temper the fury they stir in her. She has to do what she's told, even if what she's told is subject to change without notice.

Hinton likes to say that Madison is not a jail, but he acts as if she must have done something to be sent here. Every deviation from perfect conduct confirms his suspicions about her secret, violent nature. If she protests that she's been a victim of discrimination, he points to the algorithm, which treats people as an anonymous collection of data points and cannot be accused of fault or bias. The algorithm is objective. It doesn't know who you are or what you look like, he'll say, it scores everyone using the same metrics.

But for all this insistence on the fairness of the algorithm, Sara is pretty sure that what really landed her at Madison were her insolent remarks to Moss and Segura, who felt disrespected and wanted to teach her a lesson.

What has retention taught her these last few months?

That the whole world can shrink to a room.

That time is the god of all things.

That the rules don't have to make sense.

That no matter how unjust the system is, she is expected to submit to it in order to prove that she deserves to be free of its control.

SARA FINDS MARCELA ON A PATCH OF GRASS IN THE EXERCISE YARD, bent in a triangle pose. She's devoted to her yoga practice, makes time for it even when she's on double shifts or when the temperature is in the high eighties, like it is this afternoon. The other retainees have retreated to the shade of the breezeway, except for Eisley Richardson, who's doing sit-ups a few feet away, counting her reps out loud.

"You still want help with your petition?" Sara asks.

Slowly rising out of the yoga pose, Marcela stands arms akimbo, blinking at Sara. It takes her a moment to register the question. "But you said—"

"—I'll do it."

"Now?"

"Yes, now."

The library is busy, but after waiting an hour, Sara gets a seat at one of the computer stations, with Marcela standing beside her. As Sara types, she learns that Marcela DeLeón was born in Bell Gardens to a pair of schoolteachers who sat her in front of *Sesame Street* reruns while they graded papers. When she turned four, she asked for a violin—just like Elmo's. Music was at once a passion and a revelation. By the time she finished high school, she was playing backyard parties and writing her own songs.

"That's good," Marcela says.

"That's only the intro," Sara replies. "Now we have to explain why you must have your instrument, and why you must have it now." Before her retention, Marcela used to play the guitar for seven or eight hours a day, so she's lost hundreds of hours of practice. Since she's been at Madison, she's missed Sharp Jello's spring and summer tours, along with her share of merch sales and an appearance fee at a popular festival in Oregon. The band ended up using a different guitarist, and that guy is going to be with them when they start recording their new album next month. Even if Marcela were released right now and by some miracle was able to get her spot back, it would take her a long time to catch up, write new songs, and be ready in time for the band's next tour. If she can't tour, she can't make a living. Having her instrument back is the only way for her to maintain her skills and be ready to rejoin the band and support herself when she is released.

"You think they'll agree?" Marcela asks.

"It's worth a try." Sara also adds a paragraph about how music reduces stress, promotes brain function, and improves sleep. Isn't sleep why they are here, after all? It's practically in the interest of Safe-X to give Marcela her instrument; they'll get more data out of her in the end. Studies have shown, Sara writes with the confidence of someone who knows that studies can be found to support almost any claim, that listening to music before going to bed results in better and longer sleep. "There. That might work."

"Thanks," Marcela says. "I appreciate it." She saves the document to her Safe-X account. "I'm gonna go ask for clearance to send it right now."

"There's no rush," Sara replies. Petition reviews can take weeks. It took Alice nearly four months to get her headwrap returned to her.

They walk out of the library together, the petition having established a bond of sorts between them. Marcela is in a chatty mood. She tells Sara that she appreciates her help, that it's good to know there are decent people at Madison, that *some women* aren't as innocent as they portray themselves to be.

The obscure hints confuse Sara. "Spit it out," she says. "Who do you mean?"

"Lucy Everett."

"But you're friends with her, right? What happened?"

"We're roommates," Marcela corrects. "I thought she was a nice old lady. Turns out, she's a scammer." The accusation is hard to reconcile with Lucy, a widow who likes to entertain everyone at mealtimes with her stories of the Los Angeles she knew as a young girl and who can be depended upon to brighten the mood when someone is feeling down. "I know how it sounds," Marcela says, noticing the disbelief on Sara's face, "but it's true. Lucy stole names and

Social Security numbers from the real estate company she worked for, then opened new lines of credit."

"You sure about this?"

"Positive. She was clever about it, too, didn't start using the names and numbers until *after* she quit that job and started working for another company in Sherman Oaks. So it took the police a while to catch up to her. But then she got into that car accident and the case dragged on while she was in the hospital. Then I guess the prosecutor dropped charges against her."

"But how do you know she did all this?"

"Because she's getting sued by one of her victims."

"No, I mean how did you find out?"

"What happened was, she left her paperwork on her cot when she went to show Eisley where the comm pods are. Usually, she puts everything away on her shelf, but I guess she was so eager to make friends with the new girl, she got careless. I thought the paperwork was a petition of some kind, so I snuck a peek, just to see how it looked, you know, because I had to write one. Turns out, it was mail from her lawyer."

No matter how often it happens, it always comes as a surprise to discover that people are more than their public selves, that they have private entanglements we know nothing about. But why tell Sara about Lucy's legal troubles? Sara isn't a prosecutor, there's nothing she can do about them. Nor is she a victim of whatever scheme Lucy was supposedly running. So what good does it do, in the end, to share all this with her? "All right," she tells Marcela when they get to the stairs. "I'll see you later, yeah?"

Marcela stops mid-stride. "Right. I'm gonna go get clearance for my petition. Thanks."

Sara climbs the stairs to her room, finding it mercifully empty; she's had enough chatter for the day. The late afternoon light is lengthening the shadows on the floor and the heat is starting to rise. She tries to read, but her mind is restless. The revelation about Lucy is forcing her once again to unspool the chain of events that led to her retention. Maybe her dreams became suspicious because of an infraction she has forgotten about or dismissed as unimportant.

Emily has that prison sentence she served as a teenager. Marcela has a restraining order against her. And now it turns out Lucy is involved in a civil suit.

But Sara doesn't have anything like this on her record. Up until Officer Moss hauled her away, the last Friday before Christmas was just an ordinary day, filled with tedious obligations, small pleasures, minor setbacks and frustrations. If there is indeed some suspicious activity on her record, it must date back further than that. At Toya's hearing, the agents pulled out emails dating back twenty years. That is a long time to go fishing in someone's past, looking for words or actions that can be given new meanings. Sara has no idea what they might find in her own records if they looked that far back.

Then she feels it coming—the moment she spends so much of her time evading. The pain of missing her old life starts like a knife in the stomach and spreads from there to every part of her body. If only Elias wrote to her, she would have his words to live on, or live for, and freedom wouldn't seem so remote as it does now. But her birthday has come and gone, and she still hasn't heard from him. Is he starting to believe the lies they're telling about her?

The last time they spoke on the phone, he'd sounded relieved that a new speech therapist had been hired at the office, because it would lessen the pressure on his schedule. Maybe he's been busy with what's-her-name. Maybe they're together right now. Jealousy jabs her in the chest. Stop that, she tells herself. Stop it right now. She focuses on her breath, though the stifling heat makes it difficult. All she can do is sit with the pain, let her body absorb it, wait for it to subside long enough for her to be able to move again.

From: AdamAbdo@kreidlercampwalla.com
To: SaraTHussein@PostPal.com
CR Number: M-7493002
Facility: Madison
Timestamp: 02-20-09-17
Flags: LEGAL
Status: clear

Dear Sara,

My name is Adam Abdo and I am an attorney with Kreidler &
Campwalla. Your family has hired me to represent you after
Prof. Reese had to recuse himself from the case because he's
engaged to Judge Lim. Unfortunately, this means that your hearing
has been cancelled and will need to be rescheduled to a later date.

This is disappointing news, I know, and I'm sorry about this
unexpected delay. I will let you know as soon as we have a new
date for the hearing.

With my best wishes,
AA

.   .   .

From: AdamAbdo@kreidlercampwalla.com
To: SaraTHussein@PostPal.com
CR Number: M-7493002
Facility: Madison
Timestamp: 03-04-14-12
Flags: LEGAL
Status: clear

Dear Sara,

I had been looking forward to our visit this week, but I'm told you
haven't been feeling well. I hope it's nothing too serious.

I've received a copy of your most recent RAA report, and I must
stress once again how important it is that you maintain a score
below 500. We want to be ready for your hearing!

All best,
AA

.   .   .

From: AdamAbdo@kreidlercampwalla.com
To: SaraTHussein@PostPal.com
CR Number: M-7493002
Facility: Madison
Timestamp: 03-25-11-44
Flags: LEGAL
Status: clear

Dear Sara,

It was good seeing you last week. As I mentioned then, it does
happen sometimes that attendants apply the rules a little
differently from one facility to another, or that some are more strict
than others, but unfortunately there's nothing we can do about that.
Once an attendant files a disciplinary report on their Tekmerion, it
gets saved to the system and weighed against your score. So, please,
just try to follow the rules.

All best,
AA

.   .   .

From: AdamAbdo@kreidlercampwalla.com
To: SaraTHussein@PostPal.com
CR Number: M-7493002
Facility: Madison
Timestamp: 05-08-11-02
Flags: LEGAL
Status: clear

Dear Sara,

As I'm sure you've heard, the government shutdown is affecting the
RAA, and no hearings can be scheduled until a deal between the
two parties has been reached.

I will let you know when we have a new date. I'm very sorry about this delay.

Best,
AA

.   .   .

From: AdamAbdo@kreidlercampwalla.com
To: SaraTHussein@PostPal.com
CR Number: M-7493002
Facility: Madison
Timestamp: 06-01-15-22
Flags: LEGAL
Status: clear

Greetings, Sara.

I write with some good news. Your request for access to the multi-faith room has been granted, though not for the time you requested because that is during the daytime. The space is open only after the first shift, so you will have access on Fridays between 3 and 4 p.m.

The backlog is finally starting to clear and I expect your hearing will be scheduled in the next few weeks. Once again I must stress how important it is to follow the rules and keep your score under control.

Best,
AA

.   .   .

From: AdamAbdo@kreidlercampwalla.com
To: SaraTHussein@PostPal.com
CR Number: M-7493002
Facility: Madison
Timestamp: 07-07-11-38
Flags: LEGAL
Status: clear

I've just received notice that the RAA's central computer was infected by malware over the holiday weekend. Nearly 12,000 case files have been damaged or lost. I'm sorry to report that yours is among them.

The chief administrator estimates that it will take up to a month to rebuild the files, and then we will be back on the schedule.

AA

TIME PASSES. ON HIS SIXTH TRY, ADAM ABDO MANAGES TO GET Sara a hearing for eight on the following Friday morning—a prime slot, though Sara gets only one day's notice about it because the case manager at Safe-X was out sick last week and didn't update his files until he returned. It doesn't matter, Sara tells herself; there's really nothing to prepare. At dinner she can barely eat the chicken casserole on her tray, even if it's one of the better dishes from the MealSecure menu. "Don't be nervous," Toya advises. "It doesn't do any good." In the morning Sara borrows Emily's hair dryer and spends long minutes in front of the mirror, straightening out her hair, oblivious to the conversations that are taking place behind her in the locker room.

The hearing takes place in one of the prekindergarten classrooms on the first floor. There are still coat hooks at child height by the door and toy cupboards lining the wall beneath the window. The room is air-conditioned, though, a pleasant respite from the residential floor or the cafeteria. Three people sit at a table, with name cards in front of them. At the center of the table is Andrew Nicosia, whose card identifies him as an agent from the RAA. He has trendy glasses, a weak chin, and ultimate authority over the case. On the left is Pauline Ford, a senior case agent with Safe-X. She has beside her a Tekmerion, in a larger size than the kind used by attendants to report violations to the code of conduct. Completing the panel is Jamie Yuen, whose name is handwritten on the card, as if he's a replacement or a late addition. His affiliation isn't listed.

"Ms. Hussein?" Nicosia says as Sara approaches the table. "Have a seat."

The chair is steel-framed and stackable, designed for hearings with single or multiple retainees at once, a detail that strikes Sara as strange. Still, she's eager to get on with it, explain whatever needs explaining. One thought alone occupies her mind: securing her release.

With a glance at the panel chair, Pauline Ford asks, "Shall we begin?"

Nicosia consults his notes. "I believe we're expecting Ms. Hussein's attorney."

"He should be here any minute," Sara says. Where the hell is Adam Abdo? Late, today of all days. Elias chose him because, though still a junior associate with Kreidler & Campwalla, he made up for his relative inexperience with his training at a civil rights litigation clinic. She's been frustrated with his failure to secure early-release motions, but she's always been grateful that he believes in her innocence. When she talked to him about the hearing, he sounded pretty confident about her chances—though he called them "our chances."

Ford fixes her gaze on the wall clock, as if willing it to speed up time. The sour look on her face is unnerving; Sara hopes she doesn't hold the attorney's tardiness against her. At least, Yuen doesn't seem to mind: he's doodling on his notepad. From where Sara sits she can see he's drawing the room they're in, complete with its wooden cupboards and vintage light fixtures. His hand moves with the confidence of an experienced draftsman. How did he end up adjudicating retention cases?

The door opens a few moments later and Adam Abdo walks in, full of apologies. He looks different than he usually does, though Sara can't pinpoint the reason. Somehow he seems taller this morning, or perhaps it's an effect of the fitted blue suit he's wearing. "Sorry, everyone," he says, putting his briefcase on the floor and draping his jacket on his chair. "There was an accident on the freeway." He sits down beside Sara, puts a hand on her arm. "How are you, Sara?"

"On the 60?" Yuen asks. "They really need to fix that narrow lane. I almost sideswiped someone the other day."

Abdo brushes a strand of hair away from his face. His fingernails are neatly manicured, and he wears a fashionable mesh bracelet on his left wrist. No wedding ring. "The 60, yes," he tells Yuen. "There was a massive pileup, with a big rig and a boat."

"A boat! The lake's been dry for five years."

"There's always one more idiot on the road than you expect."

"Death, taxes, idiots on the road," Yuen says, flashing a smile at Abdo.

Ford clears her throat. "Well, we're glad you could join us. Shall we begin?"

"Please," Abdo says. He sits back in his chair, crosses his legs, but makes no move to bring out any documents from his bag. The confidence with which he carries himself is infectious. Sara feels encouraged, even if she can barely breathe from the anxiety that presses against her chest.

"Let's start with the Safe-X report," Nicosia says.

"Certainly," Ford replies. She slides open her screen and begins to read. "Sara Hussein has been retained in this facility since December 22 of last year. Her physical shows she's in good health, her lab tests have come back normal so far, and her psych evaluation shows no sign of psychiatric illness. However, her behavioral record remains a concern. She's had two Class A disciplinary actions in December, another Class A in February, and a Class C in April."

Wait. Sara didn't get a Class C in April—or at least she wasn't informed of it. She turns to Abdo, waits for him to object to Ford's report. From his pocket, the lawyer takes out his phone. Sara must be old-fashioned because she expected him to keep his case notes on a tablet, or even in a paper file, not on his personal device. He's probably going to pull up the most recent Safe-X report, which doesn't list a Class C in April, and take the opportunity to point out that none of Sara's disciplinary actions have ever involved a threat of violence. Her record has been spotless for the last four months, her risk score is at 502, and she's served out all her extensions. Abdo touches his phone screen, and starts scrolling.

"Any other issues since April?" Nicosia asks.

"Hold on." Sara raises a hand. "My attorney needs a moment."

But Abdo is still scrolling on his phone, looking for the file. Ford continues with her report as if Sara hasn't spoken. "No issues since April," she concedes. "However, given the number of disciplinary actions on Ms. Hussein's record, her associations with known fraudsters and suspected arsonists, and the severity of the crime under investigation, we would recommend an extension, in order to mini-mize the risk to others."

"That's absurd," Sara says. She's sharing space with other retain-ees, she's not conspiring with them. Plus, Ford is wrong about her record; no disciplinary actions were filed against her in four months. By the RAA's logic, Sara should be released forthwith. She turns to her lawyer, expecting him to object to Ford's reasoning, but instead he's writing a text or an email. "Aren't you going to say something?" she whispers.

Abdo doesn't seem to hear her.

"Thank you for that, Pauline," Nicosia says. "Jamie?"

Yuen stops doodling. "The dream data I have so far is in line with what I would expect for an individual who's been in confinement. I see numerous images of clear skies, mountains, spacecraft, flying, and so on. But I'm sorry to say that allusions to the predicted crime continue to crop up, the most recent one in September. It's pretty graphic, actually. I sent you a copy."

Yuen works for Dreamsaver Inc., Sara realizes. Is he a data engi-neer? A neuroscientist? A clinical psychologist? Adam Abdo should ask about that. But he's still on his phone. What the hell is going on? If Sara doesn't say something, the opportunity she has to present her side of the case is going to vanish. Yet she doesn't have the legal acumen to mount an effective response and she's afraid of making things worse for herself if she says the wrong thing. A lump forms in her throat. No, she has to say something, she can't sit by and let them extend her retention. "I have committed no crime," she says, barely recognizing the sound of her own voice. She's been clinging to this simple fact for months now and feels the need to repeat it. "I have committed no crime. And in any case I didn't have a Class C in April. Why are you keeping me here?"

"Because you're a murderer, Ms. Hussein," Nicosia says.

The accusation is so outrageous that Sara stands, throwing her chair back—and wakes up as she falls from her cot to the floor.

It takes her a good minute to register where she is. Her left shoul-der hurts where it hit the floor, her heart is beating ten thousand beats per minute. Rubbing her shoulder she gets back in her cot and lies in the dark, staring at the ceiling, where the moonlight dapples branches of the paloverde trees. Except for the distant call of coyotes, Madison is quiet at this hour. But she can't calm herself; doubts crackle in her mind.

Sara, a murderer?

Even in moments of pure rage, and God knows she's had a few in her life, she's never seriously entertained the thought of harming anybody. The closest she's ever come to violence was more than twenty years ago, when she was a junior in high school. With two girls from her soccer team, she'd managed to get floor tickets to a Roaring Tweedies show at the Forum in Inglewood. For weeks, they talked of little else, and because the show ran late they each lied to the others' mothers that they were having a sleepover. On the day of the concert, though, their rideshare hit traffic downtown and by the time they arrived at the venue the opening band was already playing. They wouldn't be able to get close to the stage now. Worse, Sara had trouble getting her ticket scanned. "Text us once you're in," the other two girls said, abandoning her with shocking ease at the doors.

Sara tried to get help, but the usher took one look at the pass on her phone and told her to step aside, her ticket was already used. He was an older man with skin tags on his neck and narrow eyes that seemed to expect the worst in people. "You can't come in."

"I have a pass. Look."

"It's fake. You think I can't tell?"

With the bravado of a fifteen-year-old, she cussed him.

The next moment the black suede boots she'd saved up for months to buy were grazing the floor as he dragged her by the collar toward the main gate. She was breathless from the shock of the assault, but she recovered and elbowed him until he let go of her. "Get your hands off me, asshole."

Had their confrontation ended there, it would have been unremarkable, the kind of thing that happens at concerts all the time, but Sara was so angry that he'd ruined her shoes that she shoved him. She was a midfielder on her soccer team, was used to tackling and being tackled. But the usher turned out to be more fragile than she expected, and he fell from the force of her thrust, hitting his arm on the metal railing before landing on the ground.

A bunch of concertgoers stopped to gawk. "Call security!" someone shouted, and a minute later two burly guys showed up, asking what the hell was going on.

"She attacked me," the usher said. He barely had a scratch on him, but now he was nursing his arm as if Sara had broken it. She told the security guards that he'd put his hands on her first and showed them her ticket, but even though they conceded it was valid, they escorted her out to the main gate. You're lucky we didn't call the cops, one of them said.

Sara used to have a temper on her, she'll be the first to admit that. But as she got older, went to college, transitioned to a career, she learned to maintain her calm even if she was boiling with rage. Take a beat, she'd tell herself. Count to three before saying anything. How else would she have managed to keep a job in the bourgeois milieu of museum work? Rarely does she give in to her first impulse anymore. She learned to be cautious; that was the price of the ticket.

The algorithm sees something else in her, though, something unruly and violent, and expects her to yield to these instincts. Its designers would say that the algorithm knows her better than she knows herself—an idea that makes her want to put her fist through a wall.

But she won't, she won't.

THE CAFETERIA IS ESPECIALLY LOUD THIS MORNING. FROM THE kitchen comes the hissing of an aging refrigerator, the gurgling of water in the sink, the clacking of metal trays. A maintenance worker stands on a ladder with a drill, repairing a loose camera mount on the far wall. Beneath the windows a service truck is idling, angry music blaring from its stereo. But the noise doesn't appear to bother anyone else at the table; they chatter on as usual. Lucy is complaining that the greasy food at Madison has made her put on weight; she would do anything for fresher and healthier meals. At this, Eisley perks up, but Lucy raises a hand to stop her. "Save it. I'm not talking about exercise, I'm talking about the food."

Sara takes a sip of her herbal tea. It has a stronger body and a smoother finish today, without the bitter flavor to which she's grown accustomed. "Is this a new brand?"

Alice tries it. "Tastes the same to me."

Marcela breathes in the aroma of her cup, and closes her eyes. "Hmm-mm. Such a delicate blend," she says, "with just the right hints of chlorine and soap."

The others laugh.

Yet Sara finds the tea reviving, and even flavorful. She's already used to processed meats and fake fruit, so this is only another adjustment. What else will she start liking out of sheer habituation? The toilet-and-sink combo in her room? The shower that automatically turns off after five minutes? With a clank she drops the metal cup in its slot on the tray.

"I don't care much for tea myself," Lucy says, jabbing at her fried potatoes in a quick, repetitive motion. "Apart from decent food, what I miss most is a good drink. A glass of wine with dinner, a little amaro after, a cocktail every now and then. Keeps the engines running, you know what I mean?"

Marcela sniffs. "I knew someone like that when I worked as a cater waitress. She liked to have a drink or three with dinner. I remember she always gave the same toast. *May the roof above us never fall in, and may we as friends never fall out.* She was a lot of fun, one of the best waitresses I worked with. Never complained when the guests were rude or the party ran late. Then she got caught stealing jewelry and got fired."

"Did that happen a lot?" Eisley asks.

"Stealing on the job? No, of course not. That's why we were all so surprised."

If this is a sly reference to the accusations against Lucy, Sara thinks, it seems to be working, because Lucy has gone quiet. She stabs at her food with renewed vigor, looking like she'd rather be somewhere else. Changing tables would attract the attention of the attendants, though, so she sits glumly through the meal.

The idling truck outside departs in a roar. For a blissful moment Sara thinks it's gone for good, but it stops in a different spot on the street and the idling starts again. Is it not possible to have a moment's peace in this place? She turns to Alice. "Where's Toya?"

"She didn't want to come down for breakfast. She got an extra three months, and she's taking it pretty hard."

"She must've done something," Eisley says, shaking her head.

Sara frowns. "None of us are here for what we've done, remember?"

"Right. But I mean, if they're *keeping* her here this long, then they must have something on her."

Sara suppresses the urge to snap; after all, she was once the new girl, too, she knows what it's like to cling to the belief that the system works, despite its shocking flaws. Eisley is desperate to be out when her twenty-one-day hold is completed, ergo the only people who are held longer at Madison must have done something to deserve it. She's still in denial, Sara thinks. "How hard do you think it is to make one of us look guilty?" she asks. "We're already under suspicion. Once the algorithm has a case to make, it picks out the evidence it needs from the data it can access."

"Wait. Are you an engineer?"

"No."

"So you don't know how algorithms work." Eisley looks around the table, as if she expects the others to agree with her. But she's still new around here, and the other retainees wait to see how this plays out.

"No, but I know how archives work. When you have a database of millions or trillions of items, you can't go in blind. You have to find a way to sort through the records. Like, you might start with a name, or a year, or a subject heading, and see what materials you find and what story they tell you. The problem is, if there's contradictory material and it happens to be indexed with terms you don't use or don't know about, then you're not getting the full story. I'm pretty sure the algorithm does the same thing. It's looking for data that relates to our suspicious dreams, nothing else."

Eisley seems surprised at this retort, and it takes her a moment to recover. "But obviously if they kept your friend for this long, they must have proof she's a serious risk to others. I mean, there's no smoke without fire."

"What proof are you talking about?"

"I don't know. They must have some kind of record on her."

"You're missing the point."

"Oh, yeah?" Eisley rests her chin on her hand. "Please, enlighten me."

The nerve of this woman! She knows nothing about Toya Jones, met her only a week ago, and yet she keeps making insinuations about her guilt. "I'm saying," Sara replies, her voice sharpened by irritation now, "the RAA is bound to miss exculpatory evidence because it's not looking for it in the first place."

Four pairs of eyes stare at Sara. Although the women can argue for hours on end about frivolous subjects, any mention of actual guilt or innocence makes them uncomfortable. It's too sensitive a subject, liable to bring up imperfect pasts, tense futures.

Plus, with Hinton nearby, who would want to say anything about the RAA at all?

"Now who's being loud?" Eisley asks. She takes a bite of the potatoes, then, shielding her chewing behind a dainty hand, she turns to Alice. "Didn't you tell me they charged someone a couple of months ago?"

"Sybil Wyatt."

"See?"

"No, I don't." The police came when Sara was doing an evening shift in Trailer D, but she's heard the story enough times from the others she feels as if she's witnessed it herself. "They'd told her she was in for child endangerment, but when they came they charged her with mortgage fraud after one of her business partners turned her in. So the charge had nothing to do with the algorithm."

"How can you say it had nothing to do with it? She committed fraud! The algorithm was right about her, she's a criminal. And what about the one who was arrested for assault? Gordon."

"Gorda, you mean. That's just her nickname, by the way. Her real name is Angie Moreno. That happened here, they arrested her on the residential floor. She cut her roomie during a fight." Heat rises to Sara's cheeks. "But my point is, the algorithm didn't predict shit. This fucking place drove her to violence."

"How do you know she wouldn't have attacked someone outside Madison?"

Sara has no answer to this. The very logic of this place is that it protects innocent people. Every arrest confirms the necessity of forensic observation, and every release proves that compliance is all that is required to reenter society.

"Aren't you two a ray of sunshine in the morning," Lucy whispers.

At some point during the back-and-forth with Eisley, the idling truck left. The maintenance worker who was fixing the camera mount is done; he's carrying the ladder to the door, trying not to hit any tables on his way out. It's finally quiet again. "I'm just saying," Sara mutters.

"Usually, we can't get a word out of this girl," Marcela says, "and now she's talking our ears off about archives."

Alice nudges her. "You been holding out on us, Professor. What else you got?"

"Nothing." Sara wanted to stand up for Toya, but she was also defending herself, in case one of the others casts doubt on her behind her back. No matter what the RAA says, she is not planning to commit a crime.

The bell rings. Sara was too busy talking; she didn't eat her meal.

THE HALLWAY IS DIMLY LIT, THE WALL COLD TO THE TOUCH. AS THE line for the PostPal comm pods moves, snatches of conversation reach her: one woman asks about her teenage daughter's college applications, another whispers to her husband, a third begs her brother for updates about her legal case. An hour passes before it's Sara's turn. She waits for the system to bring up her face and ID number, then dials Elias's smartphone. He picks up on the fourth ring, accepts the collect charge. Then his face fills the screen. "Is everything okay?" he asks by way of greeting.

"Everything's fine," she says, reflexively. Everything is not fine, not by a long shot. Still, she holds back her complaints, tries to start their conversation on a positive note. "How are you?"

"I'm working." He's walking down a corridor as he holds his phone, passing walls filled with framed posters of abstract art—mostly Klee, by the looks of it. The sight is nearly exotic to Sara now, so used has she become to the bare walls at Madison. Elias turns a corner, and she tries not to think about the motion sickness that handheld cameras usually give her. She tells herself to focus on him instead. "What's up?" he asks, his thick brows already knotted in anticipation of some problem.

"Nothing," she says. "I just wanted to hear your voice. We haven't spoken in a while." He opens a door and takes a seat at a desk she doesn't recognize. Finally, the picture stops moving. Elias is wearing the blue button-down shirt she gave him last year for his birthday. A badge is clipped on his breast pocket. He looks tanned, healthy, freshly shaved. "Did you get a haircut?" Sara asks.

"Last week," he says, running his hand over the top of his head. "It was getting too long."

"You look great. But where are you? This doesn't look like your office."

"I'm on the main campus, filling in for a colleague who's on sick leave. And it's Tuesday, so I have my office hours with the new hire." He clears his throat. "You sure everything's okay? Did the lawyer get in touch or something?"

"No, I haven't heard from him at all."

"So what's up?"

"Like I said, I just wanted to talk to you. Do I have to have a reason to call?"

"No, I was just asking." A phone rings somewhere in the office. He looks up, waits for someone to pick up, then returns his attention to the screen.

Sara realizes she's gripping the plastic ledge of the comm pod. Stay calm, she tells herself, take a deep breath. "How are the kids?"

"They're fine."

"That's it? Just fine?"

"Sara," he says with a sigh, "now isn't a good time for me to chat. I'm really busy at work and—"

"You haven't written me or visited in four weeks. And you forgot my birthday. How about that? You forgot my birthday. Is that a good enough reason for you to take five minutes from your busy schedule to talk to me?"

He looks up, worried that someone might have heard Sara's angry voice. Then he stands, and the nauseating movement starts up again. She looks away, keeping the PostPal screen in her peripheral vision, until after her husband closes his office door and sits down at his desk again. "I was going to send you a gift, I just haven't had a chance yet. Between work and the kids, I've been crazy busy."

"It's not about that," she says, swallowing bile. "I don't care about getting a gift, you know that. I just want to hear from you every once in a goddamn while, get a note or a visit. I just feel..." Being forgotten at Madison is perhaps her biggest fear, so rarely acknowledged that her voice fails her. The world has already moved on without her. What if her husband, too, is moving on with his life? "I want to feel," she says in a whisper, "like I matter to you."

The retainees in line behind her are eavesdropping—the argument is an entertainment for those who've never had fights like these and a consolation to those who have. But for Sara, it's just another humiliation, to add to all the others that Madison has brought her.

Elias's lips tighten. "Well, I'm sorry," he says, his voice rising now. "I'm sorry I have so much on my plate that I didn't get a chance to visit or write. I had my performance review at work. My roommate clogged the kitchen sink twice this month. And I had to take the kids to the pediatrician."

"Wait, are they sick? You said they were fine."

"They needed their shots."

"Oh, okay."

"You know, this isn't easy for me, either. Maybe you should've thought about that before getting yourself detained."

"That wasn't my fault. I didn't do anything wrong."

"It wasn't your fault the *first* time. You shouldn't've been sent to Madison. But all you had to do was follow the rules, Sara. How hard is it to follow directions? You wouldn't be there this long if you'd just followed the rules, like I've been saying this whole time."

The blame in his voice takes Sara's breath away. Her life has been stolen from her, but instead of the thieves who ran off with it, she's the one her husband thinks is at fault. Is this why he hasn't written to her in a month? Is he starting to believe what the RAA says about her, that she's secretly a delinquent, that she could be a danger to him? The shock she feels quickly dissolves into despair. If she were charged with a crime, it would be easy enough to dispute the allegations against her, or deny them, or provide an alternate explanation.

But without an actual crime she can't prove her innocence—not even to her husband, apparently. And if her own husband has doubts about her, how can she hope to convince a panel of strangers to let her out?

"Look, I didn't mean it that way," he says after a moment. "I'm just tired, and on top of it all work is insanely busy right now."

"Then I'll let you get back to it."

She hangs up without saying goodbye. Even when the screen is off, the bile continues to rise in her throat.

SAFE-X, INC.

STFOF Division
Facility: Madison
Location: Ellis, California

Patient: Sara T. Husseyn   Age: 38
Complaint: Anxiety. Requests benzodiazepine.   Timestamp: 10-16-13-03

ALLERGIES		
Allergen	Onset	Notes
TDAP vaccine	Age 21	Swelling on the arm
Pollen, grass	Age 15	Treated with antihistamine
Fragrance	Age 15	Treated with antihistamine
Dust	Age 15	Treated with antihistamine

WOMEN'S HEALTH	
Date of last menstrual period	10-12
Total number of pregnancies	2
D&C	1
Number of live births	2 [twins]
Pregnancy complications	None on record

BEHAVIORAL HISTORY			
Category	Notes	Risk (pre-retention)	Risk (in retention)
Tobacco use	never smoked	-3	0
Drug use	no, last use sixteen years ago	+1	0
Alcohol use	yes, 3-5 drinks a week	+3	0
Marital status	married	-3	0
Sexual partner(s)	Pre-retention: 1 (male), regular In-retention: 1 (female), casual	-3	+3
Birth control	yes	-3	0
Sexual assault(s)	age 19, victim	+3	+3

FAMILY HISTORY		
Disease/condition	Relation	Age of onset
Cancer (lymphoma)	mother	57
Psychiatric (depression)	father	45
Heart disease	N/A	N/A
Macular degeneration	N/A	N/A

MEDICAL HISTORY		
Diagnosis	Age of onset	Status
General anxiety disorder	15	Ongoing
Nephrolithiasis	27	No recurrence

Impression & Care Plan

Sara Husseyn is a 39 y.o. female patient presenting with complaints of anxiety. She requests a dose of benzodiazepine (Xanax. Risk +3)

Patient vitals were taken. Blood oxygen level normal. Blood pressure within normal range. Heartbeat elevated.

Benzodiazepine was denied, as supplies are reserved for sedation in situation-critical cases.

Sara Husseyn was given an opportunity to ask questions, and all questions were answered to the best of my ability. I encouraged her to email me if she has any further questions or concerns.

Signed: Adelina S. Flores.

FRIDAY AFTERNOON. SHE SITS ON HER KNEES, EYES CLOSED, reciting the āyahs she remembers being taught as a child. Her limbs are tense, and her chest is a knot so tight it hurts to breathe. Still, she tries to set aside her anxious thoughts and focus her attention on the verses from the Fātiha. It would be easier if she had company in the praying, but since Amani was released in August she's had sole use of the worship space for one hour on Fridays.

Safe-X is legally obligated to accommodate the religious needs of retainees, which it does by giving them access to a windowless storage room and an old-generation NuSpirit. It sits on a desk pushed against the wall, waiting to beam sermons in any faith or language that matches the face and file on record. It's a temperamental device, though, and today it emits no sound, no matter how often Sara presents her face to it.

She wasn't a prayerful person, in her life before, but as her detention dragged from days to months, she began to hunger for the numinous. In a place where everything she does is quantified and fed to an algorithm, where else could she find solace but in the words that are now bursting forth from her mouth in whispers? After the Fātiha, she recites Surat al-Falaq, and then al-Ikhlas, her enunciation slow and clear. Always, she fixes her mind on the language, its rhythmic syllables brimming with poetry and mystery.

And oneiromancy, too, she thinks. After all, Abraham had a vision that God commanded him to sacrifice his firstborn son; he might have done it, too, had the angel not appeared with a ram. Joseph dreamed that the sun, the moon, and eleven stars bowed down to him; years later, his father, mother, and brothers were on their knees in Pharaoh's court. Muhammad saw himself enter Mecca as a pilgrim, predicting his own triumphant return from the hegira. Entire belief systems drew moral instruction from these dreams, using them to teach the believers about the nature of faith or the promise of redemption.

Time and again, dreams have changed the world.

So who is she to say that her dreams have no meaning? If her dreams about Elias raised concerns with the RAA, then perhaps she ought to look for the reason within herself, and stop blaming the algorithm for her own impulses. She must admit—to herself, at least, since she would never admit it to others—that she's resented Elias in the past, for his impatience to start a family, his freedom from the burden of carrying twins, and even his talent at taking care of them. "You're such a good dad," his mother would say every time she visited, every single time, the unspoken part loud enough for Sara to hear.

Part of the reason Sara got herself a Dreamsaver was to be a better mother, to keep up with Elias. So yes, she resents him. And in the world of dreams, where her soul roams free, she must have done something terrible.

But surely, a voice inside her says, premonition has value only because it is so rare. Every night people dream multiple dreams, most of which have no meaning. They're little more than electrical activity in the brain, evidence that the sleeping self is alive, and at play. How many dreams did Joseph have apart from the one that predicted his rise to power in Egypt? Imagine if the sages had built religions around those, too. She can't resist a smile at this thought, and her eyes fling open. The cameras whir to adjust to her movement, and she quickly composes herself.

She has learned to wear a mask of detachment, has become so adept at it that someday, she fears, it may become her only face.

THE SKY IS HAZY, BUT THE HEAT IS RISING. VICTORIA AND THREE OF the younger retainees play cards at a table in the exercise yard, so absorbed in their game that they don't look up when a squirrel darts under a chair to pick up a carrot chip that dropped to the ground. Eisley Richardson seems to have convinced Alice to try out her fitness routine; they are doing push-ups together on a patch of grass. I should run, Sara tells herself as she steps on the track, I should get a proper workout for a change. The first lap is tolerable, but by the second she's already struggling. What happened to her? She used to play soccer in high school and as an adult went on regular hiking and backpacking trips; she should be able to handle a few laps around the track. As she reaches the curve, she sees a truck backing up to the side of the main building. The rear door rolls up with a plaintive squeak, and two men in blue uniforms jump out. They must be delivering supplies to the commissary.

As she gets closer, though, she notices they're unloading planks of wood and panels of drywall. What's all this for? If there is damage that needs to be repaired somewhere in the facility, the CRO hasn't mentioned it in his announcements.

Marcela calls out to her from the grass. "Want some company?"

"Sure."

Marcela falls into step with Sara. The shoes they were issued when they were admitted aren't designed for exercise; each footfall against the asphalt sends a shock through the feet, ankles, and knees. She's sure they're doing damage to their joints, but sitting around during yard time isn't much of an alternative, either.

"So my petition was denied," Marcela says after a minute.

"I'm sorry."

"How could they have decided already? It's only been, like, a week."

It's an unusually quick response, for sure. "Did they give you a reason?"

"The form just said 'PRIVILEGE DENIED. FILE UNSATISFACTORY.'"

So it would seem that maintaining professional skills isn't enough of a reason to let Marcela have her musical instrument. There is a perverse logic to this denial; after all, no woman who's been at Madison past the initial twenty-one-day hold has managed to keep her job in the free world. Why should a musician be treated differently than an office clerk or a truck driver? Sara feels a pang of regret at having gotten involved; now Marcela's disappointment is hers, too. "You can always try again," she says through her panting, "and give a different reason."

"It looked like an automated response. I'm not sure they even read the stuff you wrote."

Sweat is running down Sara's face and her breathing is growing more labored. After she finishes another lap, she decides to slow down and let Marcela continue without her.

The two construction workers are unloading drywall now, while the foreman takes a call on his cell phone, loudly instructing whomever he's talking to about how to get to Madison. "El giro está un poquito escondido detrás de unos palos verdes," he says, "así que debes estar atento a la bandera." A moment later, he jumps in the back of the truck and carries out a ladder. It occurs to Sara that the workers aren't repairing anything, they're building something.

Madison is expanding, she realizes with horror. The school wasn't designed to house people, let alone so many. The wait times for hearings are already long. What will it be like when more people are brought in? And what about the lines for the phones or the showers or the food?

But once dreams became a commodity, a new market opened— and markets are designed to grow. Sales must be increased, initiatives developed, channels broadened. The RAA pays Safe-X to house, feed, clothe, and surveil the people retained for their dreams. Profit flows to this company the other way, too: retainees pay to make calls, receive mail, or get personal supplies. So it makes brutal sense that Safe-X wants to expand.

She watches Marcela make the turn around the track, while she's lagging far behind. She hasn't been feeling herself lately, and last night's nightmare has made things worse. In the dream, she stands by the kitchen window, watching snow fall in big flurries outside. Weather like this calls for a warm soup. She puts a pot on the stove and pours a bit of olive oil, waits for it to spread. Each time she wants to add an ingredient, it materializes as if by magic in her right hand. A chopped onion, three garlic cloves, half a teaspoon of salt, a bunch of diced carrots. When the onions are translucent, she pours water, which gushes like a spring from between her fingers. And now the final ingredient—a heaping cup of antifreeze. Then the dream ends.

What is she to make of this? She hasn't seen snow since she was three years old. She wants to believe that the flurries represent the unusual mess she's in, which would make the antifreeze an attempt at a solution, but what if the cooking is more sinister, and she really is trying to harm her husband? Being surveilled all the time, even in her sleep, has made her unsure what to believe about herself; she no longer knows how to separate her emotions from the expectations that others have about them. Perhaps it is true what Hinton says, that the algorithm knows her better than she knows herself.

Marcela has completed her lap and caught up with Sara again. "You know what," she says, "I'm going to petition them again."

"Okay."

"I'm going to offer to teach music to the other retainees. They won't say no to an educational program."

"Go for it."

"You're not gonna help me?"

"I mean, it didn't do any good last time. It might've even worked against you."

"I don't think it's you. My score was up three points." A note of self-reproach enters Marcela's voice. "Maybe the cameras picked up something."

The workers have finished unloading the drywall. Now they sit on the bed of the truck and wait for further instructions. One of them lights a cigarette, takes a deep drag, then exhales with flourish. The other one looks across the playground at the retainees playing cards, doing sit-ups, standing on the track. He catches Sara watching him, and looks away quickly.

She heads back indoors. The sudden change in light and temperature makes her ears ring. She puts her hand on the wall to steady herself, but when she hears the squeaking of Hinton's shoes down the hallway, she has no choice but to keep moving. (Steering clear of Hinton is the most important task she sets for herself every day.) After he turns the corner, and his footfalls recede into silence, Sara stops in front of the screen where work duties are listed by location—kitchen, laundry, and custodial; trailers A, B, C, and D; groundskeeping and maintenance.

A new row has been added: construction cleanup.

.   .   .

STANDING UNDER THE SHOWER, SARA FEELS SOMEWHAT REJUVENATED. She really should make a habit of running, even though the only time she can exercise is in the afternoon, when the track is under direct sunlight and it's usually too hot. The boost of energy is worth it, though. She hasn't felt this good in ages. She finds herself making a mental list of what she wants to do before the day is over: send an email to her lawyer to ask for an update about her hearing request, pick something new to read from the library, stop by the commissary to buy toothpaste.

On the way back to her room, she comes across Toya, Lucy, and Marcela in the hallway. In one of Lucy's hands is a mesh bag with what look like her belongings—a few manila file folders, a framed picture, a couple of sweaters, some toiletry products. Has Marcela's teasing gone too far? Perhaps Lucy has asked for a room reassignment, even though the process would result in a note on her file and a bump to her risk score. "What's going on?" Sara asks, flinging her towel over her shoulder and joining the group. Immediately, Lucy's perfume makes her sneeze.

"Bless you," Lucy says, smiling at Sara. "You didn't hear?"

"No, what?"

"I'm being released."

"Now?" Sara asks, stupidly.

"Yeah. As soon as they finish processing me up front."

Sara glances at the others—she can't be the only one who's surprised by this turn of events. Lucy is a long hauler; she's been denied release several times. What changed this time around? "But when was your hearing?" Sara asks. "You didn't even tell us you had a hearing."

"This afternoon. I didn't say anything because I didn't want to jinx it."

"This afternoon?" So much for the theory that early morning hearings are successful. Lucy doesn't seem to have bothered much with her appearance, either.

Toya frowns. "But how'd you convince them to clear you?"

"That's what I asked, too," Marcela says.

"I don't know," Lucy replies with a shrug. All of a sudden she turns bashful. Her good fortune is even more apparent to her now, under the gaze of three envious retainees. "I just answered their questions."

"Come on," Marcela presses. "Just tell us how it went."

"Oh, *now* you wanna talk to me? You've been giving me the silent treatment for a week." Lucy glares at her roommate, then turns to Toya. "Look, I just told you. I answered their questions."

But now Sara wants to know, too. She wants to find out how to sound when she addresses the board. Which details she should play up, and which to leave out. She's learned the hard way that it's not enough that she's innocent; she has to deliver a convincing performance of her innocence. "Give us details."

"What I want to know is," Toya says, her voice as sharp as a knife, "what made this hearing special?"

"Special had nothing to do with it. That's the whole point. They realized I'm just a regular person, not a criminal, and they approved my release."

"So you think we're criminals?" Toya asks between her teeth. Ever since her blood pressure medication ran out, she's been as touchy as a live wire. "You're the one who committed ID fraud."

"What? Where the hell did you get that idea?"

"Aren't you getting sued by one of your victims?"

"Yes, but I didn't steal anyone's ID. I'm being sued by a customer whose information was compromised after a database breach at my old job. She's suing *everyone* at the company for failure of fiduciary duty, says we're all liable for her financial losses because we didn't protect her information. But the lawsuit is bullshit. I wasn't in charge of the database anyway, it was someone else's department."

"You didn't open credit cards with her name?"

"No, that was someone else at the company. You shouldn't listen to gossip."

"So they didn't ask you about that?"

"They asked me about all kinds of things, including that. But like I said, everyone else at my old job was sued, it wasn't about me."

"What about the dreams you had last month?" Marcela asks, her voice barely above a whisper. "Seems like they'd think twice before letting out a pedo."

The word takes Sara's breath away. But the accusation seems to touch a nerve because Lucy drops the mesh bag that contains her belongings, as if she's ready to leave it behind. Her eyes travel down the hallway toward the exit.

"Wait," Sara says, a memory suddenly returning to her. Three weeks ago, when Lucy came to borrow Emily's hair dryer, she'd lingered over the picture of the twins on her shelf. Dreams aren't real, Sara reminds herself. No matter what the RAA says, it is not a crime to dream. But when it comes to children, her own children, she isn't sure she can be so adamant. "Wait. Is that why you were asking me about my kids the other day?"

"That's sick," Marcela hisses. "*You're* sick."

"No, no, no, I was just making conversation," Lucy says, raising one hand in self-defense. Then, her voice sharper now, she adds, "You know what? I don't have to explain myself to any of you. I'm leaving this place behind, that's all that matters."

The reviving effect of the shower is gone; Sara is getting sweaty now, the towel on her shoulder as heavy as a brick. None of what she's hearing makes any sense. How can they free someone like Lucy, while keeping her locked up here? She gets the feeling that something has gone wrong, or is about to go wrong, but she's helpless to stop it.

Marcela tries to grab Lucy's arm, but Toya pulls her back just in time. "We didn't do half the shit she did," Marcela says, batting Toya's hand away, "and she's the one getting out. Does that make any sense to you?" Lucy is walking away now, but Marcela runs after her. "What'd you tell 'em, huh?" Her voice carries clear across the hallway.

"I just answered their questions," Lucy says over her shoulder. "That's all I did."

"Snitch." Marcela shoves her, and this time Lucy loses her balance and falls to the floor.

Hinton and Yee are already through the gate, whistles blowing, keys rattling. All the retainees in the hallway stand with their backs to the wall. "What the hell's going on here? Everett, you need to be downstairs for your paperwork."

"DeLeón attacked me," Lucy tells them, standing up. "That's what happened. She attacked me, she's out of control."

"Out of control?" Marcela says. "Out of control? I barely touched you!"

"I was in my room," Toya explains, hoping to avoid another write-up. "Everett came in to say she was being released."

"I was walking back from the shower," Sara says.

It doesn't matter. Hinton pulls out his Tekmerion and points it at each one of the women in turn, barely disguising his pleasure.

SAFE-X SECURITY QUESTIONNAIRE

(BASIC-10)

If you check the YES box on a question below, you must provide details on the pop-up screen.	Yes	No
1. Are you aware of any retainee who plans to harm someone at this facility?	☐	☐
2. Are you aware of any retainee who plans to harm someone outside this facility?	☐	☐
3. Are you aware of any retainee who plans to harm themselves at this facility?	☐	☐
4. Are you aware of any retainee (or retainees) planning to escape, riot, or encourage others to escape or riot?	☐	☐
5. Are you aware of any retainee (or retainees) planning to set fire or otherwise damage this facility?	☐	☐
6. Are you aware of any retainee who is using narcotics, alcohol, or any other controlled substance while at this facility?	☐	☐
7. Are you aware of any retainee who is in possession of contraband, including phones, smart devices, cigarettes, vape pens, lighters, or matches?	☐	☐
8. Are you aware of any retainee who is in possession of weapons, including guns, knives, blades, or sharp instruments?	☐	☐
9. Are you aware of any retainee who is in possession of prohibited documents or reading material?	☐	☐
10. Are you aware of any improper conduct by an attendant at this facility?	☐	☐

☐ I acknowledge that my answers are voluntary and have not been coerced by staff or visitors.

☐ I understand that answers to this questionnaire may lengthen or shorten the retention period of any named individual, including myself.

Name: _____

Signature: _____

TWO WEEKS HAVE PASSED SINCE THE SANTA ANAS BLEW IN from the canyons, but the sky still has a grayish cast. The wildflowers on the hillside droop, the bus sign is coated in dust. Sara stands at the window, waiting. At the usual time the old woman appears, lumbering up the street with her wares, but dressed today in a turquoise blue dress, with an embroidered bodice and a full skirt lined with ruffles. Sometimes she seems like the only evidence Sara has that the free world still exists, in all its capacity for beauty. Once the bus arrives, the old woman gets on, puts her bags on the luggage rack, and takes a seat. Then she raises her eyes and now she's looking right at the window. She waves.

Her heart skipping a beat, Sara waves back. The moment lasts no more than a second or two, but it's the best thing that's happened to her in days, this passing glance from someone outside.

Now she sits down with her journal. She remembers only one dream from the night before, an unusually long one that unfolds in minute detail as soon as she begins writing it. She is in a fancy hotel on the Italian Riviera, waiting for the clerk at the front desk to check availability for a room. *Mi dispiace,* he says, the system keeps logging him out. *Scuse,* it will just be another minute. She waits and waits and waits. Wouldn't it be easier if she booked the room herself? She pulls out her phone and opens a hotel app, but in a singsong voice the clerk finally announces that he has made a reservation under Sara's name for a room with a view of the Ligurian Sea. She thanks him and hurries out of the lobby, eager to move on with her day. Outside, she finds her mother waiting for her, looking just as she did when Sara was a child: petite, limber, with jet-black hair and striking, kohl-lined eyes.

"Mama, you made it!" Sara gives her mother a tight hug. "See, this place isn't as remote as you thought it was. You can get here in four hours."

But with only a glance at the fancy hotel, Faiza's face darkens. "We shouldn't stay here. Can we go somewhere else?"

"Okay. Sure."

Sara goes back to the front desk, where the clerk is snacking on baby carrots while watching television. As soon as she tells him that she needs to check out early, his demeanor changes. He slams a wrinkled dollar bill on the counter and tells her that this is the only refund he can offer. His courtesy is gone, he is businesslike.

"But the agreement says the room is fully refundable." She pulls out her phone to show him the confirmation email he himself sent her a few minutes earlier. "And for any reason."

The clerk smiles, revealing teeth yellowed by coffee. A sliver of carrot is stuck between his front teeth. "That's not what the agreement means."

For a long time she tries to reason with him: she reads aloud the line that says she can cancel one or more nights if she notifies the hotel by noon, then points to the clock on the wall. But he refuses to budge. "There's no refund on this reservation."

"Stop gaslighting me." When he ignores her again, she grabs him by the collar and shoves the phone in his face. "Just read what it says."

His glasses fall on the counter; he backs away from her.

Then the dream ends.

It isn't unusual for Sara's mother to visit her in dreams, though it's happened with less frequency as the years have passed since her death. Still, many details in the story are incongruous. Sara has never been to the Italian Riviera, for example. She doesn't rely on hotel clerks for reservations. And Italy is more than twelve hours away, not four. Unless, of course, they were traveling from Morocco rather than California. In her dream, Sara returned her mother to her home country, which wasn't possible when she died because she got so sick so fast that they were overtaken by events and had to inter her at Rose Hills. Sara never recovered from the loss, which was all the more painful because it happened only months before the FDA approved the lung cancer vaccine. She misses her mother so much.

Maybe this dream is part fantasy, part fear. The fantasy is that Sara got to see Faiza again. Sara was closer to her mother than she ever was to her father, who wrapped himself in resentful silence the summer she turned nine. That year, the Millers bought a new house with a huge backyard, where they often threw parties, often at the last moment. One day in May, they invited the Husseins over for a barbecue to celebrate their eldest daughter's admission to Georgetown. Faiza couldn't go; she was nursing a migraine. Omar said he was on a deadline for a grant proposal, but he agreed to drop the children off on his way to the lab. "Watch out for your brother," he told Sara.

The new house was huge. A dozen blue and gray balloons hung from the ceiling, untethered from the arrangement at the entrance, and on every table bouquets were wilting in the heat. Lamb kebabs sizzled on the grill. There was music, too, the adults were dancing and drinking on the terrace. The younger kids swam in the pool and as usual Zach played rough, dunking Sara into the water and holding her down until her lungs burned. She came up, panting for air, blinking in the glare of sunlight. "Stop it!" she pleaded. In a stinging betrayal, Saïd started to imitate Zach, aiming for her the next time he jumped into the water. She was relieved when one of the parents told them to get out of the pool and play hide-and-seek instead.

Sara ran to the hallway closet. Saïd tried to get in with her, but she kicked him out. "Go find your own hiding place," she told him with not a little satisfaction, closing the door slowly so it wouldn't creak. For a long time she sat quietly, the coats and jackets above her reeking of cigarettes and perfume, now and then pinching her nose to avert a sneeze. When she heard Zach calling her name from the terrace, she was reluctant to come out, thinking it another one of his tricks. Time passed. She was starting to doze off when Aunt Hiba's screaming drew her out of the closet.

This is the moment when her memory becomes jumbled and she isn't sure if she's remembering what she herself witnessed, or what she was told later, by the grown-ups. Her uncle was in the pool in his clothes, carrying Saïd out of the water. Someone yelled, "Call 9-1-1!" Kneeling on the cement, her uncle pressed his big hands on Saïd's chest, counting, counting, counting, then breathed into his mouth.

All of a sudden the terrace felt crowded, and the music stopped. But what Sara does remember, with a clarity as hard and cutting as a diamond, is the voice inside her that said *You should've let him hide in the closet with you.*

The guests parted to let the paramedics through with a gurney. They, too, tried to revive her younger brother, and failed. The police investigators said that Saïd must've been hiding in the pink flamingo float at the edge of the pool. That he must've lost his balance when he tried to get out. That he'd hit his head on the cement ledge and sank in the water. That no one had heard him because of the music.

Afterwards, Sara's father became a different man. A stranger who lived in their house. He didn't know how to cope with the loss, Sara can see that now, but his prolonged silence seemed colored by unspoken blame toward her. He started spending all his time at Caltech. When he came home, he would go straight into his bedroom, his eyes passing over her without a flicker of interest, and emerge a few minutes later, having changed into his qashaba. Then he would disappear into his office for the rest of the evening. Sara couldn't watch television or listen to music when he was working, which was all the time. The smallest interruption could set him off. He would complain that he was behind on all his deadlines, that he needed peace and quiet to finish, that no one in this house understood him. How often Sara dissolved into tears at his outbursts!

Over time, she learned not to involve him in her life. It was to her mother that she went for help with her science project, or to report that her English teacher leered at girls in class, or to get cheered up when she didn't score a goal during the entire soccer season of her junior year. Years passed before Omar crawled up from the abyss of grief, and by then Sara's relationship with him had become tainted. She let him dote on Mona and Mohsin, of course, but she couldn't quite close the distance that had opened between them after Saïd died.

As she writes, Sara realizes how much she still misses her mother. Had she only known how little time she had with Faiza, she'd have sat with her on the porch every afternoon that last summer. Faiza would sit just so, under the shade of the magnolia tree, a cigarette in one hand and her phone in the other, reading the news from home. Before moving to the United States, she had worked as a reporter for a popular magazine in Morocco, filing increasingly alarming reports about state corruption. Once, she exposed a government minister who was diverting medical equipment meant for rural hospitals to his private clinic. The story went viral, leading to a reader tip for another investigation, this one into a car-assembly plant that received subsidies to educate workers, but used the money for executive bonuses instead. Almost overnight, the DGSN became interested in her. They tailed her when she was running errands, tapped her phone, sent undercover agents to dinner parties she attended. It became impossible to find interview subjects who were willing to speak candidly to her or to travel without harassment from police officers who'd been alerted about her plans. And then she met Omar—an EMI-trained physicist who had recently landed a fellowship in California.

After she moved to Los Angeles, Faiza continued to keep up with stories from home, the ashtray by her side filling up as the afternoon hours passed. When she talked about a piece of news, the history she unraveled turned out almost always to be messier or more troubled than the article made it seem. Perhaps that is where Sara's interest in history began, on the porch where her mother smoked cigarettes, lost in memories of the people she knew in another country. This is the picture Sara always conjures when she thinks of her mother: a woman tethered to her past. Even in the dream, she returned to it.

But maybe this dream hints at Sara's fear that she is stuck at Madison, just as she's stuck in that hotel on the Italian Riviera. Nothing she has tried has worked. It's like the song says, you can check out anytime you like, but you can never leave. Perhaps her subconscious is chiding her; she should've looked more closely at the agreement she signed when she got the Dreamsaver, should've realized they'd commodify her dreams, sell them to whoever was willing to buy them. Sara has blamed herself for this lapse many times in her waking moments, too, but at the time she got the implant, her sleep deprivation was so acute, so debilitating, that she would've done anything to get some relief. No one expects a starving person to read the nutritional information on a bag of chips, so why should they expect insomniacs to read terms of service that are fifteen pages long?

Besides, even if she didn't have the neuroprosthetic she would still not be safe from the RAA. If her car had detected signs that she'd driven under the influence, they could've suspended her license. If she'd engaged in financial transactions they deemed suspicious, they could've put holds on the kind of bank accounts she was allowed to have. If she'd interacted on social media with people they'd flagged, they could've prevented her from buying an airplane ticket. After all, how else are they supposed to stop crime before it happens?

HER MIND WANDERS TO HER SHADOW LIFE, THE ONE SHE WOULD STILL have if she hadn't gotten the implant, hadn't been detained at LAX on her return from London. In that life, she's struggling to keep her eyes open while she gets the twins situated in their playpen with a set of magnetic building blocks and a few stuffed animals. The coffee maker in the kitchen beeps. She pours herself a cup and leans against the counter, sipping it as she looks out of the window at the new day. The rain from last night has left the street clean. The neighbor is walking his Lab, patiently waiting on the sidewalk as the dog sniffs the grass, his tail wagging. A woman jogs on the pavement, her face flushed and dripping with sweat, oblivious to the SUV that swerves to avoid hitting her. The leaves of the oak tree shiver when the wind picks up. As Sara finishes her coffee, the theme of *Morning Edition* begins to play on the stereo.

Or, scratch that. It hasn't rained in ten months, and the leaves of the oak tree are dry and yellow. The tile on the kitchen floor feels warm under Sara's feet. Wouldn't it be nice to go for a swim? The neighborhood Y has an Olympic-size outdoor pool, with a couple of lanes reserved for laps, and it's not too busy in the mornings. She might have time to make it there and back before she has to log on to the staff meeting at eleven. Just as she starts her coffee, Mohsin and Mona tussle over the blue dolphin that Elias's parents gave them last month. They have a dozen stuffed animals in their playpen, but of course they're fighting over that stupid dolphin, which makes a clicky sound they love. *Clickity click click.* Mohsin manages to grab the dolphin, but instead of walking away, he hits Mona on the head with it and she drops to the floor and lets out a bloodcurdling scream, like he's hit her with a brick. "Hey, buddy," Sara says, turning off NPR before the news starts. "Don't hit your sister."

"Construction has the highest number of fatal injuries of any industry."

Dazed, Sara looks up from her book. She is in the rec room, seated by the window with Toya, a bag of carrot chips open between them. From upstairs in the east wing comes the sound of construction workers calling out to each other as they pack up for the day. "What?"

"Construction has the highest number of fatal injuries," Toya repeats. "Higher than trucking or warehousing."

"I guess that makes sense, with all the tools," Sara says.

"But with a higher number of claims, there's also more cases of fraud. I remember, when I was starting out, this guy filed a claim saying he'd hurt his elbow doing construction work. The paperwork seemed legit, he had all the right medical certifications and proof of missed workdays. I called his house, just to check on a small detail, and someone answers. His teenage daughter, I think. I couldn't make out what she was saying because of the music in the background. I asked if she could turn it down, she said she couldn't because her dad was building a tree house in the backyard and the remote control was up there with him. I mean, he could've at least waited until the claim was approved." She laughs—a good hearty laugh that shows the gap between her front teeth. She's in a better mood now that she's finally received a replacement for her blood pressure medication.

Sara closes her book; she won't be able to read. When Toya gets into a talkative mood, you can't shut her up. "Did you see a lot of fraud in your time at Sanctuary?"

"Not a lot. But enough, you know."

"Enough to . . ."

"Well, to make me skeptical. Most people are honest, you know, but there are always those who try to cheat the system. I learned not to take anything at face value, even if there's documentation. First thing people do when they file fraudulent claims is attach paperwork that they think proves their lies. But as soon as I start digging, I find holes in their stories, or contradictions in the evidence, things that don't quite fit."

Sara picks up another carrot chip. "What makes you want to investigate, though?"

"The software pulls out suspicious cases for me, but then I look at the client profile, the size of the claim, the date when the policy was written. Like, if someone takes out a large policy, then files a claim less than twelve months later. That sort of thing. But sometimes it's just a gut feeling that something is off."

"You're kidding, right? You investigate based on a gut feeling?"

"I mean, yeah, sometimes."

A movement outside the window briefly catches Sara's eye; an attendant has come out into the yard, pulling his phone from the back pocket of his pants. When he turns his face toward the sunlight, she sees it's Ortega. For a moment he closes his eyes, warming his face under the sun, then turns his attention to his phone. "And you don't see why that might be a problem?" Sara asks, returning her focus to Toya.

"My job was to investigate," Toya replies. "I made phone calls or home visits, then decided on the claims. I didn't punish anyone."

"I guess," Sara says, reluctant to concede the point. She can't explain why she's so bothered by what seems like a standard procedure in Toya's profession. So what if there was no legal punishment? Making people go through a lengthy and rebarbative process based solely on a hunch isn't fair. Some people might never follow up on their claims because of the hassle, losing money that might be owed to them. That is a kind of penalty, too.

"In case you haven't noticed," Toya adds, "I work here now. That other life is gone."

All at once, Sara's irritation disappears. She tells Toya she can always go back to Sanctuary when she leaves. "You're obviously good at what you do."

"They weren't happy with the union talk, so they wouldn't want me. But even without that, they wouldn't hire me with the hole I have on my resume. As a matter of fact, no one in actuaries would."

Toya laughs silently, shaking her head at the irony. "When I come out, I'm gonna have to go in a different line of work."

"Maybe I will, too."

"Yeah? What're you thinking?"

"I'm not sure." Sara can't imagine that the Getty would have a position open for her when she comes out, and with a lengthy retention on her record, a teaching job is out of the question. She'll have to find something else. All she knows is that she can't go back to living like a bear in a nature preserve, unaware that it's being watched from hidden cameras while it's fishing for salmon or sunning itself on a rock. Surely, she's more than that. She wants freedom, not a bunch of enclosed rights. "I just want to get as far away from here as I can."

FOR ONCE, THERE IS NO WAIT AT THE COMPUTER; SARA TAKES A FREE seat next to Victoria. The headlines still mention the corruption allegations against the congressman from Arizona, but now the coverage includes pictures of the pop star with whom he was partying in Saint-Tropez last summer. The story is making the slow transition from scandal to entertainment, which probably means that in the end he will face no consequences. The drought in Wyoming and Colorado might be coming to an end, with a heavy storm expected this week. A Japanese company has unveiled its new generation of bionic prosthetics, in an ingenious, low-cost design that will make it possible to help thousands of disabled survivors of war. Then a brief item in *The Washington Post* catches Sara's eye: James Wesley, the chief administrator of the RAA, is engaged to be married.

For months, Sara has thought of this man only as the government official who claims to keep the American public safe through the application of smart algorithmic decisions. In interviews, he comes across as smart, cool, reasonable. If pushed by a dogged reporter, he might admit to a couple of problems with the current administration's approach to risk assessment, but he never fails to promote algorithmic policing as the only sensible solution to public safety problems in a society where domestic terrorists, mass shooters, and other dangerous criminals can strike with unprecedented speed and violence. The RAA stops crime before it happens, he says. He sounds like he's trying out slogans in preparation for a candidacy to elected office.

But Sara has never really thought of James Wesley as a man of flesh and blood, with family and friends and apparently now a fiancée. The report says the bride-to-be is from Pasadena, a detail that takes Sara by surprise. She went to the same high school Sara did, graduating three years later, though Sara doesn't recognize her from the engagement photo in the newspaper. The happy couple must be creating a guest list by now, debating which DJ to hire, checking availability at the Huntington Gardens or the country club in La Cañada. The thought fills Sara with rage against Wesley, who was an early advocate of risk-assessment algorithms and who now oversees the entire U.S. retention system. What can she do with this rage, though? Wesley isn't here. Day by day, her case is handled by Safe-X agents, contract employees who say they're only following the rules set down by the company.

Take Williams, for example. He looks like one of those aimless undergraduates Sara used to teach, the kind of student who sleep-walks through most of the semester, then comes to life a couple of weeks before grades are due. Right now, he's sitting in his chair by the door, struggling to keep his eyes open. A button is missing from his uniform shirt and his hair looks unwashed: he seems to be having a rough morning.

Oh, Sara remembers rough mornings. They meant late nights out, a date with someone new, a dinner with old friends, where glasses were clinked and questionable decisions were made. She remembers staying up so late there was no time to take a shower or put on fresh clothes the next day. She had plenty of rough mornings, when she was Williams's age. Years later, after she and Elias had the twins, she had a different kind of rough morning, which brought a different kind of pleasure. Mona's cooing as her diaper was changed, Mohsin's yawn as she rocked him to sleep. The way they kicked their little feet whenever she tried to wrestle them into their onesies. As she thinks of those lost moments, Sara's rage rises inside her until it oozes like pus from a sore.

Eisley Richardson walks in, takes a seat next to Sara. Now Williams stirs into wakefulness. "Aguilar," he calls out. "Time's up."

"Already?" Victoria glances at the clock above the entrance. "I came in at 7:15. I still have five minutes." She goes back to her screen and is instantly absorbed in whatever she's reading.

Without a word, Williams pulls out his Tekmerion. Maybe the rough night he had put him in a foul mood, or the Santa Anas are working on his nerves, or he enjoys the sadistic pleasure of denying a retainee the right to read about what is happening in the free world. Who knows? He points his camera at Victoria and waits for the system to pull up her file. Writing up a retainee every once in a while makes it clear to the rest of the women that they had better stay in line.

"What're you doing?" Victoria calls from her seat.

Williams doesn't answer, he's staring at his device.

"Come on," Victoria says. "Just look at the clock. I have five minutes left."

"I called Time already."

"Oh." Victoria raises her eyebrows as if to say *I must not've heard you.* She stands up readily and walks over to Williams, smiling as she tucks a loose strand of hair behind her ear. She's taller than him and wearing a different uniform, but they seem to be about the same age. "I'm sorry about that. I was just reading about the Lakers, and I guess I lost track of time. It won't happen again."

Williams seems flustered by the pretty girl suddenly towering over him.

"I didn't mean to cause any trouble," Victoria continues, touching his arm. She glances back at the computer stations, as if realizing her mistake, then returns her gaze to him. "But you can cancel it, right?"

Williams sits up straighter. "All right. Just this time."

What a performance, Sara thinks with reluctant admiration. So simple, so effective. Yet in all her time here, she has never managed it; her pride gets in the way.

THE PACKAGE ARRIVES ON A DAY WHEN SARA HAS A DOUBLE SHIFT IN Trailer D, so she doesn't receive it until late in the evening. She tears through the clear plastic emblazoned with the PostPal logo, then through a green envelope that indicates this is a premium item for which Elias had to pay extra. When the greeting card drops onto her cot, the first thing she does is bring it to her nose. She takes a deep breath, but although she can detect the scent of paper and ink and something acrid, there's nothing she can tether to her memory of home. Whatever familial smell may have lingered on the card, it was lost during the mail scanning and clearance process. Fingers trembling, she opens the card.

All around and over the HAPPY BIRTHDAY greeting, Mohsin and Mona have drawn little figures that look like tadpoles, with huge heads and sticklike arms. The drawings are in green and yellow crayons, but she can't tell which were done by Mohsin and which by Mona. The figures seem feminine to her, though, as if the twins were prompted to *draw Mama*. Did they treat it like a game, completing it on the cluttered play table by the living room window, or was it more of a chore they had to finish before dinner, without understanding its purpose? The tadpoles are full of energy, with round eyes and, at least on one of them, what look like teeth. This detail makes her smile—and then tears prick her eyes; she's missing so much while she's stuck here.

Across the bottom of the card, Elias has managed to fit a couple of handwritten lines: *We miss you so much, Sara. Get home soon.* She closes the card, feeling at once elated by this small gift and disappointed by how brief the pleasure it gave her. Now she lingers on the artwork that appears on the front of the card, a reproduction of a Yayoi Kusama screen print of a butterfly. When she was pregnant, she and Elias had gone to a special exhibit at the Broad, walking through gallery rooms covered in mirrors, each reflecting polka-dotted pumpkins. Afterwards, they'd had lunch at a restaurant nearby, and then walked slowly hand in hand toward the Metro station. This, too, is a gift, she realizes: the memory of that ordinary day. It feels like salve on the wound of their argument.

On top of all this, Elias has added a little money to her commissary account, enough to buy snacks. She runs to the commissary, as giddy as a child.

From: ZachSMiller@freemail.com
To: SaraTHussein@PostPal.com
CR Number: M-7493002
Facility: Madison
Date: October 21
Flags: LAW ENFORCEMENT
Status: Released after review

Dear Sara,

It's been a long time since we've been in touch, but I wanted to write you as soon as I heard that you're in preventive detention. I was in Los Angeles yesterday to pick up a vintage Ford Bronco that the seller refused to ship through regular channels, and I took the opportunity to visit Uncle Omar. I almost didn't go, because I couldn't remember the address, but I knew that your house was a few blocks from the old movie theater in Pasadena, so I managed to situate myself without my phone. The neighborhood looks so different than when we were growing up, especially with the noncombustible roofs and metal cladding that they have on buildings these days. Your house hasn't changed much, though.

I parked the Bronco and walked up the brick pathway, feeling like I was taking a trip back in time. I remember we used to play on the street while Mom smoked cigarettes with Aunt Faiza on the porch. The same vine was creeping up the fence. The same front door creaked as it opened. Your father looked much the same, too, except for his gray hair and the Exo-Legs he has to use on account of the stroke. I didn't even know he'd had a stroke, it's been that long since I saw him last. But he's very good at navigating that contraption, and unlike my mom he still has ALL his marbles.

We sat on the checkered sofa in his living room, drinking mint tea and talking about the old days. He showed me pictures of our moms when they were in high school, and a portrait of all of us kids from a trip to Mirror Lake when Saïd was still alive. I remember you were mad at Saïd because he'd broken your front tooth, so when we went fishing your dad paired you with me. Remember the huge rainbow trout we caught? But it wasn't until I asked about your news that he told me what happened to you at LAX. I've always hated that airport, you know, it's so disorganized and poorly run.

Sara, I'm going to be honest with you. Your dad thinks this whole thing happened because you're a difficult woman, just like your mom. He said that the way she used to talk to TSA agents rubbed off on you, and you must've said or done something during your interview that made them detain you. He hasn't had the experience with law enforcement that I have, so I guess I can see why he might think that way. But still. I told him that an arrest doesn't mean you did anything wrong. Look at me, I told him. A customer had me arrested for forging his signature on a deal, but six months later his son admitted he'd signed the papers. Who paid for the mess in the end? It wasn't the police, I'll tell you that. I'm still trying to get my record expunged.

But I didn't want to argue with Uncle Omar too much, because he seemed so frail. He kept telling me stories about the past, sometimes reaching behind him for one of the framed pictures on the console. I got a scan of the picture of us at Mirror Lake, since I don't have it, and another one of my mom when she was pregnant with me. Being in your house made me feel, I don't know, like I missed out. I wish we hadn't moved to Florida when I was ten. It would've been nice to keep all the friends I had, grow up surrounded by family, have those barbecues like we used to have, with games and music and dancing. I never really understood why we moved across the country, or why we didn't stay in touch afterwards.

By the time I walked out of your dad's house, I was feeling a bit nostalgic so I decided to take a little walk around the neighborhood. Then Mel called me. I'd rescheduled one of my weekends with the kids to travel to L.A., but she was still mad about the change and wanted to yell at me some more. This was a work trip, and anyway she agreed to the change! Now she was up in arms about it. I was so angry I could've exploded. The couples therapist we were seeing before the divorce said that I had to learn to manage my anger. Wouldn't you know, she suggested walking. Something about serotonin levels. Or was it dopamine? I don't remember. Boy, did I walk. I walked for an hour straight, trying to keep my rage in check, until it started getting dark and I had to turn around.

Anyway, I'm driving back to Florida now. With any luck, I might even be able to get there by Sunday morning and get one full day with my girls. I'm writing to you from a motel room about a hundred miles from the New Mexico border. The landscape here is not at all what I expected. It's a little greener, I guess because of the higher elevation, though the town doesn't attract much tourism anymore. Three of the resort hotels serve as climate shelters, and the others have closed down for good.

I have to catch some sleep before the next leg of the trip, but I did want to write you and offer my help. Is there anything I can do? Maybe add some cash to your commissary account? Or get in touch with someone for you? I know from experience that having some outside help or even a bit of encouragement can make a huge difference. So think on it and let me know.

Yours,
Zachariah

· · ·

From: ZachSMiller@freemail.com
To: SaraTHussein@PostPal.com
CR Number: M-7493002
Facility: Madison
Date: October 28
Flags: LEGAL
Status: : Released after review

Dear Sara,

I never heard from you after my email, so thought I'd check in
again. I certainly didn't mean any offense when I repeated the
conversation I had with your dad the other day. I was just trying
to give you a sense of how much he's still in shock after what
happened to you. And I also wanted to reiterate my offer of help.
I'm happy to add to your commissary account or get in touch with
a lawyer or a rights organization for you, though I'm sure your
husband has already taken care of that. The one piece of advice I
have is: make yourself invisible. Don't talk to the attendants, don't
make friends with the others. Keep to yourself. Stay quiet until
your hearing.

Anyway, I finally made it to Orlando after nearly a week's delay
on the highways and byways of our country. The Ford Bronco I
bought in Los Angeles turned out to have an engine problem, and
it took me forever to get it fixed and then brought to my dealership.
I had to go on the MyCourt app to ask for arbitration because the
seller refused to take responsibility for misrepresenting the car.
Luckily, I had all the right documentation, and the seller ended up
folding after just two emails from the arbitrator.

Thank goodness this business with the Ford Bronco is done,
because Mel was complaining again that I was using it as an excuse
to skip a visit with the girls. Can you believe it? I love my girls,
I wish I could spend even more time with them. Why would I
choose to be stuck with a broken car in the middle of nowhere,
Louisiana, rather than be home with them? That woman, I swear.

There's something deeply, deeply wrong with her. My mom has always hated her, and now I understand why.

But on the plus side, I have some good news: my business is getting recognized by the Chamber of Commerce next month for extraordinary service to the community. We've been sponsoring the girls' soccer team for three years and doing free shuttle rides on game days, and I suppose someone there took notice. There's going to be a fancy ceremony at the Transcontinental downtown, with the mayor and everything. I'm very excited.

Well, I won't keep you for too long. Write me back with some of your news and let me know if I can help.

Yours,
Zachariah

I N THE ONLY DREAM SHE CAN REMEMBER FROM THE NIGHT BEFORE, she's wearing a midnight blue caftan with silver embroidery trim, and walking into the lobby of the Pershing Square Building downtown. The crown moldings and mirrors have been touched up here and there, but the building looks much as it did more than a century ago. It's a shame the entrance is too small to host receptions, because it would be a great place for her photography exhibit.

The sound of the elevator doors reminds her of the task at hand: a donor event on the tenth floor. Just as she's about to enter the elevator, out come two men. One is a young politician whose face is familiar, but whose name she can't recall, and the other is Albert Finney. Albert Finney! No one else seems to recognize him—not the receptionist sitting behind the desk with her phone, nor the couple browsing the list of tenants on the building directory. Sara is awestruck; she's tempted to point the actor out to them. Look, everyone. It's the great Albert Finney! But that's not even the strangest thing about this encounter. The strangest thing is that Finney is in a yellow tuxedo, and the other guy is in a cowboy hat and fringed waistcoat.

There you are, Finney says to Sara. Come, we're about to take flight.

Uh, she says. Sure. (What else does one say to an invitation from Albert Finney?)

They step outside in the dark. The street is empty, save for a handful of giant carrots hovering two feet above the ground. What in the world? But Finney and the young politician each mount one, as naturally as if it were a horse or a mule, so Sara does the same, skeptical at first and then elated when her carrot slowly takes flight behind theirs. They begin a flyover of Los Angeles, its lights glittering like jewels laid out on black velvet. She can make out City Hall, and the U.S. Bank Tower, and the Wilshire Grand. On the freeways, the red and white lines of cars moving in opposite directions look like garlands. As they get closer to the San Gabriel Mountains, Finney raises one hand in warning.

Careful with the turn, he says, his voice barely audible above the sound of the motors.

He maneuvers his craft beautifully, angling it away from the mountains and toward the Pacific. The politician follows, letting out a howl of triumph as he succeeds. Then it's her turn. She's still not sure how to steer the damn vegetable; she was too busy admiring the sights. The Santa Anas that have suddenly picked up are making navigation even more difficult. She presses different bumps and pulls at different strings on the carrot even as the granite rock comes closer and closer into view. She's terrified of crashing, but at the last second she manages to make the turn somehow and, with relief washing over her, she follows Finney toward the ocean.

Nicely done, he says in his gravelly voice.

By the time she finishes writing this dream, she's smiling at the absurdity of it. A yellow tuxedo. Albert Finney. Giant carrots. Wait, is there something sexual about it? She's always thought Finney was sexy. Still, she finds the goofiness of the flying sequence strangely comforting. It's been a long time since she felt as free as she did in this dream, untethered from the judgment of others, unafraid to try something new.

Later, stepping in front of the mirror, she hardly recognizes herself. Who is this stranger with scared eyes and a blank face? Her uniform is immaculate, her hair pulled in a tight bun. The cameras have even trained her to stand with her limbs loose and her back straight.

Sara pulls the hair tie out, and musses up her hair. There, that's better.

DINNER IS PORK HOT DOGS, WHICH SARA GIVES TO TOYA IN EXCHANGE for the canned beans on her tray. Sara tries to eat as slowly as possible, but she knows she will be hungry later. She can hardly believe there was a time when she could order a three-course meal, every dish in it made according to her preferences, and eat it sitting on a sunny terrace while making conversation with people whose company she sought. What luxury it now seems to have complained about how tangy the salad dressing was or how salty the soup. Sara is not entirely unfamiliar with deprivation, but unlike the hunger of Ramadan, when she knew with certainty that she would be able to satisfy her cravings at sunset, the hunger at Madison taunts her all the time. One of the lights overhead flickers and Sara looks up. "Is this because of construction?"

"They haven't touched the electrical at all," Emily replies.

"Oh. Have you seen them work?"

"Just once. They have the east wing pretty much sealed up." Twice a week, Emily is assigned to a second shift with the custodial crew, and sometimes she overhears talk about goings-on at Madison.

"Do you know when they'll be done?"

"Williams said they have to be out by November 15."

Eisley looks up. "Williams, the library attendant?"

"That's the one."

The light flickers again, its reflection against the darkened windows giving the appearance of lightning in a thunderstorm. Every table in the cafeteria is full, the din of conversation at its loudest, and the heat is rising fast. At the table by the door, Victoria stands up suddenly, throwing her head back to stop a nosebleed, but there are no napkins with which to stem the flow of blood. She leaves to wash up—and one of her tablemates steals a hot dog from her tray. "This fucking place," Sara mutters, shaking her head.

Marcela turns to Eisley. "You had your first hearing today, right? How'd it go?"

"I got cleared," Eisley says. "I get out first thing tomorrow."

A stunned silence falls on the table.

"For real?" Marcela asks.

"I wouldn't joke about something like that."

"Wow."

"Who was the last Tourist?" Toya asks, looking around the table. "Anyone remember?"

Marcela dunks her hot dog in ketchup. "The medic from Temecula, right?"

"No, the medic was extended once before her release," Sara says. "The last one was Michelle Adams, the waitress. Back in May."

"You've been keeping track?" Eisley asks, fixing Sara with her weary eyes.

"It's hard not to."

"How about you, then? How'd your last hearing go?"

"I haven't had any."

"You've never had a hearing? How is that possible?"

"I couldn't get one when I had Class A disciplinary actions on my file. Then the hearing was cancelled when my first lawyer recused himself. Then there was a backlog of hearings because of the government shutdown. And then just as they started catching up, they lost my file to a glitch in the system and had to start over. I've been here longer than my last extension requires, but I'm still waiting."

"Behind me?"

"New arrivals have priority."

"That's bad luck."

"That's bureaucracy."

The overhead light has stopped flickering, but now the lamps over the service station are starting to twinkle. The malfunction bothers Hinton; he walks over to investigate.

"What's with the interrogation?" Toya asks suddenly, narrowing her eyes at Eisley. "You haven't told us anything about your case, but you're asking Sara here about hers."

"It's not an interrogation," Eisley says, washing down the last of her hot dog with a huge sip of water. "I was just curious is all."

"Toya's right," Sara says. "You never really told us much about your case. Like, you haven't even told us how you got retained."

"There's not much to tell. I was coming back from a weekend in Cabo with a friend of mine. We went there for the weekend, sat by the beach, went to a few clubs. Then on the way back, we got flagged at the border because my idiot friend had been drinking. Anyway, they ran our passports through and said my score was too high. That's all."

"That's *all*," Sara repeats, unable to keep sarcasm out of her voice. She looks around the table. "It must have been a *mistake*."

Eisley looks offended. "It was."

Sara scrapes the last of her beans from her tray. Her envy is getting the better of her, but she can't help it. Then again Eisley spent her time at Madison chattering about fitness and working in Trailer D. She never got written up, never had a delay in her case. Maybe if Sara had stayed busy and out of trouble like that, she would've been out a long time ago. She would've spent the last ten months with her family, she would've put this place behind her already.

Toya tilts her head. "So what'd they ask you?"

"Basic questions about my life. They asked about my work, my boyfriend, the trip I took to Mexico, where I went, who I saw. They were trying to reconcile my answers with the data they have. And then they cleared me for release."

She makes it sound so simple, Sara thinks. The system worked for her; therefore, it works for everyone. All you have to do is tell the truth.

"But what if they don't believe you?" Toya insists. "What if you answer their questions and find they just don't believe you?"

"I'm sorry, I don't know," Eisley says, shaking her head. After a minute, she adds, her tone more conciliatory, "I guess in some cases it takes them longer to gather the evidence they need, but they're not out to get you. They're just doing their jobs."

3

J ULIE WAKES TO THE WIND HOWLING, AND THE FRONT GATE RAT-
tling as if a mob is trying to storm the house. The ruckus must
have roused Peter, because it's not even six yet and he's in the
shower. She gropes for her reading glasses on the bedside table and
starts scrolling through the day's mail on her phone: an invitation to
the soccer parents' association meeting, two airline mileage offers, a
Brentwood fire safety update, and a tech news roundup, all of which
she deletes unread. Then she pulls up her calendar and realizes she
has a debrief at ten, a safety training at noon, and a team meeting at
two. It's only her first day back at work, and already her schedule's
filling up. And she has to host that dinner party tonight, too. She
adds a reminder to leave work early, scrolls through the news for a
bit, then toggles over to Ocean & Broadway.

She's still on the site when Peter comes back into the bedroom
with a towel around his waist, walking past her without a glance.
Beads of water dot the space between his shoulder blades; he always
misses that spot. He mumbles something as he roots around for
underwear in the dresser. "What was that?" she asks, taking off her
glasses.

"I said, what's new?"

"Oh. Remember how James Wesley is getting married? Turns out,
Jodie Franklin is four months pregnant."

"Who's Jodie Franklin?"

"You know, the new anchor for RotDotDot? It's that augmented
reality show all the kids are watching. Anyway, they were keeping
their relationship hush-hush because her divorce from her husband
hadn't been finalized, but her pregnancy forced their hand and they
had to make an announcement."

"Maybe they'll invite you to the wedding."

"Haha. Very funny."

"Why do you read that stuff, anyway?"

"Because. It's fun."

"It's fun to know who's shagging who this week?"

At least someone is getting shagged. When was the last time he even looked at her? Lately he's been using his AR contacts during sex, and she suspects he has them set to Nicki Alfonso, with whom he's been obsessed ever since she led her team to a World Cup win. Who knew hairy legs could be so titillating? She pushes the covers aside and slides out of bed, but her momentum is thwarted by the pain that shoots from her lower back through her right hip and down her thigh. She shouldn't have done twenty reps on the deadlift yesterday, not after three weeks off her routine, and her trainer did try to warn her, but it felt so good to be back in the gym she couldn't resist the temptation. Steadying herself against the bedpost, she rises carefully to a standing position. "What's with the sanctimony so early in the morning?" she says irritably. "Do I shame you when you check your football news?"

"It's not the same thing." From his closet he pulls out a light pink button-down shirt and a gray silk tie. He must have a client meeting today. "I keep up with games, I'm not interested in what the players do off the field."

"Oh, please." She slips her feet into the bunny slippers Max gave her for her birthday last month. "Just the other day, you were complaining about the Seahawks quarterback getting wasted in Vegas."

"I only complained because his partying is starting to affect their season." He turns to face the mirror, buttoning his shirt.

Peter is an attractive man, with unaffected charm and a great sense of humor. Julie has seen him command a room while she stands awkwardly against the wall, her cocktail glass sweating in her hand. Sometimes she lets herself forget this fact, but when he looks as he does at this exact moment—rested, full of life, ready to banter—it comes back to her in its haunting undeniability. She's about to change the subject when he says, "I wonder what the scientists and engineers you work with would think if they knew you read gossip sites first thing in the morning."

"All right, then. You win. You're the better person."

"It's not a competition. I was just saying."

"You're always just saying." She limps to the bathroom. "Does it ever occur to you that not saying anything is also an option?" The bottle of Tylenol is in the back of the medicine cabinet, behind Peter's probiotic supplement and antiemetic capsules. She takes two pills, washing them down with water from the sink. When she looks up, he's watching her in the mirror, trying to decide whether to push the matter or let it go.

Ruby pokes her head into the bedroom suite. She's already in her school uniform, her long hair pulled into a prim ponytail tied with a white ribbon.

"You should knock first, honey," Julie tells her. And then, less sweetly, because Ruby is ignoring her: "Or else someday you'll see something you don't want to see."

"Ugh, gross. Who's picking me up after soccer practice?"

"I'll do it, sweetheart," Peter says. "Just make sure you come out to the Wilson gate, it's easier for me to find parking on that side." He puts his arm around Ruby's shoulders, leading her downstairs to the kitchen. "Ready for your calc test this morning? You want me to go over anything with you?"

It's just like him to stir the pot, Julie thinks, then find an excuse to walk away.

She gets in the shower, standing so that the hot water hits her lower back. She feels revived by the time she gets out, but when she glances at the mirror she's startled by how pale she looks. She rummages through the vanity, finds the foundation Ruby picked out for her a couple of months ago. She dabs it on, but she must not be doing it right, because the lines around her eyes seem even more noticeable after she's done. See, this is why she avoids makeup; she has no talent for it. It was sweet of Ruby to help, though.

Or was it self-serving? Ruby didn't want to go thrifting this weekend, even though she used to beg Julie to drive her to the Goodwill in El Sereno, which she says has a better selection of vintage clothes than the one near them in Brentwood. And she said no when Julie offered to take her to a movie of her choice. Who says no to a movie? Come to think of it, it's been ages since she's wanted to do anything together. With Peter, she's not like that at all, she tags along with him whenever he asks, even when he's only running errands around town.

My daughter doesn't want to be seen with me, Julie realizes with belated clarity.

It's just a stage, she tells herself.

But being away from home for three weeks made it worse. The eyes that meet her in the mirror seem even more tired now, and the prospect of walking around in gobs of makeup doesn't help. She washes it off her face, then shuffles to the walk-in closet, where she pulls out a paisley shirt and wide-legged knit pants, the only pair she can put on without feelings jabs of pain in her lower back. For added flourish she ties a green silk scarf around her neck. It's nice to have some color on after all that time in white.

At breakfast Peter is on his phone. "I got fifteen alerts from the front-door camera," he complains, swiping on his screen and deleting emails one after the other.

"I told you, you have to take down the Mike Myers," Julie says. When Peter pulled out the mannequin in blue coveralls from the garage, she suggested he seat it on the bench out front, but he thought it would look more threatening if it was standing, so he propped it up against a pillar and secured it with strings from the rafters. It's been swinging ever since, like a convict hanging from the gallows. Everything is such a spectacle with Peter. "There's more wind on the forecast," she warns.

"Do we have to take it down?" Ruby asks from the table, where she's going over her notes for the calc test. A whole-wheat toast with peanut butter and banana sits in front of her. "Can't it wait till after Halloween?"

Peter is still deleting alerts. "All right." He can never say no to Ruby.

Max is oblivious; he has his headphones on. He's drinking some kind of synthetic fruit and vitamin mix his karate coach recommended for building muscle strength. Standing where she is by the island, Julie can see that he put the mixer in the sink, but didn't bother turning on the water. Which is an improvement over leaving it on the counter. One step at a time.

Ruby turns off her tablet and stuffs it into her backpack. "You guys know Max has an English quiz today, right?"

Peter looks up from his phone. "He does?"

"He's eleven," Julie says with a sigh. When did her daughter become such a narc? The new school she's attending has made her obsessed with tests and grades, reward and punishment. "He'll be fine."

On the screen above the island, Nimble confirms that the utility bills were paid today and that her car is due for a service next week. It also has a menu suggestion for the dinner party tonight based on the guests' dietary profiles, their tastes and calorie limits, as well as the items Julie has in the fridge: shrimp aguachile, cucumber and tomato salad, chicken-stuffed Anaheim peppers, and strawberry sorbet. All she has to do is buy the shrimp. That sounds perfect; she approves the menu, sending her order to the fish market. "Can you pick up flowers on your way home?" she asks.

"What kind of flowers?"

"Zinnias, maybe? Or roses, if they have them in fall colors. But don't get anything long-stemmed. I want an arrangement we can keep on the table while we're eating." She senses he's about to ask her more questions, so she grabs her purse and motions to the kids. "Ready, guys? Let's go."

Ruby heads for the door. But Julie has to turn off Max's playlist from the Nimble screen before she can get his attention, help him find his art project, which he left in the den last night, and then his trombone, and then his water bottle. By the time they come out of the house, Ruby is waiting in the car, leaning her head against the passenger-side window, her face beaming with the tolerance of long-suffering saints.

WHEN JULIE ARRIVES AT WORK AN HOUR LATER, PROTESTERS HELD back by barricades crowd either side of the main gate, waving signs that say MY BODY, MY DREAMS and WE THE PEOPLE, NOT WE THE PRODUCTS. There was just a handful of them when Dreamsaver Inc.'s two-tier security system was revealed in a leak to the press, but over the three weeks she's been gone their number has swelled to a couple hundred. She's not entirely without sympathy for them, she remembers well what it's like to be young and full of passion, but she wishes they'd go home already. If they thought about it, they'd realize that the system was put in place for good reason. It would be too dangerous to sell data collected from government officials, military personnel, business leaders, people with sensitive occupations.

One of the security guards motions to her to slow down so the LPR can identify her car. She hits the brakes, and in that pause one of the protesters launches a placard that lands with a thud on the windshield of her car before sliding away to the side. The LPR flashes green, and she releases the brakes, driving past the protesters without making eye contact, exactly as DI's security manual advises.

Once inside, though, she finds the campus quiet. A contractor in a green uniform is clearing leaves from the cement pathways, stepping aside to make room for a mail-delivery robot on its way to the south building. Two security guards are huddled over a broken temperature sensor, talking to someone from maintenance over the phone. A sudden gust of wind blows Julie's hair across her face. Holding it back with one hand, she faces the east building entry camera and speaks her name: "Julie Renstrom."

The doors unlock.

The main screen in the lobby is playing the most recent ad Dreamsaver Inc. rolled out, featuring testimonials from real customers who've had the neuroprosthetic implanted: a home health aide who cares for an Omaha couple in their nineties; a single father of three in Seattle; a night-shift private cop in Denver; the entire cabin crew of a New York–Singapore flight. "Payment plans are available," the Oscar-winning actress who's doing the voice-over says, sounding like she's trying to coax a reluctant child to jump into the pool.

Julie walks past the screen to the cafeteria on the ground floor, where she gets breakfast, then slides gingerly into a window chair. The Tylenol she took this morning has barely dulled the pain, and she's still hours away from being able to have another dose. A couple of years ago when she saw a pain therapist for a different injury, he suggested she use distraction techniques, like reading a book or doing a crossword puzzle or playing with a stress ball. "The goal is to think of something else, Julie," he said in his thick Bosnian accent. "To *feel* something else. A taste, for example."

The eggs are creamy, the toast is crunchy, the pineapple too sweet, the coffee heavenly.

It works for a minute or two, then the pain returns.

Outside the sky is hazy, muting the shades of green on the rhododendrons that border the courtyard of the building. Two software engineers walk by on their way to the lab. They're recent hires, brought in to code one of the new products DI is developing, and have the devotion of fresh converts; they even wear company-branded shirts. Still absorbed in their discussion, they stop briefly across from the café. Julie waves hello, but a middle-aged woman is invisible to them. She might as well be a table or a potted plant, so little do they take notice.

"Can I clear this, ma'am?"

"Yes, thank you," she says.

She rises slowly out of her chair and takes the elevator to the fifth floor. She's in the bathroom brushing her teeth when she hears a muffled sob from the stall at the far end. A minute later the door opens, and Souza from Engineering comes out. Her eyes are puffy, her lips bitten. She's another new hire, brought in just a few weeks before Julie left for her field observation, which makes this even more awkward. They lock eyes in the mirror, and Souza immediately looks away. "Sorry."

"Don't apologize," Julie replies, her mouth still full of toothpaste. This is something she has tried to teach her daughter—stop apologizing when there's nothing to apologize for. Sometimes she thinks Ruby has learned the lesson too well. Julie spits in the sink, but with her limited range of motion a glob of toothpaste lands on her shirt. Great. Just great. She grabs a napkin from the holder and starts dabbing at the stain. "What's wrong?"

"Nothing," Souza says, shaking her head.

She must've just come out of Gaspard's code review, Julie thinks. All the engineers crammed into the glass-walled conference room, presenting their projects on a huge screen, while Gaspard presides over the meeting, a remote control in hand, ready to turn off the screen if he doesn't like what he sees. The Friday reviews are supposed to be an opportunity to receive feedback, but more often than not the experienced coders use the time to deride or condescend to the younger ones. It's a hazing ritual Gaspard instituted years ago: the new hires come in as outsiders, and they come out as DIYers.

The napkin is slowly breaking into pieces; Julie gives up dabbing at the stain. If anything, it looks worse now, with paper crumbs all over it. She rummages through her tote bag, and pulls out a bottle of ice water she got at the café. "This is cold. It will help with the puffiness."

"I'm fine," Souza says lightly. She ties her thick curls into a loose ponytail and splashes cold water on her face. Her skin is a beautiful shade of brown, and completely lineless. She can't be more than twenty-four or twenty-five, one of those engineers recruited out of graduate school with promises of a good salary and a chance to develop groundbreaking technology without having to apply for government grants or submit to pesky oversight. She's pretty, too, which doesn't help in a place like this.

"Don't volunteer to go first," Julie advises. "Wait for one of the last spots to present your project. They're usually out of steam by then and they'll give you actual feedback you can use."

"What? I— It's not that."

"What is it, then?"

Souza stares at her appraisingly. She seems to want to say something, then thinks better of it. "I don't work for Gaspard," she says after a minute. "Not directly."

"Oh. I just thought—who do you work for, then?"

"McClure."

"McClure?" The name is enough to set Julie's teeth on edge. "What'd he do?"

"Nothing."

Then why is she crying in the handicap stall of the fifth-floor bathroom at 8:30 in the morning? Women used to leave anonymous notes for each other on the cubicle walls of that stall. *Don't go to lunch with Reynolds. Watch out for Ruiz. Walker gets handsy.* Then H.R. disciplined a female programmer who was caught with a permanent marker and issued a policy against leaving notes in the bathroom. But this was long before Souza was hired, and for all his faults McClure doesn't seem like a harasser.

Or maybe he is—what would Julie know? Isn't Souza a replacement for the engineer who packed all her stuff in a box three months ago and walked out without a word, never to be heard from again? Whenever someone asked McClure why she left he'd shrug and say *Couldn't cut it.*

"Come on," Julie prods. "What'd he do?"

In the mirror, Souza frowns.

Julie realizes she's pushed too far, too fast. She picks up her bag. "I was just trying to help."

FLOOR-TO-CEILING WINDOWS, A DOZEN CUBICLES, A SMALL LOUNGE. The R & D office can seem like a letdown after the ornamental glass and walnut paneling of the ground floor, but Julie feels a jolt of pure pleasure at being back. This is where she belongs, in this place where the future is waiting to be explored. Not just explored, she thinks, but shaped, like a clay pot on a wheel. Someday she'll be able to look at it and say *There, see that curve? That was me and my team at Dreamsaver Inc.*

Some of her colleagues like to work here because they make more than at another tech company; others because they believe in the lifesaving benefits of the device. But she's here because she wants to unlock its full potential. The statistics classes she took in college twenty years ago relieved her of the notion that people were ineffable mysteries. Everything they said or did could be quantified in a thousand different ways. The more she saw their behaviors laid out in linear regression models, the more she became convinced they were nothing more than discrete combinations of data. If the study she's conducting proves successful, there's no telling how wide the applications of the Dreamsaver could be.

On her desk she finds a handful of pens and pencils, two dirty spoons, a pile of books teetering dangerously close to the monitor, a set of resistance bands, and a half-empty bottle of insect repellent. Ordinarily the chaos would bother her, but after three weeks at

Madison the disarray in her workspace feels to her like she's getting reacquainted with herself. In any case there's no time to tidy up; she has to get started on her report. She faces the computer, waits for the system to recognize her, and starts typing.

The tremendous popularity of its sleep-aid devices has enabled Dreamsaver Inc. to bring to market a number of exciting services, including medical alerts, psychiatric diagnostic tools, psychotherapy assistance, and data brokerage to corporate and government clients.

But while targeted advertising remains a core strategic goal for the company, our experimental trials have not been successful thus far, in part because test subjects became aware upon waking that an image was inserted in their dreams, which led to negative feelings toward both the neuroprosthetic and the product being marketed.

Therefore, reducing ad awareness is key to cultivating positive attitudes and boosting purchase interest. In this study, we examine the feasibility and effectiveness of product placement in dreams.

The study was conducted over a three-week period at Madison, a 120-bed retention facility owned and operated by Safe-X. The facility is located in Ellis, ninety-seven miles east of Los Angeles, and was chosen for this study because it provides a closed environment, where user behavior can be observed and product sales monitored. As with previous studies, Safe-X agreed to our R & D nondisclosure agreement and was appropriately compensated for the service.

Participants: Fifty-eight women currently under forensic observation. Participants were selected based on their ages, body mass index, and access to commissary funds. Participants' ages ranged from 23 to 52 years old, with a median of 36. Their BMI ranged from 17 to 34, with a median of 25.

All participants agreed to Dreamsaver Inc.'s terms of service upon implantation with the device, constituting informed consent for this research. No administrative complaints were filed with the chief retention officer, nor reports of medical distress with the facility nurse.

Procedure: The participants were divided into two groups, matched for age and BMI. For the intervention group, an image of Katya brand carrot chips was organically embedded in eight dreams over a three-week-long period. The control group was not affected. Snack purchases were monitored pre- and post-intervention to detect changes in behavior.

Note that a similar study was conducted at the Fair View facility last August, with mixed results. While snack purchases rose on nights where a movie was shown, the difference in product sales between the intervention group and the control group was not large enough to reach statistical significance.

For this reason, the present study uses a new placement code, written by Ethan Nordell, where dream scenarios are dynamically analyzed for suitability prior to image insertion.

We also conducted field observations to determine whether users noticed product placement. Interactions with participants were recorded by means of AR contacts worn during the field visit.

Results: We analyzed snack-purchase data provided by Safe-X, via its subcontractor MealSecure.

Here we go, Julie thinks. She clicks to download the data, and starts to run statistical analyses. While she waits, she squeezes a stress ball to distract herself from the pain in her lower back. Peter says she's too accident prone, she should stop lifting weights at the gym and stick to taking walks a couple of times a day, it would get her out of the office and clear her mind. But of course he would say that, he looks no different now than when they met. An alert flashes on her screen. The first table is ready.

Fuck.

Three weeks in that shithole for these lousy numbers? She could've just stayed home, and used the time to work on a different project that would give her a better shot at the promotion she was promised two years ago, before McClure showed up, acting like he was God's gift to behavioral science. The irony is that he'd seemed interested in product placement when the idea came up at a staff meeting, but when the time came to lead the research he didn't fight her over it. He must've had an inkling how difficult it would be.

She took an enormous gamble with this study, setting aside more conventional projects in order to devote all her time to it, and all she got for her trouble was that she missed Max's fall recital, and his wrestling meet, plus his admission interview with View Prep. The sweet boy didn't complain, it was Ruby who made a huge deal about her absence, and for good measure rattled off everything else Julie was going to miss while she was out in the field. She had to remind the little brat that this wasn't fun for her either, this was work.

Pain punches her in the back. She's squeezing the stress ball so hard that her fingernails are cutting her palms.

Her phone buzzes. *Can you pick up the dry cleaning*
Can't you
I have to pick up Ruby remember
Fine

She sets the phone aside and gets two more Tylenols. On her way to the kitchen for some water, she passes the conference room, where McClure is talking to Gaspard. The way McClure leans back in his chair, hands clasped behind his head, you'd think he was chatting with a friend at a barbecue, not talking to the head of R & D. All of a sudden he pushes back from the table and goes to the whiteboard to write something, so focused on his presentation that he doesn't see her as she walks past. It occurs to her then that whatever Souza was crying about in the bathroom, it can't have been the code she's writing for McClure, because he seems too animated, too happy to have run into any problems with his project.

Don't panic, she tells herself as she returns to her desk. Don't panic.

Just look at the numbers again. The difference in unit sales between the intervention and control groups isn't significant, but at least it's heading in the right direction, with a wider margin than in the pilot study. Plus, she hasn't considered sales of comparable snacks yet, or sales by date, age, education level, or menstruation status. There's still a lot of data to go through, outliers to throw out, trends to identify, field observations to review. Who knows what she might find?

SNYDER, TREVINO, AND FAROOQI ARE THE ONLY TEAM MEMBERS IN the conference room when Julie walks in at two. To give McClure and Gaspard time to arrive without her having to ask where they are, she puts her tablet down and uses the remote to adjust the window blinds. The afternoon light is bright, but the mountains in the distance are shrouded in a yellowish haze; it must be the fire in San Bernardino County she heard about on the radio this morning. Traffic on the freeway is moving along, though, and if she leaves the office on time she should be able to make it to the dry cleaner's and the fish market before they close.

"Welcome back," Snyder says, as she takes the seat across from him at the table. He's in a soccer jersey and jeans, and on his wrist he wears a bright blue band in support of some charitable cause or other.

"Thanks." She smiles. "It feels great to be back."

"I can imagine."

"How was it?" Farooqi asks, his voice a gentle bass that makes the room feel smaller, more intimate.

"It was fine. A little scary, but overall, fine."

"Three weeks is a long time, though." Trevino coils a strand of hair around a finger as he speaks—a persistent tic. "Being quarantined with people like that."

"There were some real characters in there, that's for sure. One of them did time in state prison for assault and battery, and another one was arrested twice for disorderly conduct. A few of them had restraining orders." She shakes her head. "But for the most part, they were people waiting to have their cases cleared. There was lots and lots of waiting."

"Weren't you bored?"

"Not at all. I had to work when they worked, and I spent the rest of the time recording my observations, so I was busier than I expected."

Still no sign of McClure and Gaspard. Are they meeting somewhere in private? It wouldn't surprise her, given how close they've grown in the last few months. All this waiting is making her even more nervous about presenting the results of her study.

She is getting herself a cappuccino and an oatmeal cookie at the credenza when McClure comes in. He doesn't have a tablet or a notebook with him, a sign that whatever the other team members have to talk about is of no importance to him. That guy's interested only in himself.

"How's everyone doing?" McClure asks as he sinks heavily into a chair.

"Pretty good," Snyder replies. "Excited for the weekend. Meg and I are gonna drive up to Solvang for our anniversary."

"That's the Swedish village, right?" Farooqi asks.

"Danish, actually." Snyder explains that he heard about it from another engineer, like him a transplant from New York. Farooqi is from Connecticut, and he hasn't had a chance to see much of California, either. There's talk about what to see and do in Solvang: the windmills, the ostrich farm, the kringles.

"You could visit the mission," Trevino offers. "Mission Santa Ynez. It's one of the places where the Chumash revolted, in the 1820s. It started after a soldier beat a Chumash boy who was visiting one of his relatives in Mission Santa Ynez, and grew into a massive rebellion as word spread to the other missions. The Spanish padres had to call in the military to put it down."

"Interesting." Snyder writes it down. "How do you spell Chumash?"

Julie sips her coffee.

"How about you, Renstrom?" Farooqi asks. "Any plans?"

"Nothing as exciting." A weekend in Solvang sounds amazing right now; it's been years since she and Peter went away without the kids. Vacations are his department, but he never makes the effort to organize something for just the two of them.

At last, Gaspard arrives. "Jesus, it's freezing in here." He pulls the hood of his brown sweatshirt over his bald head before taking a seat at the head of the table. Now comes a smile, and yet Julie finds it impossible to guess what mood he's in today. Grumpy Gaspard she's used to, she finds him almost endearing, and once or twice in the last seven years at DI she's caught a glimpse of Genial Gaspard, but it's Vicious Gaspard that terrifies her.

"Let's begin with some project updates," he says. "Farooqi."

"I'm plugging along on nightmare blocking. Legal sent me another complaint they received, from someone claiming the implant makes it harder for them to wake up from recurring dreams about a domestic assault they were in years ago. Right now, I'm still logging the data and running comparisons, but I should have enough in a week or two to test blocking of user-selected concepts."

"You've been at this, what, three months now?"

So it's a Vicious Gaspard kind of day.

But that doesn't seem to bother McClure, who's scrolling on his phone. On his wrist is a neon yellow watch, and it takes Julie a second to realize it's his glucose monitor. When he joined the company a couple of years ago, he bought an extra-large bottle from the store downstairs and refilled it with water throughout the day. Julie told him to get his blood sugar level tested, because she remembered that dry mouth was one of the symptoms her aunt had when she was diagnosed with diabetes. He was relieved and thankful to have caught the condition early. They were new colleagues, then, on the cusp of a work-friendship, if not a life-friendship. But after Gaspard announced he would appoint a program manager by the end of the year, everything changed between them. McClure started to watch her, point out every mistake she made, challenge every claim, laugh at every suggestion.

Gaspard is still dressing down Farooqi. "The sooner you come up with a prototype the better. This isn't an academic problem, dude, it's the real world, all right? We have to have some kind of response if this thing gains traction, and you're not giving me anything to work with. So get me something by next week, or I'll find someone who can. Okay. Trevino."

"I'm working on improving accuracy rates for the predictive algorithm. We still aren't doing great in scenarios that fuse real and representational images. So, for example, we had one sequence where a fox was running down a hole that was shaped like a womb, except the womb was stylized sort of like how you'd see in a European medieval drawing. Or maybe Renaissance? I don't know much about art history. Anyway, the AI didn't recognize the womb as a womb, thought it was a foxhole, and assigned it an interpretation based on that."

"That's happening with the more complex sequences, correct? Longer than five GFTs?"

"Mostly," Trevino says, but his hand flies to his hair, and the vigorous coiling tells Julie he's trying to put on a brave face. "We had a few cases where it happened with three GFTs. Basically our interpretations get exponentially worse when artistic renderings appear, especially if they're woven in seamlessly with concrete objects."

"But how common are images of art, anyway?"

"That's what I thought, too. But they show up often enough to affect accuracy rates on this set."

Gaspard shakes his head. "I'll get you another set. And next time bring me your best suggestion about how to fix it, will you? I can't do everything around here. McClure."

"We already talked about it this morning." Then he turns to the rest of the team, as if reluctant to repeat himself to the plebs. "So I've been working on a social-sharing feature that will allow users to post their dreams to a circle of friends, comment on them, offer interpretations, et cetera. The feature is ready, but the question is how to calibrate it, right? How do we help users see this as a way to showcase their personality, but with enough safeguards that it won't feel like a safety violation?" He drones on about how important it is to have the right tool. "I had Souza write an app to help me test this. So I'm pretty much done with the experimental design. I'm partnering with my old lab at Tulane to find volunteers."

"It's exciting stuff," Gaspard says. The hood of his sweatshirt slips, revealing a bald head circled by a sparse fringe of brown hair. "Eric asked me about it when we had our call. He's eager to launch the new feature because the retention stuff is hurting sales. People don't want their data sold to the RAA."

"That's stupid," Snyder says. "Are they gonna give up their phones, too? Their door cameras? Their cars?"

Gaspard shakes his head. "This stuff'll blow over when the new feature launches."

Julie shifts in her chair, and pain shoots across her back.

The coffee is lukewarm, the air is cool, the light is bright.

She should've taken a few more days of rest before returning to the office. She's not quite ready for all this yet.

"Renstrom. Welcome back."

"Thank you. It's good to be back."

"How'd it go?"

Julie crosses her arms to conceal the toothpaste stain on her shirt. "It went very well. I was a bit apprehensive about the test site, but Safe-X was an excellent partner on the study, they provided security and assistance, and everything went without a hitch." Gaspard rests his chin on his palm. She needs to stop babbling and move on to the study results. "Product placement was successful for the intervention group, and so far I see no evidence of detection. Credit for that goes to Ethan Nordell, of course." She moves the cappuccino cup aside and swipes to unlock her tablet. "Now, controlling for age and BMI, we have higher sales on the featured product, though the numbers aren't large enough yet to reach statistical significance. Once I throw in menstruation cycle as a factor, I see bigger numbers, but unfortunately the sample size is pretty small. What's clear already is that exposure has—"

McClure cuts her off. "What's your p level?"

Julie pretends she doesn't hear him; it's early yet for reporting something like that, she still has to massage the data, take a closer look before tying herself down to a specific p result. But Gaspard raises his brows at her and she has no choice but to answer.

Disappointment passes across his face.

It would almost be easier if he got angry, told her she was wasting her time, and the company's resources. But disappointment means he had high hopes for the study, that like her he saw its potential. A social-sharing option is exciting, sure, but image insertion is the future. She knows it, Gaspard knows it. It's time to take a risk, she thinks, follow her hunch.

"I did notice something, though," she says quickly, before she loses her nerve. "Actually, it could be a big thing. I collected three dreams featuring carrots—actual carrots, not the packaged product—and for that individual I'm seeing a nice little spike in unit purchases.

Now of course, it could just be a coincidence, but what if her brain translated Ethan's code in a more idiosyncratic fashion and came up with its own execution of what we asked it to do?"

And just like that, she has Gaspard's attention.

IN THE EARLIEST FOOTAGE THE SUBJECT APPEARS GAUNT, HER KINKY hair pulled in a bun that brings out the sharp angle of her jaw. Her face is blank and her eyes remain cast down, but soon it becomes clear that she's paying careful attention. When she speaks it is only to offer crucial advice—that Julie should accept a job assignment— then resumes her silence.

Her unease seems to disappear over time. In later clips she looks straight into the AR contacts whenever Julie speaks, though she still doesn't engage much in conversation, whether the subject is food or fitness or work. It's only when the subject of Toya Jones's extension comes up that she stirs, becoming agitated in her friend's defense.

In the final clip she is aggressive, maybe suspicious.

Is it cheating, to want to know more? The profiles that Safe-X gave Julie include only the names, pictures, and biometric data of the fifty-eight participants in the study, but now she wants to find out everything she can about Sara T. Hussein—her tastes, habits, pre-dispositions, the synaptic connections that translated the inserted image into something different, and just as effective.

If Julie could conduct a postexposure interview with her, she might be able to have additional context for the dreams in question. But how to go about something like this? Post-study contact with the participants wasn't part of the agreement, so she would need to get some kind of permission from the chief retention officer. That could take a while, especially if she has to negotiate payment. Maybe she should cut the red tape, find a way to talk to Sara without disclosing her reasons.

Just then Ethan Nordell appears at the entrance to her cubicle. He's in a T-shirt and jeans, with a string of mala beads around his wrist. How does he manage to look so relaxed when he has so much responsibility? But then again, he's always been even-keeled; it's what she likes best about him. She stands up to give him a hug.

"So, this is it?" he asks, pointing at her screen.

Julie nods. She clears the guest chair and they sit side by side while she shows him the three dreams she pulled out.

He whistles. "What did Gaspard say?"

"He was definitely interested, but then McClure suggested that maybe your code—"

"No." Nordell shakes his head. "No, no. There's nothing in what I wrote that would've modified the image like this. Can you play that last one again?"

Julie hits the restart button.

"This could be big."

Julie nods, feeling gratitude wash over her. Nordell has always been a good sounding board for her, going back to their days at Stanford, long before she met Peter. Sometimes she misses grad school, when they spent so much time in the lab together they could finish each other's sentences.

"I should get going," Nordell says, standing up. "Should we bring anything tonight?"

"Just your lovely selves."

"All right then." He waves at Julie as he heads out. "See you later."

MELISSA WARD-NORDELL IS ON HER THIRD GLASS OF WHITE WINE BY the time dinner is served. Julie feels a little light-headed herself, though she's better at holding her drink. She should've served some hors d'oeuvres, she realizes, maybe the mushroom puffs that have been sitting in the freezer since Labor Day or that organic artichoke dip the kids like so much, but she was so late getting home that she barely had time to change her shirt. She had to call Ruby from the car to ask her to iron the linen tablecloth and set up the table. And after all that, Peter forgot to marinate the chicken for the main course so it took another hour for the food to be ready. Everyone is ravenous. When Melissa reaches for the bread, she nearly topples the sunflowers Peter brought home from the florist.

"Let me get these out of the way," Julie says, standing up. Pain shoots down her leg; the long commute home has made her worse. She places the flowers on the sideboard and limps back to the table, lowering herself carefully into her chair. The bread is delicious, the tablecloth is pretty, the wine is chilled.

"I think you're getting tipsy, honey," Nordell tells his wife.

"You like me when I'm tipsy," she replies.

They smile at each other like teenagers.

Julie excuses herself and goes across the hall to the den, where she left her purse when she came in from work. The Percocet is in a green enamel case decorated with a gold serpent, an antique she bought years ago, when the kids were in diapers. They're splayed on the sectional now, watching a horror movie and eating pizza with the Nordells' eight-year-old daughter. As she passes them again, Julie notices Ruby staring. "What?" she asks.

"Nothing," Ruby says. She pulls a piece of pepperoni glistening with grease from the slice on her plate and drops it into her mouth.

"How was your calc test?"

"I already talked to Dad about it." Her eyes return to the television screen, where a young Drew Barrymore is on the phone, screaming with fear but not daring to hang up on the caller.

It was Max's choice to play a classic movie tonight. Julie should've suggested something less scary, for the sake of the Nordells' daughter at least, but she was too tired to think of an alternative. The speakers practically rattle when Drew Barrymore screams.

"God, she's so dumb," Ruby sneers.

"Did it go okay?" Julie asks. "Your test?"

"It was fine."

Why do I bother, Julie thinks. She walks back across the hall to the dining room. It is pitch-dark outside and without the yard lights the entire scene is reflected in the windowpanes, as if they are staging a play in which they are actors and audience all at once. Peter is telling the Nordells that he made the shrimp aguachile from an old family recipe his Mexican grandmother gave him. "Abuela used to make it for us whenever we visited her in Guadalajara."

Julie takes a bite and, for a brief, blissful moment, the fiery taste of the chiles consumes all of her attention. When she got to the fish market after work they were already out of Louisiana Organic Farms Shrimp and although the vendor said this brand was just as good, she's not so sure. The shrimp is a little chewy, it seems to her, but probably no one else has noticed it, they're all eating. With a bit of food in her, Julie feels herself relax a little. She drains the rest of her wine, and fills up her glass again.

"Easy there," Peter says.

She glances at him, then takes a huge sip. "I've had a long day."

Nordell folds a tortilla around the shrimp on his plate. "I wish they wouldn't schedule so many meetings on Fridays. It gets so busy. Did you hear that McClure got put on administrative leave?"

Julie nods. She swirls the wine in her glass, debating whether to tell Nordell that it was she who spoke to H.R. this afternoon. He might find her behavior underhanded, and think less of her. But enough was enough. She couldn't stay quiet anymore about McClure; she had to act to protect Souza.

Melissa looks up. "Which one's McClure?"

"You don't remember him?" Nordell says. "Tall guy, red hair? He was hired by Gaspard the month before you quit."

"But why was he put on leave?" Peter asks.

"Wait," Melissa says, holding up a finger. "Was he the one who left half-eaten tubs of ice cream in the freezer?"

"No, that guy's not at DI anymore," Nordell tells his wife. "I think he went to Nabe. McClure's the one who had a gallon-size water bottle."

"Oh, right."

"Why was he put on leave?" Peter asks again, staring at Julie.

She frowns. What does he care all of a sudden? He usually finds shop talk boring.

"Well," Nordell replies. "There's only two reasons for that. And let's just say he never handled anything financial."

A scream of horror and delight comes from the den, followed by the movie's theme music. Julie touches a button on her phone and lowers the television volume. "I told Gaspard from jump that McClure wouldn't be a good fit."

"Is that why you were late coming home?" Peter asks.

"No," Julie says, reaching for another tortilla. "I was late because I had to pick up your dry cleaning."

"I don't miss dealing with H.R. issues," Melissa says. "Like, at all. It didn't happen very often, because most people aren't litigious, but every once in a while H.R. had someone who'd make noises about suing and they'd call me to sort it out. I hated it."

"Well, you don't have to do it anymore," Nordell says.

Melissa fills her glass again. "And thank God for that."

"Thank the IPO," Nordell says with a laugh. He looks lovingly at his wife.

The shrimp is spicy, the tortilla is warm, the wine is sweet.

"It sucks for McClure, though," Peter says. "Getting news like this on a Friday."

"There's no good day for news like this," Julie replies, running her hand flat on the linen tablecloth. There are still creases everywhere. "Does anyone else smell smoke?"

Melissa sniffs the air. "No, I don't smell anything."

Julie touches the NaarPro app on her phone, and is relieved to see that it has already activated the air filtration system in the house. Outside, the wind picks up, rattling the front gate.

"McClure was always a bit of an ass," Nordell continues. "I remember he had a problem with Liu, a couple of years ago."

"What kind of problem?" Julie asks.

"Something to do with a division-wide memo he sent, right around the time when we had that issue with the warehouse workers. I forget the details, but Liu complained about him all the time. I guess he had it coming."

That he did, Julie thinks. It's not her fault he's not a team player. Maybe if he'd stayed in his lane and stopped trying to upstage everyone, he'd still be at DI right now.

"Me, I always liked him," Peter says. "He was one of the few people to talk to me at you guys' office parties. And now he's probably gonna be out of a job."

The concern on his face appears genuine. McClure's been trying for months to steal the promotion she's been expecting. If Peter paid any attention to her when she talked, he'd know that.

Peter looks around the table. "Anyone want seconds? There's more in the kitchen."

"By the way," Julie tells the Nordells, "Peter's grandmother wasn't Mexican. She lived in Mexico for the first seven years of her life while her parents were stationed at the U.S. embassy there. Then she moved back to Virginia. She's about as Mexican as I'm French. He got the recipe from Nimble."

Peter looks at her for the first time. "Julie."

"What? You don't need to make up a story about the recipe. The food tastes great without it."

"You don't get it. The story *improves* the taste. Plus, my grandmother considered herself Mexican." He looks around the table. "And who am I to contradict her?"

"Well, three cheers for the chef," Melissa says, raising her glass. "It was delicious."

"Because I used Abuela's recipe."

Melissa laughs at Peter's stupid joke; she has a lot of tact. It served her well when she worked at DI, Julie thinks, especially when one of the business people talked about their weekends of drinking and debauchery. Nordell picks up on his wife's cue, and raises his glass to the chef as well.

"Except the story's not true," Julie insists.

"Goodness. You're acting like I committed a crime."

Not a crime, she wants to say. But that doesn't mean it's right. Peter loves to exaggerate, doesn't he. Twist her words and make her seem like she's crazy. She takes a long sip of wine. The knot between her shoulders is loosening, finally. Her husband's voice seems to come from far away. "I just don't understand why you make things up."

"What's that? Your words are getting slurred."

"I said, I don't understand why you make up stuff," Julie says, reclining in her chair, stretching her legs under the table. For the first time today, the pain is gone. She closes her eyes, luxuriating in a freedom she has not tasted in so long. The room is warm. Her lips tingle. "I definitely smell smoke."

4

THE LIGHTS TURN ON, THE FIRE HORN BLARES. SARA SITS UP, dazed and frightened all at once. She waits for an evacuation order from the chief retention officer, or some kind of safety announcement, but neither comes. Is it a false alarm? No, the lights have stayed on and, beneath the mustiness that clings to the walls and the smell of sweat and sleep, there's a whiff of smoke. The last two wildfires that swept through this part of the state didn't trigger the sirens, though the sky grayed with ash and smoke for days. This one must be close. Sara pushes the covers aside.

Emily is already at the window, with her face to the glass pane and her hands cupped around her eyes. Outside, the wind is an angry, drawn-out howl. "It's blowing west," she says. "But it's still dark out, I can't make out much."

If Emily is right about the wind, then the smoke will reach Sara's husband and children soon, if it hasn't already. Years ago, Elias fell into the maddening habit of silencing his devices at night before plugging them in in the kitchen, so he might not receive the phone alerts until he wakes in the morning, might not check that all the windows in the house are properly sealed, turn on the air purifiers, and pack an evacuation bag.

From the hallway comes the hum of conversations—wild guesses about the direction of the blaze, mixed in with stories about past fires. After a while a consensus seems to build: if this fire really posed a serious threat, the CRO would have ordered an evacuation. "What do you think?" Sara asks her roommate. "Are we in any danger?"

"Depends on the speed of the wind." Emily sucks her teeth. "Plus the temperature, the humidity level, the kind of crews they're using, things like that. But if the siren got triggered, it's not looking good."

They stand at the window together, watching the sky lighten from charcoal to ash.

A few minutes later, the bell for device check rings. Hinton comes through the gate in a mask. And not a cheap one, either—a high-quality respirator that he must have kept in his locker downstairs, saving it for a day just like this. It squashes the lower part of his face and makes his eyes look wider, as if caught in a moment of surprise. He rushes through the neuroprosthetic scan and ends up having to go back and re-scan one of the retainees in 204. When he finally gets to 208, Emily blasts him with questions. "So where did the fire start?"

"Is it a surface fire, or more like crown?"

"What percent contained?"

"Are they calling up the state crews?"

The scanner beeps, and Hinton moves to Sara.

"Are you evacuating us?" she asks.

He fixes his surprised eyes on her. Though the mask hides the lower part of his face, it seems from the crinkles on his temples that he might be smiling. What's so funny about this situation? If they're marooned here, so is he. But before she can ask him anything else, he goes across the way to 209.

Sara returns to her room. In all the time she's been at Madison, she's never seen Hinton rushing through device check like this. It's his favorite part of the job: the moment when the women stand at attention while he holds the scanner that gives them credit for a night of compliance. Maybe what she took to be a smirk is only his way of hiding his fear. Maybe there's some truth to the stories about the burn scar on his neck, the lost home, the dead German shepherd. She makes her cot, tugging at the pilling blanket, while across the room Emily fumes. "Why bother with the siren?" she says, her voice brimming with indignation. "What's the point of a siren if there's no evacuation?"

"For the attendants."

"I figured. Ever heard of a rhetorical question?"

Emily has been irritable ever since she was pulled off breakfast duty and placed on custodial services, which she hates. This morning she's especially irate, ranting about poor emergency training and missed fire drills, lapses she took it upon herself to bring to the CRO's attention in an email at the start of the summer. The response she received seconds later informed her that Safe-X is in compliance with all of the state's safety protocols and emergency procedures.

When Sara returns to the window, Emily looks up from her cot. "See anything?"

"Not much." The sky has lightened to orange. The jackrabbits that live on the mountain seem to have fled, and the only movement comes from the bushes swaying in the hot wind. Beyond the hill, the horizon is a line of red. Sara waits for a few minutes, but the bus isn't running this morning. The old woman must've called on family or friends and made plans for a possible evacuation, but here at Madison the retainees are entirely at the mercy of Safe-X. Sara's thoughts flit back to her family. She has to talk to Elias, she has to find out if he and the twins are safe.

Promptly at 6:30 she walks to the PostPal comm pods downstairs. She counts thirty-seven women ahead of her in the line; it might be hours before her turn comes. She sits with her back to the wall, wraps her arms around her knees and closes her eyes. A few minutes later she hears the jingle of keys, and Hinton appears at the corner. He tells the women to disperse, but the mask muffles his voice and the retainees pretend not to understand his orders. For a moment he surveys the line, then walks into the PostPal office.

The news is carried from mouth to ear until it reaches Sara: Hinton has ordered the comm pods closed for the day. "The whole day?" she asks in disbelief, stepping out of the line and craning her neck to look. Sure enough, the overhead lights in the glass booths are being shut off one by one. The women whose calls have been interrupted step out into the hallway.

"All day," Alice confirms. She was five spots ahead of Sara. Now she's closed the book she was reading and is holding it to her chest as if for comfort.

"Can he do that?" Sara's left leg has fallen asleep. She rubs it with one hand while with the other she steadies herself against the wall. "I mean, they're a separate company, aren't they? He doesn't work for them."

"I have no idea what just happened."

"Has he ever closed PostPal booths before?"

Alice chews on her lower lip. "He closed them once last year, I think it was in November, but it was only for an hour or two because the PostPal guys were here to fix something. He's never shut them down for a day, and definitely not on a day like this."

Sara walks up to the PostPal office entrance, where some of the women have gathered, trying to find out what happened or asking for a refund of their interrupted calls. No rule has been broken, they argue, so why are the pods being closed today? Because communication is a privilege, the attendant on duty replies, and privileges can be taken away at any moment. The grumbling continues until Hinton steps out of the office. From the back of the crowd someone calls out, "Thanks a lot, asshole."

Hinton pulls his mask down to his chin. "Who said that?"

No one answers. The women disperse quickly, before he gets the urge to point his Tekmerion at one of them. He stares at one of the domes on the ceiling, as if willing it to speak the name of the woman who cussed him out, then adjusts his mask over his nose. He'll have to go to the observation deck to review the footage.

"I need to check on my kids," Sara says as he walks past her.

"Not my problem."

"Wait." A shiver of discomfort runs down her back when he turns to look at her. There is something deeply unsettling about his eyes, which never seem to blink or waver, but remain fixed on their target with military precision.

"What is it?"

"They're gonna know you're shutting down their booths."

"Is that a threat?"

"I'm just saying, there's a wildfire. They're probably expecting a higher call volume on a day like this." She searches his face for a reaction, but even with the mask she can tell he's untroubled. "I wonder what'll happen when they notice that their pods have been shut off."

"Nothing," he says with a chuckle. "Nothing'll happen. You think anyone at PostPal cares what goes on in here? They have hundreds of facilities, most of them bigger and more profitable than this one."

She tries to swallow, but saliva sits in her throat like chalk. "They'll notice the shutoff, is what I'm saying."

"Not a shutoff, an outage. Outages happen." He shifts on his feet. "Look," he says, his tone suddenly serious. "I can't have the hallways packed with people. It's not safe, not today."

She doesn't want to beg—and yet. "Please. I just want to check on my family. Please."

"And I want to be somewhere else." He tilts his head. "But we don't always get what we want. Such is the nature of life."

As if their situations were the same. As if he were separated from his children, kept in the dark about his family's well-being, prevented from using the phone in the middle of a wildfire. But never mind moral principle or basic fairness: even by appealing purely to his self-interest, she can't convince him to keep the booths open. She presses her lips together, holding back from screaming all the ugly words that come readily to her.

AT BREAKFAST SARA CAN'T BRING HERSELF TO EAT, THOUGH IT IS A Friday and scrambled eggs and fried potatoes are on the menu. The light streaming in from the windows bathes the cafeteria in orange tones, coppering the faces of everyone around her. The heat is stifling; it feels as if they're sitting in an oven. Marcela coughs into her elbow, then takes a long sip of tea to tamp down the urge.

Emily arrives with her tray. "The fire started yesterday near Lake Perris. But it spread real fast because of the wind."

"Lake Perris?" At least it's far from Elias and the kids, Sara thinks. "But they're containing it, right?"

"Nope. It's three and a half miles away from here."

"Jesus."

Toya rubs her nose. "Is it just me or is the smell stronger now?"

Emily casts an appraising look on the half-empty dining room. "They should've had an emergency plan in place, with designated team leaders who can execute it when the time comes. They should be giving us masks, at least."

All of a sudden the lights go out. The hum of the service station, the hiss of the refrigerator, the whirr of the cameras—all these stop at once, too. Whether the shutdown is a preemptive measure by the state or a sign that the fire has damaged the power grid, Sara has no idea. She watches as Hinton goes to the door, pokes his head in the darkened hallway, then after a moment returns to his phone, this time holding it up to find a working signal.

"I asked about masks at the infirmary," Marcela says after a minute, before being overtaken by another fit of coughing. Flores runs the infirmary, where under ordinary circumstances the women can get pads or tampons at no expense if they agree to have their periods tracked. "She said she didn't have any for retainees."

"I can make masks for all of us," Sara whispers. "I can use my sheets to make masks for all of us."

Silence falls on the table. An entire section of the Safe-X handbook is devoted to prohibitions against destruction of company property, and the corresponding punishments for each offense. In the kitchen, a retainee is still washing meal trays at the sink, the clattering getting louder and more aggressive as the pile beside her rises.

Marcela asks, her tone straining to be hypothetical, "Where would you get scissors?"

"I'll find something," Sara says.

"In the laundry room?"

"We don't have any tools there. But I'll figure something out."

Williams rushes into the cafeteria just then, his shoes squeaking on the vinyl floors. He brings some kind of news to Hinton, who listens with his head cocked to the side and his hand cupped behind one ear. The two men continue their palaver at the window, looking worriedly at the orange sky. Williams is about to leave when Hinton calls him back and makes him adjust his mask snugly over his nose. It's an oddly protective gesture, coming from Hinton.

And still no announcement from the CRO.

"We're fucked," Emily says.

"No. I'm going to make masks for all of us," Sara says again. Sensing that the other women agree, or at least that they do not disagree, she shares the idea that came to her when she sat down and found a thick layer of ash on the table. We are wasting our time waiting for help, she says. It might never come, or it might come too late, which amounts to the same thing. Have you noticed that the construction workers aren't here this morning, she asks. They must've been held back from work today, which means we are close enough to the fire that it isn't safe for them. If it isn't safe for them, how can it be safe for us? We have to make face masks to protect ourselves against exposure, just like the attendants. And then, she says, lowering her voice even further, we need to go down to Receiving and take control of one of the service trucks. We have to get out of here.

"Count me out," Toya says.

Of all the objections to her proposal, Sara hasn't anticipated that the first, and the swiftest, would come from her closest friend at Madison. It's a dangerous plan, yes, but they themselves are in danger. If they're not evacuated, they'll burn to death, and that's if the carbon monoxide doesn't kill them first. "But why? You want to just sit here and wait?"

"Do you know how many rules you'd be breaking? What the attendants will do when you get caught? When, by the way, not if. Even if you leave this place without getting caught, you'll head into the city without papers, without food, without money. When you're clear of the fire, you'll part ways with the others. You'll want to go home, to your husband and children, and they'll be waiting for you there." All of this Toya says dispassionately, as though she were outlining to a customer all the reasons why his insurance claim is being denied. "If you leave Madison, you won't be going to another retention center, you'll be going to prison."

"This *is* a prison."

"No, it's not." Technically, retainees have more rights than prisoners. They can vote in local, state, and national elections, even if the unpredictable length of their confinement means that most don't bother changing their voter registrations, if they're registered at all. They can also conduct limited banking transactions, a privilege that comes down to being able to charge commissary items or various PostPal services to their families' credit cards. The finer distinctions between jails, prisons, public safety centers, commitment clinics, and retention facilities seem to matter a great deal to Toya all of a sudden. "It's not a prison."

"Whatever you say."

"Who cares about the difference," Emily puts in, "if we're all gonna be burned alive?"

"That's right." Sara turns to Alice. "What about you? Can you help us get out of here? I bet you'd know how to jump-start one of the trucks in Receiving."

Alice raises her palms. "I never said I broke into trucks."

"I'm asking if you *can*, not if you did. Can you jump-start one or not?"

"What's going on with you?" Toya asks, putting a concerned hand on Sara's arm.

Sara shrugs. "Isn't it obvious?"

"Listen to me," Toya says. "Right now, we're a problem for them. If we leave, they become a problem for us."

"Suit yourself. But I'm not going to sit here and wait to be killed."

Marcela has another coughing fit, and Alice has to give her some of her own tea to wash it down. Across the cafeteria a table of younger retainees erupts in a loud argument, with Victoria getting up in a huff and moving to another spot; Hinton notices the brou-haha, but instead of going over to investigate, he walks out of the cafeteria altogether.

"I can get you a blade," Emily says. "For the masks."

Another surprise. Emily is the only one in the group with a crimi-nal record, which lengthens the extensions she receives whenever she is written up. She has the most to lose from breaking out; yet she's the only one willing to act. "That would be great," Sara replies. "Anyone have commissary credits? We'll need to buy bottled water."

Toya, Alice, and Marcela look down at their food.

"I guess it's just you and me, then," Sara tells Emily.

She picks up her tray and heads to the busing station. Never before has she wanted more keenly to get away from this place, with its crushing indifference, its petty and ever-shifting rules.

THE COMMISSARY IS SOLD OUT OF SNACKS, BOTTLED WATER, AND BAT-teries. With the credits she has left on her account Sara buys what liquids are left—a canned fizzy drink and an apple juice—and waits while the clerk tallies her balance with a hand calculator. I should've gone to the store before breakfast, she reproaches herself, I shouldn't have delayed. Walking away with her purchases she notices that a few retainees are clustered in small groups at the windows to the exercise yard. On the other side of the smudged glass, a Safe-X agent stands with his hand shielding his face from the orange glare of the sun, eyeing the sky as if he could divine the future.

Back in their room Sara finds Emily working on a disposable razor with her tweezers. The razor has a pivoting head, so she has to steady it against the mattress while she pulls at the metal staple that holds the cartridge in place, but after a half dozen tries the staple comes off. She taps lightly on the handle, and three shiny blades drop onto the blanket. "There," she says. "Take one."

With the blade Sara cuts a square piece of fabric from her sheet. She places a strip of toilet paper across the middle, folds the fabric over it, and loops a rubber hairband around either end. "How's this?" she asks as she fits Emily with the mask. "Good? Can you breathe?"

"Kind of."

"Do you smell smoke?"

"Not so much," Emily concedes.

"Then it's working." Sara quickly makes a second face covering and puts it on, adjusting the straps until it fits snugly. The reflection that meets her in the mirror reminds her of the pandemic of her childhood. Unlike some of her classmates in school she never minded wearing masks: they concealed her bouts of acne, the rage she felt whenever a boy told her she needed to smile more, her impatience with strangers who asked, "So what are you?" She couldn't have known that the skill would come in handy so many years later.

Sara stands at the window again. The sky is a bright orange, and the cloud of smoke has edged closer—she can see only twenty feet past the bus stop on the highway. "Look," she says, pointing outside. "It's getting worse."

"If they don't get us out right now, we won't be able to make it. I can't believe the CRO is AWOL on a day like this. And Hinton's disappeared, too."

"You still want to do this, right?"

Emily gives a quick nod. Her comic books and pictures are already packed in her pillowcase. "The Receiving gate isn't a good idea," she tells Sara. "It's crawling with attendants. We should get out from the kitchen. There's a door in the back that leads to the lot where they park their cars."

"All right." Sara bundles her journal and the drinks she bought into her pillowcase.

It is a short walk downstairs. Mercifully the hallways are busy, the power shutoff having relieved retainees of their trailer duties for the day, and no one pays them much attention. Blending with the traffic they make their way to the cafeteria, now empty of diners. "This way," Emily says, leading Sara past the service window. She enters a key code at the kitchen door and a moment later they are inside, standing before the magic door.

Which requires another key code.

Now what?

Emily tries the same code she used a moment earlier, but the light flashes red. She runs her index finger on the keypad and, though it's clear that the numbers 2, 5, 8, and 0 have been pressed a hundred times, there's no guessing what the correct permutation might be.

Sara's eyes sting; the smell of smoke is stronger by the door than anywhere else in the building. This is no time for codes. She runs back to the kitchen to look for a metal spatula or a can opener, but all the drawers are locked. The stainless steel countertop is bare, the dishwashing station empty. Is there a toolbox in the walk-in cooler? She steps inside—and finds Hinton doubled over next to a stack of crates.

Their eyes meet, though she isn't sure he fully registers her presence because he's having so much trouble breathing. A pained wheeze escapes from his throat. His face is red, his neck has retreated into his shoulders.

He's having a panic attack, Sara realizes.

She takes a step toward him. It would be easier for him to breathe if he took off his mask, but she doesn't dare touch him and in any case he's already looking away from her as if in shame, facing the boxes of dehydrated eggs as he struggles to take in as much air as his lungs will allow. The wheezing dies—he's stopped breathing altogether. His hand flies to his holster, out of instinct it seems. Doesn't he realize that the heavy gear on his belt is a greater danger to him at this moment than she will ever be? All she wants is to leave this place.

She runs back out to the kitchen, and grabs the only movable item she can find: one of the meal trays from the service station. It will have to do. Back at the door, she starts hacking at the keypad with it, but the lock just won't break.

"Leave it," Emily says after a minute. "Leave it. Let's just go to Receiving."

They cross the empty cafeteria again and come out into the hallway, where the screens that display work assignments are black. As they turn the corner, they bump straight into Yee, who's carrying gallon-size containers of water in each arm. It takes him a second to regain his balance. "We're not meeting in the cafeteria," he tells them, his voice distorted by his N95. He's put on a neon yellow vest over his uniform; an orange whistle dangles from his neck. "Go to the auditorium."

"Now? We're evacuating?"

"I need everyone in the assembly area, ready to leave. If you see any other residents, tell them to meet us there."

Turning the corner the two make their way to the main hall, where they find dozens of retainees, some standing in groups, others sitting on the floor, waiting under the Arnautoff mural. A couple are wearing masks fashioned out of paper towels or sanitary pads. But no one seems to know when the buses will get there.

The heat continues to rise as more retainees pour into the hall. Feeling light-headed, Sara opens the fizzy drink and sips from it while gazing at the Arnautoff mural. The green lettuce seems exotically lush this morning, and the earth a rich, damp brown. It's a bucolic scene that always manages to make her nostalgic for a past she's never known, a time that seems more innocent than the present. But as the laborers kneel in the furrows, they're watched by the foreman in blue dungarees, and later by the artist in his studio, and later yet by her, the process transforming them from people into objects.

Maybe past and present aren't all that different, she thinks. The strange thing—the amazing thing, really—is that we've managed to find work-arounds to surveillance: we speak in whispers, look for camera blind spots, pass contraband through toilets or showers, even as we know that breaking the rules may lengthen our confinement.

And I have broken the biggest rule of all, she realizes: trying to escape this place.

Meanwhile, retainees have continued to trickle into the main hall. Victoria is the last one to arrive; she finds a spot next to Alice. The air is electric, charged with impatience. How much longer must they wait? Is the evacuation happening or not? The attendants are running around, the power outage having rendered their Tekmerions useless. One of them has gone to the office to get a current list of retainees, another is looking for a manual counter.

The distant drone of vehicles brings people to their feet, and a few minutes later Ortega appears with a bullhorn. "We'll be evacuating to Victorville," he announces. "You must report to the exercise yard, where you'll be checked and led in groups of forty-two to the buses. Do not bring any personal items with you. I repeat, do not bring personal items with you. Your medications have to be packed in clear plastic bags. Proceed in two neat lines toward the yard."

An immediate and frenzied rush follows this announcement. Sara walks, half carried by the crowd, and elbowed and kicked along the way, to the exercise yard. White ash blankets the grass like snow, and the trailers' doors rattle in the hot wind. Beyond the chain-link fence a giant cloud of smoke sits on the horizon.

Hinton and Williams wait by the first bus, with zip ties dangling from their belts.

7.1. Loss, alteration, or destruction of company property is strictly prohibited and will result in an incident report and an extension of the retention period.

7.2. Extensions for loss, alteration, or destruction of company property can range from 21 to 84 days.

7.3. Depending on the severity of the damage, additional sanctions may be imposed, including the loss of commissary privileges.

7.4. Retainees are responsible for reimbursing Safe-X for any lost, damaged, or destroyed item according to the schedule below:

Sheets: Up to $300
Pillowcases: Up to $50
Blankets: Up to $400
Towels: Up to $75
Socks, bras, underwear: Up to $50 each
Uniforms: Up to $300
Shoes: Up to $200

SARA WAKES TO THE DRIVER CURSING AT TRAFFIC. THEY HAVE been on this back road for the last three hours, after finding the freeway entrance closed. She wipes spittle from her mouth and looks out of the barred window at a landscape of rock and brittlebush. The sun is a faint orb in a tangerine sky, and the light is dim. The woman sitting behind her leans close, her breath hot against Sara's neck. She speaks in a whisper, because talking on the bus is against the rules. "Got a tampon?"

Sara shakes her head. She's brought nothing with her, because Hinton confiscated her pillowcase at boarding. The loss of her journal is enough to bring tears to her eyes again. She turns her face to the glass and weeps quietly, wiping her tears with the palm of her hand. Everything has been taken away from her. Not just the life she had before, with a million pleasures and luxuries she can scarcely remember, but also the rope she's braided patiently over the last few months, and with which she hoisted herself from the depth of despair every morning. What will Hinton do with her journal? Read it to pass the time on his lunch break? Throw it into the trash without a look? Turn it in to the RAA as material evidence in her retention case? Each alternative seems as intolerable as the next. That journal belongs to her, and her alone.

The bus comes to an abrupt stop, its brakes hissing painfully. The driver leans on his horn until the car ahead of him begins moving again. Sara's bladder feels full, she wishes she could relieve herself. "How far are we from Victorville?" she whispers to Emily, who sits beside her with her pillowcase in her lap. It was Jackson who processed her for boarding, and she let everyone in her line keep their belongings. If Sara had been in *that* line, instead of Hinton's, she'd still have her notebook. "Do you know?"

"The sign back there said Hesperia."

So not too far, Sara thinks with relief. She closes her eyes again, hoping for sleep, but the driver hits a pothole, and it feels as though someone has punched her in the bladder. She should've used the bathroom before they left Madison, but the thought never occurred to her, so anxious was she to leave. Now she slouches in her seat, trying to find an angle that will lessen the pressure she feels. Her big toe is throbbing with pain from being stepped on during the frenzy to get on the bus, and her arm hurts where someone pulled her back.

The driver stays on the small road for another two hours before getting back on the freeway. Finally the cloud of smoke is behind them, the sky is a pale yellow. At least Elias and the kids are safe from the fire, she consoles herself, at least they're safe at home. Has the CRO sent them notice that she's being evacuated? Have they been told where she is being taken? The CRO is quick to get on the loudspeaker about shift changes or broken pipes, but today he's left the attendants in charge of handling the evacuation.

Late in the evening they reach Victorville and drive another five miles, past gas stations and fast-food joints and a nature preserve, to a beige stucco facility that still bears, carved above its front doors, the words VICTORVILLE HIGH SCHOOL. At the parking-lot gate, there is another wait while Safe-X agents give instructions to the driver, hollering so their voices can be heard over the roar of the engine. Finally the bus pulls up to a building in the back of the retention compound.

With guns pointed at them the women are untied, then marched into a gym, where cots have been arranged in rows under bright industrial lights. There are no sheets or blankets. The line to use the only toilet stretches the length of the hall. CONGREGATING IN THE RESTROOM IS STRICTLY PROHIBITED, a sign says—a warning that is repeated in Spanish and Chinese. As Sara waits her turn she shifts on her feet, hums to herself, bends forward with her hands on her knees, but ten feet away from the bathroom door she can hold it no longer and soils herself. An acrid smell rises from the orange puddle slowly forming at her feet.

"Hey," someone yells behind her. "Watch it."

Sara keeps her eyes averted. When next the restroom door opens, the woman ahead of her in the line yields her position. Inside, Sara cleans herself as best as she can. Not even when she was pregnant with the twins did she feel as much pain in her bladder as she did today. She thinks wistfully about the individually sealed dose of ibuprofen she stuffed in her pillowcase, a precious commodity under any circumstances, let alone on a day like this. Why couldn't Hinton have let her keep her things? What difference would it have made to him? She rinses her pants in the sink, wrings them, and comes out of the bathroom in her underwear.

From the back of the line, someone whistles.

Sara's face turns hot. She covers the puddle with the paper napkins she got from the dispenser, then moves the tissue papers around with her shoe, mopping up the urine. The other women step away from her in disgust.

Afterwards she has to walk across the gym with her wet pants in her arms. A guard with a trolley is handing out power bars, but she feels too self-conscious to stand in front of him half-naked. She looks for a cot, but they have all been claimed already, so she finds a spot next to Emily, lays her pants to dry, and curls up beside them for the night.

An hour later, the lights are turned off.

SARA OPENS HER EYES TO FIND HINTON STANDING BEFORE HER, flanked by two prison guards in brown uniforms. Have they come to escort everyone back to Madison? She scrambles to cover her bare legs with her pants, still wet from the night before. Her bruised knees stick out, the nail on her big toe is broken. The overhead lights are blindingly bright, and the stink of unwashed bodies hangs in the air. All around the gym, the women are rising from their cots, wiping sleep from their eyes, getting ready for device check. Why is Hinton towering over her like this? In his hand is her dream journal, with a dozen neon-colored page markers sticking out of it.

So he's read it. And he's brought it with him this morning to torment her. Enraged, she tries to grab the booklet, but he lifts it out of reach with one hand, while with the other he places a leather strap on her wrist. Sara lets out a yelp of surprise. What is happening? In a swift motion, Hinton tightens the strap around her wrist and unfurls the rest of the leash. "What are you doing?" she manages to ask. Her chest is tight, she feels out of breath. "What are you doing?"

With the leash Hinton pulls her to a standing position and leads her, bare-legged and barefoot, toward the door. The two guards follow behind, a hand on their holsters. From their cots the other women stare.

"Where are you taking me?"

"To the cage. Where you belong."

"No!" She pulls back violently at the leash—and wakes when her elbow hits the wall.

THE SMELL ISN'T SO STRONG AT FIRST; IT MIGHT BE NOTHING MORE than the foul odor from the bathrooms that haven't been serviced, or the fetid scent of a hundred and eight women who've been locked in a windowless gym for the past eleven hours. Sara tries to find a comfortable position on the vinyl floors, tries to go back to sleep. But as time passes, the smell becomes more distinct.

Smoke.

She sits up, alarmed. Under the LED lights of the cameras mounted along the wall, she can see wisps of smoke filtering from the vents. Emily has woken up, too. "Fire!" she yells in a voice that carries clear across the gym. "Fire!" She walks along the aisle, shaking the women awake. One by one they rise from their cots.

Sara runs to the nearest camera and waves her arms like a madwoman, trying desperately to get the attention of whoever is watching from the other end. Some of the women go to the door and bang on it with their fists. "Fire!" they yell. "Open the doors!"

Smoke continues to seep through the vents. Sara is struggling to breathe, her cloth mask is useless. She joins the crowd at the door, trying to push it open. Then someone unlocks it from the other side, and she is crushed under the weight of other bodies. She takes a hit on the head—and wakes on the floor of the gym.

ZACH STANDS IN THE DRIVEWAY, UNDER THE SHADE OF THE MAGNOLIA tree, his inhaler bulging out of the front pocket of his jeans. It is a sunny day in June, school has just let out for the summer. "My turn to be the zombie," he says.

"No, my turn," Saïd replies. He just got a haircut, his ears stick out.

Zach and Sara protest at once. Saïd has already gotten two turns, and wasn't he it when they played Red Light, Green Light? *That's not fair.* Inside the house, the kettle is whistling on the stove. Their mothers must be making mint tea, getting ready to watch their TV show together.

But Saïd ignores the complaints. He contorts his face, tilts his head, and starts walking out of step across the driveway. His eyes bulge, his movements are jerky. Whether the others like it or not, the game has begun. He tries to catch Zach first, but Zach is too tall, too agile. So Saïd goes for Sara. As they tussle, she falls to the ground, and blood gushes out of her knee. "Mama," she calls. "Help!" But no one comes to her aid and she has to kick and pinch and elbow her brother in order to free herself. As she tries to release Saïd's grip on her, she realizes that his face has turned into a skull.

"ROUGH NIGHT?" EMILY ASKS IN THE MORNING. THE INDUSTRIAL lights have come on, the cameras whirr as they follow the movements of the women rising from their slumber. Marcela is doing sun salutations, Alice is unfolding her headwrap, Toya has turned her face to the wall, trying to sleep some more. Somewhere outside, a truck beeps as its driver goes into reverse. "You look a little pale."

"I haven't had anything to eat, is all," Sara replies. Her pants are still damp and smelly. To think that she once stood every morning in her closet, undecided about which shirt to pair with which skirt, or what piece of jewelry might best complement the dress she picked out. After a moment of hesitation she slips her pants on and walks to the restroom. Sleeping on the floor has left her with pains and aches all over her body, but it comes as some relief that there's no smoke, that the only scent in the air is that of the women around her. Maybe the fire has been contained.

The line is mercifully shorter than the night before, but by the time her turn comes there's no soap and the napkin dispenser is empty. She washes her face and hands, fretting all the while about the smell of urine that lingers on her. As she steps out of the bathroom, she bumps into Toya, who carries a little ziplock bag with her medications. "Morning."

"Morning."

Toya puts a hand on Sara's arm. "Emily told me what happened."

"We had to try something."

"You had a bad day. Everyone does, at some point. You're lucky you didn't get caught."

Sara nods. Someone pushes past them to get out of the bathroom; it's the woman who sat behind Sara on the bus; her pants are wet, and stained maroon. The gym where they're being housed has no supplies of any kind. Sara is about to ask Toya if she can spare an Advil for the broken nail on her toe when Victoria comes to the door. "Are you two coming or going? Don't just stand there. You're blocking the way."

Toya goes in, Sara comes out.

Moments later a bell rings. Two Safe-X guards walk the length of the warehouse, telling the women to pick up their things, straighten their cots, keep the alleys clear. Once the safety check is completed, another guard orders the women to stand. But instead of the neuroprosthetic scanner at Madison, he uses a simple counting device.

At least there's that.

FOR FIVE DAYS THE WOMEN REMAIN IN THE GYM. BEING SEGREGATED from the other retainees at Victorville—most of them men under investigation for future gun crimes—they can't use the television room or the exercise yard or the comm pods. Meals consisting of stale sandwiches and salty snacks are brought on trolleys by two guards, who are immediately assailed with questions each time they hand out the food. Is the fire contained? Have you notified our families? Can we make phone calls? Can we get some soap? How about a change of clothes? And the most common, the most pressing question: When will we get out of here?

There is no air-conditioning, and the little ventilation they get is from the doors that open to let guards in and out. The crowding around the food trolleys gets especially intense on the second day. "Get back," one of the guards yells at the women. "Make a single fucking line." With a flick of the wrist he unlocks his baton and raises it, which is enough to force the retainees to comply, but the heat and the rank smell of the women have made him pale and a minute later he faces the wall and throws up.

From then on, the retainees are ordered to remain six feet away from the trolleys. No one who approaches without verbal permission from a guard will be given any food.

Rumors run wild. The firefighters are slowly gaining control of the fire. No, they're losing the battle, and the entire town of Lake Perris is gone. The freeways have reopened. No, only the 10 and the 5 are open, the other freeways are still closed. Governor García is going to grant some compassionate releases on account of the wildfire. No, you must've heard wrong. Retainees evacuated from another Safe-X facility have been put in a cramped activities room, we're lucky to be in the gym. Bitch, you call this luck?

And so on.

The uncertainty is compounded by boredom; Sara would do anything for a book. After hours of cajoling, Emily allows her to read the unfinished comic book, which turns out to be not about the pyromaniac superhero so much as it is about Rina Campoy's relationship to her mother, a burlesque dancer who travels the country with members of her company. The work is exhausting and precarious, so she leaves Rina in the care of an uncle whose nine-to-five job she believes will provide a more stable lifestyle. The uncle is a struggling scientist for a weapons corporation based in Washington, D.C., and when he needs volunteers to test his experimental serum, he secretly uses his niece. As Rina grows up and her powers become evident, she spends much of her time trying to reconnect with her mother.

"What part are you at?" Emily asks, after every few pages. The rash on her neck seems to be clearing. "Do you like it?"

"It's not at all what I expected."

"In a good or bad way?"

"In a great way." If only she'd been in the same line as Emily when they were being processed for boarding, she could've kept her journal. She could be writing a letter to Elias, or recording all that she's seen of this facility, or jotting down the horrendous dreams she's been having since she's been brought to Victorville. What will the RAA's algorithm make of these nightmares?

On the sixth day the guards finally bring some news: the women are to get ready; they will be driven back to their retention center this morning. This time, the bus driver takes the main road, speeding past apartment buildings and strip malls toward the freeway. Sara leans her forehead against the barred window. The sky is gray, the trees bend under the heat. When they exit the freeway, they pass a cluster of damaged structures in the little town of Ellis—a gas station, a tire shop, and two adjoining convenience stores.

Ellis used to be known for its tool factory, which once supplied farms throughout California with modern equipment; there are still murals here and there celebrating the workers who built the town, proclaiming it the place where "imagination meets creation." But these days the factory is home to a Twenty-Thirder community—a subject of frequent complaints among Safe-X attendants, who blame it for the general dilapidation of the town.

Without slowing down, the bus crosses old railroad tracks to the eastern part of Ellis, where all the structures have remained safe from the fire. Including Madison.

Welcome back, residents. This is your chief retention officer speaking. It has been a rough week for all of us, but we are grateful to our first responders for keeping us safe. I'm happy to report that our facility has not suffered any damage, and that all residents have remained safe.

Unfortunately, the evacuation has caused us to miss our deadline on the Vox-R contract, so those of you assigned to Trailers A and B will be going on twelve-hour shifts starting tomorrow to make up for lost hours. Remember, anyone who wishes to pick up overtime hours can do so by filling out a form at one of the kiosks outside the main office. Training takes only twenty minutes.

In addition, we are experiencing some staffing issues due to the impact of the wildfire on our employees. The exercise yard and the recreation room will be closed until further notice. We are still working on getting the commissary restocked.

THE FIRST THING SHE NOTICES ON HER RETURN TO THE RESI-
dential floor is the cameras hanging limply from their cords,
their glass eyes gouged out. Someone must've taken advan-
tage of the power outage and the chaos of the evacuation to destroy
the surveillance equipment upstairs. Whoever the vandal is, Sara
thinks, she's a hero. Not being watched, even if it's only on the second floor and only until the cameras are fixed, feels to her like a sip
of freedom. It won't quench her thirst, but it'll keep her going. And
even though the toilets reek and the floors are blanketed with ash,
she has a room, with its bed and blanket, its framed picture of the
children, its little window.

This is another thing Madison is trying to teach her, she realizes.

Be grateful for the little you have, a voice inside her says. You never
know when they might take even that away.

Still, the return to the retention center is rough. A weird stomach bug, which some of the retainees contracted when they were
at Victorville, seems to be spreading fast. It has already laid up five
women, and that means their shifts will be reassigned tomorrow, on
top of the extended shifts the CRO just announced. There are not
enough clean uniforms to go around for everyone, the infirmary is
out of tampons, and the smell of rotting food has spread from the
cafeteria to the rest of the facility. Dinner has been pushed back to
seven to allow time for the kitchen to be cleaned.

But at least there are showers.

Be grateful for the little you have.

For two hours Sara waits her turn. The water, when it hits her
skin, is nothing short of a miracle. She lathers and scrubs and rinses
for five luxurious minutes. Then the timer beeps, and she wraps her-

self in a towel and steps into the pale light of the locker room. The bruise on her arm has grown purple, the broken nail on her big toe has fallen off. She rubs lotion all over her body, massaging the areas that are still sore from the nights she spent on the floor of the gym. She brushes her teeth and applies cream to her face, but no matter how long she takes with her anointments she has to put on her dirty uniform again, its smell somehow more revolting than it was before.

But at least there are comm pods.

Be grateful for the little you have.

On her way to call Elias, she passes the Case Management office, where Gardner is removing the Halloween decorations that have been hanging from the service window for the last month. He's already peeled off the glow-in-the-dark skeleton and the black netting, and now he's unhooking the string of orange bulbs. A roll of paper towels and a spray bottle sit on the counter. "Hussein," Gardner says as she passes him, "H-U-S-S-E-I-N."

It's a running joke to him; he makes it whenever he sees her. The first couple of times Gardner did this, Sara asked him why he was spelling out her name. Was there an update in her case? Then for many weeks she ignored him, thinking that withholding her attention would make him stop. But today something comes over her, and she laughs along with him, throwing her head back and slapping her knees. It is a scornful laugh, a laugh that says nothing can touch her after what she's been through these last few days, not even the petty cruelties of small clerks.

Gardner stops what he's doing to stare at her.

Sara stares back, her lips still stretched into a smile.

"Keep it moving, all right?"

"Sure thing." She walks down the hallway, noticing at once how good it feels to move her limbs after five days in lockup.

Be grateful for the little you have.

But something has shifted in her, she realizes as she waits in line. The filth and stink of her uniform, which persist even after she's washed herself, are giving her a new clarity about her situation, its false hopes and stubborn misconceptions. She's been so focused on her case, from its absurd start through its successive delays, that despite being at Madison for ten months she's failed to see how much she has in common with the other retainees. Not just the struggle to be free or the rage against stupid rules, but the vulnerability that this place has exposed in them. It comes to her then that facing her vulnerability is the only way to remove pretense from her interactions with others, and allow her to rely on the friendships she has made.

Finally her turn comes. She dials, her heartbeat quickening as she imagines Elias at work, hearing his phone ring, but finding it buried under the usual clutter on his desk. It will take a second or two for him to locate it, press the green button, and sink into a chair to talk to her. But after a few rings, the call goes to voicemail.

Her disappointment is short-lived. On her return to her room she finds out she has mail—an express package from Elias, dated two days before the evacuation. It contains respirator masks, bottles of water, energy bars, hand sanitizer, disinfecting wipes, and a miniature first-aid kit, each wrapped in plastic. Maybe Elias doesn't write her as often as she likes, and, yes, they hit a rough patch, but he's trying to show he cares. He's taken the trouble—as well as the expense, which these days they can scarcely afford—of ordering these items from the only commercial site approved by Safe-X.

Yet Sara remains puzzled by the arrival of the package. If her husband was keeping an eye on the Perris fire, and had time enough to ship her some emergency supplies, then why wasn't the CRO prepared? And if he wasn't, then someone higher up at the company? Safe-X maintains hundreds of facilities spread across twenty-two U.S. states. Surely they have the logistical means to handle an emergency. They're traded on the stock exchange, for God's sake. Why didn't they evacuate the women until the last possible minute, and to an overcrowded retention center ninety miles away? Whether it's indifference or malice she has no idea.

But she knows she can't be grateful for it.

THE CAFETERIA IS FULL TO CAPACITY, THE WINDOWS ALREADY STEAMED by the time Sara and Emily get their trays and join the others at their usual table. The hum of conversation is a perfect current, drowning individual voices in its ebb and flow. Dinner is spaghetti in a meat sauce, served with a kid-size apple juice and a cheese stick. It takes

Sara a couple of tries to unwrap the cheese stick; they haven't had anything to eat since they left Victorville, and her hands are shaking with hunger.

"Our room was searched while we were gone," Alice says.

"The cots were turned over," Toya cuts in, eager to tell the story herself. "Pillows and sheets all over the place, a total mess. But the weird thing is, our photos and papers and things are untouched. Even my origami birds are where I left them."

"I wonder what they were looking for," Sara says.

"They searched 203 and 209, too."

"Was anything missing in those rooms?"

"Nope."

Sara takes a bite of cheese. 203 is Linh Nguyen and Claire Lopez, and 209 is Ana Guerrero and Stephanie Michaels. They're all long haulers with a history of disciplinary actions. "They're trying to identify the saboteur," she says.

"The what?" Emily asks.

"Whoever broke the cameras. They're looking for what she might've used to cause so much damage to their cameras." She finishes the cheese stick in two quick bites, then picks up her spork. "But even that doesn't make sense, because they should've searched the entire floor, not just those rooms."

Emily sucks her teeth in mock disapproval. "You can tell Hinton's not on duty."

Sara's thoughts flit to her journal. Before coming down to dinner she went to check the trash cans by the back gate, but they had been emptied already, the only garbage in them remnants of the attendants' lunch. If she wants to find out what happened to her notebook, she'll have to ask Hinton. "Maybe he has the day off."

Emily frowns. "In the middle of the week? That's not like him. Anyway, maybe it wasn't the attendants who turned the rooms upside down. Maybe it was someone looking for shit to steal or trade."

"If it's another retainee," Alice says, looking suddenly aggrieved, "they had plenty of time to go through our stuff. We were on the last bus back, 'cause we got delayed behind a truck at the freeway exit."

"A lot of good it did them." Toya laughs. "I don't have anything worth stealing."

"But still, that's messed up," Alice continues. "You think you know people, but really you don't. I mean, look what happened with Lucy Everett."

Marcela looks up from her food. "Don't mention that bitch again. I want to eat in peace."

"*Soo*-rry," Alice says, raising her hands. "Speaking of which, did you all notice that the screens in the hallway haven't been updated? They still show the hearings from last week."

"They haven't pushed the button is all. You're up again soon?"

"In December. But I wonder what'll happen to the people who missed their dates because of the Perris fire."

Sara takes a sip of apple juice. "They'll go to the back of the line. Like it was with me when the government shut down." Madison is run like a factory, she thinks. The conveyor belts move twenty-four hours a day, seven days a week. It doesn't matter if there's a snowstorm or a tornado, if there's a presidential election or a championship finals game, if a worker is sick or pregnant or injured: the conveyor belts keep moving. Every retainee is processed through Safe-X's software, which keeps track of dates, infractions, and extensions. When a hearing with the RAA is marked MISSED, the retainee goes back in line to wait for the next available hearing—assuming she's not written up for bad behavior in the meantime.

"God," Alice says, wiping tomato sauce from the side of her mouth, "I just hope there's not another fire before my hearing."

Marcela chuckles. "Or a flash flood."

"A mudslide."

"A blizzard."

"An earthquake."

"Come on, guys. That's not funny."

The women eat their sticky, greasy spaghetti without complaint; it's the first hot meal they've had since they were evacuated last week. How relieved we all are to be back to our narrow rooms, Sara thinks, our hot showers, our square meals. But in a day or two we will want more, and then what? "We have to stop the conveyor belt," she says.

Marcela puts her hand over her nose; the stench from Sara's uniform is powerful, and rifling through the trash cans before dinner didn't help. "What're you talking about?"

"We have to stop working. This place can't run without us, and the longer they hold us, the more money they make. That's why they're always writing us up, and when we follow the rules, they come up with new ones for us to break." She looks around the table. "But if we refuse to work, their costs go up, and their revenue goes down. They might decide this facility isn't profitable enough, and close it. And anyway even if they don't, why should we help them keep us locked up in here? Why should we contribute to our own detention? We should make *them* pay for having us here. We have to stop working." She pauses to take another sip, moving the straw around the bottom to catch every drop.

"Easy for you to say," Marcela says, cutting a meatball in half. "I bet you have money in your commissary account. And when it runs out, your husband can send you more."

"Not really," Sara replies. When she turns in her damaged sheet to the laundry office, she'll be hit with a financial penalty for damaging company property, so any money she might receive from Elias will go first to repaying Safe-X before it can be put in her commissary. In any case, she doesn't want to ask her husband for more money, because he already has two mortgages to pay, her student loan to service, diapers and formula to buy, not to mention the upkeep for the Volvo he bought on a whim before their lives took an unexpected turn. Even after taking in a paying roommate and cycling through his credit cards, he's been struggling. The truth is, they'll be paying debt from her retention for years to come. "But you understand what I'm trying to say?"

Alice's eyes dart to the attendant station, where Ortega sits, looking at his Tekmerion. He's a lanky guy who ordinarily works the main gate, checking visitors' credentials and biometrics, but tonight he has been put on cafeteria watch. Then Alice asks, her voice dropping even further, "You want to go on s-t-r-i-k-e?"

Sara becomes aware she's taking another huge risk. It is foolish to tempt fate again, after miraculously escaping notice last week. But how else can she survive this place? She has to take a chance on the other retainees, joining her life to theirs. "Yes," she says, the acknowledgment making her face flush.

"Let's just eat in peace," Marcela pleads. "Can we do that? Can we eat in peace?"

"I'm up again soon," Alice says somberly, her voice so low Sara has to lean over the table to hear. "I don't want any problems."

"We just got back today," Marcela adds, her tone halfway between horror and admiration, "and you're already looking for trouble."

Something about the phrase takes Sara back to her childhood, to those awful years spent watching herself, not daring to jump around, make a mess, be loud, get in a fight, or even bring home a bad grade lest her father lose his temper. Even now, the idea that she might be to blame silences her, makes her feel alone.

"That's not what this is," Toya counters. "She's talking about collective organizing, which is a protected right."

Gratitude washes over Sara. "Yes, exactly."

"Except in this place. Prisoners don't have a right to s-t-r-i-k-e."

"I thought you said this wasn't a prison."

"It's not." Toya tilts her head. "But it's not *not* a prison, you know? The courts haven't ruled on retention centers, so it's kind of a gray area."

"Oh." Sara feels deflated again.

"The only way to find out," Toya adds, with mischief gleaming in her eyes, "is to go ahead and do it. See what happens."

Marcela dips her cheese stick in the spaghetti sauce. "Can't we just eat in peace?"

"Look, I don't want another extension," Alice says. "I can't take any more of this shithole, I just can't."

"We get it," Toya tells her, patting her arm. "You've made yourself clear."

All of a sudden Ortega gets up from his chair, his Tekmerion in hand.

The women fall silent, but Ortega walks past them to a table where five younger, rowdier retainees are eating. Still looking at his Tekmerion, he touches Victoria on the shoulder. "You've been selected for blood and urine tests," he tells her.

Victoria's usual bravado is gone. She points to her tray, asks if she can finish her meal, please, she's only halfway through. But Ortega won't budge. After a minute she gets up and follows him to the door, where another attendant stands, waiting to escort her to the infirmary. A moment later, the din of conversation picks up again.

"So what about you?" Sara asks Emily. "You've been awfully quiet."

Emily shrugs.

"Just look what happened last week," Sara presses. "They weren't prepared for the evacuation, didn't even give us masks. We barely made it out."

"But we're not in any danger now." Emily has lost her appetite for adventure, it's clear.

Sara turns to Alice and Marcela again, but they give her the same studiously neutral expressions they reserve for the cameras. She and Toya will have to do this on their own.

THE NEXT MORNING IT IS WILLIAMS WHO WALKS THROUGH THE GATE at six, dragging his heels, leaving long, dark streaks on the gray floors. He runs through device check at a leisurely pace, at one point stopping to chat with Victoria, though she doesn't seem particularly interested in talking to him; she goes back to her room as soon as her scan is complete. But this isn't the only thing that feels out of the ordinary, and it takes Sara another minute to tease out what it is: the cameras that track everyone's movements are dead. She can stand over the white line, chat with her roommate, laugh about her situation or cry over it without feeding morsels of information to a greedy algorithm.

"Where's Hinton?" she asks when Williams brings the scanner to her head.

"Out sick."

"How long will he be gone?"

"Don't know."

"What's wrong with him?"

"What do you care?"

"Just wondering."

Where is her notebook? It's one thing for an AI to digest data from her dreams, spitting out predictions as it goes, but another for the senior attendant at Madison, a man she despises, or tells herself she despises, to read the narrative of her dream life, entertaining himself with the impressions and memories and questions she has so carefully recorded. She would do anything not to cede that power to him.

But maybe she's wrong, she tells herself consolingly, and Hinton hasn't bothered to look at her notebook. His mind was on the fire, surely, and he was eager to evacuate. So he tossed it away, maybe in the garbage can in the attendants' locker room, and now it's some-where in a landfill, buried under mountains of trash that seagulls are picking through for anything edible. She lingers over that image, disturbing as it may be, for the assurance it gives her that her secrets are safe.

The thought that Hinton might have turned in her dream journal as evidence to the RAA is so depressing that she packs it away in a far corner of her mind, never to be brought out again.

She returns to her room and wraps herself in her blanket. Madison isn't properly insulated; it's always either too cold or too hot. Emily eyes her from the mirror above the sink, where she's washing up. "So you're not going to work?"

"No. That's what I told you yesterday."

"I thought you were just talking, and got carried away." She dries her face, then stares at Sara for a minute. "Your score'll go up if you don't work."

"I've been working for eight months, look where it got me."

After Emily leaves for her early shift, Sara washes up and goes to the window. The sky is slowly lightening to silver. White clouds sit like cotton balls on the horizon. The creosote bushes that border the road tremble in the breeze, but it seems the jackrabbits and road-runners that ordinarily live on the mountain have yet to return. The bus stop is empty. Perhaps the old woman hasn't returned to Ellis from wherever she was evacuated. Or, a more tragic possibility, her house has been damaged in the fire, the straw she uses to make her baskets feeding the flames, and she can't return home yet.

Like me, Sara thinks. Home feels so remote to her these days that it's become less a place than an idea, whose expanse she can hold in her mind but no longer inhabit. Madison is where she lives now, where for the safety of others her impulses and dreams and desires are contained.

A moment later the bus comes down the street, the driver not bothering to slow down at the stop sign, and Sara turns away from the window.

She wants to find out more about the fire, but when she goes down to the library she has to wait until the breakfast bell rings before people begin to leave and a seat at the computers opens up. The photographs in the *Los Angeles Times* look like snapshots of the apocalypse: red and orange skies looming over San Bernardino, evacuees sitting in gridlocked traffic, frightened horses being herded onto a trailer, trees shorn of leaves and burned black. Worse are the pictures from Lake Perris, where the whole town burned to the ground.

Even in Ellis, she discovers, the damage is far more extensive than what she glimpsed from the obscured window of the Safe-X bus. The fire has claimed some fifty buildings on the eastern side of town, including a grocery store, a pharmacy, and two fast-food restaurants, but also a historic pool hall, built in the same architectural style as Madison, and which had been used by a local community organization as a space to provide services for the elderly. At least two people have died, and dozens suffered injuries and smoke inhalation. Sara tries to find out more, but Ellis is too small of a town to command much coverage in the *Times,* and after clicking and scrolling for a while without success, she turns to the rest of the news.

The congressman whose corruption allegations dominated headlines a few weeks ago has disappeared from the front page, replaced by a television actor who's been caught with an underage girl. The pharmaceutical company that makes Cerephy is standing firm on the cost of its dementia-treatment pill, despite mounting pressure from advocates and families of Alzheimer's patients, who accuse it of rank extortion. Tensions continue to rise between the two private water companies in California, and there is speculation about a hostile takeover.

Disappointingly there is no news on the RAA. Instead, the paper is running an editorial on criminal justice reform, which calls retention a humane tool for reducing violence because it saves American communities both the trauma of the crime and the cost of prosecuting it. It's time to leave antiquated notions of punishment behind, the editorial concludes, and expand our bias-free, science-based crime prevention system.

Sara tries not to think about this system, and focus instead on Madison. She doesn't want to contribute to Safe-X's bottom line any longer. What a shame that Toya is the only one in her group who agrees with her about the necessity of the strike. She was hoping to find more support, at least among her friends. Still, even if her efforts are too small to be of consequence, she has to start somewhere.

I have to do this for my own sanity, she thinks. My self-respect.

She returns to her cell, finding it empty. The solitude feels like a wonderful novelty after the week at Victorville. Sitting on her cot, she eats one of the power bars Elias sent her. She chews slowly, savoring the taste of nuts and caramel, and with her fingernail picks out all the crumbs that fall on her blanket. The hint of apricot she detects beneath the caramel brings back memories of her mother, who used to make jams and compotes every summer. The house smelled of fruit and sugar for days, while the top shelf in the pantry slowly filled with mason jars labeled in her neat handwriting. Even now Sara associates that fruity scent with happiness, with a time in her life when her family was whole, mother father daughter son, in a cluttered cottage not far from campus, with a magnolia tree out front and a lemon tree in the back.

But after Saïd died, Omar's questions about the accident lingered over the house like a foul smell. Why did Sara's mother stay home on the day of the Millers' party? He got headaches all the time, and he still went to work. Why did Aunt Hiba go to the store for more ice? The children were left unattended for over an hour. Why did Uncle James have to play music at such a high volume? Saïd must've cried for help, thrashed in the water, made some kind of noise. What was he doing outside, anyway? The children had been told to stay inside. Why did Zach give up looking for Saïd? They were supposed to play together. And the worst, the most painful question of all: Why did Sara not let her brother hide in the coat closet with her?

Omar was well versed in the role that chance played in shaping the cosmos, yet he had trouble accepting its minute effect over his own life. He wanted to apportion blame for the accident and, dissatisfied with the answers he got, he retreated into pained silence, spending as much time as he could in his lab. The Millers decided to move, putting an entire continent between them and Omar's denunciations.

But Sara's poor mother accepted her guilt without complaint or protest, and set about redeeming herself. She was always on watch, fearful that in a moment's inattention something might happen to her only surviving child. She never let Sara walk home from school or take the bus with her friends, instead shuttling her in the car anywhere she needed to go. She scheduled regular visits to the pediatrician and treated even the mildest cold as though it might be a sign of pneumonia. Sara's friends were the subjects of stealthy, yet thorough investigations into whether they used drugs or alcohol. At times the attention could be suffocating, and in order to get away from it Sara had to lie to her mother.

Maybe "lie" isn't the right word, Sara thinks. She just taught herself to be careful what information she shared, and with whom. As a teenager she created two social media accounts, one to use with her friends and one curated for her mom, and proved so adept at keeping them separate that she made a habit of it. Her well-behaved self was what she showed to the adults in her life, so that her more troubled self could roam free with the friends she trusted. Hearing her mother click her tongue in disapproval every time she scrolled through Zach's Printastic feed confirmed Sara's belief in the necessity of her choice. "That kid's gonna get in trouble," Sara's mother would say, inhaling deeply from her cigarette.

What an irony that Sara is now under retention, while Zach is writing to her with advice. But is it true, as he said in his email, that it was Saïd who chipped her front tooth when they were playing the zombie game? That afterwards her father had tried to keep the peace by pairing her with Zach during their fishing trip? No, no, no. Saïd was only six or seven at the time; it had to have been Zach who pushed her down on the driveway. In any case, Zach seems to have turned his life around now, even getting an award from the Chamber of Commerce in Orlando for his service to the community.

The sound of hammering from the other end of the building

interrupts her thoughts; the construction workers are back this morning. It seems there are more of them, too, because the noise is louder than before. They must be trying to catch up on lost work-days. There haven't been any new admissions this week, Sara real-izes. Perhaps the CRO is waiting for construction to be completed before admitting new cases. According to Alice, who heard it from someone in custodial, bed capacity will increase to 184. How the same cafeteria, showers, library, and infirmary will serve nearly fifty percent more retainees, Sara has no idea.

She's discarding the wrapper from her breakfast bar when Jack-son appears at the door. She wears new prescription glasses, with tortoiseshell frames that make her look like a prep school matron, the impression somehow undermined by her multiple earrings and the electric blue of her nail polish. "Hussein," she says, "get to work. You're late."

"I quit."

"What? No one told me." Jackson scrolls through the work sched-ule on her tablet. "You're still listed here, see."

Sara's gaze falls on the tablet, where a color-coded grid shows a list of retainees, their work assignments, current locations, and performance metrics, the numbers rolling at an astonishing speed. Again she's reminded of colonial censuses, the piles of ledgers main-tained by small clerks across the empire, and that made the extrac-tion of labor more efficient. The whole enterprise depended on careful note-taking, on accounting for every native with the highest degree of accuracy. "That's so strange," she says, her voice rising to indicate surprise. "I filled out the form on the day we evacuated. Maybe it got lost when the power went out?"

"Great, just great. My schedule's already messed up after last week, and now you're quitting on me." With one finger Jackson types Sara's name on her device, waits for the profile to load, and enters the date. Then, reading from the prompt, she asks, "What's the rea-son for resigning from your assignment?"

"I just told you, I quit."

"That's not on the list." She scrolls through the pull-down menu again. "I'll just select UNWILLING TO WORK."

What a distinction, Sara thinks. Resigning is what innocent people do, out there in the free world, but here she's a retainee, which means that the impulse to quit can only come from laziness or ineptitude or insubordination. Now it can be used to charge an additional penalty anytime she breaks a rule at Madison.

"If you don't like Trailer D," Jackson continues, toggling from tab to tab, "I can move you to custodial full-time. I need more bodies there."

"No, I'm okay."

"What about your Monday and Wednesday shifts in laundry? Don't tell me you're quitting those, too."

"I am."

"Lord have mercy," she whispers, shaking her head. She follows the prompts to the final screen and marks Sara as having refused alternate assignments offered to her. Then she puts away her device and makes a show of waving a hand in front of her nose. "Girl, a shower wouldn't kill you."

"I did shower. I just can't get a clean uniform yet."

"Well, it's gonna take even longer now. I have to find someone to replace you," Jackson says, walking away. Just as Sara sits down on her cot again, she returns. "I almost forgot. You have a visit this afternoon at two."

"For real?"

"Do I look like I'm kidding? Be downstairs by 1:45, all right?"

IN HER FILTHY UNIFORM SHE GOES TO THE POSTPAL OFFICE. SHE WALKS through a metal detector, gets a neuroprosthetic scan, and submits to a pat-down, after which the attendant ushers her into the waiting area. Signs posted at the entrance say that ALL CONVERSATIONS ARE MONITORED and VISITS ARE A PRIVILEGE. Rachel Cosgrove from custodial is already waiting, sitting with her hands clasped over her stomach and her head resting against the wall. Her brown hair is parted down the middle, revealing two-inch gray roots that make her look older than she otherwise seems. On the clock above the door, the red hand moves sluggishly across the dial.

"Who're you waiting for?" Rachel asks.

"My husband."

"I'm waiting for my daughter. My eldest. She's driving down from Fresno."

"That's a long ways from here" is all Sara can think to say.

"It was easier on her when I was at Fair View, 'cause that's in Tulare County. Now she has to get up at five in the morning to make it down and back in one day. She's a hospice nurse, she only gets one day off a week."

"Fair View?"

"Where I was the first time. I was in three months."

Sara doesn't want to hear more; she folds her arms across her chest and turns her gaze to the wall. Rachel gets the hint, and an expectant silence falls between them. A cockroach emerges from behind the garbage bin, scurries across the floor, then ducks behind the bench. Time passes. A sign beneath the observation window says KEEP HANDS IN VIEW AT ALL TIMES and another says VISITS LIMITED TO 30 MINUTES, NO EXCEPTIONS.

Sara starts to count the signs; there are sixteen of them, warning, instructing, forbidding, or ordering. She doesn't dare move.

Then a few minutes after two, another attendant appears. She leads the two retainees down a gray corridor to the visiting room, where Elias is chatting with a pretty blonde in a jean skirt and platform boots. The perfume on the woman is familiar; it's a scent Sara used to wear when she was in high school, but had to forgo once her allergies became more pronounced. Mohsin is toying with the tassel that hangs from the blonde's purse, while Mona sits in Elias's lap, playing with his car key fob.

At the sound of the door opening, all four look up. Elias stands, carefully depositing Mona on the floor, and comes toward Sara. Regret washes over her—she should've worked the laundry, she could've had a chance of getting clean clothes this afternoon, she could've looked more presentable. She has to fight the urge to run back to her room, to keep her filth hidden from her husband. "Thank God," he says as they embrace. "I was so worried. Are you all right?"

"I'm okay, I'm okay," she replies. "I'm sorry about the stink."

"Don't worry about that." He rubs her arms, as if to make sure she's really there, standing in front of him. "I'm just glad they brought you back. They told us you were all transferred to another facility, but they wouldn't tell us where or give us much information. Angie and I were just talking about that."

"Who's Angie?"

Elias tips his head toward Rachel Cosgrove's daughter, who is leading her mom to a table across the room. They sit down, and are immediately engrossed in their own conversation.

"Did you have to evacuate, too?" Sara asks.

"Oh, no. But clinic was cancelled for the week because of the smoke. I stayed home with the kids. They went a little feral. Yesterday was the first day I could take them to the park. I think that's why they didn't mind the drive out here so much."

Sara scoops up Mona. Her hair is a tangle of curls, thicker and darker than the last time Sara saw her, more than six weeks ago. But drawn by the tassel swinging from Angie's purse, Mohsin has followed her to the other table. "Hey, buddy," Elias calls out to him. "Leave that, please. Come say hi to Mama. Come."

After some hesitation Mohsin returns. "What happened here?" Sara asks worriedly, running her finger over the huge scratch on his cheek.

"Mona happened. They were stuck at home too long, they started fighting."

"Let's go over here." Carrying Mona, Sara picks the table farthest away from the Cosgroves. She sits down, with Elias across from her, and the clear plastic bag required by Safe-X between them. In it are the twins' diapers, a changing blanket, a few toy cars, and a stuffed parrot.

"Your dad wanted to come," Elias says. "But his Exo-Legs are being serviced and I didn't want to wait. It was hard enough getting a visit through the system for today, I didn't want to reschedule."

"He can come on his own, you know. I haven't seen him since August."

"Well, it's not as easy for him," he says, rummaging through the clear bag for the toy cars. His fingers are long, his skin unblemished. Little tufts of hair sprout beneath his knuckles.

"Did he have to evacuate?"

"No, he was fine. He just couldn't go on his walks like he usually does."

"So he could've come."

Though Elias has laid out toy cars on the table for him, Mohsin picks up the Volvo key fob and puts it in his mouth; Elias takes it out. It's a small act, performed probably a dozen times a day with a toddler, but in its ordinariness it contains everything Sara has missed over the last year. "Come here, buddy," she asks her son, patting her other knee, but Mohsin doesn't pay any attention, he's far too busy trying to get to the key fob again. "You want some chocolate from the machine?" she asks. A shameless bribe.

"No, no, they can't have chocolate," Elias says with a frown. "Not until they're two."

"Right," she says, her face burning with embarrassment. "Of course. Sorry."

She smooths down Mona's polka-dot dress, parts her hair with a finger, and without brushing out the curls she winds each side into a bun, all the while cooing to her. The smell of her little girl is intoxicating; she buries her nose in her daughter's neck and inhales.

For a while she tells Elias about Victorville: the dirty bathroom, the moldy bread, the women who had to walk around with bloodied pants, the cruel withholding of news about what's happening outside the facility. Then the door opens, and a Safe-X attendant walks in. He stands in front of the first vending machine, which sells fruit cups and juices, checking its inventory against the numbers on his tablet. He starts whistling a tune, which Sara recognizes as a lullaby, though she can't quite remember its name.

"So I talked to Adam Abdo," Elias says.

This is the moment she has come to expect in every visit, but also to dread, because while the legal details her husband reports vary, the message remains the same.

Elias tells her that just in the last month the lawyer handled two cases that are similar to hers, and was able to win release for both of his clients at the twenty-one-day mark. He tells her it's crucial that she keep her record clean, that she stay out of trouble, that she follow all the rules, because once they go before a judge, Abdo is confident he can get her out. He tells her there's no reason why her case can't proceed like those others. "But it's crucial," he concludes, "that you keep your head down. Just follow the rules."

She can't tell him about her attempt to escape during the fire, she realizes. Even if she's evaded notice for it, which she isn't fully convinced she has, she's still in violation of the handbook because she tore up her sheet. Elias is working hard to keep up with the bills, and now she's saddled him with a $300 penalty. She's stopped wearing her hair in a bun, her uniform is filthy. She hasn't maintained the standards of grooming and cleanliness that Safe-X mandates. Worst of all, she's resigned from her job, and is trying to convince the others to do the same.

Sara kisses her daughter's cheek. "Did you miss Mama?"

Mona examines Sara's hair, puts a strand of it in her mouth, then gets bored and drops it. Her hand burrows in the neckline of Sara's shirt, looking for a necklace to play with. A moment later she wants to get down from Sara's lap. "Stay, baby. Stay."

"Did you hear me?" Elias asks, his voice tinged with impatience.

"Yes, I heard." She gets Mona the stuffed parrot from the diaper bag. "Does your parrot have a name?"

"Parrot," Mona says, like it's the most obvious thing in the world. She pushes a button on the stuffed animal, and its red wings make a fluttering sound. Another button, and it squeaks.

"Adam said you'll get a hearing this month. December at the latest. He says they're not going to want to carry the backlog from the shutdown into next year, because James Wesley has his eye on a Senate seat and he won't want any scrutiny over his awful numbers. What, you don't believe it?"

"It's not that." She shakes her head. "It's just that how things sound out there has nothing to do with how they actually work in here."

"I understand. But hang in there. Adam says it can't be much longer now."

The attendant has stopped whistling. He's propped his glasses on his forehead and is typing something on his tablet. Across the room, Angie lets out a loud sob. She rests her head on her mother's shoulder, and weeps unguardedly. Rachel whispers some words of comfort, but the crying only gets louder. The twins turn to watch, mouths open.

"Why she cry?" Mohsin asks.

"Because she's upset, buddy," Elias replies. "She's sad."

"Why?"

"She misses her mama."

"That her mama?"

"Yes, that's her."

Mohsin starts for the other table, but Sara stops him with a hand on the shoulder. "I think they'd rather be alone, honey." With a cry Mohsin wrestles himself out, and Elias has to run after him. "I'm so sorry," he tells the Cosgroves.

"It's okay, Elias," Angie replies. She wipes her pretty face with a tissue and smiles at Mohsin. The strap of her leopard-print shirt has fallen off her shoulder, but she doesn't readjust it. Sara isn't an especially jealous person, but today she is nearly overcome with envy for Angie's clean clothes, the bauble that dangles from her necklace, the pleather shoes that give her an extra two inches. Clearly Elias and Mohsin have both taken a liking to her. "It's okay. He doesn't bother me."

"Come on, buddy," Elias says, leading Mohsin back to their table and taking his seat across from Sara. In a whisper, he tells her that Angie's wedding is scheduled for December, but apparently her mom got into a fight with her roommate and won't make it to the wedding. That's probably why Angie is crying.

"How do you know?"

"We were talking before you came in."

"Ah." Sara pulls her son onto her lap. "You're such a sweet little boy," she tells him, giving him a kiss on the cheek. She smooths down his shirt, where yellow hibiscus and plumeria flowers float on a sea of blue. "I wish I could've gone to Hawaii," she says after a moment.

"We'll go someday," Elias says. "After you get out."

"I missed my chance." The feeling that life is passing her by hits her with such force she nearly doubles over from the pain. What has happened to her? In less than a year she has become someone she can hardly recognize, scared and filthy and stuck in an institution. She's tried to follow the rules, she's tried so hard, yet suspicion still hangs over her. She can't seem to shake it. How does she look under the lens of the cameras on the wall? From this side she's just a wife and mother trying to spend time with her family, but to the merchants of data from the other side she's a QUESTIONABLE trying to pass for a CLEAR.

The attendant is finished with the inventory; he puts his tablet in his back pocket and walks out, whistling his tune again. Mohsin reaches for a toy truck, revs the engine on his palm, then sets it down on the table. Mona is pressing the buttons on her stuffed parrot one after the other; the parrot whistles and chirps and clicks—a cacophony that seems to absorb her completely.

When Sara looks at Elias again she finds him staring. Does he sense that she's withholding something from him? All he wants to talk about is keeping her record clean, being docile, doing everything she's told in order to win her freedom. Why get into a fight and ruin this visit? He'll find out soon enough about her dark and obdurate nature, which not even ten months in retention have been able to correct.

"What is it?" Elias whispers, taking her hand. "Tell me."

"Oh, nothing," Sara says, interlacing her fingers in his. He has beautiful hands, she thinks, hands that have never labored with tools or harsh chemicals. She's never thought much about them before, but now their beauty is clear to her. Such things those hands could do to her between rustling sheets. Such things they did. She misses them every day. "I'm sorry."

"About what?"

"This," she says, her chest filling with new sorrow. She has tried to comply, she has tried so hard, but the truth is she can't follow the rules. Nor does she want to. "Everything."

Then another attendant enters the room, locks the door in open position, and stands with his arms on his hips. A female voice comes on the loudspeaker. "Your visit is complete. Please collect your belongings and proceed to the exit."

Elias puts the toys into the plastic bag, and picks up Mona. "I guess this is it."

"When are you coming back?" Sara asks, with Mohsin still in her arms.

"I'm not sure. My missed appointments have to be rescheduled, so it'll be a little while." With a glance at the Cosgroves, he adds, "Just please remember what the lawyer said, okay?"

"I won't forget." Sara puts Mohsin down, but now he grabs her knee and refuses to let go.

"Give me your hand, buddy," Elias says.

Sara bends down to her son's level. "I love you," she whispers into his ear. Quickly she pries his little hands from her legs while the attendant watches from the door.

Elias and Sara embrace, then he turns around and walks out behind Angie Cosgrove.

The clock says that thirty minutes have passed, but that seems like a lie.

Sara's room feels stiflingly warm when she returns. She splashes water on her face, then uses the toilet. There is spotting in her underwear. Her period is two days early; it must be the stress. She goes to the infirmary to report her period and ask for a pad, then takes her laundry back to the clothing office, where to her relief there is no line at all. But when she stands at the service window, she finds Victoria lounging in a chair with a comic book in her hands. "We ran out of clean uniforms again," Victoria says without looking up. "Try again tomorrow."

SAFE-X, INC.

Short-Term Forensic Observation Facilities Division
Facility: Madison
Location: Ellis, California
Timestamp: 11-08-09-02

Minutes compiled by: MeetingPro

The Safe-X staff meeting was called to order at 09:02 a.m.

Present: Chief Retention Officer ████. Senior Attendant Jackson. Attendants Yee and Ortega. Junior Attendant Williams. Case Manager Gardner. Administrative Assistant Doyle. Nurse Flores.
Absent: Senior Attendant Hinton
Guests: None.

CRO ████ asked how everyone was doing and if anyone had to evacuate.

Attendants Williams, Jackson, and Ortega raised their hands. Attendant Ortega said that his family is still with his wife's sister up north because his littlest has asthma and the air quality is still so bad in Ellis.

CRO ████ said it had been a tough week for sure. He wished to personally thank the staff for their professionalism during the evacuation of the facility, and he welcomed everyone back.

APPROVAL OF OCTOBER MEETING MINUTES

On a motion by CRO ████, with a second from Senior Attendant Jackson, the meeting minutes of October 8 were unanimously approved.

CRO REPORT

CRO ████ managed to procure some heart and diabetes medications through a short-term agreement with Fair View, but regular shipments are not expected for another four weeks.

Work on the ward expansion has resumed. CRO ████ had previously tied payment to timely completion of the project, so the construction company is sending a larger crew to make up for lost time. He is happy to say the project remains on deadline.

CRO ████ reported that the resident survey that was contracted for last month was completed successfully. No surveys are planned for this month, but he expects another one to start as early as the first week of December.

ATTENDANT REPORTS

Attendant Jackson reported that work contracts are running behind schedule due to the evacuation. The extended shifts will not be enough to meet deadlines.

CRO ████ asked how many shifts are vacant at the moment.

Attendant Jackson responded that there were 23.

CRO ████ asked why the numbers are so high, given that shifts have been extended.

Attendant Jackson replied that five residents are in the infirmary with the stomach flu.

CRO ████ asked Nurse Flores if they're really sick or if they're using this as an excuse not to work. He asked her to remember who she's dealing with.

Nurse Flores responded that she is trying to limit the spread of the virus.

CRO ████ asked how long it takes to get over this stupid virus.

Nurse Flores responded usually three days.

CRO ████ reminded Nurse Flores that he is running a retention facility, not a hospital. He asked Nurse Flores to apply careful judgment before admitting people to the infirmary.

Attendant Yee reported that all the cameras on the second floor are broken.

CRO ▮▮▮▮ said he was well aware, but what have you done about it.

Attendant Yee responded that he doesn't have purchase authority in the system.

CRO ▮▮▮▮ asked where Senior Attendant Hinton was.

Attendant Yee responded that he has been out on medical leave since the evacuation.

CRO ▮▮▮▮ expressed surprise that Senior Attendant Hinton had that many sick days available, but in a way that makes sense. CRO ▮▮▮▮ said he would get Senior Attendant Hinton on the phone today.

CRO ▮▮▮▮ asked if Attendant Yee had found who committed the vandalism.

Attendant Yee responded that he had conducted an investigation, but so far he did not have any leads.

CRO ▮▮▮▮ reprimanded Attendant Yee for his handling of this whole situation. He said he would order the camera replacements right away and urged everyone to use any and all available means to identify the vandal. This was a top priority, he said.

ADJOURNMENT

There being no further business, CRO ▮▮▮▮ moved that the meeting be adjourned. The motion was seconded by Attendant Jackson and carried unanimously. The meeting was adjourned at 09:46 a.m.

S HE STANDS OUTSIDE HER CHILDHOOD HOME. THE MAGNOLIA tree is bare, the paint on the front beams is peeling. It is a sunny afternoon in June, yet all the lights are on in the living room. There her mother sits by the window, reading the newspaper with a magnifying glass, the oxygen tank that her oncologist recommended propped up against the coffee table. Across from her, Saïd plays a game on his phone, swiping furiously as he chases a moving target across the screen. His cheeks are puffy and gray, and at his feet water is pooling into a puddle. The sound of a wind chime makes Sara turn around. Across the street, in a house that looks like a replica of her own, Elias sits on the porch with the twins, reading a book to them. The blooms on *his* magnolia tree are as big as saucers. "I really miss your mom," he tells the kids.

The next moment she is at her desk at the Getty. Around her, cubicles have slowly emptied; she is the last one in the office. She clicks through a slideshow on her screen, making sure the order of the photographs in her exhibit is correct and proofreading each caption. One of her favorite pictures appears—B386, showing three little girls leaning against a stone wall in the village of Chauen, a suspicious gaze directed at the Spanish photographer who has pointed his camera at them. With a surge of horror Sara notices that the caption is wrong. It says the picture was taken in Martil in 1929, when it should be Chauen in 1921. It's a good thing she caught this mix-up now; the exhibit will open in just two weeks. She logs in to the library, where she can find the correct caption in the catalogue, but no matter what search terms she uses or how long she scrolls through the archive, she cannot locate the master file. She picks up the phone to call a colleague for assistance.

The line rings and rings and turns into the morning bell.

Sara sits up, feeling worn out from the frantic search in her dream. Her imagination has once again taken her back to the moment she was retained: she's eager to fix whatever mistake landed her at Madison, but can't find the data point she needs to correct in order to prove her innocence. She hates these dreams, finds them stressful. On the other hand the earlier dream is just as morbid, placing her somewhere between the home of the dead and the home of the living. Usually when her mother visits her in a dream, it is a comfort. This time, it feels like a warning.

She steps into the bright hallway, where the other women are already lined up.

The gate opens with a loud buzz, and Hinton appears.

Sara never thought it possible to be relieved at the sight of this man, but that is exactly how she feels when she sees him walking down the hallway, his keys jingling with every step. Down the line he goes, taking his time with device check.

She is supposed to stand still, eyes fixed straight ahead, but instead she leans against the doorjamb and watches him. He isn't the lean, athletic man she first laid eyes on last December; there's an incipient stockiness to his build, the first hint of middle age. A trail of orange paint cuts across the pocket of the fleece jacket he wears over his uniform. She continues to stare openly at Hinton as he applies the scanner to Emily's neuroprosthetic. His eyes are puffy, his skin flakes along the jawline. And are those silver roots on his sideburns? She didn't know he dyed his hair!

The scanner beeps, Emily goes back inside.

On Hinton's neck is a fresh tattoo of a small grizzly bear, in a design identical to the one on the state flag. The bear is supposed to represent strength and bravery, two qualities she doesn't particularly associate with Hinton. As usual he smells like instant noodles, but beneath the food it seems to her she detects a note of alcohol.

Hinton puts the scanner to Sara's implant. "Jesus, you stink," he says, crinkling his nose. "I don't know how you can stand it, it's disgusting."

"At least I don't smell like cheap booze."

Their eyes meet.

"What'd you do with my stuff?" she asks.

He whistles. "I didn't know you were a writer."

Whether this is a sign of admiration or contempt, she has no idea, but it's clear he's read her notebook. She's spent the last week entertaining this exact possibility, so she expected to be prepared for it, yet it feels like a kick in the stomach. All those pages she wrote about the memories her dreams brought up, the hopes she nurtured, her desires and frustrations with this place—he's read everything. She feels light-headed, has to steady herself against the doorjamb. "So you still have it," she manages to say. "Please give it back to me. Please."

The word *please* elicits an amused smile from him. "If you dream of having sex with me, all you had to do was ask."

Though her back is turned to her room, Sara knows Emily is listening. Across the hall, at the doorway of 209, Ana and Stephanie chuckle. They'll tell the others and, because no story resists embellishment when it travels, rumor will have her sleeping with all the attendants by the end of the day. Another abasement inflicted by Hinton.

She's known a lot of Hintons in her life, especially in the world of museum work. Her own department, an all-women group that includes several archivists with graduate degrees and twenty years of experience, is run like a fiefdom by a man who was brought in from outside the institution three years ago. Jim Klass had a habit of making sweeping changes, and whenever he was challenged about it he would sideline the women who disagreed with him, dropping them from meetings or berating them over insignificant details when they did attend. It took Sara a while to understand that her boss loved to exercise control at work because he was so lacking in it in his private life: for years he had been involved in a lawsuit against a baby-food manufacturer that he accused of having caused his younger son's autism. Perhaps as a result of this protracted and expensive suit, he tended to view every discussion as an argument that had to be won decisively by one party or the other. The only time he backed away from one of his faddish initiatives was when one of the women under him had leverage.

Hinton moves to leave, but Sara puts a hand on his arm. "Wait," she says. "Why were you hiding in the walk-in refrigerator?"

He swats her hand, but the grin on his face has disappeared. Now we're talking.

WITH THE SCAN FINISHED, SHE RUSHES DOWNSTAIRS WITH EMILY. There are already three people waiting outside the clothing office, even though it's only 6:15. They join the line, Emily teasing her already, asking how long she's had a crush on Hinton, and Sara shaking her head, saying, "Don't even." But it's fine. It's fine. She's been fortunate in her roommate, she knows, and after so much time together she's learned to trust her. Emily could've filled out several Basic-10s if she'd had the inclination, but so far she's kept everything she's seen or heard to herself.

The line reaches the end of the corridor by the time Victoria arrives on duty. Her hair is in a bun, but instead of the standard low knot she has braided and pinned hers into a more elaborate updo, apparently without fear that an attendant might dock her for improper grooming. On her lips she wears red lipstick, one of the most expensive items in the commissary. Sara can't recall her wearing it before; the wine-dark color suits her, though it also makes her look older than the twenty-two years she celebrated not long ago.

With a thunderous roar, Victoria rolls up the service window.

Sara picks up her laundry bag, eager for the line to move. It is a chilly morning, but made cheerful somehow by the sound of the rain, the first of the season, which falls with great abandon on the world outside. The patter is invigorating, as if she herself were a tender plant, its leaves scorched, now opening itself up to receive sustenance.

Emily's turn comes. Eyes fixed on Victoria, she holds out her bag. "Morning."

"You can just put it down," Victoria says, pointing at the counter. "Fill out the form."

"Right. Sure." Emily faces the screen, taps out her request, then swivels the tablet back. "I like your lipstick," she says.

Victoria nods distractedly. She catalogues the items Emily turned in, and gets replacements. "Next."

Sara puts her mesh bag on the counter and quickly fills out the form on the tablet before turning it over for inspection. The piles of laundry lining the back wall are short, but she is relieved to see that uniforms are still available. She will get one this morning.

Victoria makes a note that one of the sheets has been torn. "Oof. That's gonna cost ya."

"Yeah, I know."

She regards Sara with new interest, but after a moment brings her fresh linens, a shirt, a pair of pants, underwear and socks. "It's good you came early," she says. "We're not expecting another delivery of uniforms today."

Sara clutches the clean clothes tightly to her chest.

"Laundry service is slower with you out," Victoria continues. "And now Toya. What's going on with the two of you? You came down with the quitting disease at the same time?"

Victoria has been at Madison, what, five or six months? Not quite a long hauler, but not a newbie, either. By now, she's realizing there are only three things she can do: obey, resist, or withdraw. Everyone tries to obey the rules, in the beginning. But inevitably, even when they don't mean to, they break one. Safe-X makes its largest share of profits not from the observation period of twenty-one days that the RAA has mandated but from the postponements it generates through its complicated disciplinary system. Intentionally resisting the rules has the same result as unintentionally breaking them—higher risk scores. But withdrawing their cooperation at least lets them exercise what power they have and strike back at the company that's keeping them here. Victoria has been here long enough to understand that.

"I wouldn't say it's a disease," Sara says, tilting her head. "It's more like a good fever. Like when your body's immune system is fighting a virus." She smiles. "It's nothing to be afraid of."

But Victoria's attention seems to have shifted already. "Next."

Sara heads straight to the locker room, where she discards her dirty uniform and steps into a shower stall. Clean clothes haven't been a concern before, but being deprived of them for so long has opened her eyes to just how removed she has become from her life in Los Angeles. She's starting to think back on that life with the nostalgia she has for the years she spent in Berkeley during college, or London during her year abroad, places she no longer inhabits but that have left a trace on her character. As this place will. She'll always be a retainee, even if she leaves Madison tomorrow. This, too, she has in common with the other women here.

As she steps out of the shower, she finds Ana styling her hair at the sink. Drops of the gluey product she uses have fallen on her growing belly, staining the clean shirt she just got from the clothing office. "Shit," she whispers, and shifts to her side against the sink. Emily faces the mirror in her bra, carefully applying cream to the base of her neck, the folds of her armpits, the inside of her elbows. The red bumps all over her upper body look like markers on a map. "It just keeps getting worse," she complains. "I don't know what to do anymore."

"Maybe it's the soap you're using," Sara says.

"I stopped using soap."

"The water, then."

"Nothing I can do about that."

Sara puts on her underwear, shirt, and pants, pausing at each item to savor the feeling of its cleanliness. "It could be one of these products," she says, pointing to the janitorial cart that Marcela has left in the passageway.

"It was bad before I got put on custodial."

Ana washes her hands at the sink. "Well, then, you're allergic to retention."

"Sounds about right." Emily puts her shirt back on, then rolls up her sleeve so the tattoo on her arm shows. Staring at the mirror, she flexes her right bicep; the helmeted figure of the firefighter quivers. A look of satisfaction passes over her face. "At least I look good, right?"

"Right," Sara says with a smile.

Marcela comes into the locker room just then, and places the spray bottle of glass cleaner in its space on the cart. "Jackson is waiting for you outside," she tells Emily. "Says she needs you to report to the laundry room right away. It's an emergency."

Joy draining from her face, Emily glares at Sara as if it's her fault, then leaves.

"How are you feeling?" Sara asks Ana. When they were at Victorville the poor woman had to station herself outside the bathroom to make it easier to reach the toilet. "Still getting morning sickness?"

Ana nods, puts a protective hand on her belly. "I feel like it's getting worse."

"It's probably the stress," Sara says. "And the food here isn't helping. You know, it would be easier on you if you didn't work. If you could get proper rest."

Ana chuckles. "That'll be the day."

"I'm serious." Sara takes her time gathering her filthy clothes into her mesh bag. "Why shouldn't you rest? You're in your third trimester now, right? If they say you're a danger to your baby, the least they could do is let you rest so you can keep it safe. You have to think about your health, you know, because they're not. Let them pay to run this place, they have all the money they need for that. There's no need to contribute to your own detention."

But when Sara tries to catch Ana's gaze in the mirror, she looks away.

ANOTHER FOOD SERVICE WORKER HAS BEEN FELLED BY THE STOMACH flu, so Alice has been moved from Trailer C to cafeteria duty. She works the service window at lunch, handling both the hot wells and the cold foods by herself. Sweat seeps through the edges of her headwrap, darkening its pale green to an emerald color around the hairline. Sara asks how the day is going, asks if the mac and cheese has pork in it, if that green stuff is creamed spinach, but Alice won't look her in the eye. That's how it's been ever since Sara mentioned a strike. Alice quickly fills out the tray, her attention on the warmers, determined to prove herself a model employee.

Sara carries her food into the dining room, and finds Toya eating alone at a table by the far wall. She has styled her hair à la gamine, with a part down the side, and refreshed its color to charcoal.

"You look great," Sara says as she sits down. Whatever the handbook may claim, their bodies are their own, and every act of self-expression, however small, is a refusal to cede dominion over it. Her gaze travels across the cafeteria; it's half-empty today.

"Jackson staggered the trailers' lunch breaks," Toya explains.

"Still trying to make the new deadline for Vox-R?"

"And she might. She got two newbies this morning, and already put them to work."

The day is dark, made for brooding, yet Sara feels chatty, and apparently so does Toya—she relays a rumor that Hinton and Yee got into a loud argument outside the library, an occurrence they both find utterly unusual because Hinton never loses his temper. At all times he maintains a patrician attitude toward the junior agents, giving them direction or advice. He's been acting strange since the evacuation.

"I hope you two are happy," Emily says as she sits down with her tray. She starts to eat, jabbing angrily at her mac and cheese. "It's insanely hot in the laundry room, and the thermostat isn't working today."

"It never did."

"You could've at least waited until the schedule eased up. That nasty stomach bug is still going around." She raises herself from her seat to survey the dining room. "Where's Marcela?"

"She's fine," Toya replies. "I saw her leave when I was coming in. She got called to clean up vomit in the infirmary."

"That's gross." Emily shakes her head. "Do you know how much laundry there is right now? Claire and I can't catch up."

"That's the point," Sara says. "This place can't run without us."

"Look, I get what you're trying to do, I really do. But this is just stupid. You're not gonna change anything about this place. You're just making things harder for the rest of us."

"That's not what we want," Sara replies.

"You're free to work," Toya says with a frown, "and we're free to not."

"Well, *you* not working affects *me* working. Did you stop to think about that?"

Sara puts a hand on Emily's arm to reason with her, but all of a sudden Victoria appears. "Is this seat taken?"

Emily's face lights up. "It is now."

Victoria sits down and, while the other three women watch, goes about wiping down her tray and spork with a medicated wipe she pulls from a brand-new package. She's fastidious about it; the process takes a couple of minutes to complete. Only then does she begin to eat. Her fingers are long and dainty, though her nails are bitten to the quick. "All this starch is killing me," she complains. "I feel so bloated."

"What're you talking about?" Emily replies. "You're so tiny."

"I used to be, anyway," Victoria says, in a tone that suggests she's used to getting compliments about her looks. She takes a spoonful of mac and cheese and chews it slowly. Then, pointing her spork at Toya, she says, "I like your hair like this. Makes you look younger."

Toya touches the ends of her hair. "You think so? It's not too short?"

"Not at all. My mom wears it like this."

"Well, then," Toya replies, her voice sharpened by irritation, "I guess your mom has good taste."

"Oh, she does. She has excellent taste in everything except men."

Emily chuckles. "What about you?"

"I do okay." Victoria grins. "Not just with men." She turns her gaze on Emily. *You intrigue me,* her eyes seem to say, *how come I didn't notice you before?*

What a flirt, Sara thinks, not without admiration. In her mind a picture forms of Victoria at a backyard party, in a sundress and with her hair finally free of its bun, surrounded by a clump of suitors eager to impress her.

"Did I hear you got moved to laundry?" Victoria asks.

All of a sudden Emily is at a loss for words.

"They put you with Claire Lopez, right?"

Another nod.

"And you like working in laundry?"

"Well." Emily swallows her food. "I mean, it's work. There's not much to like. But it's all right."

"Is it now?" Toya says with a laugh. "It's not too hot in there for you, what with that thermostat not working?"

Emily flushes. She gives Toya a look that says *Please please please shut up.*

Listening to the banter, Sara becomes curious about Victoria Aguilar. "You're new in the clothing office," she says, taking a bite of the mystery meat that sits next to the mac and cheese, and steeling herself against the taste. "Weren't you in groundskeeping? Why'd you switch?"

"I didn't want to be out in the sun all day," Victoria replies.

"I see."

"But you know," Victoria adds, "what you said this morning got me thinking. So many people are sick with the stomach flu right now that it would only take ten or fifteen of us to quit for this place to shut down."

Sara has always thought of Victoria as a performer, what with her mime routines and the card games she likes to play in the exercise yard, but up close it's clear that there's more substance to her. Where others have avoided talk of the strike, or ignored it altogether, she seems unafraid of it. Not just unafraid, but downright eager. "Why'd they make you take that urine test?" Sara asks.

"I guess someone filled out a Basic-10 on me."

"But why'd they report you, do you think? Did you make yourself some enemies around here or what?"

Victoria shrugs. "Probably."

"Some people don't need a reason to snitch," Emily puts in, her voice suddenly grave. "They do it for kicks, that's all. They get off watching someone else being punished."

"Exactly. But it didn't matter. My test was clear."

"See?"

"Anyway, I think you're on to something," Victoria continues. "I never wanted to work for these people anyway. I was told I'd be here three weeks, and it turned into five months. I'm sick of it. Let them figure out how to run this place without our help."

"You got a point," Emily says.

"It's amazing, isn't it," Toya says with a glance at Sara, "the paths that people have to travel before they see the light."

FALL MIGHT BE HERE, SARA THINKS AS SHE WALKS AROUND THE TRACK. The sun is out, and hot enough to burn the eyes, but there's a bite to the breeze that blows across the exercise yard. The women are lifting weights, playing cards, eating snacks, all in white uniforms that, no matter how dirty they might become, stand out against the blacktop.

Meanwhile, Jackson sits under the breezeway, smoking a cigarette, lost in her thoughts. She's waiting for the shift change at 1:30, when Walsh will come out to relieve her and she can go back to her office, there to worry about her looming deadline. She hasn't bothered with earrings today, either, and her nail polish is chipped.

The attendants spend so much time monitoring us, Sara thinks, it never occurs to them that we've been monitoring them, too. We learn their schedules, their tastes, their habits and quirks. Sometimes even their fears. Sara continues walking around the track, but a minute before the shift change, she heads indoors to the administrative office.

Her skin breaks into goose bumps; the office has AC, so it's a good ten degrees cooler than the rest of the building. One wall is painted a cheerful yellow, its only adornment the stylized lightbulb that serves as Safe-X's logo. Another wall bears various plaques and commendations, many of them for Hinton, whose eyes follow her from six framed portraits at once. Fear burns in her stomach, but it's the good kind of fear, the fear you get when you're about to do something you should've done long ago.

Hinton has just arrived to relieve Williams. He's still getting settled at the desk, finding a space for his water bottle and his fleece jacket. Doyle, the administrative assistant, is chattering on the phone, her back turned away from the service window.

"Excuse me," Sara says.

Doyle swivels on her chair. She's a pretty woman in her forties, with freckles dotting her face and a silver ring through her septum. "Hang on," she tells whoever is on the other end of the line. "What is it?"

"I'd like to file a grievance." Sara's voice is clear, every syllable enunciated.

"Material or administrative? I only handle material complaints."

"For one of the attendants? I guess that would be administrative."

Doyle points to the kiosk ten feet from the service window. "Don't you see the sign that says Administrative Complaint? Or is it that you can't read?"

"Thank you," Sara says cheerfully. She moves to one of the kiosks, waits for the system to recognize her face, and follows the prompts on the screen. WHAT WOULD YOU LIKE TO REPORT? *Misconduct.* DATE OF INCIDENT. *October 30.* TYPE OF INCIDENT. *Dereliction of duty.*

Before she can click to the next tab, Hinton is at her elbow. "What're you doing?"

"Filling out a grievance."

"Stop it," he hisses.

"Give me my journal, then."

"I don't have it."

"You threw it out?" The shock of this nearly takes her breath away. She turns back to the tablet and clicks on the next screen, typing quickly on the digital keyboard. NAME OF OFFENDER. *Hinton.* INCIDENT DESCRIPTION. *While Madison was on alert for the Perris fire, and the attendants were preparing for the evacuation, Senior Attendant Hinton abandoned his post and went to hide in . . .*

"Stop it," he says again, pulling her away from the screen to stop her from typing. "Stop and listen to me for a second. I didn't throw it out."

"Where is it, then?"

"I had it when we evacuated. Put it in the trunk of my car. But I couldn't go home, 'cause of the fire. I had to spend a few nights at my cousin's house in Upland before I could go back to my place." His voice turns angry. "My roof was damaged, all right? And I can't get anyone to come out and look at it for another three weeks, so I've been a little busy dealing with that. I don't give a shit about your precious little book, I'll get it back for you."

"When?"

Doyle has stopped talking on her phone. She's hunched over her keyboard, pretending to work while eavesdropping on their conversation. Somewhere down the hall, a door opens and closes.

"When I have a day off. It's a heck of a drive to Upland, in case you didn't know."

"You just said you had it in the trunk of your car."

He heaves a sigh. "I left it at my cousin's house. Like I said, I had a lot on my mind with the fire and everything. I'll get it for you next Sunday."

"I can't wait that long."

"I said I'll get it for you, and I will."

Sara wavers, and in that moment of hesitation Hinton touches the CANCEL button on the form. "It's always better to resolve grievances informally. That's what it says, right there in the handbook. Section 8.4. Look it up."

Good morning, residents. This is your chief retention officer speaking. As of this morning twenty-two residents and three staff members have caught the norovirus, bringing the total number of cases to thirty-one. I am placing this facility under a public health emergency. [a cough] Excuse me. If you have gastrointestinal symptoms, you should immediately report your case to Senior Attendant Jackson. She will be making shift reassignments across the facility to ensure that we can meet our commitments.

Please try to isolate from others if you're sick, and make sure to drink plenty of fluids. All residents should wash their hands with soap, avoid sharing utensils or personal care products, and maintain good hygiene. Disinfectant spray is available at the commissary for those who wish to clean their rooms.

Fresh linens may not be available at this time. Residents who need them should do their own washing at the utility sinks in the exercise yard. A limited supply of soap is available for this purpose on a first-come, first-served basis.

Once again, this facility is under a public health emergency. We need everyone to work together if we want to stop the spread. *Please* do your part.

EASY FOR HIM TO SAY, SARA THINKS. THE CRO MANAGES THIS facility and four others from his home, where he can work undisturbed on finding new contracts for Safe-X, negotiating terms and conditions, and ensuring that profits continue to rise. The smooth baritone of his voice may be familiar to Sara, but she has never spoken to him or seen him up close—he doesn't interact with individual retainees.

Fifteen minutes after his announcement, the commissary sells out of pink bismuth and electrolyte drinks. The small bottle of hand sanitizer that Elias shipped to Sara before the wildfire becomes a high-value commodity: she is offered lip balm for it, then ramen noodles, beef jerky, carrot chips, a battered copy of *The Metamorphosis*.

The book is impossible to resist.

She is pleased with the trade, but walking back to her room she passes Linh throwing up in 203, and worries she might have made a mistake. Maybe she should've kept the hand sanitizer. Getting sick is the last thing she needs. But aren't soap and water better at warding off contamination? All she has to do is be extra mindful about washing her hands. She'll be fine.

She spends the morning reading, taking special pleasure in being able to underline a passage she likes or circle a word or a phrase that surprises her. In her life before, she had hundreds of books, so many that they were piled in leaning ziggurats along the wall of her bedroom. She walked past them every day, but it is only now that she understands what luxury it is to own a book.

If Sara feels sick, it is for home. Home is a baby's sock under the coffee table, wildflowers on the hallway wallpaper, a window that opens to let in fresh air. Home is the sweet babbling rising from the double cribs after she turns off the light, and the barking of the neighbor's dog late at night. There he goes again, Elias complains, he's going to wake the kids. Home is the warmth of her husband's body against hers whenever she stirs at night. The music of Miles Davis on a Sunday morning. A bowl of apricots, still damp after a rinse. The squawk of seagulls at the drive-through down the street. Elias saying "Want to take a walk? I'm feeling cooped up all of a sudden." Rooms that aren't scorching hot, rooms that aren't freezing cold. Water in a tall, clear glass.

She reads until her attention is drawn by a conversation taking place in the corridor not far from her room. Jackson and Ortega are helping a civilian who stands on a stepladder, pointing a miniature flashlight at one of the broken Guardian cameras. It must be a technician from the video-surveillance company, sent here to assess the extent of the sabotage. He pokes at a camera with a miniature screwdriver, then whistles in admiration. Whoever did this knew what they were doing, he says. It would've been enough to rip the cords, but they also broke the lenses and cut off the emergency batteries. There are twenty-two cameras in the hallway of the residential floor; every one of them will have to be replaced.

"Damn," Ortega says. "How long is that gonna take?"

The technician consults his tablet, then issues a verdict: two weeks.

"That long?"

"Sorry, man. We're dealing with shipping delays right now."

Sara smiles as she returns to her cot. Had she been working her usual shift in Trailer D she would never have heard this valuable piece of information. Two weeks will give her time to talk to everyone on the floor about the strike.

So far, though, her efforts haven't gained much momentum. Toya, Emily, and Victoria are the only retainees who've quit their jobs. The others are afraid of getting into trouble, or they're sick with the norovirus, or they need the paycheck, or they're so tired from the extended shifts that Jackson has scheduled to meet the new Vox-R deadline that all they want is a moment of peace and quiet before lights out.

At the cafeteria she eats lunch with the other strikers, noticing at once that Alice has elected to sit in the opposite direction from them. Marcela is working through lunch; she's been asked to clean up the infirmary again. But many of the tables are empty, Sara notices, which makes it easier for the cameras to record conversations, even if they're practiced at keeping their voices hushed. For now, silence is the only protection.

She tries to eat as slowly as she can; today's serving of turkey casserole seems even more frugal than usual. She finishes the cup of tapioca pudding on her tray, running her thumb on the rim to catch the last bit. Only after she's licked her finger does she realize what she's done. Who knows where that cup has been? The service counter, the tray, the seat, the table—all these are potential vectors of disease. The meal turns stressful, a protracted exercise in remembering anything else she might have touched.

While her friends head outside, she goes to the bathroom to wash up, but there is no soap and the paper towel dispenser is empty. She rinses her hands in scalding hot water, counting to thirty before she turns off the tap, and dries her hands on her shirt.

Walking through the main hall afterwards, she passes a clump of retainees talking beneath the Arnautoff mural while a janitorial cart sits beside them. One of the women suddenly detaches herself from the group, puts a hand over her mouth, but can't stop herself from spewing a thick stream of green bile, which lands on the floor, spattering the other retainees' uniforms. "I'm sorry," she says helplessly. It all happened so fast that no one in the group had a chance to get out of the way. Sara quickens her pace, giving the group a wide berth as she leaves the main hall.

She is relieved when she finally reaches the exercise yard; there is enough space here to avoid unnecessary contact with others. It is a sunny afternoon in November, and the air smells faintly of the hot tar that a city crew spread on the highway yesterday.

Jackson has left the shade of her post under the breezeway. She's walking the perimeter in the opposite direction from Sara, stopping every once in a while to chat with one retainee or another. By the time Sara finishes her third lap, Jackson is talking to Victoria, who has lingered at a table with her deck of cards after Toya and Emily left. Sara comes to stand at the light pole nearby, using it to steady herself as she does her stretches, all the while eavesdropping on their conversation.

"So why'd you quit your job?" Jackson is asking.

"Didn't feel like doing it anymore." Victoria picks up the deck in her right hand and peels off cards one after the other with the thumb of her left hand. Her movements are languid, yet proficient. A can of Coke sits in front of her, the metal casing sweating in the heat.

"I can always put you somewhere else. Maybe custodial?"

"No, thanks."

"If you're worried about the virus, I'll find you another spot. It doesn't have to be custodial."

Victoria stacks the cards in front of her and makes as if to stand.

But Jackson takes a seat at the table. "Want a cigarette?"

Victoria hesitates. Then: "No, I'm all right."

Jackson lights up, letting out a huge puff of smoke. "So who put you up to it?" she says, crossing her legs and holding her cigarette aloft. She is at pains to look relaxed, but instead she looks affected.

"I'm not up to anything. I don't know what you're talking about."

"You don't? Because you and Emily Robbins quit within minutes of each other. That girl is up to no good, you should know that by now if you know nothing else."

Victoria splits the deck in two, and riffles the cards together. Then, her movements swift and precise, she creates a bridge and squares the cards together again. Casino style. "No one put me up to it, boss," she says with a chuckle. "And definitely not that old cow."

"Uh-huh."

Victoria fans the deck on the table. "Pick a card."

Jackson pulls one, looks at it, then puts it back. "If you don't want to take a full shift, I can get you a half shift two or three times a week. Nice and easy."

Victoria shuffles the deck, then fans the cards again. She pulls out an ace of spades. "This your card?"

Jackson nods. "So how about it? A half shift three times a week?"

"Nah, I'm good."

"All right, then. But just so you know, your score's gonna go up again. Which is a shame." She stands up, dusting off her knees. "I thought you were one of the smart ones."

Jackson returns to the sentry post under the breezeway, from where she surveys the retainees scattered across the yard, two or three of them exercising, but the others just resting or getting some sun before having to go back to work. Then she pulls out her Tekmerion.

Sara comes to sit at the table. "Will you show me how you do that trick?"

Victoria takes a long swig from her soda. She shuffles the cards again and fans them in a wide arc in front of Sara. "Keep your eyes open," she says with a smile.

Sara picks a card, then puts it back.

"See where my thumb is?" Victoria asks. "That's how I mark the card you picked. Then I just shuffle the deck like this, see, fan it, and voilà. This is your card, right?"

"Yes, it is. Nicely done."

Victoria demonstrates a few more plays, the tricks becoming more elaborate and harder to spot as time passes. When the sun reaches their table, she shields her face with one hand, but soon she heads back to the main building, leaving Sara alone.

On the other side of the exercise yard, a huge white truck beeps as it reverses toward the service entrance. Two construction workers in dusty uniforms appear at the gate, guiding the driver to where the vehicle should stop. They load their materials and equipment into the bed of the truck then drive off, trailing a cloud of exhaust.

The yard gets quiet again.

By the looks of it, construction is nearly done. Twenty new rooms will be opened, each housing two retainees, or sometimes three. All Jackson has to do is wait, Sara thinks; she'll have a fresh batch of workers to assign in a few weeks, or maybe just days. Yet she's determined to fill up every spot on her schedule, even in the middle of an outbreak. Jackson seems troubled by the possibility of a strike—worried, even—despite the fact that she's a lowly worker, too, replaceable the moment she outlasts her usefulness to the company.

TEKMERION REPORT

Report: A765-4920
Timestamp: 11-14-03-29
Attendant: Jackson
Subjects: Sara Hussein, Victoria Aguilar

At approximately 3:30 this afternoon, I observed Retainees Aguilar and Hussein talking in the exercise yard. Retainee Aguilar showed Retainee Hussein one of her card scams, the three-card monte. Retainee Aguilar demonstrated the scam three times, after which Retainee Hussein tried it successfully.

EJ

MEMO

From: Eugenia Jackson
To: CRO ▮▮▮▮▮
Timestamp: 11-15-08-05

Please find this week's schedule attached. The vacancies due to the public health emergency are highlighted in yellow, those due to releases are in green, those due to resignations are in red. Trailers are running at 72% capacity, with contract completion projected at December 15 for Vox-R and January 8 for NovusFilm. Staffing areas that have become critical (below 50% capacity) are custodial and laundry work, which retainees have been avoiding because of the norovirus. To improve work operations, I request approval for the incentives below:

- Priority access to food service line
- Extended visiting time (15 extra minutes, redeemable at next family visit)
- Expedited processing of outstanding petitions
- Preferred medical service (access to NSAIDs if requested)
- Reassignment to room with a window (depending on availability)

Please let me know at your earliest convenience which of these you would be willing to approve.

Yours sincerely,
Eugenia Jackson

cc: Andrew Hinton

AN HOUR AFTER BREAKFAST, HER STOMACH STARTS TO HURT. Maybe I'm just reacting to the ambient panic, she thinks, maybe it's gas or indigestion. She drinks water from the fountain, careful that her lips not graze the spout, but a few minutes later her mouth fills with bile and she has to throw up, barely reaching the toilet bowl in time. The eggs and potatoes she had this morning come out, in eruptions that surprise her with their violence. A stream of orange vomit sluices down the toilet to the floor.

"Oh, boy," Emily says from her cot, where she's been drawing her comic book since she quit her job. She has borrowed Victoria's pillow, using it to prop up her drawing pad, and over this new setup she watches Sara. With a socked foot, she pushes to the edge of the mattress the pack of sanitizing wipes Elias sent, and which they've been sharing since the start of the outbreak.

Sara wipes the toilet and floor as best as she can, washes her hands, then lies down on her cot. Soon she is shivering under the blanket. The last time she was sick was with a cold she'd caught at a friend's wedding, the spring before her retention. She'd spent two days at home, snug under her duvet, watching movies, and when Elias brought the twins from daycare he also brought her that chicken soup she liked from the deli down the street and some flowers to cheer her up. Back then she'd felt sorry for herself, being stuck in bed when she could be playing with the kids or going out for a walk. But her retention has erased that kind of aimless self-pity. She has to withstand the pains and aches in her body.

SHE WALKS INTO THE MAIN HALL, PAUSING AS ALWAYS TO ADMIRE THE Arnautoff mural. She has a thick book under one arm, a biography of Sayyida al-Hurra that she needs to return to the library before it closes. Hinton comes out of the sentry post just then, wearing blue dungarees, but no shirt. From shoulder to wrist his arms are bandaged, and his face is puffy—perhaps a side effect of whatever medication he has been put on for his injuries. "Huthein," he calls out to her. His speech is distorted, the sibilants mushy for lack of teeth. What happened to him? "Thay where you are," he says. "Wait."

"What is it?"

Three retainees on their way back from the cafeteria stop to watch.

"What'd I do?" Sara asks. "I'm just going to the library, that's all."

"I thaid, wait." Hinton steps inside the attendant post and presses a button, whereupon two police detectives instantly materialize at the entrance to the main hall. One is tall and skinny, the other short and fat, just like in the movies. This isn't real, Sara thinks, this isn't really happening. When one of them takes a cigarette out of his mouth, and stubs it under his foot before walking up to her, she almost laughs.

But as the detective gets closer, a sick feeling comes over her. She looks at her hands, and finds that instead of a book, she's holding a can of fuel.

A big, red, five-gallon can, enough to set fire to the whole place.

How did it get here? Only a minute ago, she had a book. Now she has the gasoline, material evidence that she's the criminal they've been alleging she is all this time.

The three retainees watch and whisper amongst themselves.

"Sara Hussein," the short cop tells her, bringing out handcuffs, "you have the right to remain silent."

SHE IS SCROLLING THROUGH NABE AT THE PARK WHILE THE TWINS play in the sandbox. Elias has gone to buy coffee from the cart across the street, leaving her to watch the kids. He's taking his sweet time, she notices. It's an early morning in winter, but the sun is already hot. "Come out of there, guys," she tells the kids after a moment. "Let me put some more sunscreen on you." She rummages through the tote bag that sits beside her. In it are diapers, wipes, a small bottle of lotion, an empty Altoids tin, some tissues, cheese snacks, a bottle of water, bobby pins, anything and everything except sunscreen. She forgot it at home—again.

And the award for the worst mother of the year goes to . . .

God, she needs coffee. At least she has the kids' wide-brimmed hats, she didn't forget those. "Come out of there, guys," she tells the kids. "Let me put these on you." Mohsin shakes his head no. With a bright yellow plastic shovel, he digs a hole in the sand, drops his shoe in it, and starts shoveling sand over it. Mona helpfully pours water over it from her watering can. There goes another pair of shoes, Sara thinks. She really, really needs coffee. Why is Elias taking so long? "Come out for a second, please," she says. "Let me put these hats on you."

Mona uses her rake on a different patch of sand, while Mohsin crawls to a new spot, directly under the sun.

"Come out of there, please."

It's as if they can't hear her.

"I'm not gonna tell you again," she says between her teeth. Stepping into the sandbox she picks up her son and, over his screams of protest, gets his hat on him. As she's about to put him down, she realizes she's wearing white from head to toe—widow's white.

The park turns into her apartment, the sandbox into the living room rug. The imam has arrived with a piece of paper for her to sign, so he can proceed with the funeral arrangements. All around her are friends and neighbors who have come to offer condolences on the sudden death of her husband. It's unbelievable, they say, shaking their heads. He was a good swimmer; he might've made it out of the river if he wasn't carrying two backpacks.

In the corner Elias's mother wails, points a finger at Sara—who wakes up with a start, eyes crusty with dried tears, and has to throw up again.

FOR TWO DAYS SHE LIES IN BED. THE WORLD OUTSIDE HER ROOM CEASES to exist, and the only news she hears comes to her secondhand, from Emily. The housing expansion is complete, the construction workers are gone. Ana's boyfriend proposed to her when he came to visit this morning. Supposedly he dropped on one knee and gave her a candy ring, bought from the vending machine. It's kind of sweet, right? Another fire has erupted, this time in Klamath, where it's already burned 80,000 acres. Why doesn't Governor García activate the Western States Firefighting Alliance? That's exactly what the treaty is for, situations like this—he's making containment harder the longer he waits. That idiot Williams is still trying to chat up Victoria, he won't take a hint. Another thirty-five people have caught the virus, and one threw up on her keyboard in Trailer C. She couldn't run out to the bathrooms in the main building, and there are no trash cans in the trailer.

Sara feels more settled on the third day. After morning device check she has stamina enough to clean herself up and make her bed. It is a cool morning in November; she shivers as she stands at the window, waiting for the old woman. A lanky teenage boy appears at the bus stop instead, dragging a metal cart filled with straw goods. He has long black hair that he wears in two neat braids, and narrow shoulders that disappear under the bulk of his jacket. Maybe the old woman has been hurt in the fire, and now her grandson, or her nephew, or a neighborhood kid is in charge of selling her wares in her absence. Standing at the bus stop he stares at his phone, never looking up from it no matter how long Sara waits at the window. Then the bus arrives and carries him off.

Every day is a struggle, Sara thinks. We need friends if we are to make it through.

Across the room Emily is gathering her things for a shower. So far she's managed to dodge the virus: she jokes that her mother's cooking has given her a stomach of steel, she can handle anything. After she goes down to breakfast, Sara reads a few pages of *The Metamorphosis*, then puts it away, stacking it neatly above her letters. With any luck, she might have some mail today. She runs a finger on the framed picture of the twins, then yawns and stretches her arms above her head. She really is feeling better this morning, she might even be able to eat.

But at the cafeteria, the smell of the oatmeal makes her nauseous, and the growling from her stomach sounds like a preemptive protest. It feels good to be out of her room, though, to go through the motions of an ordinary day, even if she can't eat. She carries her tray to one of the tables by the window, where Emily and Victoria are chatting happily. "Where's everyone?" Sara asks as she sits down.

"Toya and Alice are both sick," Victoria tells her. "I don't know about Marcela."

They resume their conversation. It sounds like they're talking about Reno, a city Sara associates with a lyric from a country song, but that Emily knows quite well, having grown up only a few miles from the border with Nevada. "I used to work as a cashier at the ski resort in Reno, back when it still snowed there, but what I really wanted was to work at the casinos, 'cause the pay was better."

"Doesn't pay much, actually," Victoria replies. "I made most of my money in tips. I got licensed so I could work in San Manuel, and on a good day I could clear eleven, twelve hundred in cash."

"Where's San Manuel?"

"You know, up in the Mojave?"

Emily shakes her head. "I've never been. When did you work there?"

While the two chatter, Sara looks out at the grounds, where one of the gardeners is showing the other how to spread fertilizer on the lawn. The ritual is one of the constants of her childhood: every November, gardens up and down the street from her parents' were covered in a pungent, brown mixture, the stench lasting for days. It will be unpleasant to sit outside today, when all she wants is to feel the sun on her face; she's desperate for some fresh air after three days in her room.

The squeak of rubber shoes on the vinyl floors makes her turn away from the window. In quick, determined steps, Hinton and Williams approach her table. What will they come up with this time? She's been surprised, these last few months, at how inventive the attendants can be in interpreting the handbook. If you loiter, you're lazy. If you rush, you must be up to no good. One day your hair is messy, another your nails are too long. Hinton is better at this game than all the others combined, and now that she's not working she knows she's more of a target than ever.

But the attendants don't look at her at all. Williams is pointing his Tekmerion at Victoria.

"What're you doing?" Victoria asks, amused.

Standing at Williams's elbow, Hinton waits as the system pulls up Victoria's file. "Enter it as a Class A," Hinton orders. "And then when you get to the next screen, I'll show you the box for vandalism. It's not obvious on this software update."

"Okay," Williams replies. He starts typing, his lips moving silently, like a child working out a math problem.

"Wait, what?" Victoria says, jumping up to her feet. Sunlight strikes her face, bringing out her almond eyes, her perfect cheekbones. But it's the fierceness of her expression that makes her stand out. "What vandalism?" she asks, ignoring Williams and addressing herself to the senior attendant. "What're you talking about? I didn't do anything."

"You broke the cameras upstairs," Hinton informs her, his eyes never leaving Williams's Tekmerion. "That's gonna cost you 180 days."

"180? Are you fucking serious? I didn't touch your cameras. I was downstairs that morning, you can ask anyone."

"She was downstairs," Emily volunteers. "I saw her."

"Robbins, stay out of this," Hinton hisses. "We'll get to you another time."

Victoria turns her attention back to Williams. "Come on, Cary." Her tone suggests she's disappointed in him, but he can still make up for his blunder if he reverses course. "You *know* I didn't do this. I was downstairs the whole time. How can you write me up? You don't have any proof."

"I have a witness report," Williams says, chin tilted in protest. But he averts his eyes, as if he doesn't trust himself to face Victoria. Confidence drains from his face. His thumbs are poised uncertainly over the screen.

Hinton intervenes. "See the button that says MORE? Click on that. Go ahead, click. Now scroll through and hit NEXT for the next page. There, you see where it says VANDALISM?"

"Got it. Thanks, boss."

"What witness are you talking about?" Victoria asks. "Give me a name. Give me her fucking name and let's see what she has to say." She looks around the dining room, daring the informant to come forward. A long minute passes, the only sound the splash of the power faucet in the kitchen. "See? Somebody's making up shit about me and you're writing me up without any proof."

"She was downstairs," Sara tells Williams, recalling the day of the evacuation. "We both saw her. She was playing cards with Alice, you can just ask her if you don't believe us."

"Alice Carter's out of commission," Hinton says. "She's been taken to the ER."

"The ER? Is she all right?"

Victoria moves a step closer to Williams. "Someone must've lied about me."

"And you know all about that, don't you."

"I'm not a snitch," Victoria says between her teeth. "Fuck off with your accusations already." She looks like she's going to punch him, then thinks better of it. She takes her tray to the busing station, where she dumps it and stomps out of the cafeteria.

"Phew," Williams says, his face pink. He seems pleased with how it all turned out. "She's got a temper on her, that one."

Hinton nods. "Let me know if you have any more trouble with the system."

"Sure thing, boss."

Williams leaves, and Hinton returns to his station, looking disappointed that the excitement is already over. Around the cafeteria the women slowly go back to their food, their idle chatter.

Sara takes a deep breath. The revolting smell of the oatmeal reaches her again, and she has to push the tray away. 180 days! That's probably the longest extension she's heard of since she's been here. She waits for the conversations around her to get loud enough for her to speak. "This is revenge. Because she keeps ignoring his advances."

"Williams's had his eye on her for a while," Emily says, scraping the last of the oatmeal from its slot on her tray. The sound makes Sara's skin crawl, it's all she can do not to grab the spork. Emily finishes eating, licking the last of the oatmeal from her utensil. "But also, she did it."

"What? How do you know?"

"I just do," Emily says with a grin. "It's gonna take a couple of weeks to replace all the cameras, that's why they're so pissed."

"But I *saw* her with Alice. We both did."

"That was much later, when we were all waiting for the buses. She'd already taken care of the cameras by then."

"That's amazing." Victoria Aguilar is whom they have to thank for the private conversations they've been able to have on the residential floor since they got back from Victorville. They've enjoyed other small pleasures, too: sitting in their underwear when the rooms get too hot, or bartering for items they need, or staying up when the lights are out. "*She's* amazing."

"Right? I really like her."

Sara laughs. "Yeah? What about Clara?"

"Oh, you have it wrong," Emily replies, though she sounds like she's trying to convince herself. "It's not like that at all. We're just friends."

"If you say so."

SHE RETURNS UPSTAIRS AFTER BREAKFAST. THE FLOOR IS STILL DAMP from this morning's cleaning, the air thick with the scent of synthetic pine, but she can still detect the sour smell of disease. Too many people have been up all night vomiting. At the door of 234 she stops. Alice's cot has been stripped of its sheet and blanket, and her pillow taken away. Across the room Toya lies on her side with one hand shielding her eyes. The light from the window is placid, the rays of a mild sun on an ordinary day. "Hey," Sara whispers as she steps inside, "you awake?"

Toya takes her hand from her face. Her eyes look jaundiced, her lips pale.

"How're you feeling?"

"Like hell."

"Your first day?"

"Second." Toya raises herself slowly on one elbow until she makes it to a sitting position. On the shelf above her bed are a couple of library books, a few origami birds, and a picture of her with her husband, their eight-year-old bichon frisé, Monty, between them. "I guess I should be grateful I'm not in the ER."

Two retainees walk past 234, arguing over something, followed a minute later by Marcela pushing the janitorial cart, where the mop bucket sloshes with dirty water. She looks exhausted, perhaps she's getting sick herself.

Sara leans against the doorjamb, too tired to continue standing, but too wary of Alice's bed. "What happened to her?"

"She was in bad shape, she couldn't even get up when she needed to throw up. I told them, but by the time they came to check on her, she'd passed out. She told me once that she'd had hernia surgery a while back, but I don't know if that has anything to do with it."

"And it's the norovirus, not something else?"

"As far as I know."

"Well, at least she gets to be out of this place for a few days."

"Always look on the bright side of life."

Sara laughs and with her thumb points to the picture of the bichon frisé. "All this time I thought you'd named your dog after Monty Clift."

Footsteps draw her attention back to the hallway. A man wearing a face mask and surgical gloves is visiting, flanked by Hinton, Jackson, and Yee. Walking down the hallway, he stops at nearly every room, sometimes asking questions that the attendants take turns answering. Is he some kind of doctor? No, he has stopped to examine the broken cameras, shaking his head slowly as Hinton explains that it will take another few days for the replacements to arrive. "The vendor had a *force majeure* situation," he says, raising himself slightly on his heels.

"What situation?"

"There was a Category 5 hurricane in Malaysia, sir? The flooding has affected the factory where the cameras are made, hence the delays in shipping."

But the man is grumpy. "For what they're charging us, they should've delivered them by courier overnight."

Maybe it's an accountant, Sara thinks.

The group moves to 222, where both occupants have been sick with the virus, and are sleeping on soiled sheets. This time it is Jackson's turn to explain that there is still a shortage in clean laundry, exacerbated by the fact that she can't fill every shift. "I sent you a memo about this, sir," she says. "I can manage in the trailers, but I can't get extra shifts in laundry or custodial. The residents are afraid of handling contaminated material."

This doesn't appear to satisfy the visitor. "We're not gonna get this place running properly again if we can't get the virus under control."

"It's the chief retention officer," Sara whispers, suddenly recognizing his baritone.

Curiosity about the man they've been hearing from only through his occasional audio announcements is enough to push Toya to stand next to Sara at the door of her room. The CRO is a short man in his forties, dressed in jeans and a blue button-down shirt with the sleeves rolled up. His arms are covered in dark, fuzzy hair. But although she can now match a body to the voice on the loudspeaker, she still doesn't know what he looks like, his face being shielded by a surgical mask. Still, watching him dress down the attendants gives Sara a rush of satisfaction.

"I can get you more linens," the CRO says. "I'm placing an order anyway for the new wing. Where's Ortega?"

"Out sick."

"He's out, too?" Now the CRO sounds angry. "Was he eating in the cafeteria?"

This is against the rules, everyone knows that. The attendants glance at one another before Hinton replies for them. "I don't think so, sir. He could've caught it anywhere in the facility."

"Okay," the CRO says, in a tone that suggests he's heard enough, he has all the information he needs to make a decision. The group reaches 231, diagonally from where Sara and Toya are standing. "This looks bigger than on the feed," the CRO says, with surprise in his voice. He pulls out his phone to take a picture. "I think we can fit another cot in here."

Sara steadies herself against the doorjamb. She must've misheard the man; he can't possibly be thinking of adding more retainees to this wing, when he has an entire new wing to fill and they're in the middle of an outbreak. Toya lets out a sigh; standing up by the door has tired her. She returns to her cot, but almost immediately she has to rush to the toilet bowl. The sound of her retching makes the CRO turn around, taking notice of 234 and its stripped-out cot.

"234A is the one that got sent to the ER, right?" he asks.

"Yes, sir," Hinton replies.

"So who's this, then?"

"My name is Sara," she says, her heartbeat quickening. There is so much she wants to say: she's innocent of any crime, she shouldn't be under retention, she's already been at Madison far longer than would be necessary to decide her case. And she's not alone: almost everyone here has been in limbo for months, and in a few cases years. "Sara Tilila Hussein."

"The resident from 208," Hinton puts in.

"What's she doing here?" the CRO asks.

"I wanted to check on my friend."

"Shouldn't she be at work?"

"I quit."

The CRO isn't looking at Sara at all. Now he's waiting for an answer from Jackson.

"Sir, as I explained in the me—"

"I know what you put in your memo. And as I said in *my* memo, you need to show some initiative. Figure it out. Or do I have to do everything around here?"

Meanwhile, Toya has finished rinsing her hands. She sits on her cot, leaning forward so she can watch through the doorway.

"I mean, just look at these two," the CRO says. "Look how weak and filthy they are. How do you expect to get this situation sorted out when you guys can't maintain the most basic hygiene?"

"We don't even have soap," Toya says from the doorway.

The attendants glare at her. *Shut up if you know what's good for you.*

If the CRO heard her, he gives no indication, moving on to the next room, where he asks about the broken pipes. The attendants follow at his heels, providing updates or explanations.

The encounter was brief, but it knocks the breath out of Sara. She has to sit down on Alice's cot, with her elbows on her knees and her head tucked between her hands. What just happened? The CRO is the most powerful agent at Madison, the only one with the discretion and authority to decide how it should be run. But he didn't seem to see her. She's not even sure he heard her name.

From: EisleyRichardson@me.com
To: SaraTHussein@PostPal.com
CR Number: M-7493002
Facility: Madison
Timestamp: 11-14-09-12
Flags: NONE
Status: clear

Dear Sara,

I heard on the radio last week that Madison had to be evacuated during the Perris fire, so I thought I'd check in on you, see how you're doing. The damage from the fire is much bigger than anyone anticipated. I hope no one was hurt!

All is well on my end. I'm back at home now, falling into my routine again, although I've been cooking a lot more than before. I used to think meal prep was a chore, but I've come to realize just how much pleasure I get from eating meals I've made myself.

Anyway, write me back and let me know how you all are doing.

Eisley

               .   .   .

From: EisleyRichardson@me.com
To: SaraTHussein@PostPal.com
CR Number: M-7493002
Facility: Madison
Timestamp: 11-16-10-32
Flags: FINANCIAL TRANSACTION
Status: clear

Dear Sara,

I never heard back from you, and it's only this morning that I realized you might not have any funds left in your PostPal account. I wish they'd allow people who've been released to donate what's left of their funds. It seems like a waste, doesn't it? Anyway, I went ahead and added some money to your PostPal. Write me back with your news.

Eisley

        ·   ·   ·

From: EisleyRichardson@me.com
To: SaraTHussein@PostPal.com
CR Number: M-7493002
Facility: Madison
Timestamp: 11-17-21-27
Flags: FINANCIAL TRANSACTION
Status: clear

Dear Sara,

I wonder if there' a problem with the system, and you're not seeing my messages. Woud you just let me know if you've recieved them?

Julie

        ·   ·   ·

From: EisleyRichardson@me.com
To: SaraTHussein@PostPal.com
CR Number: M-7493002
Facility: Madison
Timestamp: 11-19-09-45
Flags: NONE
Status: clear

Dear Sara,

I hope I haven't offended you by adding a little money to your PostPal account. I was just trying to help.

Eisley

BUT WE WEREN'T FRIENDS, SARA THINKS. IF ANYTHING, EISLEY Richardson had been increasingly hostile as her retention period was coming to an end, finding ways to justify everyone else's repeated extensions. The conversation during her last night at Madison had been especially contentious; she was leaving the next day and was confident in the system. How strange that she's writing to Sara now. And not just one message, but four. What explains the sudden interest, the needless expense?

Perhaps it's survivor's guilt. Now that she's safe at home, surrounded by family and friends, she's starting to cope with the distress and isolation that her retention forced on her, and realizing how lucky she has been to get out. She's trying to make amends for her past behavior. Fine, Sara thinks. And she'll take the commissary funds, she's not too proud for that. She needs all the help she can get with her debts, and maybe in a few weeks she can afford shampoo again. She jots down a quick thank-you note and, with an eye on the clock, logs out before PostPal charges her for another thirty minutes of usage.

She ponders all this as she heads to the clothing office (no clean uniforms, come back tomorrow) and from there to the library, where she wanders the stacks. The charitable association that provides books to Madison has sent a fresh batch of GED study guides, a series of horror novels that were popular three decades ago, and a complete set of Penguin Classics recycled by a shuttered college in Vermont. Sara pulls out *Jane Eyre* from the shelf and reads until a seat at one of the computer stations opens up.

The *Los Angeles Times* is still covering the damage that the Perris fire has caused across two counties in Southern California, though the news is relegated below the fold, as most of the front page is taken up with a poultry inventory problem that started when two plants in Minnesota shut down over meat-safety concerns this summer, and cascaded into a turkey shortage that will affect Californians in the coming holiday season.

She clicks over to the national page, where she is greeted by news about James Wesley, who has formed an exploratory committee to decide if he should run for a U.S. Senate seat. In the photograph that accompanies the article, Wesley is shown stepping off a private plane, with his arm at his fiancée's back, leading her toward a waiting black limousine. He smiles at the photographer, his eyes faintly visible behind sunglasses, trying to project the confidence that his hoped-for job demands. She hates everything about this man, and especially the fact that he belongs to the exempt class: whatever crime or injustice is revealed to happen under his watch, he won't suffer any consequences.

Her thoughts flit back to the messages she received this morning. Eisley is a far better person than me, she thinks. If I'd gotten out in twenty-one days, I'd have put this place behind me, moved on with my life. And I wouldn't be writing to people I barely knew. Maybe she was drunk? That would explain the typos, the chummy tone, that name she signed with.

Sara opens a new window. A search for "Eisley Richardson" returns two million results, a remarkably small set these days, but far too large to be of any use to her. She narrows the search to California, and gets a hundred thousand hits. Better, she thinks. There's an audiologist in Sacramento named Eisley Richardson, and a math teacher in Torrance, and a horse breeder in the Central Valley.

When she adds the name "Julie" the search narrows to just three hundred results, all for a teenager who died in a boat-racing accident twenty-five years ago. There's a picture of her in one of the newspapers, but she's a redhead with green eyes, she looks nothing like the Eisley Richardson that Sara knows. She scrolls idly through the article, reading about this young girl whose competitive spirit led her to take enormous risks with her life. There's another picture of her further down the article, this time with her best friend, whom the caption identifies as Julie Renstrom. There must be a mistake, because this Julie Renstrom looks exactly like the retainee who was released from here a couple of weeks ago.

Sara enters the name "Julie Renstrom" into the search.

All at once she has the curious sensation of being back in her childhood home, playing under the magnolia tree with Zach and Saïd. Every time she calls "Marco," Zach replies, "Polo," but no matter how quickly she turns in his direction, she can never tag him; he's too stealthy. Saïd has no guile, though, and the moment he responds "Polo," she grabs his wrist. "You're it!" she says, delight raising her voice nearly to a scream. Now she can remove the blindfold from her eyes.

For a moment the world is blurry, and then it reveals itself to her with shocking clarity.

That is how she feels now as she rushes, breathless, out of the library. So many details take on another meaning: Julie Renstrom's arrival during off-hours; her assignment to 258, next to the emergency exit in the back; how quickly she fell in step with the general routine; how eager she was to ask the other retainees questions about their lives.

But why did DI send Julie to the retention center? It can't have anything to do with the hardware; the devices are checked every morning, and she wouldn't need to assume a false identity if she were only investigating a problem with the implant. It has to be a software issue, Sara thinks as she ascends the stairs.

But the company already has their dreams, so what do they want?

They want more, is what she can guess, more than collecting and storing and weighing and interpreting the dreams of every person who has ever used a Dreamsaver. The only way to increase profit continually is to extract more from the same resources.

Toya is still curled up on her cot when Sara arrives in her room. "I need to talk to you," she says.

5

NEXT EVENING. SARA AND TOYA LINGER BY THE CUBBIES IN the locker room, under the sign that says THIS PROPERTY IS SUBJECT TO INSPECTION WITHOUT NOTICE. The air is stale, the smell getting stronger with each garment Alice takes off. Her sweater, her pants, her headwrap pool at her feet. She has just returned from the hospital, where she was treated for complications from the virus and told she needed to rest, but eager to keep up her good score she worked a twelve-hour shift today. They have cornered her here, where they can talk undisturbed.

"You're saying she was a snitch?" Alice asks.

"Not a snitch," Sara replies, with a glance at Toya. The revelation about Julie Renstrom has given them an unexpected edge; they intend to use it. They spent the day strategizing, debating whom to approach, and how, and when. Alice Carter was first on their minds; she's been at Madison for more than a year and in that time has shown herself to be a kindred spirit. "Or not exactly a snitch. She's a scientist who worked for DI. Works for them still, according to her profile."

"So she was, like, watching us?" Alice asks. Isn't that what the implant does, her tone suggests, and the Guardian cameras, and the temperature sensors, and the attendants. What difference does it make if there's one more person watching?

"But she was doing it in secret," Toya insists. "She had no reason to watch us in secret, right? Not with all the data they already collect. My guess is, she was testing something on us. Like we're goddamn guinea pigs."

Sara is still mad at herself for not realizing this sooner. She watched Julie Renstrom come and go for three weeks, and yet she didn't really see her. Or she saw only the parts that she was meant to see. Had it not been for an email slipup, the veil might never have been lifted from her eyes. "And if they sent her here," Sara says, a thought suddenly crystallizing in her mind, "then they probably sent others before her. For all we know, there might be another one here right now."

Alice checks that her shampoo is in her toiletry bag, then zippers it up. "That's crazy."

Not crazy, Sara thinks. In fact, it's the opposite of crazy; it's the parasitic logic of profit, which has wormed its way so deeply into the collective mind that to defy lucre is to mark oneself as a radical, or a criminal, or a lunatic. Entire generations have never known life without surveillance. Watched from the womb to the grave, they take corporate ownership of their personal data to be a fact of life, as natural as leaves growing on trees. Detaining someone because of their dreams doesn't exactly trouble Americans; most of them think that the RAA's methods are necessary. Blowing the whistle on Dreamsaver Inc.'s illegal behavior might make headlines, might even cause a scandal, but that doesn't mean it will change anything for retainees, or at least not for those in the locker room right now. They can't afford to wait for other people to save them. "That's why we have to strike," Sara continues. "Enough is enough."

Alice wraps herself in her towel and starts toward the showers.

Sara puts a hand on her arm. "How about it?" she asks, hoping for a sign, however small, that they're getting through to Alice. She tries flattery. "A lot of people look up to you, and if you join us, maybe they will, too."

"You don't understand," Alice replies, shaking her head. "My score is down to 515 now. I can't screw it up. I can't."

"CAN YOU MOVE YOUR LEFT KNEE UP A TINY BIT?" EMILY ASKS. "THERE. That's great." Minutes pass, during which the only sound is that of the pencil on the sketchbook. Sara stares at the ceiling, ruminating over her defeat. Alice has been extended a dozen times, so she'd thought her indifferent to the dangled carrot of release, but clearly she's miscalculated. She needs to work with long haulers, yes, but she should've started with those who've recently been slapped with an extension. The punished might be more receptive than the hopeful. A musical note interrupts her thoughts. "Did you hear that?" she asks, raising herself from the bed.

"Hear what?" Emily says. "Don't move, you were perfect like that."

A second later, it happens again. It sounds like an A note. She stands up.

"Oh, man," Emily says, tapping the pencil on the pad. "I was almost done and then you moved."

Another note. This time it sounds like a D. Sara comes out of her room and walks in the direction of the music. She hears a G, played again and again. A minute later she is at the door of 202, where Marcela is hunched over a maple-colored Gibson guitar. It is a beautiful instrument, and a well-worn one, too, with scratches that testify to many years of use. The guitar case sits on the opposite cot, unassigned since Lucy was released, and on its side is a huge sticker of a pink brick—the logo of Sharp Jello. Marcela is so absorbed in her tuning that she doesn't notice Sara standing at the door of the cell.

"Marcela," Sara calls after a moment.

Marcela looks up. The joy on her face has transformed it; she looks ten years younger, her eyes shine with pleasure. "My petition was approved."

Her fifth try, Sara thinks. How will she convince her to join the strike now? This is another complication she hasn't anticipated, she realizes; as she makes one move, Safe-X will counter with another.

THERE IS NO TIME TO WASTE. SHE HAS TO ORGANIZE FASTER AND BETTER, or else her efforts will fail before they've even started. Working with Toya, Sara draws up a list of long haulers who got in serious trouble in the last few weeks, some for dealing contraband and others for a nasty fight in the rec room. There are twelve names on the list, but once Sara removes those who are laid up in the infirmary, she is left with nine, which she splits with Toya.

She starts with Elaine Coleman and Jeannie Kowalski, down the hall in 257. It is late in the evening, the time when everyone is getting ready for bed. Elaine is working on a puzzle, her reading glasses perched on her nose, while Jeannie is braiding her long hair. "Knock, knock," Sara says, and when Elaine nods, she steps inside.

257 has no window, but being at the corner it is slightly larger than the other rooms. The air smells faintly of the antiseptic cleaner that Jeannie managed to get, under mysterious circumstances, right when the outbreak started. Sara stands in the space between the cots, and tries to make her case. She talks about the long hours they work, the money they make for Safe-X, the state of the cafeteria, the showers, the laundry, the ridiculous rules that keep them here, working even more hours, making even more money. The only way out is to withhold their labor. Let the attendants do the work, she concludes.

Elaine lets out a snort. She sits cross-legged, with her half-completed puzzle laid out on a piece of cardboard, staring at the picture on the box—an autumn scene, with red and yellow leaves dominating the composition.

Sara persists. "You used to teach math, right?"

Elaine has been at Madison for thirteen months, and before that she worked for twenty-two years as a schoolteacher for LAUSD, so she's seen a strike or two in her day.

"Remedial algebra," Elaine replies, trying to place a piece on the puzzle. The piece doesn't quite fit, and she pulls it out. "I was better at teaching Calc A and B, but the chair liked to stick me with the bigger classes and assigned the smaller ones to his girlfriend. A lot of good it did him, too, 'cause she ended up cheating on him with one of the music teachers. Actually, they were both cheating, the music teacher was married to someone who worked for the dis—"

"My point is," Sara cuts in, "we'll only get anywhere if we hit their profit margins."

"Maybe we can get some goddamn AC in here," Jeannie says, turning to look at Sara for the first time. Jeannie gets hot flashes that nothing seems to soothe. Even now her face is pink, her shirtsleeves damp at the armpits. "Sometimes I feel like I'm gonna die."

"AC, sure," Sara says.

"And longer showers." Standing up to face the small mirror above the sink, Jeannie loops a rubber band at the end of her braid. "And more time in the yard."

Better conditions of retention aren't exactly what Sara has in mind—she wants Madison to close altogether—but she has to start somewhere, and after listening to Jeannie rattle on about everything that needs improvement, she brings up what she has learned about Julie Renstrom.

"Wait, are you serious?" Elaine sits up.

"Remember how surprised we were when she stayed here only three weeks? Now you know why. She was testing something."

"Are they allowed to do that?" Jeannie asks.

"Doesn't matter if they are," Elaine tells her. "The point is, they already did."

"Wasn't she in 258?" Sara points to the left wall. "Next door to the two of you."

Jeannie shakes her head. "She was in here all the time."

STEPHANIE MICHAELS IS THE NEXT NAME ON THE LIST. SHE'S A THEME-park attendant who's been at Madison since February and has worked in different jobs throughout the facility: dishwasher, service worker, librarian, custodian, maintenance worker. This afternoon Toya has invited her to the poker game she's playing with Victoria and Emily at one of the tables, a game that seems no less contested for having no financial stake. When Sara takes a seat, Jackson comes out from under the breezeway to walk the perimeter.

"Jackson's in trouble," Sara begins.

"Hmm-hmm," Stephanie says. She stares at the cards in the middle of the table, trying to remember which ones Victoria and Emily have already played. A nine of hearts, a jack of spades, and a three of diamonds lie at the top of the pile. The cards have gotten thin from use, but no one has enough money for another deck.

"The outbreak messed up her schedule," Sara continues, "and now six of us aren't working."

"Imagine if more people went on strike," Toya adds.

"Can you just let me focus?" Stephanie says. "I'm trying to play a game here."

A moment later, Victoria folds. The others continue for another few rounds, and when they lay down their cards Stephanie has three nines, Toya has two pairs, but Emily has a full house. "You've been getting better," Sara tells her cellmate.

Emily turns modest. "I got lucky."

From the road comes the sustained honk of an angry driver, drowned out a moment later by the sound of tires screeching on the pavement. Jackson walks by the table, eyeing the players as she passes them, then returns to the breezeway. Sara stretches her arms, the fresh air is invigorating.

While Victoria shuffles the deck, Sara makes her case to Stephanie. We have to stop working, she says. It's the only way.

"How about it," Toya says. "You want to join us?"

"Who's in already?"

"The four of us," Toya replies, pointing around the table. "Plus Jeannie Kowalski and Elaine Coleman."

The short list of names fails to impress Stephanie. "Yeah, I'm not interested," she says. "It's too risky."

Victoria leans forward on the table. "You know what else is risky? Life. Life is risky. Go ahead, Sara. Tell her about Eisley."

Sara recounts what she discovered, but Stephanie is in disbelief that DI would send an undercover scientist. "There must be another explanation," she says. And when Victoria starts dealing cards for a new game, she makes up an excuse and leaves.

TEMPER YOUR EXCITEMENT, SARA CHIDES HERSELF. YOU'RE PUSHING too hard, too fast. This is something her mother used to advise her all the time: anything worth having is going to require some patience. Yet when she returns to her room after yard time the sight of the broken cameras reminds her how much Victoria has already sacrificed; she has to make the most out of the opportunity that her young friend has created for all of them. She decides to try the next names on her list, Rita Mason and Carol Warren in 248.

Rita used to be a clerk for a shipping company, while Carol did bookkeeping for a chain of restaurants. A few months into their retention, they started a little commerce in pepper, which some retainees use to flavor the bland cafeteria food, trading it in different-size packets in exchange for whatever items they need or want. Their room has a miniature fan, which whirrs from the shelf, and a battery-powered reading light. "How're you two feeling?" she asks. "I heard you got the bug."

"She gave it to me," Carol says, pointing to her cellmate without looking at her.

"You don't know that."

"I know you don't wash your hands when you use the toilet."

"That's not true." Rita looks up at Sara. "It's *not* true, you know. She's just mad that she got sick after holding out for ten days and now she's looking for someone to blame."

"Well," Sara says from between their cots. "The way I look at it, this thing wouldn't have spread so fast if we hadn't been caged—not just here but at the other jail, too."

"Right. That's how it started." Rita turns to Carol. "So if you're looking to blame someone, blame Michelle. She caught it in Victorville and brought it here."

"That's not what I mean," Sara says, shaking her head. "I'm talking about accountability, not blame." She's off on a tangent again, she realizes. The last thing she needs is a philosophical debate, she has to turn this conversation around before it gets out of hand. She tells them about Julie Renstrom's fake name, her real job and secret goals.

"See what I told you," Carol says, turning to Rita.

"You knew?" Sara asks.

"I mean, I didn't know this, exactly. But I knew something was off about her. The way she never looked at the attendants, I thought that was strange. Usually newbies try to reason with them, ask them questions about how things work, see if they can get help on their cases, but she never did. She only ever talked to us."

"Well, you had her number," Rita says. Her complexion has turned pallid, the vein across her forehead is a bluish green. She seems to be struggling not to throw up.

"This is one of the reasons we're organizing," Sara says. She tells them about the importance of doing this now, while the stomach flu is still wreaking havoc on the work schedule. With just a few more people joining the strike, the impact will be felt.

"Sure," Carol says. "Okay."

"Yeah?" Relief washes over Sara. With Toya bringing in Maggie Rivera and Yolanda Brown, they are up to ten, enough to attract the attention of any retainees who've had a complaint or a grievance about Madison.

Which is all of them.

ERIC HOLLINS ANNOUNCES DREAMSOCIAL, PRODUCT TO LAUNCH EARLY NEXT YEAR

THIS IS A RUSH TRANSCRIPT.
THIS COPY IS NOT FINAL AND MAY BE UPDATED.

Every once in a while, an innovation comes along that is so revolutionary it makes you wonder how you've managed to live for so long without it.

Ten years ago, when we launched the Dreamsaver out of an office sandwiched between a tattoo parlor and a cannabis shop, my mom called me in a panic, worried about how I'd be able to pay back all the money I'd borrowed from her and my dad. I told her not to fret, this was going to work.

But how do you know, my mom asked me.

It's a gut feeling, I told her.

I knew, deep in my gut, how transformative it would be for so many insomniacs like me to get a full night's sleep. To feel rested and rejuvenated in as few as five hours. I knew the freedom that would come from being able to control sleep.

The rest, as they say, is history. Our product has saved countless lives, and our customers have told us as much. In my office I keep dozens of their testimonials, some of them handwritten notes, like the one I received from the labor-and-delivery nurse who was afraid she was endangering patients because she couldn't concentrate at work. You've given me my life back, she said.

If helping people get some rest had been the only thing that DI ever accomplished, I would have considered myself lucky. But

I'm extremely fortunate to be able to say that we are launching a product that will once again revolutionize sleep.

And today I can tell you that I have that same gut feeling I had years ago.

Not only will our newest Dreamsaver reduce the ratio of sleep to rest, not only will you be able to get the physical and mental health benefits of a full night of sleep on just three and a half hours, but it will also allow you to share your dreams with your family and friends.

Allow me to demonstrate.

[Video screen lights up, a dream begins to play. The dreamer is riding a horse, holding it by the mane rather than a bridle. The trail is rough, and barely marked, but eventually the rider comes out to a green meadow with a waterfall on the right-hand side.]

This is a feed from my own Dreamsaver. I have chosen to make this dream shareable with my wife and children, plus my good friends Angela and David. I'm going to scroll so you can see the comments. "Is that Nova Scotia?" my wife is asking. That's where we honeymooned twenty-two years ago. It looks like it could be, but in my memory it feels like a place I hadn't been before.

My friend Angela offers an interpretation. "You're moving through a rough patch. But your handling of the horse and the lack of bridle suggests you're doing it without effort." Very astute.

"Can I go zip-lining there?" And that's from my teen. [Audience laughs.]

As you can see, users have full control over how little or how much of their dreams can be shown, and to whom.

You can also subscribe to feeds. Those of your friends, or those of a public figure, like your favorite actor or a football player you like. On this screen, you can see that I'm subscribing to Therm X's feed. I've been a fan for years, and it's nice to see how creative he is, even in dreams.

[Video screen turns off.]

In a world that so often divides us, our dreams can connect us.

By sharing our dreams we can relate more intimately than ever before. We can understand one another on a level that was previously unavailable to humanity. And that is how I know that this is a product unlike any other, a product that will change forever how we interact with those around us, and allow us to move through life with more grace and empathy.

[Female voice-over starts.]

DreamSocial. Share a dream. Help a dreamer.

S HE PASSES A BANK OF SCREENS IN THE GROUND FLOOR HALLWAY. This afternoon it's filled with public health messages and calls for volunteers to pick up additional work shifts. She stops to read the names of the lucky women who are receiving visitors today: Claire Lopez, Ana Guerrero, Stephanie Michaels, Toya Jones. All visits are marked as ON TIME, except Toya's, which is listed as CANCELLED.

Well, that's strange. Toya's husband is as punctilious as she is; he schedules his visits a month in advance, always taking a half day off from his job at the Veterans' Administration to drive out here to see her. Could this be retaliation against her for joining the strike?

Emily warned them that this might happen, told them that when she was a teenage inmate in Lassen County, the guards took away visiting rights from anyone who got in trouble. "But we're not in trouble," Sara pointed out. "We have a right not to work."

Now Sara stares at the screen, the letters and figures blurring before her. Is she prepared to give up the rare visits she gets from Elias and the twins? She might not last long if the choice is between working for Safe-X and seeing her family.

Maybe something happened to Toya's husband, she tells herself. He ran into some car trouble, or something came up at work. Maybe he had to take Monty to the vet. Toya did say her dog was fourteen and was having hip trouble.

In this way, having reassured herself, she heads to the library to return her books. The autumn day is fading to an early dusk, the light from the windows is weak. She places the books on the return shelf next to Ana, who's checking a catalogue of donated titles against the censored materials list.

At this hour, there is no wait at the computers. Sara opens the *Los Angeles Times,* and finds most of the front page taken up with coverage of a hurricane in Northern California. San Francisco is affected, as is Fremont, where her brother-in-law lives.

Before she can finish the article, Williams is at her elbow. "You're done."

"What do you mean?" By her estimation she still has another twenty-eight minutes to go.

"I mean, you're done. You've lost library privileges."

"But why?"

He holds up his Tekmerion. "You're not cleared to be here. Come on. Get going."

Legs weak, she stands up. The library is her only connection to the free world; losing it removes any pretense about her situation. She has no rights at Madison, despite what the handbook may say; she has privileges only, which can be revoked at signs of defiance.

Later, she commiserates with Toya over the day's losses. They are outside the cafeteria, waiting for dinner service to start. "It's just a fluke," she says, in a weak attempt to cheer up Toya. PostPal is notoriously prone to mistakes and hiccups, so the cancellation of Toya's visit could be just another example of the chronic malfunction that characterizes the entire retention system. "Remember how they marked me as unavailable, back in February?"

"But no one else's visit was cancelled."

"PostPal isn't Safe-X," Sara continues. "They have no idea who's on strike."

"How do you explain cutting your library access, then?"

Sara has no answer to that. The line isn't long, the stomach flu having claimed another dozen retainees in the last twenty-four hours. As they reach the service window they are surprised to find Jackson serving mac and cheese. She ladles the orangey goop onto a tray and with a tired sigh slots a kid-size juice box into a compartment. Behind her, in the back of the kitchen, another attendant in a hairnet is opening a MealSecure container with a box cutter, unpacking the fruit cups inside onto the industrial table.

When the attendant comes out, Sara sees that it's Hinton.

Good morning, residents. This is your chief retention officer speaking. I am happy to report that fresh linens and uniforms are available in the clothing office. Soap dispensers have been refilled throughout the facility.

At 4 p.m. today Nurse Flores will be conducting an inspection to ensure that every resident is in compliance with the hygiene rules outlined in Section 2.1 of your handbook. Anyone found to be in violation is subject to a written reprimand and/or an extension.

Starting today, residents who have recovered from the norovirus will be temporarily reassigned to laundry and custodial, with shifts running from 7 a.m. to 10 p.m. Senior Attendant Jackson will continue to make adjustments as necessary.

The case numbers at this facility are starting to plateau, and I'm confident that the worst of this crisis is behind us.

The weather today is partly cloudy, with a low of 60 and a high of 72.

THE NEW CAMERAS ARE INSTALLED ON A CHILLY MORNING IN November, twenty-two translucent domes with built-in microphones, emotion-tracking software, and optical zoom. But the CRO must not be entirely satisfied with the images they beam to the control room, because he has put a raft of new measures in place. The number of foot patrols doubles across the facility. A janitorial closet, notorious for being a blind spot, is bolted shut. The seating limit at cafeteria tables is cut by half, to four residents per table, presumably to allow for clearer sound capture. And all this, Sara thinks, because the strikers total twelve.

"Maybe he's feeling the pressure," she tells Toya. They are in the showers, shivering as they wash under the lukewarm water, one of the lightbulbs flickering above them. They speak with urgency and little preamble, aware of how precious their time away from the cameras is. Yet this constraint also lends their meetings a rare intimacy.

"How many people are out sick?" Toya asks. "I counted thirty-two."

"Thirty-three, I think. One of the newbies is out."

"Okay, so let's say thirty-three. And with our twelve, that's forty-five. I don't see how they're gonna make the deadline for Vox-R. They're gonna have to push it a third time."

"If we keep it up," Sara says as the water shuts off, "the CRO will have to pay a penalty for breach of contract."

As they're toweling off at the lockers, Marcela walks in with an industrial-size soap container and starts to refill the dispensers at the sink. The few times they've approached her about the strike, Marcela was unsympathetic, afraid of losing the guitar it took her weeks to get. But the story about Eisley Richardson has been making the rounds, no doubt with added lurid details, and when they bring up the strike again she seems less adamant.

"I'll think about it," she says.

Progress, Sara thinks.

Then, one after the other, the strikers lose access to the commissary. No matter how often they present their faces to the scanner, or the angle they use, the system responds with USER NOT RECOGNIZED. Victoria shrugs it off; she had only pennies left in her account. But Emily has been locked out of the money for her art supplies, Toya for her cigarettes. So they have to barter for the things they need, using what little luxuries they've managed to procure during their retention—a bobby pin, a pencil, a face mask.

Bartering is forbidden, the CRO announces one morning.

The attendants keep an especially close eye on Sara. Whenever she walks into another retainee's cell, Hinton arrives within minutes to conduct a surprise inspection. If she goes to the exercise yard, Jackson comes out from under the breezeway to watch her. If she takes a shower, she finds Yee waiting outside the locker room, asking her why she's dawdling.

The heat on her is such that she's afraid to use words like *strike* or *boycott* and must resort to codes like *crossword* or *cricket*. That she is losing the ability to communicate in ordinary language seems to her only the latest absurdity in a long series that started nearly a year earlier. Or perhaps it started before, but content with the small pleasures and enclosed freedoms of her life, she didn't notice.

SHE IS PUTTING A CLEAN SHEET ON HER COT ONE AFTERNOON WHEN Hinton appears in the doorway. Her first thought is of her cellmate, who for the last few days has been fretting about increasing retaliation, but it seems her turn has come first. What bogus charge will the senior attendant try to pin on her in order to slap her with an extension? What obscure violation will he reveal? Without realizing it she takes a step back, and finds herself standing on the dirty linens that have been cast to the floor. She moves again, this time closer to the other cot, and hits her knee on the metal, sending pins and needles down her leg. "Shit."

Hinton watches from the doorway, his eyes never leaving hers.

"What is it?" she asks, her voice flat. "What do you want?"

From the zipper pocket of his fleece he pulls out the notebook. "I drove all the way to Upland to get it for you."

It's a standard composition notebook, but it has her name on the front cover and that blot of blue ink on the side where her pen once leaked. Her heart leaps with joy; it's as if a dear friend she hasn't seen in months has suddenly appeared at her door.

As she steps forward to claim it, he withdraws it again. "On one condition."

"What is it?"

"Get back to work."

"No."

"No?"

"That wasn't the agreement we had."

"Well," he says, "consider our agreement unilaterally amended due to one party failing to meet their obligations."

This fucking guy. Always trying to sound sophisticated, and always at the worst moment. "I never promised you I would work," she replies. "And by the way, there's no rule that says I *have* to work. This isn't a prison, remember? I haven't been convicted of a crime, and I can't be compelled to work by any correctional entity, whether public or private. You should know this, it's in the handbook."

"You know I lost my mom to cancer, too." He flips through her journal, as if looking for a specific passage he wants to reread. More than half the pages are covered with her neat handwriting, and the frequent thumbing through has made the booklet thicker. "Breast cancer, in her case. It happened fast, she was already at Stage 4 when they diagnosed her. I was just a kid, it messed me up for a while."

Is he seriously asking for her sympathy, after everything he's done? She looks at him searchingly. His face is somber, his eyes cast down. In all the time she's known him, he's never revealed anything about his private life. Losing her mother set her adrift for years; the grief would've sunk her if it'd happened when she was a child. But is he even telling the truth? Maybe he's lying again, trying to create the illusion that they have something in common. It's his way of saying *I understand you, I've been in your shoes, now it's time for you to be in mine.*

When he raises his eyes again, she meets them with a blank face.

A long minute passes.

"I see what you've been doing here," Hinton says, changing tacks. "You're collecting evidence. Presenting your own stories, your own interpretations. It's gonna make a big difference to your case when the time comes." He makes a show of flipping through the journal, then closes it with a snap. "So do you want it?"

Of course she wants it. "We agreed that you'd bring it," she says cautiously, "and in return I wouldn't fill out a grievance. That's what we agreed on. That was the deal."

"That was the deal three weeks ago. Things are different now. The CRO doesn't care about the mess of the evacuation anymore, I can tell you that. He has other priorities now."

She swallows, though her mouth feels dry. The leverage she once had has vanished, and now she feels a rush of regret that she didn't fill out a complaint immediately on her return from Victorville. How foolish of her to make a deal with Hinton. What was she thinking? What made her believe he could be trusted to keep his end of the bargain?

"If you go back to work," Hinton continues, smoothing out a dog-eared page with his thumbnail, "sooner or later the other residents will, too."

"If the others don't want to work, that's their choice."

"You're underestimating your powers of persuasion. If you go back, I think you'll find that the others will, eventually. Then I give you your notebook, and you can go back to writing your little stories. This place runs smoothly again. Everyone wins."

Look after your own interests, in other words. That's what her lawyer says, what her husband says, what her cousin says. It's what she tried to do for months—minding her business, following every rule, trying to appear more compliant, more deserving of freedom than others stuck in this place. But what did that achieve, in the end? She's still stuck here, still marked as a QUESTIONABLE. And in the meantime she's been depleted of her dignity. Only in the last few weeks has she been able to regain some measure of self-respect. To give it up now would endanger her survival.

"Here." Hinton holds out her journal. It is the only record she has of the past 340 days, the only way she can counter whatever story the RAA has concocted about her. "All you have to do is go back to work."

Prison is a place beyond shame. She uses the toilet in front of her cellmate, showers in open stalls, receives mail that the attendants have already pawed through for anything valuable or forbidden. To abandon the other women who joined the strike would mean not only accepting this shame as ordinary, but validating it. "No. Keep it."

She turns around and continues making her cot.

"You're a real pain in the neck, you know that?"

SARA SITS IN THE HALF-EMPTY CAFETERIA, SHIVERING IN HER UNI-form, waiting for the dim light of a November morning to reach her table. Having been relegated to the end of the service line, she's received no eggs, only a small serving of potatoes and a piece of toast. Toya managed to get the last cup of herbal tea, which she holds for a moment between her hands to try to warm them. While they eat, they talk about their suspension from the library, and the commissary, and the television room, and soon, they fear, the exercise yard.

The strike has given them purpose these last few days. It has nurtured their hopes, shielded them from gloom. But without access to the rec room or the library, how will they occupy themselves during the eighteen hours from lights on to lights out? Boredom is dangerous. If they want the strike to have a chance of succeeding, they have to find ways to keep themselves and the others busy.

"We could start a zine," Sara suggests.

"Didn't they deny a petition for one?" Toya replies. "Last month, remember?"

"Right. But I think that petition was for distributing printed materials inside the facility, wasn't it? We can skip all that. I mean, we can't afford to print and distribute a hundred twenty copies, anyway. We can write the zine in longhand, a single copy, and pass it around. They can't stop us from doing that."

"Maybe."

For a while they discuss the contributions they might make, or seek from others, writing that could not only keep them and their fellow strikers entertained, but also sustain them in some small way, give them what relief there is in knowing that they're not alone. The more they talk, the more Sara becomes animated by the idea of a collaborative zine.

Emily and Victoria arrive, engrossed in a conversation about photography, of all things, Victoria saying it was a hobby she got into when the casino where she worked closed for two weeks after a cyberattack on its computer systems, and how much she misses it. "I know how you feel," Emily replies. She used to take pictures of people and objects she wanted to draw in her comic, keeping the photographs as references, but here at Madison she can't have a camera, and it makes the work less precise, more complicated.

"But you have plenty of models," Sara teases, thinking about how her roommate hasn't been asking her to pose lately, now that she's become close with Victoria. "How would you like to draw a new comic? A one-page strip about this place?"

The idea seems to appeal to Emily, though she worries about paper, which she has been rationing ever since she lost access to the commissary. They talk about other practicalities, like whether they should use ink or erasable pencil, collate with staples or yarn. Ever since the strike began, they've had to adapt to limited resources, a constraint that, paradoxically, has made them more creative.

Hinton walks into the cafeteria just then, flanked this morning by Williams, who has looped his thumbs into his belt, as though he were merely an observer sent to shadow the senior attendant on his rounds. Together they move to the attendant station by the far wall, where they confer in hushed voices with Yee. A fourth attendant appears, joining the huddle.

All talk about the zine stops, the entire table watching and waiting. Across the cafeteria, the air becomes electric with expectation.

And then Hinton walks over to their table, his deputies trailing behind him. "You and you," he says, pointing to Sara and Toya. "Stand up and come with me."

Toya and Sara exchange a glance. What will he charge them with this time? They've barely been up for a couple of hours, they haven't had time to break any of the new rules the CRO has imposed. "What is this about?" Sara manages to ask.

"Come on, Hussein. Up, up, up. I don't have all day. Stand up and come with me."

Panic seizes her. This isn't a write-up, she realizes, which in any case he could fill out right here on his Tekmerion; he wants to take her somewhere else, to take both of them somewhere else, and he has brought reinforcements with him. "Where are you taking us?"

Hinton touches the zip ties at his belt. "Don't make me cuff you. You wouldn't like it." And then, with a wink at his deputies, he adds, "Or maybe you would, I don't know."

Williams chuckles.

But Emily reaches across the table and touches Sara's arm. It's going to be okay, the gesture says. Don't be afraid, we're all in this together. Whatever happens, don't be afraid.

Sara and Toya stand up, one after the other. The junior attendants clasp their arms, as if they might try to escape, and lead them behind Hinton out of the cafeteria.

RETAINEE DISCIPLINARY REPORT
Name: Sara T. Husseyn
Retainee: M-7493002

Timestamp	Status	Infraction	Attendant
12-24-09-05	UNEMPLOYED	Failure to follow case manager's directions	Hinton
12-24-09-06	UNEMPLOYED	Loitering in Hallway A-2	Hinton
12-24-09-06	UNEMPLOYED	Unauthorized hairstyle	Hinton
12-29-06-10	UNEMPLOYED	Failure to stand behind line during device scan	Hinton
12-29-06-10	UNEMPLOYED	Using profane language vs. attendant	Hinton
1-15-12-34	UNEMPLOYED	Unpermitted entry to multi-faith room	Hinton
1-21-07-13	UNEMPLOYED	Attempt to access unauthorized reading material	Williams
1-28-11-44	UNEMPLOYED	Using profane language vs. attendant	Hinton
02-01-07-31	EMPLOYED	Tardy—Trailer D	Jackson
02-14-19-45	EMPLOYED	Loitering in locker room with Resident Jones	Hinton
10-18-16-55	EMPLOYED	Fight in hallway B-1	Hinton
10-29-12-31	EMPLOYED	Unauthorized hairstyle	Hinton
11-12-07-02	UNEMPLOYED	Damaged property (sheet)	Jackson

6

THE TWO AGENTS SIT SIDE BY SIDE AT A DESK. ONE IS A GRAY-haired man in a linen blazer and jeans, with two tablets and a phone laid out in front of him. The other is a young woman dressed from head to toe in black: frock, stockings, shoes. Even the row of pearls around her neck is black. The choice seems deliberate, a sartorial way of conveying that, even if she's only in her twenties, she's in a position of power. The fragrance she has on is light and citrusy, but after so much time in retention Sara finds the scent overwhelming. She sneezes.

"Ms. Hussein," the man says, in a voice that grates like sandpaper. "Have a seat."

Sara takes the only chair across from them.

"I'm Agent Bradley," the man continues. "With me this fine morning is Agent Mendoza. We will be conducting your evaluation and providing a recommendation for the RAA. Any questions before we begin?"

"My lawyer isn't here."

Bradley puts on the reading glasses that dangle from a black cord around his neck. "Mr. Abdo, correct? This is an expedited assessment, though."

"I don't understand."

"You don't need a lawyer for this. We just want to ask a few questions."

"I have a right to a lawyer."

"Of course, you do. But this is an expedited assessment."

"I don't know what you mean by that." With a glance at the door, Sara asks, "Is that why I wasn't given any notice about this hearing? Hinton pulled us from the cafeteria in the middle of breakfast and brought us here. I didn't have time to call my lawyer."

"Let me back up for a minute," Agent Bradley says. "The RAA has taken note of the backlog of cases at this facility and has charged Themis Legal Services with providing expedited assessments for select retainees. These assessments take no more than ninety minutes. Of course, you have a right to decline and wait for a regular hearing, whenever there's an opening in the RAA's schedule. Is that what you'd like to do, Ms. Hussein?" Bradley asks, peering at Sara over the rim of his reading glasses.

So this is why they're meeting in the music room of the annex, half a block down the street, instead of the first-floor classroom at Madison, where everyone else had their hearings. The desk is set up on the dais where teachers once conducted students in choir or violin, with Sara's chair so near the edge that she must be careful not to move it or else she'll fall backward. As in the main facility, the walls of this room, including the sconces and wainscoting, were painted a cool white, trading historical charm for blank purity.

Bradley and Mendoza are still waiting for Sara to decide. Either she answers their questions, and gets a chance to finally go home, or she goes back to waiting for who knows how long until her hearing is scheduled. "It's entirely up to you," Mendoza says. "You've been here a long time."

"343 days," Sara replies.

Bradley's eyes travel to the clock on the wall, then settle on her again.

Should she agree to the expedited hearing or wait for the regular one? Nothing about the agents' demeanor tells her which alternative is better for her case.

"And aside from the Class As in December and January," Mendoza continues, "you've had a pretty clean record for the rest of the year." She scrolls on her tablet, then stops. "Well, there's that Class B on October 18, but that one's a little harsh."

"Hinton?" Bradley asks.

Mendoza nods. "The footage shows that the fight was between retainees Marcela DeLeón and Lucy Everett. You and Toya Jones were bystanders, as far as I can tell."

"I tried to *stop* the fight."

"You were being a Good Samaritan," Mendoza continues.

Why are they being so reasonable all of a sudden? The headache starts as a slow, steady beat along Sara's right temple. She presses a finger there, feeling for the incipient pain, wishing she could have a glass of water, but save for the agents' tablets and phones, the desk is bare.

"You don't have a criminal record, either."

"No."

Mendoza looks up from her tablet. "Like I said, it's a pretty clean file."

"So why am I still here, then?"

At this, both agents turn to their tablets again, and it dawns on Sara that they've taken her question for consent. The assessment has begun.

"The algorithm is holistic," Mendoza says. "It considers two hundred sources. Legal and financial, of course, but also familial, educational, reputational—"

"You have an R-785," Bradley cuts in, without regard for his colleague's attempt to give the introduction she has so clearly rehearsed. He scrolls through the bill of retention on his tablet. "The police at Heathrow received a harassment complaint made against you by a passenger on a December 22nd flight from London to Los Angeles. Later that same day, you have an R-97, making a false statement to an RAA officer."

"But I already explained what happened at Heathrow. I called the flight attendant because the guy next to me was choking, I never harassed him. It was the crew who decided to get him off the flight, not me. My lawyer has filed a counter-complaint with British police about this." If only she could get the word out to Adam Abdo. Her gaze travels to the door, before returning to settle on Bradley. "And as for the RAA officer, I never lied. I explained to him that my employer was covering my trip, which they were supposed to do once I turned in my receipts. He just misunderstood."

"The data doesn't lie."

"It doesn't tell the truth, either."

"I wasn't finished, Ms. Hussein. You also have an R-471, for troublesome dreams. They are what caused the RAA officer's concern."

"What dreams?"

"For example," he says, consulting his tablet, "on May 12 of last year, you had a dream that while your husband was in the bath, you added Xanax to his cup of tea."

She has no memory of this dream. It would've made more sense if in the dream she'd put the pill into her own cup of tea rather than Elias's, but dream logic isn't real logic. She wants to point this out to Bradley, but he's busy rattling off her suspicious dreams.

"—Then on October 9, you had a dream that you pushed him into the river."

"It was a nightmare," she replies. If anything, it was triggered by the RAA's accusations, which upended her life and tormented her for eleven months, adding a psychic burden she has found hard to carry. That is why her brain started working out different simulations in her dreams, but never coming up with anything more damning than an accident at the river.

"—A couple of weeks later, you had a dream about poisoning the soup."

She swallows. "I would never hurt Elias. This was just a dream."

"Every murder starts with a fantasy," Bradley says, his jaw tight.

You should've taken Hinton's offer, a voice inside her says, and accepted the journal. You could look up every dream he's brought up, offer your own story for each one. She closes her ears to the suggestion. She wants to be free, and what is freedom if not the wresting of the self from the gaze of others, including her own? Life is meant to be lived, to be seized for all the beauty and joy to be wrung out of it; it isn't meant to be contained and inventoried for the sake of safety.

"And to be clear, it's not your dreams alone," Mendoza adds. "The algorithm is considering your dreams in conjunction with your other behavior."

In the second before Sara answers, the labyrinthine pathways of data leading to this moment suddenly light up: dozens of texts she sent to her friend Myra, complaining about Elias's unbridled spending; footage of their argument outside the Volvo dealership; her attempts to get one of his credit cards cancelled; late-night searches for a couples therapist.

Mountains of data that testify to her most intimate frustrations, her most shameful resentments. Like a fortune-teller reading tea leaves, the algorithm made up stories as it was going along, until it found one that was plausible enough to please its audience. Sara presses her fingers to her temples, trying to stop the throbbing. "I don't know how many times I can say it. I would *never* hurt my husband."

"The RAA takes risks of domestic violence seriously," Bradley says.

Mendoza takes out one of the long pins that keeps her hair in a severe bun on her nape. With a fingernail she scratches a tender spot on her scalp, a look of relief blooming on her face. "How would you interpret these dreams, then, Ms. Hussein? Tell us."

"I wouldn't interpret them *literally,* for starters. My husband and I have our problems, like any other couple. That doesn't mean I would wish him dead, much less that I had any plans to murder him." She shakes her head. "I have a mortal fear of water. I'm sure that's why it appears so often in my dreams."

"You're saying that we need to interpret these dreams in context."

"That's right." Sara sits back, but her movement unsteadies the chair and she nearly falls backward. Groping at the air, she regains her balance. "And the context," she says, as she shifts her chair, "is that my husband and I were trying to adjust to being new parents. We never expected to have twins. It was a radical change to our lives, and it required so much of us. My dreams, well . . . they must've reflected my anxiety about being a mom and my frustration with him, that's all."

"But what if you've been suspected of something like this in the past?" Mendoza asks. Her voice is soothing, like a therapist trying to coax some understanding or revelation out of a stubborn patient. "Wouldn't that be relevant context, as you say? You were interviewed in connection with the death of your brother, isn't that right?"

It takes Sara a minute to parse what Mendoza is implying. Memories of that summer party thirty years ago in Pasadena return to her, jumbled up even more than usual by the gravity of the agents' accusations. The intolerable heat that afternoon. The smell of the jackets in the hall closet where she hid when they started playing hide-and-seek. The dollar she found when she started digging through one of the jacket pockets. And then the blinding light when she came out. All the adults standing around the pool. Her uncle kneeling over Saïd's body, giving him CPR. For months afterwards she had dreams that Saïd was still alive, that he'd only been away at summer camp or having a sleepover with a friend. Now the agents are digging through that painful time in order to make a case. "My brother drowned in a pool when we were kids." Her voice is shaking, she realizes, both at the memory and at the realization that the algorithm might have detected what she's worked so hard to keep buried for three decades—her guilt.

The algorithm knows so much about her already, going all the way down to the nucleic acids that twist in a helix inside her cells. Is it so strange that it has identified her true nature? "It was an accident," she says.

"But the police interviewed you," Bradley insists.

"I was nine years old." Her head is throbbing. All she wants is to close her eyes, shut out this room and everyone in it, and yet she must remain alert, must choose her words carefully if she is to persuade them to release her. "And I didn't see anything, I was hiding in a closet. I suppose the officers did talk to me that day, to figure out what happened, establish a timeline, that sort of thing. But I didn't…" She shakes her head. How can she convince them she is innocent, if she herself isn't sure she isn't responsible? "They said my brother had been trying to hide in an inflatable and fell in the pool. The medical examiner ruled the death an accident."

"You understand why we have to take this seriously, Ms. Hussein. It's not just your husband's life that may be at stake here. There are children in the home."

This guy reminds Sara of her old doctor. He would start typing clinical notes from the moment he stepped into the exam room, barely looking at her as she described the symptoms that had brought her to see him. I know what it is, he'd say. He was so sure his diagnosis was correct that he would put in a referral or send out a prescription order before she was finished talking about her illness. That's the kind of listening Bradley is doing at the moment: a listening keyed only to specific words. "If you're planning on detaining every woman who's had arguments with her husband," she says, "you're going to have your hands full."

"You're not every woman."

What a bizarre thing to say. Is she expected to behave exactly the same as every other woman in their database, or else she'll arouse suspicions? She is Sara Tilila Hussein. She's never pretended or even wanted to be anyone else.

But that is the trouble. The merchants of data who've spent decades building a taxonomy of human behavior find outliers troublesome. By definition outliers aren't predictable, which also means they're not profitable. Soon, their actions become aberrant, their ideas peculiar, their lives transgressive: they are delinquents.

"Is that it?" she asks.

"Is what it?"

"Is that the substance of your accusation?" she asks. Rage has entered her voice, but she doesn't care. These agents know she has been at Madison for nothing more than a minor squabble at the airport in London, a poorly phrased statement, a few dreams, a connection to something that happened thirty years ago. How can they admit this late in the process that she was detained not because her dreams showed that she was planning to commit a crime, but because an RAA agent who was intent on putting her in her place seized on her nightmares? Now a crime has to be identified. And if not identified, then manufactured. That is why they're digging into her past, all the way to her childhood. They have nothing else. "You're saying I'm a danger to my husband, even though he himself has denied it?"

"Well," Bradley says, and returns to scrolling on his tablet. "There is the matter of your cousin." A subtle tilt of Mendoza's head suggests that she finds this line of investigation useless, though she is reluctant to contradict Bradley. He continues, blithely unaware of her signal. "I see here that he's been in touch with you, but in your interview with the RAA you said you hadn't seen him in years."

"I haven't. I can't stop him from writing me."

"And anyway his score has dropped considerably," Mendoza says, before toggling to another tab on her screen. "Is it your contention, then, that you're not a danger to your husband? That you're a law-abiding citizen?"

"Yes. No. I mean, I'm *not* a danger to my husband, *and* I obey the law."

"Because your record at this facility indicates otherwise."

But didn't they say earlier that her file was clean? Or was that a lie? Doubt gnaws at her, depleting the confidence she has tried to project. She doesn't know how to respond. Everything that comes out of her mouth seems objectionable to these agents, another reason to keep her in retention. She has no idea when this will end. Perhaps never. Perhaps she will never regain her place among the living.

The door flies open just then, and a man in a paisley shirt and blue jeans steps inside. The ease with which he strides across the room conveys he is familiar with these proceedings; he has been watching from the other side of the camera mounted on the wall. "I can speak to the resident's record at this facility," he says, in a voice that Sara recognizes as the CRO's.

Bradley looks flustered. "Oh, hello."

Mendoza stands up to offer her hand, and Bradley follows suit. "What a nice surprise."

"Thanks," the CRO says. "Sit, sit. Make yourselves comfortable."

"We were getting ready to assess Ms. Hussein's residential record," Mendoza tells him.

"Right." The CRO nods. "Hinton and I discussed this case at length yesterday. We were pleased to note that the mandated retention period has been completed, and all the Class A extensions have been served. It's a fairly clean file."

"My concern is the recent uptick of indiscipline, specifically the Class B last month."

"Well, I think Hinton can be a little, shall we say, enthusiastic at times. He would be the first to admit it." The CRO pauses, waits for a chuckle from Bradley.

Mendoza frowns. "But it shows—"

"It's my professional opinion," the CRO says, "that there's no need for further retention."

Sara watches, breathless. If this was his opinion, why did he not say anything before? Only after she has become an obstacle to the smooth running of his facility has he taken an interest in her case. She's shocked he even knows her name; certainly it is the first time he has spoken it. Her gaze travels to the door again, where on the other side Toya is waiting for her own expedited hearing with Themis Legal Services.

"But how do we put it in?" Mendoza asks.

"We'll do a TLS-78," Bradley tells her, his voice taking on the condescension of an expert toward his young charge. "Release recommended due to inconclusive data."

"That sounds suitable," the CRO replies. "Thank you both for accommodating us on such short notice."

Bradley gives a nod of acknowledgment. He is typing quickly on his screen, filling out Sara's release papers, and submits the paperwork with a decisive tap. Then he raises his eyes to the clock, thinking ahead to the next hearing.

Is this really happening? Sara wonders, her pulse thrumming with anticipation. She's waited months for this moment, but now that it has arrived she's stunned by how it came to be. The CRO contrived to keep her and others here as long as possible, but now that she's disturbing the peace at Madison he's contriving to get her out. It seems so mechanistic, so baldly cruel, that she has trouble understanding it. But what the mind cannot comprehend, the heart has enough sense to feel. The rage she has bottled up comes unsealed, and before she realizes what she's doing she cusses the CRO—a word so nasty it instantly brings color to Mendoza's cheeks.

If he is surprised, the CRO doesn't show it. He is pulling up a document on his own tablet, which he now hands to Sara. The document is only a paragraph long; it says that Sara releases Safe-X of legal, medical, and financial liability for the time she has spent at Madison. She also agrees not to disparage the company or its leaders in any form of communication, or take any action that could result in harm to its reputation.

An impossible choice, if it can even be called a choice. No matter what she decides, she has to leave people behind, her family or her friends, and carry the guilt of it with her forever. What should she do? The CRO is pressing the tablet into her hands, saying, "Here, sign right here," and Bradley stands up, dusting off his jacket, ready to move on to Toya's hearing.

Only Mendoza is waiting, with something like pity in her eyes.

This is it, Sara thinks.

She touches her finger to the screen—and she is free.

As she moves toward the exit, she finds Hinton waiting in the doorway, with a plastic bag in his hand. All the personal items she kept in her room are inside it, even her journal. "They'll process you out in Room B," Hinton says, pointing her down the hallway.

She takes the bag from him and turns away.

"Hope you had a pleasant stay with us," he calls after her.

SARA COMES HOME TO A DIFFERENT APARTMENT. THE CEILINGS are too high, the windows too large, the walls cluttered. And the colors! Everything is bright: the Taznakht rug in the hallway, the children's drawings on the refrigerator, the balloon bouquet topped with an inflatable purple star that says WELCOME on one side and BIENVENIDOS on the other. After only a couple of minutes standing in the living room she gets dizzy and has to sit down. Elias asks if she's okay, but his voice is drowned out by the buzzing in her ears. He brings her a tall glass of water and stands by the coffee table to watch her drink it. It tastes so clean that she drains it in one long draw. "Can I have another one?"

"Sorry?" he asks, leaning in closer.

"Can I have another one?"

"You can have as many as you want."

Such abundance. She has forgotten what it feels like. From the other side of the coffee table, Mohsin is watching her. He is used to seeing her in the gray visiting room at Madison; she must seem out of place to him here. Nor does she look the same without her uniform. Earlier in the day, in the parking lot at Union Station, he allowed himself to be picked up, hugged, petted, kissed, but after a while he clawed at her face and pushed her away. Afraid of how she might look under the cameras, Sara didn't insist, though her body ached with want. Now her son sips warm milk from a green cup, humming to soothe himself, all the while eyeing her with the skittish curiosity of a civilian for a booted invader.

"Watch Kiki?" Mona asks.

"Now? Why don't you sit next to Mama for a bit? She missed you."

"No, Kiki."

"You've already seen it a million times."

Instantly her eyes mist. It's remarkable to witness. "Kiki?"

With a sigh, Elias puts an animated movie on the living room screen. Before the title credits are finished rolling, Mohsin has dropped into his toddler chair on the rug. Mona picks up her cup of milk from the table. Both of the children are drowsy with fatigue, the drive from the station having taken longer than necessary because of an oil spill on the freeway.

The television blares. Why are cartoon voices so high-pitched? Mona giggles as a penguin in a Hawaiian shirt cannonballs from a glacier into the sea, splashing his friends in icy water. Carrying her sippy cup she clambers onto the sofa. The movie is so familiar to her that she mouths the penguins' dialogue while she drinks her milk. Then, getting sleepy, she nestles her head on Sara's lap.

"I really think we should get you seen by a physician," Elias says. Hearing about the undercover DI scientist has made him anxious to find out what exactly has been done to her; several times he has asked Sara if she ever ran a fever, if she had aches or pains these last few weeks. "We can try the neurologist my dad was seeing last year. Just to be safe, you know."

"No," she says, softly patting Mona on the back. The prospect of putting on a white gown, sitting on a papered table, and submitting to an exam feels like an extension of everything she is desperate to leave behind forever. Besides, she is not sick. "I'm fine, I promise."

Elias removes a sweatshirt from the armchair and sits down. The shirt belongs to his roommate, a graduate student at UCLA, who offered to stay with friends for the weekend when he found out Sara was coming home. The apartment is cramped, with his bicycle taking up space in the hallway and his books piled up against the wall.

"Are you hungry?" Elias asks after a moment. "You want something to eat?"

"Yes, please."

She slides Mona onto the sofa, using cushions as guardrails, and follows Elias to the kitchen. On the counter is the Nimble screen, with all their devices listed—their phones, the television, the fridge, the oven, their car, the kids' tablets—and the precise location of each. How can she disentangle herself from such an elaborate web? She is free now, she reminds herself, she can do anything she wants.

She can sever the sticky threads that still entrap her, however long it might take her.

The microwave beeps. Elias sets a plate of picadillo and rice and a fresh glass of water on the table for her. She begins to eat, taking small bites to make the food last.

"How is it?" he asks as he takes the seat across from her. "The meat's not too dry?"

"Not at all." She finds the meat juicy, the green peppers flavorful, the onions practically exotic. The knife and napkin sit by the side of her plate, unused.

An anguished howl makes her jump out of her seat.

"It's just the neighbor's hot water pipe. She's been having plumbing issues."

"Oh." She returns to her meal, and after a minute becomes aware that her husband is watching her from the corner of his eye. She is not herself anymore, she knows. Or not her old self, at any rate.

As time passes she grows restless, waiting for device check.

But there is no bell—a silence that now feels like mercy.

IN BED SHE TURNS TO HER SIDE, HER HUSBAND NESTLING AGAINST HER in warm sheets that smell of lavender soap. He loops his arm around her waist and kisses the nape of her neck. It's been nearly a year since she's been kissed like this, and it feels wonderful—yet also strange, especially after his hand burrows hungrily under her shirt.

She doesn't know what to do with herself, whether she should say something or keep quiet, turn around or remain in place. Her skin breaks into goose bumps. Out of nowhere the image of her narrow room comes back to her, the hunger for human touch she felt every day, especially early in the morning or late at night. A knot forms in her chest. Elias draws her even closer to him, whispers her own name into her ear. She can feel his erection through her pajamas.

"Wait," she says, pulling away from him.

"Sorry." He clears his throat. "It's just, it's been so long."

She turns around to face him. The scent of his skin is familiar; he smells like home. Yet there is a hint of danger between them that she finds difficult to put into words. For nearly a year, she's been fighting suspicions that she's a threat to him; now she's almost afraid to touch him.

But they're alone, she tells herself. The curtains are closed, their devices are in the other room. No one can see them. Eventually she takes his hand in hers, runs her thumb across his knuckles. They stay like this for a while, facing each other in the dark, before she brings her lips to his, setting off a hot jolt of recognition, then a current of pleasure.

What a wondrous thing a body is, holding within it tender memories that can be unlocked only by the touch of another. In the unshackling her limbs unstiffen, come to life timidly at first and then with a force that surprises her, and she rediscovers the feel of his skin against hers, the sweet taste of his tongue, the way their legs entangle under the sheets. She remembers what it's like to surrender to the moment, to savor not just the joy she's receiving, but the joy she can give, too.

"YOU MUST'VE BEEN DREAMING," HINTON TELLS HER AS HE SCANS HER neuroprosthetic. The first cold snap of the season has made his face ruddy, restoring his good looks, and on his uniform sleeve he has a new gold stripe. He pulls out his Tekmerion to write her up for being late for device check.

"I wasn't." Didn't he hear the news of her release? She looks down the hall. Perhaps she can get one of the other retainees to back her up. But the ward is empty; everyone has already gone to work.

"It's all right," Hinton says, now in a conciliatory tone. "It happens a lot in this place. Get to the infirmary, they'll want to do a psych exam. Find out why you're imagining things."

"I'm not imagining things. The CRO said I was free. I signed all the paperwork."

"Right."

"He did," she insists. "You can check with him if you like."

"Why would I do that? I have you right here on this screen." He finishes his report, then puts the Tekmerion back in his pocket.

"I'm telling you, he signed the papers. I'm supposed to be released." Her gaze turns toward the gate. Should she just make a run for it? He can't stop her from leaving, she's free. Not just free, under observation, but free free.

"No, you're not," he says with a laugh. "Not after this."

With an anguished cry she wakes in her bed, Elias shaking her shoulder. "Honey," he whispers, "honey, honey, you're having a nightmare."

Before she can fall back asleep she has to wait for her heartbeat to slow down. She has to relinquish control, learn to trust her body again, knowing it will return her to the safety of this bed. She nestles her head against Elias's shoulder, and he strokes her arm to comfort her as she drifts off to sleep.

TIME IS NO LONGER DIVIDED INTO SMALL SLIVERS, THE PRECISE USE of each dictated to her by Safe-X, but in shapeless morsels she can consume as she likes. There is no rush, she has to remind herself as she washes up in the morning. Take all the time you need. She averts her eyes from the clock, finds pleasure in mundane tasks, like picking out a T-shirt and a pair of jeans, throwing the windows open, smoothing the flowered duvet over her bed.

Her father is waiting in the living room when she comes out. "Welcome home," he calls out, activating his Ambulator Exo-Legs to get to her. He wears a tattered T-shirt with NASA's meatball logo on it and a baseball cap that has long lost its color, but beneath his unkempt appearance is a vigor she never noticed in his visits to Madison. He folds her into his arms, the tenderness of the gesture taking her by surprise, and now a sob catches in his throat.

She finds herself patting his back in consolation.

All his life her father has weighed every decision he made, holding himself as a model, yet for all his careful calculations he is one of the unhappiest people she has ever known. He buried a child and a wife, and for the last year watched her struggle to prove that she deserved to be free. The relief that so clearly consumes him now is an expression of love, she realizes, however belated or imperfect it may be. Her safe return is a rare moment of grace.

The television is on—another cartoon, though this time Mohsin is ignoring it in favor of the building blocks that Elias has laid out on the play mat. Mona has wandered off to the deflating bouquet by the window and is trying to grab one, threatening to topple the entire display. "Baboon," she cries. The velvet clips on her pigtails are coming loose.

Sara rushes over to help. "Balloon," she corrects as she works to unfasten one cord from the rest. "Bal-loon. What color is it, baby?"

"Yellow."

"That's right." Sara loops the balloon ribbon around her daughter's wrist. "So it won't fly away."

Her father motors back to the coffee table. "I brought you these," he says, pointing to the pink mums in a tall mason jar, "from my backyard."

"They're lovely," she says, bending to smell them. She's missed small touches of beauty like this, realizes now how necessary they are to life. "Thank you."

While she sips her tea he tells her about his gardening projects, the beds he set up for radishes and sugar snap peas, the grow lights he's considering at the advice of Mrs. Ma, his new neighbor, the movie they saw last week. The chatter is unusual. It occurs to her that perhaps he's working up the courage to tell her something and when he mentions Mrs. Ma a third time, it comes to her that this is the reason, or at least a reason, for his dwindling visits this fall.

The morning passes like this, in companionship and long conversations that touch on everything except her retention, as if her father and her husband are afraid that speaking of it might extend its hold on her life, on all their lives, when all they want is to put it behind them and move forward. In the end it is Sara who brings it up, because the silence about it bothers her, makes her feel she has something to be ashamed of, when really she doesn't, and she says, "I should call Toya."

After their Themis hearings, the two of them had been processed together, then released to the bus stop across from Madison, Toya in the athletic clothes she was wearing at the casino where she was detained and Sara in the flannel shirt and jeans she had on during the flight from London. Neither of them could make a call; their devices were out of battery.

Dizzy with freedom, Sara sat on the metal bench, pressing her shoes into the ground, amazed at the sight of her own laces. When shock finally gave way to anticipation, she went to look at the schedule posted on the pole and began eyeing the road, waiting for the bus.

This was what the old basket-seller did every morning, before she disappeared. Sara turned her gaze to the building, instinctively looking for her own window, the fourth from the right. The joy of being free was tainted by the pain of leaving Emily and Victoria and the others behind, and the crushing urgency of getting them out.

Toya zippered her sweater against the breeze, then came to stand by the pole next to Sara. The two of them were free because they'd managed to disrupt what passed for normal at Madison. The only way to get the others out was to keep on doing it. Even if it wasn't apparent to them right now, they had to work together to find a way.

"I should call Toya," Sara says again, "see how she's doing."

Her husband and her father stare. She can't be serious, their eyes say, not after what she's been through, what they've all been through, she should think of her risk score, stay away from any QUESTIONABLES in order to maintain her good standing. But what they don't see, what they can never truly see unless they had been, like her, confined and controlled, is that isolation is the opposite of salvation, that she owes her release to the women who joined together to say no.

Freedom isn't a blank slate, she wants to tell them. Freedom is teeming and complicated and, yes, risky, and it can only be written in the company of others. The work she started at Madison isn't finished. She intends to see it through.

Her father and her husband are still staring at her, as if unsure how to handle the delinquent newly returned to their home. Contradict her, and start another argument? Or stay quiet, and let her tick up her risk score again?

But now a curious thing happens. Her father pulls out his smart device. "If you're going to call," he says, "use my phone." At eighty-one years old, his risk score is exceedingly low, and it continues to drop month after month. By offering his phone, he's shouldering some of the hit that being in regular touch with a QUESTIONABLE might cause Sara. It's a protective gesture, a fatherly gesture, perhaps the first she has seen, or allowed herself to see, in decades.

This is also what Madison has given her, even as it has taken so much from her—the knowledge that she isn't alone, that she doesn't have to be.

The road ahead is still uncharted. She wants to watch her children blow out the three candles on their birthday cake. She wants to help her friends get out of Madison. She wants to sever her ties to OmniCloud. She doesn't know how to navigate this new road, but she knows she has to try, and that she can only do it alongside others.

She takes the device from her father, types Toya's name, then hits CONNECT.

Acknowledgments

In writing this novel, my eye was on the future, but my research was into the past. The following sources were particularly useful: *The Third Reich of Dreams* by Charlotte Beradt; *The Great Book of Interpretation of Dreams* by Muhammad ibn Sirin; *I, Pierre Rivière* by Michel Foucault; *Discourse on Voluntary Servitude* by Etienne de la Boétie; *The Age of Surveillance Capitalism* by Shoshana Zuboff; and *Acres of Skin: Human Experiments at Holmesburg Prison* by Allen M. Hornblum. The phrase "precaution, not punishment" was inspired by the finding in *Wong Wing v. United States* that immigration detention was "not imprisonment in a legal sense." The terms of service that appear at the end of Part 1 are an amalgam of standard agreements used by various tech companies. The town of Ellis is fictional; pre-crime is not.

I started working on *The Dream Hotel* in 2014, but had to set it aside to finish another novel. The isolation of the Covid pandemic, and the extraordinary grief of that time, led me to pick it up again. I'm grateful to the Radcliffe Institute at Harvard University for the Catherine and Mary Gellert fellowship, which was critical to the completion of the manuscript. Thank you especially to my cohort of fellows, scholars in a broad range of disciplines, whose talks were the highlight of every week.

Thank you to my agent, Ellen Levine, for her steadfast support over the last eighteen years; to my editor, Naomi Gibbs, for her astute comments on the manuscript; and to my publisher, Lisa Lucas, for her unstinting encouragement. Thank you to my publicists, Michiko Clark and Kimberly Burns, for taking such good care of my work. Thank you to Bobby Degeratu for research assistance, especially on legal cases involving dreams. Thank you to Aaron Bady, Souad Lalami, Tochi Onyebuchi, and Scott Martelle for their notes on an early draft. Thank you, most of all, to Alexander Yera, whose love and encouragement makes my work possible.

About the Author

LAILA LALAMI is the author of five books, including *The Moor's Account,* which won the American Book Award, the Arab-American Book Award, and the Hurston/Wright Legacy Award; was on the longlist for the Booker Prize; and was a finalist for the Pulitzer Prize. Her most recent novel, *The Other Americans,* was a national bestseller, won the Simpson/Joyce Carol Oates Prize, and was a finalist for the National Book Award. Her books have been translated into twenty languages. Lalami's writing appears regularly in the *Los Angeles Times, The Washington Post, The Nation, Harper's, The Guardian,* and *The New York Times.* She has been awarded fellowships from the British Council, the Fulbright Program, the Guggenheim Foundation, and the Radcliffe Institute at Harvard University. She lives in Los Angeles.

A Note on the Type

This book was set in Janson, a typeface named for the Dutchman
Anton Janson but actually the work of Nicholas Kis (1650–1702).
The type is an excellent example of the influential and sturdy
Dutch types that prevailed in England up to the time William
Caslon (1692–1766) developed his own incomparable designs from
them.

Composed by North Market Street Graphics,
Lancaster, Pennsylvania

Printed and bound by Friesens
Altona, Manitoba

Designed by Betty Lew